THE FLYING CAVALIER

BOOKS BY GILBERT MORRIS

THE HOUSE OF WINSLOW SERIES

The Honorable Imposter
The Captive Bride
The Indentured Heart
The Gentle Rebel
The Saintly Buccaneer
The Holy Warrior
The Reluctant Bridegroom
The Last Confederate
The Dixie Widow
The Wounded Yankee
The Union Belle
The Final Adversary
The Crossed Sabres
The Valiant Gunman
The Gallant Outlaw
The Jeweled Spur
The Yukon Queen
The Rough Rider
The Iron Lady
The Silver Star
The Shadow Portrait
The White Hunter
The Flying Cavalier
The Glorious Prodigal
The Amazon Quest
The Golden Angel
The Heavenly Fugitive
The Fiery Ring
The Pilgrim Song
The Beloved Enemy
The Shining Badge
The Royal Handmaid
The Silent Harp
The Virtuous Woman
The Gypsy Moon
The Unlikely Allies
The High Calling
The Hesitant Hero

CHENEY DUVALL, M.D.[1]

1. *The Stars for a Light*
2. *Shadow of the Mountains*
3. *A City Not Forsaken*
4. *Toward the Sunrising*
5. *Secret Place of Thunder*
6. *In the Twilight, in the Evening*
7. *Island of the Innocent*
8. *Driven With the Wind*

CHENEY AND SHILOH: THE INHERITANCE[1]

1. *Where Two Seas Met*
2. *The Moon by Night*
3. *There Is a Season*

THE SPIRIT OF APPALACHIA[2]

1. *Over the Misty Mountains*
2. *Beyond the Quiet Hills*
3. *Among the King's Soldiers*
4. *Beneath the Mockingbird's Wings*
5. *Around the River's Bend*

LIONS OF JUDAH

1. *Heart of a Lion*
2. *No Woman So Fair*
3. *The Gate of Heaven*
4. *Till Shiloh Comes*
5. *By Way of the Wilderness*
6. *Daughter of Deliverance*

[1]with Lynn Morris [2]with Aaron McCarver

06B

GILBERT MORRIS

the FLYING CAVALIER

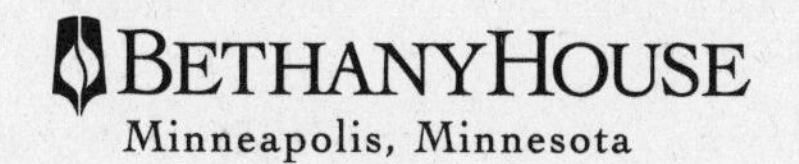

Minneapolis, Minnesota

Cover illustration by Dan Thornberg
Cover design by Josh Madison

Published by Bethany House Publishers
11400 Hampshire Avenue South
Bloomington, Minnesota 55438

Bethany House Publishers is a division of
Baker Publishing Group, Grand Rapids, Michigan.

Printed in the United States of America

ISBN-13: 978-0-7642-2967-1
ISBN-10: 0-7642-2967-2

The Library of Congress has cataloged the original edition as follows:

Morris, Gilbert.
The flying cavalier / by Gilbert Morris.
p. cm. — (House of Winslow ; bk. 23)
ISBN 0-7642-2115-9
I. Title. II. Series: Morris, Gilbert. House of Winslow ; bk. 23.
PS3563.O8742 F59 1999
813'.54—dc21 99-6518
CIP

To Jean and Harry Sanburn

Thanks a million for all
you've done for me and Kay.
It is good to find people like you
in a world which has forgotten to care.
May the Lord bless you richly
all the days of your life.

GILBERT MORRIS spent ten years as a pastor before becoming Professor of English at Ouachita Baptist University in Arkansas and earning a Ph.D. at the University of Arkansas. A prolific writer, he has had over 25 scholarly articles and 200 poems published in various periodicals, and over the past years has had more than 180 novels published. His family includes three grown children. He and his wife live in Gulf Shores, Alabama.

CONTENTS

The House of Winslow

★ ★ ★ ★

THE HOUSE OF WINSLOW

★ ★ ★ ★

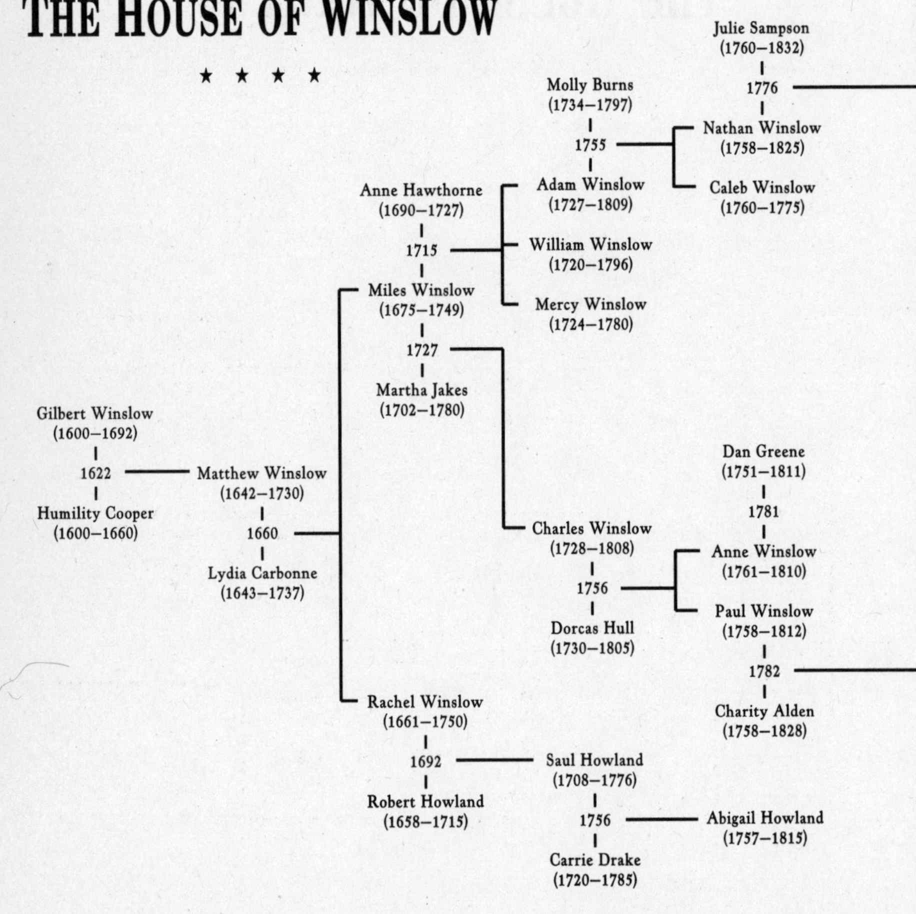

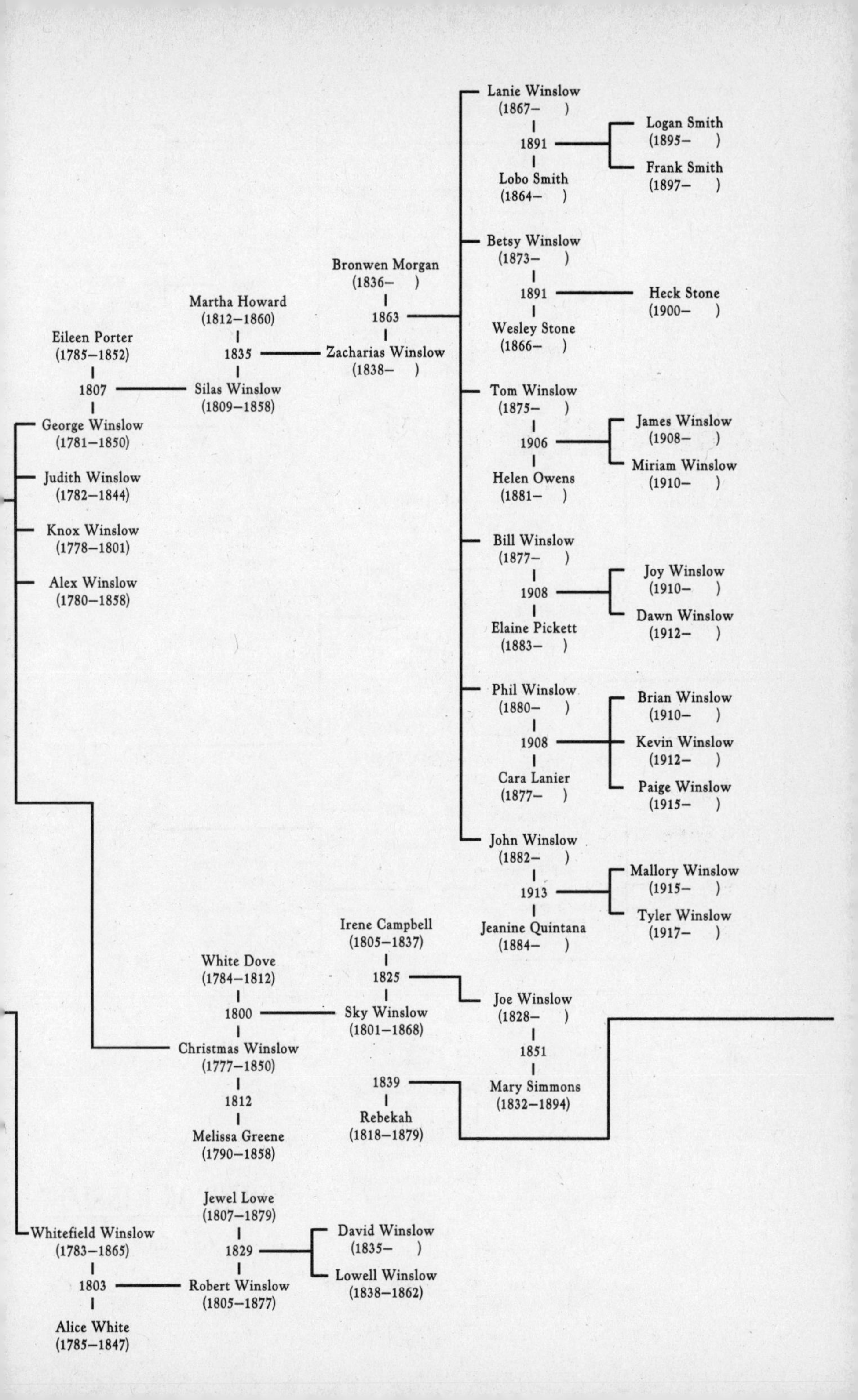

Lanie Winslow
(1867–)
1891
Lobo Smith
(1864–)
Logan Smith
(1895–)
Frank Smith
(1897–)
Betsy Winslow
(1873–)
1891
Wesley Stone
(1866–)
Heck Stone
(1900–)
Bronwen Morgan
(1836–)
1863
Zacharias Winslow
(1838–)
Martha Howard
(1812–1860)
1835
Silas Winslow
(1809–1858)
Eileen Porter
(1785–1852)
1807
George Winslow
(1781–1850)
Judith Winslow
(1782–1844)
Knox Winslow
(1778–1801)
Alex Winslow
(1780–1858)
Tom Winslow
(1875–)
1906
Helen Owens
(1881–)
James Winslow
(1908–)
Miriam Winslow
(1910–)
Bill Winslow
(1877–)
1908
Elaine Pickett
(1883–)
Joy Winslow
(1910–)
Dawn Winslow
(1912–)
Phil Winslow
(1880–)
1908
Cara Lanier
(1877–)
Brian Winslow
(1910–)
Kevin Winslow
(1912–)
Paige Winslow
(1915–)
John Winslow
(1882–)
1913
Jeanine Quintana
(1884–)
Mallory Winslow
(1915–)
Tyler Winslow
(1917–)
Irene Campbell
(1805–1837)
1825
Joe Winslow
(1828–)
1851
Mary Simmons
(1832–1894)
White Dove
(1784–1812)
1800
Sky Winslow
(1801–1868)
1839
Rebekah
(1818–1879)
Christmas Winslow
(1777–1850)
1812
Melissa Greene
(1790–1858)
Jewel Lowe
(1807–1879)
1829
Robert Winslow
(1805–1877)
David Winslow
(1835–)
Lowell Winslow
(1838–1862)
Whitefield Winslow
(1783–1865)
1803
Alice White
(1785–1847)

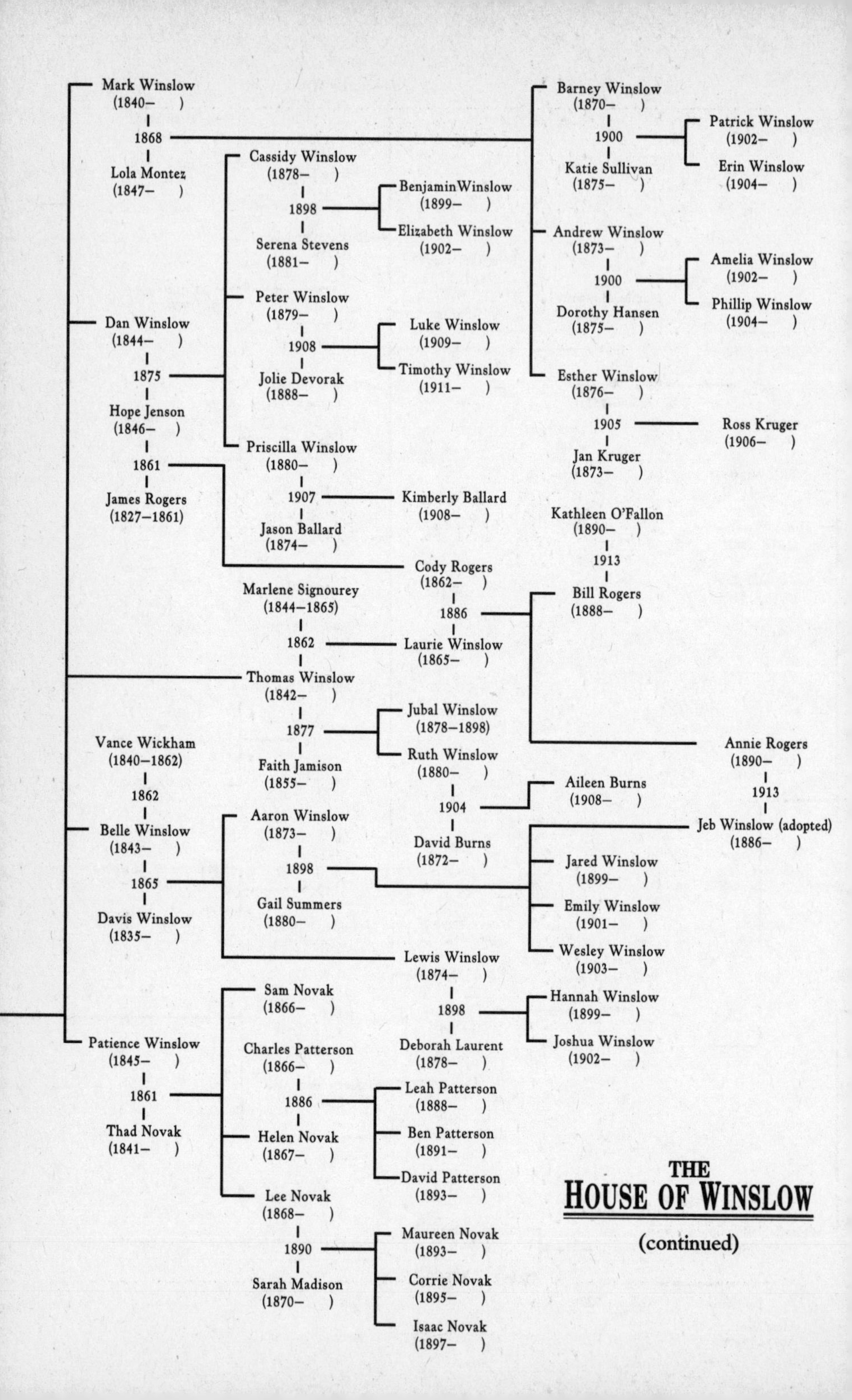

Mark Winslow (1840–)
1868
Lola Montez (1847–)
Barney Winslow (1870–)
1900
Katie Sullivan (1875–)
Patrick Winslow (1902–)
Erin Winslow (1904–)
Andrew Winslow (1873–)
1900
Dorothy Hansen (1875–)
Amelia Winslow (1902–)
Phillip Winslow (1904–)
Esther Winslow (1876–)
1905
Jan Kruger (1873–)
Ross Kruger (1906–)
Dan Winslow (1844–)
1875
Hope Jenson (1846–)
Cassidy Winslow (1878–)
1898
Serena Stevens (1881–)
BenjaminWinslow (1899–)
Elizabeth Winslow (1902–)
Peter Winslow (1879–)
1908
Jolie Devorak (1888–)
Luke Winslow (1909–)
Timothy Winslow (1911–)
Priscilla Winslow (1880–)
1907
Jason Ballard (1874–)
Kimberly Ballard (1908–)
1861
James Rogers (1827–1861)
Cody Rogers (1862–)
1886
Kathleen O'Fallon (1890–)
1913
Bill Rogers (1888–)
Annie Rogers (1890–)
1913
Jeb Winslow (adopted) (1886–)
Marlene Signourey (1844–1865)
1862
Laurie Winslow (1865–)
Thomas Winslow (1842–)
1877
Faith Jamison (1855–)
Jubal Winslow (1878–1898)
Ruth Winslow (1880–)
1904
David Burns (1872–)
Aileen Burns (1908–)
Vance Wickham (1840–1862)
1862
Belle Winslow (1843–)
1865
Davis Winslow (1835–)
Aaron Winslow (1873–)
1898
Gail Summers (1880–)
Jared Winslow (1899–)
Emily Winslow (1901–)
Wesley Winslow (1903–)
Lewis Winslow (1874–)
1898
Deborah Laurent (1878–)
Hannah Winslow (1899–)
Joshua Winslow (1902–)
Patience Winslow (1845–)
1861
Thad Novak (1841–)
Sam Novak (1866–)
Charles Patterson (1866–)
1886
Helen Novak (1867–)
Leah Patterson (1888–)
Ben Patterson (1891–)
David Patterson (1893–)
Lee Novak (1868–)
1890
Sarah Madison (1870–)
Maureen Novak (1893–)
Corrie Novak (1895–)
Isaac Novak (1897–)
THE HOUSE OF WINSLOW
(continued)

PART ONE

Lance and Noelle

★ ★ ★ ★

CHAPTER ONE

CHRISTMAS IN PARIS

★ ★ ★ ★

Snowflakes as fluffy as down and as large as gold coins drifted silently down out of slate gray skies, muffling the streets of Paris in a three-inch carpet of pristine white. The sun had remained hidden behind clouds all day, and the city on the day before Christmas in the year 1908 lay still with that strange silence that comes with a gentle snowfall. The carpet of glistening white had muted the clatter of the hooves of horses and the rattling of wheels from the coaches that plied the streets, and Noelle Laurent was delighted with the winter scene. Making her way along the Champs Elysées, she glanced skyward, where myriads of flakes danced in the amber glow of the streetlights, which were just barely necessary at this time of day. "This is *my* day," she murmured. "No wonder I was named after it. Mama must have known I would love Christmas so much."

Noelle was wearing a lightweight blue woolen overcoat that reached almost down to her high-laced shoes. On her head was perched a felt hat, and the dark brown curls that escaped were covered with the white flakes. Her dark brown hair highlighted her face, and a piquant expression gave her an air of excitement as she threaded her way down the street before turning finally into a shop. The bell over the door jingled loudly, and she was met by a rotund woman with bright, merry eyes who greeted her at once.

"Ah, Mademoiselle Laurent! I am surprised to see you this late."

"I have to get a few more things, Madame Douvey." She laughed then for no real reason except for the sheer pleasure that ran through her. "I suppose it's a good thing Christmas will be over after tomorrow. I've spent every sou I have on gifts!"

"There is a story by a man named Dickens—an Englishman," Madame Douvey smiled. "It is about a very wicked, stingy, and greedy man named Scrooge."

"Oh yes! *A Christmas Carol*. A fine tale indeed!"

"Certainement! It ends by saying Scrooge learned to keep Christmas better than any man in England." Madame Douvey chuckled, and the action sent her massive frame quivering. "If that is so, then you, Mademoiselle Noelle Laurent, know how to keep Christmas better than any woman in France! Now, what can I show you?"

"Oh, I just need a small gift for my sister. She's so hard to buy for. She doesn't care anything about clothes or jewelry."

The two women moved through the shop, which was almost empty now. Outside the last rays of the sun were fading. By the time Noelle stepped out into the street with her purchases, the darkness was complete, broken only by the faint glitter of tiny specks of light. She looked up and smiled to herself. "Such tiny stars overhead," she murmured. "So you will have to do, Monsieur Streetlight."

The snow was drifting down harder now in long slanting lines, and the cold bit at Noelle through her light coat. A quick glance revealed that there were no cabs available, so she turned and made her way down the street. She grasped awkwardly at several bundles, holding them to her breast, her mind moving ahead to the pleasantries of the following day. Finally she saw a cab some twenty yards ahead. At the same time she caught a quick glimpse of a tall man stepping out of a shop, intent on engaging the cab.

Oh, I have to get into that cab! she thought with alarm. Cabs were scarce on Christmas Eve, as most of the drivers were home with their families, she supposed. Noelle broke into a fast pace and closed the distance, but when she was no more than twenty feet away, her foot encountered a sheet of sheer ice. Uttering a wild cry as her foot slid out from under her, she threw the packages skyward. As they fell she windmilled, waving her arms wildly as she attempted to keep her balance. But she went down, and instantly she felt her right ankle twist under her. *I've broken it!* she thought. A sharp pain shot through her ankle as she struck the pavement, catching herself partially on the heel of her right hand. Helplessly she lay there biting her lip against the pain for a moment, then struggled to get up.

A strong hand closed on her left arm, and another came around her shoulders, pulling her to a sitting position. "Well, that was a bad one! I hope nothing's broken."

Noelle caught a glimpse of the man's face and answered in English. Though the pain seemed to grow even worse, Noelle Laurent managed to say, "I think my ankle is broken, monsieur."

"Oh, I say! That is a bad one! You'll have to go to a doctor."

"Oh, I must go home!"

"You can't go home with a broken ankle! There must be a doctor or a hospital somewhere. I don't know the city."

"My . . . father is a doctor, and he will be at home now. If you could help me to get home."

"Why, certainly. We'll take this cab right here." He lifted his voice and said, "Driver, open that back door, will you?"

As he did, Noelle saw his face clearly, a clean-cut jaw and firm lips. He was very tall, she knew that much, and now she saw that he was wearing some sort of uniform. English, no doubt, although she could not identify it. Although she could not determine the exact color of his eyes, they were probably blue like those of most Englishmen. She had no time to examine him more closely, but as he suddenly bent over, she could not help but notice his handsome features. She felt his arms go under her knees, then behind her back.

"I'm going to pick you up and put you in this cab. I'll be very careful of your ankle."

"Thank you, monsieur." Noelle felt herself lifted as if she weighed no more than the snowflakes that kept drifting down. His arms were strong, and she automatically, without thought, put her arms around his neck to help him bear her weight. It was an intimate position, and, despite the pain, a humorous thought ran through her. *What a romantic way to start Christmas. . . !* She had no time to think about this further, for carefully he bent over and gently placed her inside the cab.

He shut the door, retrieved her packages from the sidewalk, then came around and got in beside her. "You'll have to give directions to the driver."

"One sixteen Rue Crozat," she said in French.

"Oui, madame." The driver was a short, slight man muffled up in a fur coat, and his hat was pulled down almost over his ears. "Will madame be all right?"

"It's mademoiselle—and yes. Just get me home."

"Certainement, mademoiselle."

The cab protected them from the wind and the snow, of course, but it was still cold. It was a very small cab, and Noelle felt the pressure of her rescuer's arm against her own. She looked at him and asked, "Your name, monsieur?"

"Lance Winslow." A slight pause, then he said, "Lieutenant Winslow of the RFC."

"The RFC? What is that?"

"The Royal Flying Corps."

"Oh, it is with the flying machines, non?"

"It is with the flying machines, yes. How's your ankle?"

Carefully Noelle moved her toe up and down. With a grimace she bit her lower lip. "It's very painful, Lieutenant—but not broken, I think. Only badly sprained."

"That was quite a fall you took back there. Is your home near here?"

"Not too far. I'm sorry to put you to such difficulty. No, that is not the word. Trouble?"

"No trouble or difficulty, either." Lance Winslow turned to examine the young woman and added, "I have nothing else to do."

"On Christmas Eve you have nothing else to do but rescue clumsy young women?"

The smile that lit Winslow's face touched his eyes. He was, Noelle saw, one of those men whose eyes revealed what they were feeling with perfect clarity. *He would not make a good cardplayer. His eyes would give him away every time.*

"Nothing at all. I'm a long way from home."

"Ah, that is so sad. Especially on Christmas."

The two said nothing else until finally the driver pulled over in front of a three-story brownstone. "We are here," he announced as he got out and threw the door open.

Noelle made an attempt to lean forward, but the tall officer simply reached out and pulled her back firmly. "You wait right here. I will announce to your parents what has happened." He hesitated, then said, "Do they speak English as well as you?"

"Yes, of course. We all speak English very well. My father interned in Grey's Hospital in London." She gnawed her lip in a worried manner. "Do not alarm them if you can help it, Lieutenant."

"I'll do my best."

Getting out of the car, Winslow went up the first steps very carefully, for they were piled with at least four inches of white, fluffy snow. A brass knocker on the door caught his attention, and he banged it firmly several times. Looking back, he saw the young woman peering out at him anxiously. *Pretty thing, I wonder how old she is.* At that point the door opened, and a young woman stood before him. He was not an expert at gauging the ages of young people, but he thought probably she might be twelve or thirteen. "Hello," he said. "Are your parents home?"

"What is it you want?" the girl asked.

For a moment Lance hesitated. He really needed to talk to the parents, and fortunately at that moment a man with dark hair streaked with gray came into the foyer. He examined the tall man with one quick gaze and spoke a few words in French. Seeing the incomprehension in his guest's face he immediately said, "Yes, monsieur. What can I do for you?"

"Doctor Laurent?"

"Yes, indeed." Concern came into the doctor's eyes. "Is there a problem?"

"It's your daughter." Lance saw alarm leap into the man's eyes, and at the same time a woman came to the foyer. She was considerably younger than her husband, he thought, and by the look on her face, she had heard his last statement.

"What is it?" she cried out. "Is there something wrong with Noelle?"

"Don't be alarmed," Lance said quickly. "She twisted her ankle and was unable to walk, so I brought her home in a cab."

"Oh, that was very kind of you, monsieur," Doctor Laurent said immediately, relief washing into his eyes. "Is it serious?"

"She says it's not broken, but it's pretty painful." Lance hesitated, then said, "I'm Lieutenant Lance Winslow."

"We're grateful to you, Lieutenant." The doctor moved forward. "I will bring her in."

"No need for that, sir," Winslow said. "I can carry her."

"Oh yes. Please do, Lieutenant," Mrs. Laurent said.

"Bring her into the study where I can take a look at that ankle."

"Certainly, Doctor." Lance turned and carefully walked down the steps once again. He did not care to break his own leg in his attempt to help the young woman. Moving to the cab he opened the door and said, "Just swing your legs out. I think I'd better carry you in."

"Oh, I think I could walk with a little help."

Ignoring her statement, Lance simply reached in and picked her up again. He turned back to the cabdriver and said, "Wait for me, driver."

"Oui, monsieur. I will wait until I get paid. That is for certain."

Lance grinned and turned to face the young woman he was carrying. Her face was only inches away, and he could see that she had lovely features. "Pragmatic chap, isn't he?"

"Most cabdrivers are." Noelle was very conscious of his arms around her. As he carefully carried her up the stairs, she turned to see her parents and her younger sister, Danielle, waiting anxiously at the door. "It's all right," she assured them. "It's just a twisted ankle."

Reaching the top of the landing, Lance entered the house. The younger sister closed the door, and he said, "Thank you very much."

"You're welcome, Lieutenant."

"Right this way, if you don't mind," Dr. Laurent said.

Lance followed the doctor and entered a very attractive parlor. It was a large room with blue-and-green wallpaper on the walls, hardwood floors with a large multicolored area rug, and high ceilings painted a bright white. There were three large windows with white sheer lace curtains and blue-and-white drapes falling softly to the floor. The furniture was ornately carved and made of the best woods, he could see, and was covered with various shades of blues and greens. A fire was burning brightly in the fireplace, and the sparks sent a myriad of colors reflecting from the cut glass of the lamps and mirrors in the room.

"Right here on the couch."

Lance carefully placed Noelle down so that her back was against the end of the settee, her legs stretched out in front of her.

"Thank you very much." Noelle managed to smile despite the pain. "The next time I fall, I'll make sure you're around, Lieutenant."

"Glad to be of service, mademoiselle."

Stepping back, Lance watched as the doctor carefully removed the shoe and then with sensitive fingers manipulated the swollen foot.

"That hurts? Yes, of course. Now. Can you move your foot this way?"

"You are a soldier, Lieutenant?"

Lance looked down at the young girl and smiled. "Yes, I am an English soldier."

"My name is Danielle. I've always loved to read about soldiers and battles." Danielle was a younger version of her older sister. "It's so romantic."

"Well, I'm sorry to disillusion you, Miss Danielle, but being a soldier isn't always romantic. It can be just as boring as what you do. Your schoolwork, for example."

"No, that could not be," Danielle said. She was fascinated by the tall soldier who stood before her. His wedge-shaped face was lean, and he had a determined chin. His skin was very fair, and his eyes were a very peculiar shade of light blue, almost like that of a certain wild flower Danielle loved to collect. "Have you fought in many battles?"

Lance suddenly grinned and wanted to reach out and tweak her nose. He resisted this impulse but shook his head. "Not a one. Not yet, anyway."

"How is she, Pierre?" Katherine Laurent was standing beside her husband, anxiety etched on her face.

"It isn't broken, Katherine, but it is a very bad sprain." Turning his eyes toward his older daughter, Pierre Laurent said, "You're going to have to stay off this foot for several days. No weight at all on it, and I'm going to put cold compresses on it."

"Cold compresses! I'm freezing now!"

Doctor Laurent laughed. "Then I'll put on hot compresses." He stood to his feet and said, "Katherine, please fix our guest something. Hot tea and some of that cake you made."

"Oh, I wouldn't want to intrude," the lieutenant insisted.

"Oh, you must stay, Lieutenant!" Danielle brightened up. "Mother, may I fix tea for the lieutenant?"

"Certainly. Go along with Danielle, Lieutenant Winslow," Katherine smiled. "Pay your driver, and as soon as we get this clumsy daughter of mine patched up, perhaps we can all have a little time to visit and get acquainted."

Lieutenant Lance Winslow was exceedingly glad for the invitation. He had nothing to look forward to but a small lonely room in a hotel. He had made few friends since he had come to Paris, and now he willingly said, "I wouldn't want to leave until after I find out how Miss Noelle is." At that Winslow excused himself to go outside to pull Noelle's packages from the cab and pay the waiting cabdriver. Upon returning to the foyer, Winslow shook the snow from his boots, then handed the packages to Danielle.

"Come along," Danielle said quickly. She left the room and Winslow followed her into a large and well-furnished kitchen. "We can make your tea here," Danielle said firmly, "and then we can take it into the parlor."

"That would be very nice. How old are you, Miss Danielle?"

"Almost fifteen."

"Almost? How long until your birthday?"

Danielle looked startled and then giggled. "Nine months," she said.

"Well, I remember when I was your age I did the same thing. I wanted to grow up so fast, I suppose the day after I was thirteen, I was claiming to be almost fourteen, too."

"I'm very mature for my age," Danielle said as she busied herself pulling together the tea set and putting a kettle of water on the stove to boil. "Everyone says that. I don't feel at all comfortable with young people of my own age. All my friends are older."

"What are you going to be when you grow up?"

"A scientist or, perhaps, a doctor like my father."

"A noble ambition." Lance Winslow sat back. He took off his overcoat now and his hat, placed them on a chair, then leaned back to enjoy the warmth of the kitchen. He carried on a light conversation with Danielle and discovered that she was, indeed, a precocious young woman. If he had been blind and had not been able to see her, he would have assumed from her conversation that she was at least seventeen or eighteen. "Do you have any young admirers, Danielle?" he asked mischievously.

"Pouf! They are camels!"

"Camels?"

"They are silly! As I told you, Lieutenant, people of my own chronological age bore me." The kettle was boiling now, and with considerable aplomb, Danielle poured the tea, then asked, "Sugar or cream?"

"Both, I'm afraid. Everyone says I just ruin the tea."

"You should drink it as you like. I'm afraid this is not the English tea that you are accustomed to."

Lance smiled. "I'm sure it will be excellent."

Indeed it did prove to be excellent tea, and he enjoyed himself a great deal sitting back and talking with the young girl. She had a lively expression and her mind was very quick. He was on his second cup when Katherine Laurent came into the kitchen.

"Now I think we can all have tea," she said.

"Is Noelle going to bed?" Danielle asked.

"Not right away. She'll have tea with us in the parlor. Ah, you've already prepared it. Will you bring the tray in, Danielle?"

"Certainly, Mama."

Following his hostess down the short hallway and turning back into the parlor, Winslow saw that Noelle's ankle was now thickly bandaged. She was sitting still with her back at the end of the settee, and she gave him a wan smile when he entered.

"I'm bandaged up so tightly I won't be able to move for a week."

"You'll have to have a wheelchair, I'm afraid, for a day or two, and then a cane for at least a week or more." Doctor Laurent turned to Winslow and smiled. He shrugged his shoulders, saying, "She is headstrong, I'm afraid."

"That's the kind way he has of putting it. He usually says I'm as stubborn as a mule."

Noelle's face, Winslow saw, was made rosy by the heat of the fireplace. For the first time he had a chance to examine her at leisure. Her hair was still damp from the snow that had now melted, but it was luxurious and had a pronounced curl to it. Her eyes were rich, dark brown and wide spaced. Somehow he knew those eyes could laugh, and yet they had a pride in them he liked to see in a woman. Her spirit glowed in her, somewhat as if live coals were behind her eyes. She was a beautiful woman, and he found himself unable to look away from her for more than a few seconds.

Over the tea and cakes that Danielle served, Lance found himself telling them about his life in England and telling them more about himself.

"I left the university to join the army," he said. "My father was a soldier," he added. "He was killed in action."

"And you always wanted to be a soldier like your father?" Noelle asked, her eyes fixed on him.

"I suppose so. I never really thought of doing anything else."

"What is it you do in the army?" Danielle asked.

"Well, at the moment I'm one of the few in our army who believe in airplanes as a military weapon."

"Ah, the airplane! A very interesting invention," Doctor Laurent murmured. He sipped his tea and then said, "But how could they serve as a military weapon? They are up in the air and not very far at that, from what I read."

"Right now they can't go very high or stay up long, but I believe they're going to change the nature of warfare. Can you imagine"—Lance leaned forward and his eyes seemed to glow—"what it would mean to a general to know exactly what the enemy was doing and to know it within twenty minutes? As it is now, an officer has to send a message by a courier on a horse. The courier must travel over all kinds of territory. He may get shot and killed, and the message may never arrive. But in an airplane it's a different story."

"Are you a flier yourself, monsieur?" Katherine asked with interest.

"Oh yes. That's how I became interested. In any case, I think the French fliers are the best in the world, so I persuaded my commanding officer to send me over on a mission to pick the brains of some of your aviators."

"Pick the brains?" Danielle leaned forward at once. "What does that mean, 'to pick the brain'?"

A laugh went up and Lance grinned. "It means to find out all they know, Miss Danielle. So that's what I've been doing."

"And have you been successful?"

"Well, I've met some of the best fliers and pilots in France. Unfortunately, some of them don't speak English, and I don't speak French, so it's been a little bit difficult to communicate."

"Perhaps I could go as your interpreter, Lieutenant," Danielle piped up, her eyes bright. "I speak very good English!"

"You certainly do, Miss Danielle. I wish I could speak French as well."

"What about your family?" Noelle asked.

"I have very little. I have no brothers or sisters, and my mother remarried a solicitor named Briggs. They live in Scotland, so I don't see them too often."

"Oh, that's so sad!" Noelle said impulsively. "And to be away from your own country among strangers on Christmas Eve."

"Why don't you have Christmas dinner with us tomorrow?" Danielle piped up.

"Danielle, don't be impertinent!" her mother exclaimed.

"I'm not impertinent! You'd like to, wouldn't you, Lieutenant Winslow?"

Winslow suddenly found himself wishing very much that he could do exactly what this young woman suggested. He hesitated, saying, "Well . . . I'm not at all sure . . ."

Doctor Laurent, seeing the loneliness in the young man, said, "We would be most happy if you would join us for Christmas dinner tomorrow, Lieutenant, if you have no other plans."

"My only plan was to eat a bowl of soup in a restaurant somewhere. I'd be most grateful to be in your home, Doctor."

At that Winslow rose, and said, "And now I must be going."

As soon as Lance Winslow had left, Danielle came and sat down flat on the floor before her sister. "And now. Tell me all about it. Everything!"

"I twisted my ankle and he helped me get home," Noelle smiled.

"That's not the way it was!" Danielle's eyes were dreamy. "Isn't he the handsomest thing you ever saw?"

"Very fine looking indeed," Noelle said. She reached out and pinched her sister's arm sharply. "Danielle, I don't want you to become infatuated with the lieutenant."

"I never get infatuated! That's for children!"

"Never infatuated! Why, you've gone off into fits of it ever since you were ten years old!"

Danielle got to her feet and said huffily, "Infatuation is for children!"

As Danielle walked off with her back straight, Noelle shrugged her shoulders and smiled toward her mother who had taken all this in. "She's incurable, isn't she, Mother?"

"She's just young."

"Was I like that when I was fourteen?"

"No. You were much more sensible." A worried look came into Katherine Laurent's eyes. "Danielle is very impressionable, though." Then she laughed. "But she has some reason this time. Lieutenant Winslow is extremely handsome and so tall!"

"He was very nice," Noelle said thoughtfully. She was silent for a moment and then shook her head. "He's so alone in the world."

Katherine suddenly came over and leaned down. She put her arm around her older daughter, Noelle, and said, "Now don't you go getting infatuated!"

"Me? Don't be silly, Mother!"

"That's not being silly. That's being realistic. A man in uniform does have a certain attraction for a woman. I remember when I was your age, I couldn't help looking at a handsome soldier."

"Well, I'm glad you married Father instead of a soldier. He's always home, not off fighting in some war."

At that moment Doctor Laurent came back and said, "Now, we've got to get you into bed. I should have had the lieutenant put you there. But I'll have to do." He picked her up with a grunt and said, "You've got to go on a diet. You're getting too big. . . ."

CHAPTER TWO

ROMANCE ABOVE THE CLOUDS

★ ★ ★ ★

"Dani, you're going to wear all of your clothes out changing them so much!" Noelle leaned against the back of the settee, her foot propped up, and gave an amused glance at her younger sister, adding, "That dress is too old for you. I told you so when you bought it."

Dani gave Noelle an indignant glance. "It is not too old for me!"

"Yes, it is. Mother said so when you tried it on at the store. You just pressured her into it."

The dress in question was definitely too old for a fourteen-year-old, even one as mature as Danielle Laurent. It was a day dress with a loosely cut, high-waisted bodice and a high neckline with a collar of small frills. It was a bright yellow color, except for a panel of rose-colored silk set in just under the bosom. Craning her head to look at herself, Danielle said defiantly, "It's just right for me!"

Noelle made a gesture of helplessness and smiled toward her mother, who had entered to watch the scene. "I was just telling Dani that dress was too old for her, but she doesn't agree."

"Well," Katherine said, studying the dress carefully, "it probably is, but by the time she's sixteen, it will be just right. How's your ankle?"

"It hurts."

"Perhaps you ought to take some more laudanum."

"No, that stuff makes me sick!"

"Then perhaps I'd better put a cold press on it."

"Oh no, Mother, it's fine. Now that I'm propped up, it'll be better soon." Noelle was wearing a simple green dress cut close to the figure with a high décolletage and a neck encircled with a muslin collar. Her hair was carefully done, for her mother had worked hard at it earlier that day. Noelle had slept little the night before, and her father had finally medicated her until she had fallen almost into a stupor. Now faint dark circles shadowed her eyes, and lines of pain etched the corners of her mouth. She had set her foot down about using a wheelchair and had managed to get to the parlor by holding on to the shoulders of her mother and sister.

"I'm going to change dresses," Danielle said abruptly. "I'm going to wear my pink silk."

"Well, please make up your mind!" Katherine Laurent said with some irritation. "You are doing it again, Dani! You're infatuated with Lieutenant Winslow."

"I never have infatuations!"

This statement caused Noelle to laugh aloud. "What a thing to say! Why, you've had infatuations on actors, policemen, and artists. Not to mention Charles Stratton, the soccer player who lives down the street."

Danielle gave her sister a withering look and then flounced off. They heard her footsteps on the stairs, and Noelle said thoughtfully, "She's very impressionable. I worry about her sometimes."

"Oh, I was the same way when I was her age, but she'll outgrow it. Young girls are always that way."

"I wasn't."

"No, that's right. You weren't. But you were always more steady than Dani." At that moment there was a knock at the door, and the women heard Danielle's steps come flying downstairs. Noelle smiled and said, "She'll never wait for Marie to open the door."

Danielle was at the door very quickly. She opened it and smiled, saying, "Good morning, Lieutenant."

"Good morning, Miss Danielle." Lance stepped inside and pulled his overcoat off, handing it to the maid who had appeared. He thanked her and then gave Danielle a more critical look. "What a beautiful dress. Is it new?"

"Well, yes, it is. I purchased it to wear to a ball, but I thought I'd wear it for Christmas instead."

"You look very nice in it."

Danielle flushed rosily and then smiled. "You look nice, too."

She looked with admiration at his uniform, which consisted of a dark khaki tunic with brass buttons set off by an extra-wide leather belt with a smaller one going over the right shoulder. The uniform was completed with light tan jodhpurs and brown boots that came almost up to the knee.

"Well, I don't have a chance to wear a dress uniform very often," Lance said. "Besides," he grinned, "I knew you'd look pretty, so I wanted to come up to your standards."

Danielle's flush grew even more rosy, then her mother suddenly appeared, saying, "Don't keep the lieutenant standing outside, Dani! Bring him in!"

Lance moved down the beautifully decorated foyer, turned to his left, and went at once to Noelle, who was sitting on the settee. She put out her hand and he took it, and in a gesture he had never thought himself capable of, he bent over and kissed it. He had read somewhere that men kissed the inside of a woman's wrist, but he was not sure about this. He felt rather awkward and unsure of himself, but he saw the warm approval in Noelle's eyes.

"So good to see you, Lieutenant," she murmured.

"It's good to be here. Thank you for your kind invitation to spend Christmas with your family."

"It is our pleasure. You got here just in time. Marie tells me that the meal got done earlier than she thought, so we can go right into the dining room."

At that moment Doctor Laurent entered the parlor. He wore a single-breasted morning coat fastened in the front with two buttons. It had a narrow collar and a striped tie. "Good morning, Lieutenant," he said cheerfully. "Or it's almost afternoon."

"I hope I didn't come too early."

"Not at all. I'm starved," the doctor smiled. "Smelling the aroma of roasted goose always brings hunger pangs."

At that moment Marie appeared at the door. She was a tall woman with an austere look and ran the household with an iron hand. "The food is on the table. Will you please come now."

"Our master's voice," Katherine smiled. She looked over with some consternation at Noelle, asking, "Pierre, how are we going to get Noelle to the table?"

"Oh, I can hobble along."

"You don't need to put any more weight on that foot!" Doctor Laurent said sternly. "Lieutenant, perhaps you would be so kind."

"Why, of course!" Lance moved over and said, "If you're ready, Miss Noelle."

A rich pink suffused the face of the young woman, but she nodded. "I hate to be such a bother."

"No trouble at all. I broke both my arms once when I was a young man. I was all kinds of bother." Leaning over, he slipped his arms around her and lifted her easily. He carried her into the dining room and set her carefully down in one of the chairs. "There you are," he said cheerfully. "Perhaps you could hire me to be your personal porter until your ankle heals."

They all sat down, and, as Marie had said, the food was on the table. Glancing around, Lance said, "This is a lovely room." The room was a large area of about sixteen by sixteen with a high white ceiling, cream-and-blue wallpapered walls, and a large Persian carpet covering almost all the floor. The mahogany furniture was all large, massively carved, and polished to a high gloss. Two large floor-length windows were covered with dark blue curtains and tied back with a gold brocade rope that hung down into a large tassel. A small white marble fireplace sent out an ample amount of heat. The table was covered with a white embroidered tablecloth and was set with fine china and crystal side pieces. Lance Winslow thought, *This room is like the family—warm and graceful.*

"My wife has good taste," Pierre said, noting Winslow's study of the room. "She keeps buying furniture, but I tell her one day we won't need anything this fancy. After we leave Paris we'll have to sell much of it."

"You're leaving Paris?"

"Someday when I retire from my practice. Both Katherine and I come from small villages. We'd like to move away from the hustle and bustle of the city life."

Marie cleared her throat, and hearing the sound, Pierre Laurent laughed quietly. "That's a signal from Marie to ask the blessing and get on with the meal—so we will do so." Bowing his head, Laurent uttered a quick prayer, and then as soon as the amen was said, he picked up the carving knife and fork, and said, "Now, since I am the surgeon I will carve the goose."

It was a lovely Christmas dinner indeed! The meal consisted of roast goose, rich chestnut stuffing made with lots of butter, potatoes with gravy, peas and pearl onions in a butter cream sauce, fresh loaves of bread lathered thoroughly with rich butter, preserves, cakes with rich rum sauce topped with raisins and currants, and hot black coffee.

As the meal progressed, Winslow inquired more into the Laurents' possible move to the country. He turned to Noelle and Danielle, commenting, "I don't suppose that will please either of you. There won't be much of a social life."

"That's what I keep telling Father," Danielle spoke up at once. "I'd hate to be stuck in a little town with nothing to do."

On the other hand, Noelle nodded, saying quietly, "I would like it very much. I like the quiet atmosphere of a small town much better."

"I'm from a small town myself. Everyone knew everyone. Big cities like London and Paris confuse me."

The talk went around the table, and finally Doctor Laurent, who had finished his meal, signaled Marie for another cup of coffee. "What is your thinking on the current political scene, Lieutenant Winslow? Being in the military, you must be very apprehensive about what is happening in Europe."

Winslow instantly grew serious. He nodded, saying, "It's not just the military that should be concerned. It's all of us, Doctor Laurent. I'm afraid these are troubling times."

"Indeed they are, and due to get worse, I think. Your entire mission here, as I understand it, is to find ways to use the airplane as a military weapon?"

"Yes, sir. Basically that's it."

"Are your countrymen so certain there will be a war?"

"They don't always say so publicly, but privately there is great concern. I'm sure you are aware of the two armed camps that are dividing Europe."

"Yes. It started back when I was a younger man with the alliance between Germany and Austria-Hungary."

"That is true, sir, and it is getting worse. Bismarck was satisfied with Germany's boundaries, but the kaiser is not. He wants a war, and when a leader such as he wants a war badly enough, he will find a way to get it."

"When Wilhelm the First died, a friend of mine wrote, 'Lord abide with us, for the evening draws nigh.' "

"Yes. Wilhelm the Second brought his own troubles."

"I don't understand all this," Katherine said, shaking her head. "It's so confusing."

"It is very confusing, Madame Laurent," Winslow said. He was silent for a moment, and all of the Laurents studied the chiseled face of the Englishman. He appeared meditative and there was grave thoughtfulness in his light blue eyes as he seemed to be having troublesome thoughts. "I don't know if you're aware of it, but Russia and France have agreed to unite if either is ever threatened by aggression."

"That is so," Doctor Laurent said quickly. "And sooner or later Germany will have trouble with Russia."

"Yes. And then France will be drawn in."

"That will be a sad day for our country."

"And for England, for she will be drawn into it, too. As a matter of fact, the United Kingdom became attached to the Franco-Russian combine in 1904. So . . ." he said, and then he managed a smile that made him look younger, "your country and mine are tied together."

As all this talk about politics went on, Danielle fidgeted impatiently. Finally she said, "Come. It's time to open the presents."

"What makes you think you have a present?" Doctor Laurent said, his eyes twinkling. "You've been a naughty girl."

"I have not! I've been good!"

"Well, I suppose you have. Once again, Lieutenant, may I trouble you to help Noelle to the large parlor?"

As Lance carried Noelle to the larger of the two parlors, he was acutely aware of her youthful beauty and of the fragrance of her lilac perfume. She turned once suddenly to face him and their eyes met.

She smiled then, saying quietly, "I'm sorry to be such a burden."

"I assure you, Miss Noelle, you are no burden at all." He entered the larger parlor decorated with dark, rich colors. The walls were papered in a dark red-and-gold flecked paper, the ceiling was painted white and very high, and the floors were covered with wall-to-wall carpet in dark reds, greens, and black. The windows were covered with dark burgundy velvet coverings, and the overstuffed furniture was done in golds, greens, blues, and reds, all soft hues to the eye and to the touch. He ensconced his burden into an overstuffed chair, then took a seat beside her.

The giving of gifts and the squeals of delight from Danielle made Lance Winslow smile with pleasure. He had not celebrated a Christmas like this in years, not since he had been a very young man. As he observed the love and playful bantering of the Laurent family, the thought came to his mind, *I hope someday I can have a home just like this. How they care for one another*. He was surprised when Danielle came over with a gaily wrapped package.

"This is for you, Lieutenant."

"Why, I certainly wasn't expecting a present, and I didn't bring any for you."

"Open it," Danielle urged. Her eyes were bright, and she looked very pretty. In fact, she had been the instigator of rounding up a present for their guest. She had pestered her father until he had managed to come up with a solution. Several years ago he had been given a beautifully designed razor with mother-of-pearl and set with a gold crest. Pierre Laurent had used the same razor for over twenty years and was reluctant to give it up, beautiful though the new one might be, so he had finally consented to Dani's persistent persuasions.

As Lance opened the box and picked up the razor, his throat suddenly became thick with emotion. "It's a beautiful gift, and I will use it as long as I grow whiskers." He opened it and admired the gleaming steel.

"It's as good as the scalpels that I use. It's made from the finest Swedish steel," Doctor Laurent said. "I hope you'll enjoy it, Lieutenant."

"I certainly will, and I'll treasure it always." He looked up at each of them and said, "Your gracious invitation and this gift are very special to me. Enjoying the day with all of you sure beats being at a hotel by myself. I thank you all."

Noelle was touched by the loneliness of Lance Winslow. "You must come often and visit our home while you are in France."

"With your parents' permission, of course, I will," he said, nodding toward her father.

"Certainly," Doctor Laurent said. "It will be our honor."

The day went more pleasantly for Lance Winslow than any he could remember. He spent a great deal of the time playing games with the family, and Danielle's squeals of delight as she beat him at draughts were amusing. He took a liking to the young girl immediately and once said quietly to Noelle, "I wish I had a younger sister such as yours. She seems so . . . so . . ."

"Excitable, impressionable, and totally unable to contain her feelings," Noelle finished for him. "Dani is a dear girl, indeed. We all love her very much."

"She's very pretty."

"Oh yes. She'll be a beautiful woman."

"It runs in the family," Lance said. Then as her eyes opened with surprise, he added, "Your mother is a lovely woman." Then he grinned, saying, "And you are, too, Miss Noelle. Pardon my impertinence, but I think I'm a little bit intoxicated."

"But you haven't had any alcohol."

"No, but just being in a home like this is intoxicating for an old soldier like me."

"Old soldier, indeed! How old are you, Lieutenant?"

"Well, I'm twenty-one." He blushed as her merry laugh rang through the room and then shrugged his trim shoulders. "I make myself sound like Methuselah, don't I? And how old are you, if I may ask?"

"I'm twenty and Danielle is fourteen."

"Going on fifteen," Lance smiled. "She's already informed me of that. She's a very precocious young woman." He leaned forward and studied her face. "You have a very marvelous family. I hate to say it, but I'm almost glad you twisted your ankle. Otherwise I would be sitting in an empty café somewhere eating a bowl of soup."

The two sat there talking for a while, then he finally rose to leave. "Were you serious about my coming back?"

"Why, of course!"

"Then you may see more of me than you think. I'll call tomorrow to see how your injury is." He reached out, took her hand, and squeezed it. "And after your ankle is well, I hope that we might go out some evening. Perhaps you can show me the sights of Paris."

"That would be delightful, Lieutenant Winslow. Good night."

After the lieutenant had gone, Noelle sat with her foot propped up. It was throbbing, for she had put more weight on it that day than was proper, but her thoughts were not on her ankle, but the pleasant day she had enjoyed with a very handsome officer. When her father came in later, she said, "He's very nice, isn't he?"

"Very nice, indeed." He sat down beside her and asked, "How's the ankle?"

"A little pain but not bad."

"You'll have to stay off of it."

"Lieutenant Winslow asked if I could go out and show him a little of Paris as soon as my ankle is better."

"And you would like to do that?" her father asked, a twinkle in his eye.

Noelle smiled, saying slowly, "Yes. I would like to very much, Papa."

★ ★ ★ ★

"Are you certain you're able to be on your feet?" Katherine Laurent had come to stand behind Noelle, who was putting the final touches on her hair.

Noelle put the brush down and turned to smile. "Why, of course I am, Mother. It's perfectly well now." This was not exactly true, but the ankle was much better. She had improved rapidly, and now, at the later part of January, she had only a slight twinge to remind her of the bad sprain. She got to her feet and said, "Lance wants to take me to see something. He won't tell me what it is."

"You two have seen quite a bit of the city," Katherine said. "What is it this time?"

"He won't tell me. He just said it was something very special."

Thirty minutes later Lance arrived. The weather had modified, so he was not wearing an overcoat. He looked very dashing in his olive uniform, and when Noelle came to greet him, he grinned. "Ready for the big surprise?"

"I can't imagine what it is. We're not going to the zoo, are we? Not in January."

"Something better than that." Lance turned to Katherine, saying, "I will have her home early, madame."

"You two have a good time."

When they were outside, the cold bit at Noelle's cheeks. She was wearing a long, double-breasted overcoat fastened with large buttons and a flat hat with a small crown. Lance helped her into the cab that was waiting and then leaned forward and whispered the directions to the cabbie, who spoke some English.

"You're certainly making a mystery of this," Noelle said, smiling.

"A woman likes a man of mystery."

"Who told you that? You haven't been reading those awful romance novels, have you?"

"They're not awful at all. I'm a very romantic fellow."

"Are you, now?" Noelle giggled suddenly. "I don't think men who are romantic have to announce it."

"Well, actually I feel like putting a sign around my neck that reads, 'I'm a very romantic fellow.' "

Noelle leaned back in the cab, enjoying the conversation. He was very amusing, this Lance Winslow, and she knew he was becoming very fond of her. He had not tried to kiss her, but somehow her intuition told her that it would come soon. He would not tell her anything about the destination as he teased her, threatening to blindfold her at one point.

Finally the cab pulled up, and Lance got out and then helped Noelle. He paid the cabdriver, then turned and said, "Well, here we are."

"But—what is it, Lance?"

They were standing beside a large field that was thickly strewn with airplanes of all sorts. A large crowd had gathered, and most of them were bundled up to the ears against the cold weather. The air was filled with the sound of engines buzzing and roaring. Lance took her arm and said, "It's the International Paris Air Show—the first one ever. There are pilots and planes here from all over the world. It's really one of the reasons I came here. I was talking with the pilots all day yesterday. Come along. I'll give you a tour."

For the next two hours Noelle was treated to the sights of airplanes such as she had never dreamed. Most of them looked like flimsy kites to her with their canvas or silk-covered wings, with the pilot sitting in the middle exposed to the air.

"They look so . . . so flimsy. They're very dangerous, aren't they?"

"One pilot I met here named René Thomas has had twenty-seven crashes."

"Mercy! How is he still alive?"

"Well, I think he's broken most of his bones, but he loves the adventure of it. Look at this plane here. Now, that is an airplane for you."

"What kind is it?" Noelle asked.

"That's a Farman Pusher biplane. Look at those ailerons!"

Lance explained what an aileron was and pointed out the fine points of the craft, which had a four-wheeled undercarriage made of lightweight wood.

Lance enjoyed her company as they toured the rest of the airplanes, and the afternoon went pleasantly enough. Finally he said, "I have a surprise for you, as I told you."

"Isn't this it, coming to the air show?"

"Not all of it. Come along." He led her through the maze of planes and said as he went, "I know your ankle must be aching, but you won't have to stand on it much longer." The two arrived in front of one of the planes that looked no more sturdy than the others. A medium-sized man with a dark, olive complexion and a droopy mustache straightened up and smiled as the two approached.

"Ah, my English friend."

"Monsieur Blériot, may I present Mademoiselle Noelle Laurent. Miss Laurent, Louis Blériot, the finest pilot alive."

Blériot was a rather solemn-looking man, but a glint of humor danced in his eyes. "I bet you say that to all the pilots."

"Not at all, monsieur. I would not mislead mademoiselle, and I am sure you will be the first to cross the Channel."

"You mean fly across the English Channel?" Noelle exclaimed. "In *this?*"

"Ah, you do not understand, mademoiselle." Blériot spoke in French, and Lance caught little of it, but he tried to follow along as the French pilot explained the virtues of the two-seated craft.

Finally Blériot winked at Lance. "Is the young lady ready for her first flight?"

"What!" Noelle gasped, staring up at Lance.

Louis Blériot laughed. "You have not told her, then?"

"No, I haven't," Lance said. "Monsieur Blériot has kindly consented to let me take his plane up. You will be my passenger."

Staring at the flimsy airplane, Noelle had an impulse to laugh and refuse, but she had an adventurous spirit and a streak of daring in her. She smiled and said, "Monsieur Blériot, you are too kind."

Quickly the two men worked on the plane, and a short while later, Noelle found herself seated in the wicker seat just to Lance's left. The engine ran roughly and then leveled off. Waving toward Blériot, Lance moved the controls, and the airplane taxied out. Noelle held on tightly to the arms of her seat, and as the plane picked up speed, she wondered, *What in the world am I doing here? Father would have a fit!*

And then the ground seemed to drop away, and Noelle caught her breath. She could hear little but the snarling roar of the engine, and the cold wind bit at her face, making it numb.

"Are you afraid?"

Noelle turned to face Lance, who was leaning over and had shouted into her ear. "Not as long as you're here," she shouted back.

And then the plane rose. After the initial shock of being off the ground, Noelle took delight in the ride. It was something she had never dreamed of. She looked over and saw the Eiffel Tower rising clearly out of the city. "Look. There's the street where you live—and there's your house!" Lance shouted.

"Oh, it is! It is! Wait until I tell Father!"

Finally, in a great sweeping curve, Lance brought the plane back high over the field. Down below, the planes with their bright covered fabrics broke the solemn earth colors of winter. Lance suddenly leaned over, and removing his left hand and putting it behind the seat, he placed it on her left shoulder. His touch surprised Noelle, and she turned to him. His face was only inches away as he pulled her closer and put his lips almost against her ear. "I planned all this just for one reason."

"Planned what, Lance?"

"Getting you up here all alone."

And then Noelle's heart beat faster. His arm tightened around her, and she saw that he intended to kiss her.

"I brought you up here so that I could tell you that you're the loveliest woman in the world, and that I'm falling in love with you."

He brought her around to face him with the strength of his left arm, and Noelle put her hand up on his shoulder. And then, high above the earth, higher than Noelle had ever imagined, Lieutenant Lance Winslow kissed her. Although the temperature was cold, his lips seemed warm by comparison and she lost all sense of time. She could only imagine what was in his heart, but she knew that her own was stirred as it had never been stirred by a man. For that one moment high above the earth Noelle Laurent knew deep in her heart she loved this man. He was a foreigner, and they were very different in many ways. Everything seemed against such a romance, but the love she felt was greater than the differences.

Finally he removed his lips and laughed aloud. "You're a woman who can disturb a man, Noelle. I'd better pay attention to what I'm doing or we'll crash." He made a sweeping circle, and as he lined up the plane with the field, he turned to her. "Are you angry?" he asked anxiously. He did not want anything to go wrong with this woman, and he watched her face, searching for some sign of regret.

But Noelle suddenly reached out and struck him on the shoulder with a light blow. She laughed aloud and shook her head. "Some men," she said, delight dancing in her eyes, "will do anything to get attention."

★ ★ ★ ★

As soon as Noelle returned home, Danielle, of course, begged her sister to tell her all about her outing with Lieutenant Winslow. Finally, with some exasperation, Noelle told her about the air show and the airplane ride.

"Oh, I wish I could have gone up!" Danielle said. "You have all the luck."

Danielle kept pressing for details until Noelle smiled, saying, "He kissed me when we were up in the airplane."

Danielle stared at her sister for a moment silently, then she bit her lip and abruptly left the room. As she went to her own room, she threw herself across her bed, and hot tears rose in her eyes. "Why couldn't it be *me?*" she whispered, pressing her face against her pillow. "Why couldn't I be the older sister?"

CHAPTER THREE

"If I Have You—I Have Everything!"

★ ★ ★ ★

Spring had finally come to Paris with a burst of almost furious energy. As May came to an end, the parks seemed to explode with bright blossoms, and the grass was so green it looked like a carpet of emeralds. In contrast to the dark political cloud that hung over England, the season had a halcyon quality to it that seemed to override the fears that abode in the hearts of so many.

Danielle Laurent gazed out the window with a disconsolate air as Noelle and Lance got into a taxi. As the vehicle pulled away, she turned and complained, "Lance never spends any time with anyone but Noelle!"

"Well, that's only natural," Katherine Laurent said mildly. She removed her glasses and rubbed her eyes, placing the embroidery in her lap. Studying her youngest daughter, she said, "They're engaged, Dani. They need time to be alone."

"Well, it wouldn't hurt Lance to pay a little attention to someone else! Just because they're engaged doesn't mean everybody else has dropped dead in the world!"

"Don't talk like that!"

Danielle suddenly burst into tears and ran out of the parlor, leaving her mother to stare after her. "Something's got to be done about that child," she murmured aloud. She and Pierre had talked more than once about the unnatural obsession Danielle seemed to have for Lance Winslow. At first it had been mildly amusing, for Danielle had formed schoolgirl attachments to young men before. However, this time it was different. Her other attachments had been, for the most part, to famous men whose pictures she saw in periodicals and newspapers, mostly actors. But after Noelle and Lance had become engaged, both Katherine and Pierre had expected Danielle to pass through that stage. To their dismay, it had not gone away. In fact, it had gotten worse. Now Katherine bit her lip and thought, *I've got to talk to Pierre. Dani's moodiness is getting serious. I'll be glad when Lance and Noelle get married and move to England.*

★ ★ ★ ★

As usual, Lance had taken Noelle to the airport, where he had put on a pair of coveralls and allowed her to watch him as he worked with one of the mechanics tearing down an engine. As Noelle sat on a chair under the shade of the hangar, she was amused. *It never occurs to Lance,* she thought, *that a woman might not be fascinated by watching an engine being disemboweled.* Still there was affection with the thought, and she was content to be with him. Their engagement had happened rapidly, and her parents, to her relief, had approved of her marrying an Englishman. It would mean, of course, that she would be moving to England. There was a natural regret over that, but still they were very fond, indeed, of their daughter's future husband.

Her thoughts were interrupted as overhead an enormous dirigible floated over, its motors making a snarling sound. It seemed too large to fly, and she saw that it was a German craft. Lance had pointed them out to her more than once, for they seemed to be everywhere. Once he had told her, "The Germans are forging ahead. Mark what I tell you. One of these days those things will be dropping bombs and killing people."

Now as the dirigible settled down toward the earth, Noelle watched as men ran out, grabbed ropes, and anchored the monstrous aircraft. The canopy, which was suspended underneath, soon disgorged the pilot and crews. "Lance, do you really think those awful looking things will really become practical?" she asked.

Looking up from a stubborn bolt that refused to become disengaged, Lance wiped his brow, leaving a black mark on his forehead. The perspiration flowed down, and his hair was matted. Casting his eyes over to the airship, he said, "They already are. Those things are all over Europe. Count Ferdinand von Zeppelin talks about what great passenger ships they'll be, and they've flown great distances already. Why, I saw a poster the other day with a map showing their stops. Just like a train."

"Well, that would be good, wouldn't it?"

Standing to his feet, Lance came over to stand beside where Noelle was seated. She looked cool and very pretty, but his thoughts were on the massive craft that was being tethered. "I can see one thing," he said soberly. "How big a bomb do you think this airplane would carry?" He motioned toward the frail airplane from which the engine had been removed.

"Why, I don't have any idea."

"Maybe a hundred pounds, but look at that Zeppelin. Why, it could carry plenty of bombs, and as far as hitting something, look how easy it would be, Noelle. That thing can hover in air just like a hummingbird! Just imagine if it came over Buckingham Palace. Why, the king wouldn't have a chance!"

"Do you really think that will happen, Lance?"

"I think it might," he said quietly. "I've been talking to some of the German mechanics. They're going full speed at developing military aircraft of all kinds." He shook his head, and disgust showed on his lean face. "And we're doing nothing in England and France."

"France had better come up with some fighting aircraft because my country is so far behind, I don't think we'll ever catch up."

For a time Lance went back to working on his engine. Finally, when he had helped the mechanic install it back into the craft, he came over to Noelle, wiping his hands on a dirty rag. "Let me clean up," he said, "and we'll go get something to eat."

An hour later they were at a sidewalk café on the Champs Elysées. They were both hungry and ordered a large luncheon. "Do you miss English cooking?" Noelle asked.

"Yes, I do, although everyone says French cooking is the best in the world. I guess," he grinned, "I just would like to have some plain old English roast beef."

"I'll have to learn to cook all over again. Not that I can cook much anyway. Marie does most of that."

Reaching over, Lance took Noelle's hand. "You'll be a wonderful cook," he said. "Everything you do is wonderful."

"Little you know! Except for a cake or two, I've never fixed anything for you!"

"I'll eat it no matter if it's burned to a crisp."

For a time they sat there enjoying the mild breeze that stirred occasionally, and finally Lance said, "I have news for you. I got a letter this morning from headquarters." He looked at her and turned his head to one side. "I don't know whether you'll like it or not."

"What is it, Lance?"

"I'll be leaving here soon. I have to return to my station."

"Oh, Lance, do you have to go?"

"There's a civilian speaking," he smiled broadly. "Of course I have to go. Orders are orders."

"Then we'll have to be married at once. When do you have to leave?"

Lance stared at her and shook his head with admiration. "I wanted to ask you, but it seemed to be rushing it. I've only got two weeks."

"Two weeks is enough. We'll have a June wedding."

"June is a good month for weddings," Lance said. He had learned to love this girl more than he had thought possible. At times the intensity of his feelings for her almost frightened him. He had learned to control fear in the air and was a man of steadfast character. Still, just the thought of losing her sent a cold chill down his spine. He held her hand then and said, "There's no one like you, Noelle."

"Oh, there are plenty like me."

"No. You're the only one for me. I could never love anyone else."

"I like to hear that, and you must tell me often."

"It's true enough." He squeezed her hand, then brought it to his lips and kissed it. "If I have you," he said quietly, "I have everything."

Noelle reached out and put her hand on his cheek. "You have your moments, Lance Winslow," she murmured. "Indeed, you have your moments!"

★ ★ ★ ★

The Laurent household turned into a hive of furious activity. Katherine Laurent, like all mothers, wanted to have a very formal wedding, but the shortness of time limited them somewhat. Nevertheless, by the time June 2 came, all the arrangements had been made. On the day before the wedding, Lance came for a final visit. He was wearing a freshly tailored uniform, and as he stood before his future mother-in-law, he said, "I wish I could wear one of those fancy wedding suits that I see in the society pages, but I didn't think I should spend the money."

"Of course you shouldn't, Lance," Katherine said. She came over and stood before her tall soon-to-be son-in-law, looking up at him. "You look very handsome in your uniform. All of Noelle's girlfriends are going to be alive with envy."

"Well, I've worried about one thing, Katherine. I'll never be a rich man. You understand that."

"You'll be a general one day. I'm sure of it." Katherine smiled and patted his arm. "In any case, I wanted to tell you how fond Pierre and I are of you. Noelle couldn't have picked a better husband."

A warm feeling washed through Lance and he reached out and hugged Katherine. "It's good of you to say that," he whispered. "I'll do my best to make her happy."

At that moment Danielle came in, and she stopped abruptly upon seeing Lance. "Hello," she said in a small voice.

"Why, hello, young lady." Lance went over and stood before her. "All ready to be the bridesmaid tomorrow?"

"Yes."

Lance gave a quick look at the face of the young girl. Usually Danielle was cheerful and full of life, but there was a lackluster quality about her today. "Hey, tomorrow's my wedding day. You've got to cheer up. It's the bride who is supposed to be nervous!"

Danielle did not answer. She hesitated for a moment, then turned and walked away without another word.

"What's wrong with her? Is she sick?" Lance asked with surprise.

"You don't know?"

"Know what?"

"Oh, she's got one of those schoolgirl affections for you. What do they call it? A crush."

Surprise caused Lance to blink. "Why, that's not possible!"

"Possible. It's not only possible, it's so. If you were French, you would have seen it a long time ago."

"Why, Katherine, it's ridiculous. She's just a child!"

"No. She's not *just a child,*" Katherine said, and her lips drew together in a tight line. "She's halfway between being a girl and a woman, and now the woman in her has taken over. Pierre and I have been very concerned about it. So has Noelle. She's never mentioned it to you?"

"Never said a word." Lance was thoroughly shocked. "But surely it will pass away."

"Of course it will. We had just hoped it would be before now. But, as you say, it will pass away. Don't let a foolish young girl's impossible dreams spoil your wedding day. You'll have a daughter of your own one of these days. Just remember they can be very foolish."

Later on Lance spoke to Noelle about Danielle. "Your mother tells me that Danielle's behaving rather foolishly."

Quickly Noelle looked up at Lance. "Yes, she is," she said. "She's always been impulsive. It's not the first infatuation she's had. Don't worry about it."

But Lance was looking closely at Noelle. "You're worried about it. I can tell."

"Well, a little bit."

"Did you ever have one of those things? Crushes."

"Oh, half a dozen, but I got over them very quickly, and so will Danielle." Forcing herself to smile, she reached up and pulled his head down and kissed him. "There, that's the last kiss you get until after we're married."

"And what about afterward?" Lance teased her.

"That will depend on how good you are. Now go."

★ ★ ★ ★

Even with such little time to plan, Katherine Laurent managed to give her daughter Noelle a beautiful wedding.

As Lance stood in the front of the church and watched Noelle come down the aisle, he thought, *There's no other woman in the world like her*. And as she came to stand beside him, he smiled and received her smile in return. Then they both gave their vows, and afterward when he kissed her, he said, "If I have you, I have everything."

It was something he often said to her. He had first said it that day at the airport when they had seen the German Zeppelin, and it had become very precious to Noelle. As they turned and went out of the church, she caught one glimpse of Danielle's face and for a moment allowed herself to become disturbed. Then she thought, *Lord, you'll have to take care of my sister. I've got a husband now, and he's going to get the best I've got to give him.*

That afternoon they boarded the steamship that would mark the beginning of their honeymoon trip. Lance had requested extra leave and planned a tour through England and Scotland to see his mother.

That night as Noelle was lying in the bed, Lance came to her, took her in his arms, and said, "You may get tired of hearing this, Noelle, but I love you probably more than a man should love a woman."

Noelle was wearing a gleaming white satin gown, and as he lay beside her, she felt a glow of possession. "How could a man love a woman too much?"

"I don't know," he said. He kissed her and then whispered, "If I have you, I have everything."

Noelle returned his kiss and then put her arms around his neck and hugged him tightly. Tears came to her eyes, and she whispered, "I hope you'll always feel that way, sweetheart."

★ ★ ★ ★

The honeymoon was wonderful, and when it was over, Lance and Noelle knew that their love was everything they had hoped it would be. They treasured each other's company more than they could imagine. Neither had ever been so at home with a human being, and more than once Noelle would stop and say, "Lord, you have given me just the husband I needed, and I thank you for it."

They had settled down in a small apartment in Hastings, and Noelle had at once set about becoming an English housewife. Sometimes Lance was gone for several days and he was rising in importance in the service. Noelle learned to cook and spent much time at the fish markets down on the coast and in the greengrocers' shops. She became a regular customer, and was greeted warmly by the English shopkeepers and fishermen.

They enjoyed their time on the weekends, and when Lance could squeeze out some days off, they went on short trips throughout the countryside. Once Noelle said, "I believe I'm seeing more of your country than I ever saw of mine."

One day in July Lance came running in, his eyes bright with excitement. "It's happened!" he cried. Picking Noelle up, he swung her in a wide circle.

Almost breathless, Noelle demanded, "What is it? What's happened?"

"It's Blériot. You remember the pilot we met on our first outing?"

"Certainly I remember Monsieur Blériot."

"Well, he's done it! He's crossed the Channel! The first man to fly across the English Channel."

"Oh, how exciting! Did you get to see him?"

"See him! I was there when he landed! England's going crazy."

"What does it all mean, Lance?"

"It means, for one thing," Lance said soberly, "that England's protection is gone."

"Her protection?"

"Yes. Up until now we were in a fortress here. We could only be attacked by ships, but now planes can leave France and attack us from the Continent." His jaw grew hard and he nodded. "That means we have to have airplanes that can fight them off, and soon, I'm afraid."

Lance was so excited about Blériot's success, he insisted they both go and congratulate him at once. It took some doing, but Lance used his influence, and they were able to meet with the newly famous pilot. Blériot smiled at once when being introduced and shook his head. "Ah, you think I would forget such a lovely lady? I remember you well, madame."

"Congratulations, Monsieur Blériot. I'm very proud of you, as is all of France."

"And England as well, Louis," Lance said.

The two had a short visit with the pilot, then he was soon dragged off by the powers that be to receive proper accolades.

Later that night when the two had gone to bed, Lance held Noelle in his arms and talked about what the Channel crossing meant.

Noelle listened contentedly, her head on his chest. When he finally grew silent thinking about all that had to be done in his job, she said, "I have news for you."

"What is it?"

"There are going to be three of us."

Instantly Lance gave a great cry of joy. "You mean it?"

"Are you happy? Is it too soon?"

"Too soon? Why, what a silly you are!"

"It will tie you down."

Lance held her tightly, joy running through him. "I hope it's a girl," he whispered. "Then I'll have to change my little speech."

"What speech is that?"

"The one where I say if I have you, I have everything."

"And what will you say now?"

He kissed her and held her tightly, then murmured, "If I have you two, I will have everything. . . ."

CHAPTER FOUR

No Longer a Child

★ ★ ★ ★

Ever since Danielle Laurent had begun planning her trip to England, she had carefully crossed off each succeeding day. Now she leaned forward and made a careful X over the sixth of May and noted the date, 1914. She hesitated for one moment, and her mind went back to another time. She remembered suddenly how when Noelle and Lance had left after their wedding to go to England, she had crossed off day after day on another calendar. Now that time came rushing back to her, and she suddenly straightened up and moved over to the window to stare outside.

"That seems like a lifetime ago," she murmured, and a pang came to her that she had thought to be done with forever. She could not help but remember then how as a fourteen-year-old she had wept night after night. Finally after weeks of despair, she had burned the calendar and decided to put her feelings for Lance Winslow out of her mind forever. Now she turned suddenly and walked across the room to the full-length mirror and studied herself analytically. What she saw was a relatively tall, attractive young woman with a wealth of abundant light brown hair, a pair of well-shaped and cool brown eyes set in an oval face. Her eyes went downward, and she noted the trim, womanly figure, more shapely than that of most young women. She was wearing a light green cashmere dress with a wide collar decked with velvet rosettes, and the vest was of oriental silk threaded with gold. She turned to study the skirt that fell to the ground in a bell-shaped fashion, then suddenly shook her head impatiently. "I was just a child then," she muttered. "Why do I think of those days?"

Turning quickly she moved across the room and began packing her bag. It was to be a two-week visit, so she packed her undergarments, gowns, and stockings as carefully as she could. She could hear the birds singing outside, and finally when she had finished packing the bag and closed it, she went to look out the window again. It was a favorite view of hers, and she had spent many hours daydreaming here since her family had moved from Paris two years earlier. Her father had done what he had long yearned to do, escaped the pressures of big-city life to live in a small village. Belleville was only twenty miles from Paris, so shopping trips or visits to medical association meetings were simple enough. As for Danielle, she had actually enjoyed being in a small town, to her surprise. The whole family had quickly found their place within the small community, so that now they were well content with their lot.

A squirrel suddenly appeared in the large plum tree that rose up level with Danielle's window. A smile touched her lips, and she murmured, "I'll have to remember to get Georgette to feed you, not that you need it. You're getting fat." She smiled at the antics of the squirrel for a time, then a knock at the door caused her to turn around. "Yes. Come in."

When the door opened, her father came inside and smiled. "Well, are you ready for your journey?"

"Yes, Papa. I'm all packed."

Pierre Laurent came over and smiled at this younger daughter of his. "That's a pretty dress for traveling. Is it new?"

"No. I've had it over six months. I just never had an opportunity to wear it."

"You don't get out enough." Pierre shook his head. "You've gotten to be an old woman, Danielle. Why, you ought to be out attending parties and balls every night." Danielle smiled, for it was an argument they had had often. Her father and mother had been disappointed that she had not thrown herself into the social life of the village. Aside from church and a few parties, she had made few contacts. Now she reached up and patted her father on the cheek. "I'll have a party every night while I'm visiting Noelle and Lance."

"You might look around. I understand there are plenty of young men over in England." He winked at her and settled back on his heels, adding, "What you ought to do is have a rousing romance."

"I will, Papa. I'll find a young man full of romance who will jilt me incredibly."

Pierre laughed. Danielle, though she had grown quieter than he had expected since she was a young girl, was still able to poke fun at herself. "You'll never be an unmarried spinster!" he declared. "Just not possible."

"Do you have the letter for me to take to Noelle?"

"Yes. Right here." Reaching inside his coat pocket, Pierre pulled out two fat envelopes, one for Noelle and one for Lance. "And don't forget the package for Gabby. I don't suppose I'd know her. We haven't seen her for two years. Let's see. She's how old now?"

"She's just turned four." A wistful look swept across Danielle's face. "Children change so quickly. She was such a doll when they were here on their last visit."

"I wish she could have come more often, but now it doesn't appear that there'll be a great deal of visiting. I'm glad you're going, though. I know Noelle has begged you to come for a long time." He asked curiously, "Why didn't you go before this? You've had plenty of time."

Indeed, Danielle had little excuse for not going to England. She had decided to become a doctor and had qualified as a nurse. Now she assisted her father in his work as a village medical man in Belleville while continuing her studies. Truth was, which she had never admitted even to herself, she did not want to see Lance Winslow. As the years had passed, she had managed to put her feelings for him away, convincing herself they were simply foolish, girlish infatuations. Still something in her had changed in those days when she had first met him. There had been enough young men interested in her that she might have chosen among several very acceptable suitors. Once she had almost reached the point of agreeing to become engaged, but abruptly, without any explanation, she had broken off the relationship. Now she said, "Oh, Papa, it's getting late, isn't it?"

Fumbling with a gold watch that he extracted from his vest pocket, Pierre stared at it and exclaimed, "Yes, indeed! I'll get your suitcase. The taxi is probably waiting."

As they went down the stairs, they were met by Katherine, whose hair in the past five years had become quite streaked with gray. She refused to dye it, however, as many of her friends had, and now said, "Come along. You don't want to miss your sailing."

Danielle turned to say to the short, chubby maid who had come carrying a smaller valise, "Georgette, I'll miss you."

"And I'll miss you, mademoiselle."

"Don't forget to feed the squirrels and the birds."

"No. I won't forget. They'll be fat as pigs when you come back."

Danielle reached over and patted the maid on the cheek, for she had strong feelings for her. Georgette had been with them for the last couple of years and had taken over when their housekeeper, Marie, had refused to leave Paris for the country.

"I wish you'd let us take you to Calais to put you on the ship," Pierre said. He shook his head, adding, "It doesn't seem right shipping you off in a taxi."

"Why, Papa, it will be fine. There's no point in you and Mother having to make that long ride there and back. We can say good-bye here." She reached up and put her arms around him and kissed him, then did the same for her mother. "I'll be back before you know it. When I come back I'll bring pictures of everyone."

"Try to get Noelle to come on a visit and bring Gabby with her. I know Lance will be too busy, but they could come and stay for a few weeks or even a couple of months."

"I'll try, but you know how it is with them. They can't seem to survive being out of each other's sight for a day or two. Good-bye. I love you."

Settling down inside the taxi, Danielle leaned out and waved, watching until her parents disappeared from view. She thought ahead to the time when she would arrive and wondered if Lance had changed a great deal. On their last visit he seemed not to have aged at all, and now she resolutely thought, *I've got to spend all the time I can with Noelle and Gabby. The way things are shaping up here on the Continent, there may be a war soon, and then that will end the traveling back and forth across the Channel.*

★ ★ ★ ★

The small ship that plied its incessant voyages from Calais to Dover was not particularly romantic. Danielle had made one extended voyage on the *Lusitania*. She had enjoyed it more than she had thought, but the *Babette* bore little resemblance to the floating palace. There were no enormous ballrooms with curving stairs, nor were there ornate dining facilities. She stood on the bow of the *Babette* enjoying the hot sunshine and the smell of the salt brine. She had always loved the tang of the sea, and now she shook her hair loose and let the breezes blow it behind freely.

"Enjoying your voyage, miss?"

Danielle turned to see a tall young man in a uniform who had come up to stand behind her. He was a rather homely young man with an engaging smile and a pair of alert gray eyes.

"Yes, I am. You do this all the time, I suppose?"

"Yes, I do. Back and forth just like a tennis match. Dover to Calais, Calais back to Dover. But I won't be doing it long, I don't suppose."

"Oh?" Actually Danielle was glad for the chance to talk to someone. She had not spoken to anyone on the ship, and now she smiled and asked, "What will you be doing?"

"Going in the regular navy. I think I'm getting a commission. What with the war coming up, they need lots of men."

Danielle's brow clouded for a moment, and she shook her head slightly. "There may not be a war, don't you think?"

"Oh, there's bound to be a war!" The young officer spoke cheerfully as if speaking of a cricket match.

There was nothing in his demeanor to indicate anything like fear, and as he chattered on in an amiable fashion, Danielle thought, *If the war comes, his ship may be sunk, and he may be dead in the bottom of the sea. But it doesn't seem to bother him.* Cautiously she approached the subject. "War's a terrible thing, isn't it?"

"Oh, of course it is very terrible."

"Doesn't it ever occur to you, Lieutenant, that you might get killed?"

"Can't worry about things like that, mademoiselle. Besides, they always told me I was born to be hanged. Can't drown if I'm going to be hanged, can I now?"

Danielle shook her head and said, "I don't think it's quite that simple, Lieutenant. I don't know much about war, but I know that men die."

"Why, people die every day, miss. A ship went down two weeks ago off the coast of Newfoundland. Two hundred and twenty people went down. What's the difference between that and war?"

Danielle was not sure. She had worried a great deal about the war and talked with her father about it. Somehow she knew that this blithe acceptance of a monstrous thing, if it ever came to pass, would put millions in shallow graves, and it disturbed her greatly. "Are you a Christian, Lieutenant?" she asked suddenly.

Dismay swept over the young man's face. "Why, I was christened when I was a baby, so my mum tells me."

"But that's a little different, isn't it? I mean christening isn't the same as being a Christian."

"Ain't it now? Why, I thought if one just got christened and did the best he could and went to church when it was convenient and was a decent chap, that would settle it. God wouldn't condemn a fellow if he did all that, would He?"

Danielle was herself a devout believer. Most French were Catholic, of course, but there was a strong Protestant church that her family had always gone to. It had not been easy, sometimes, to be outside the mainstream of religion, but Danielle had a thorough knowledge of the Bible at her command. She began quietly to give her testimony to the young sailor, who stood there staring at her with astonishment. He had actually approached her, she knew, because it was something he would do with any attractive, young woman on the ship. Now she saw that he was rapidly becoming very nervous, and inwardly smiled. *He certainly didn't come to get a sermon. He wanted a girl*, she said to herself. *But at least he'll hear one sermon.*

"Well, that's very interesting, miss. Ah, excuse me, please. I have duties to perform."

Danielle watched the sailor as he rapidly made his way down the deck and disappeared down one of the stairways. "Well, that's one way to get rid of an unwanted young Romeo," she murmured, but then she thought again of what might become of this young man if war came. She strolled around the deck of the small ship, and within two hours, she heard one of the passengers say, "Look, there's Dover. See the white cliffs?" At once she turned and saw a thin line darkening the horizon. Danielle had heard of the white cliffs of Dover all of her life, and now as the ship rapidly approached, she stood there looking at the cliffs that rose up out of the mainland like tall sentinels guarding the coast of England.

Finally she went below and checked her bags to make sure she had all of her things, then engaged a steward to carry them topside.

The ship slowed, and she could feel the throbbing of the engines like a mighty heartbeat as the ship moved into the harbor. It was crowded, it seemed, with ships of all kinds, some large, some small, and the white sails of the sailing vessels seemed like the wings of doves as they flew over the blue-green water. The billowy clouds overhead were as white as the sails, and Danielle became apprehensive as the ship came to a stop on a wharf. She made sure that her baggage was being handled and then waited until the gangplank was lowered. She let the other passengers crowd off. There were not a great many of them, not more than thirty or forty, but finally she took a deep breath and moved down the gangplank. Her eyes swept the docks and at once picked out the tall form of Lance Winslow. He stood almost half a head taller than the others around him.

When he saw her, he smiled instantly and lifted his hands, calling out, "Danielle! Danielle! Here I am!"

When she stepped off of the gangplank, Danielle found herself suddenly confronted by Lance, who reached out and hugged her, picking her up off the ground.

"Lance, you're squeezing me to death!" Danielle protested. He was the same as she had remembered and seemed not to have aged a day except for a few lines around his eyes that only made him look more masculine. "My stars! Look at you! You've grown up again! Every time I see you, you get more gorgeous!" Lance grinned. "Here. Are these your bags?"

"Yes. That large one and the small gray one over there."

The two went out past the dock to the street outside, where Lance stored her baggage in a small red automobile. "Get in here," he said, opening the door. And when he had settled her, he went to the other side and, stepping in, started the engine. It made a riotous roar, and he grinned at her. "Loud, isn't it? Louder than some of the engines in the planes I've been flying."

"It's a beautiful car."

"Well, let's hurry. Noelle and Gabby are chomping at the bit to see you. They wanted to come, but we all wouldn't fit in this machine of mine."

As Lance threaded his way through traffic, which included automobiles, buses, and lorries, as well as wagons and horse-drawn carriages, he peppered her with questions about the trip and about the family.

Danielle gave him a quick review, stating that her father and mother were both well and she herself had never been more healthy.

Suddenly Lance took his eyes off the road. They had passed through the center of Dover, and now he turned to say, "What about you, Danielle?"

"What about me?"

"I mean is there a faint tinkling of wedding bells out there in the future?"

Quickly Danielle met his eyes and then turned away and looked at the line of shops that were flashing by. "No," she said, barely audible above the roar of the engine. "Nothing like that for me."

An hour later, they arrived in front of a small brick house, one of six in a line, all of them two-story. "Here we are," Lance said and shut the engine off.

He jumped out, but before Danielle could get out, she heard her name and looked up to see Noelle coming out with Gabby by her side. As soon as she got out, Noelle hugged her enthusiastically. Then Danielle turned and saw that Gabby was examining her with curious eyes. "You wouldn't remember me, Gabby, but I'm your aunt Danielle."

"I remember," Gabby said. "You gave me a doll."

"You still have that doll? Well, I brought you some more presents, even though it's not Christmas." She knelt down and studied the face of her young niece who resembled Noelle so much. Danielle looked up at her sister and smiled. "You'll never be able to deny her. She's you all over, Noelle."

"That's a mercy. She could have been a mutt like her dad," Lance grinned, as he lifted both suitcases out.

"Well, she's very pretty. Now, you and I are going to have a wonderful time, aren't we? You're going to show me all your dolls."

"Oh yes!" Gabby beamed. She was a very outgoing child with a warm smile.

As they all made their way inside, Noelle suddenly reached over and hugged Danielle. "I'm so glad you've come," she said warmly. "I've been so lonesome for you."

★ ★ ★ ★

"Do you think Danielle has enjoyed her visit?" Lance asked. He was sitting on a high stool watching as Noelle peeled potatoes. "Here. Let me help you with those."

"You'd cut your finger off. How could you fly your smelly old airplanes then?"

"They're not smelly."

"They are. They smell like castor oil."

"Well, that's because there's castor oil in the gas mixture. Here, let me show you how to peel a potato." Taking a potato and a knife, he proceeded to shear away the brown exterior and then held it up. "You see."

"I see you've put the best part of it in the garbage. Your peelings are too thick." For a moment Noelle paused and nodded her head. "Yes. I think she's had a good time."

"She hasn't gone out much, has she? I thought she might find a young fellow here to court her. I've sure brought enough by here."

"You have, a regular parade. I could have told you that was useless."

Lance held the potato in his hand and, reaching over, picked up the saltshaker and salted what was left of the potato generously. He took a bite of it and murmured, "I wonder why potatoes don't taste good raw? They're good every other way." Then he tossed the potato down into the bowl and said, "I wonder why she's never married. What do your parents say?"

"Just that she's very quiet and doesn't go out much. They don't know how to explain it."

"Well, I'll bring George Bentley by tomorrow. Women are crazy about him. Big, good-looking fellow. I don't think you've ever met him."

"I remember Bentley. You might as well save yourself the trouble, Lance. He's not her type."

"Well, what is her type?"

For a moment Noelle was quiet. She had observed her sister carefully throughout the days she had been in England, and it had become clearer to her that Danielle had shown little interest in the young men Lance had tried to foist off on her. She had never forgotten how taken Danielle had been with Lance, and although she and her mother had not talked about it in a long time, Noelle knew that in some strange way Danielle had never gotten over her crush on Lance. It grieved her heart, but Noelle knew she could never tell Lance. She remembered mentioning it to him once, and he had been incredulous. Now that Danielle was twenty, and those days were long passed, all she could say was, "She'll come out of it one day and find a fine husband and have a good family." She reached over then and pulled his head down and kissed him. She winked saucily, saying, "But her husband won't be as good looking as mine."

"Of course not. How could he be?" Lance suddenly reached out, put his arms around her, and the potatoes went rolling on the floor as she dropped the bowl. He ignored her protests and said, "Romance is more important than supper."

And it was then that Noelle looked at him and repeated what she had heard him say many times. 'If I have you, Lance, I have everything!"

CHAPTER FIVE

LET SLIP THE DOGS OF WAR

★ ★ ★ ★

After Danielle returned to France, Lance threw himself into a whirlwind of activities. He saw clearly the approaching threat of a great European war on the horizon and was determined that England would be strong in the skies.

When Noelle asked him how things stood as far as military strength and planes were concerned, he said, "As far as I can tell, the French have the head start. They're the most air-minded nation in all of Europe. Why, they have over two hundred and fifty planes, and they've won practically every air show they've entered. They've got a new airplane called the Nieuport, designed by a French engineer. It's the prototype of what all the small fighting planes will be like."

"But what about Germany?"

"Well, they've been lagging behind the French for some time. Most of the time they just steal French designs. They've got a plane called the Albatross that looks good, but I'll tell you the danger. There's a young man named Anthony Fokker, a Dutchman. He's the son of a wealthy coffee planter from the East Indies. The fellow is a genius, I tell you, and I wish he were on our side."

"What about England?"

A grimace swept across Lance's face. "Well, believe it or not, we're depending on a cowboy named Samuel Franklin Cody."

"Oh, a relation of the Buffalo Bill Cody I've read so much about?"

"No. No relation at all. He's an older man. I think he was forty-seven before he first flew any kind of plane. Comes from Texas and was a gold prospector in the Klondike and a Wild West showman. Like Buffalo Bill. You'd like to meet him. He'd be interesting for you."

"What's he like?"

"Oh, he wears shoulder-length hair, Western boots, and a huge hat. Carries a pistol, too, at his side, a Colt, and likes to shoot it behind hangar doors. He's scared us all to death, and he isn't that good a shot."

"But he builds airplanes?"

"The strangest thing I've ever seen. He can't read or write, but he has an instinctive flair for aeronautical engineering. The trouble is he wants to build huge planes. He was hired over here at the army balloon factory. As a matter of fact, he helped build the first army dirigible."

"Oh, the one that flew over London?"

"That's the one. Ran out of gas and had to be carted home. What he's done for us is get us started in airplane building. He built British army airplane number one, a huge craft with a fifty-two-foot wingspread. We called it a flying cathedral, and it was practically worthless. But it got other people to work on better designs. You remember that man I brought home, Kenneth Haviland?"

"Oh yes. I liked him very much," Noelle said.

"Well, he and a man named Thomas Sopwith are the bright stars for our air force. Haviland built the B.S.1." Here Lance grew excited. "It flies ninety-two miles an hour, and it'll be marvelous for a single-seated scout and a fighter plane. Why, one could shoot down balloons with it, I do believe, if we could mount a machine gun on it somehow. And Sopwith made a small plane that was able to climb fifteen thousand feet in ten minutes."

"What are the other nations doing, Lance?"

"Let's see. . . . There's a fellow in Russia called Igor Sikorsky. He's fooled around with helicopters—planes that are able to fly straight up and down with a rotor blade, but he's been making fixed-wing machines. Two years ago he came up with a four-engine biplane. It had an enclosed passenger cabin, a pantry, a toilet, and even interior heating. Why, it even had a promenade deck. Look," he said, "I'll show you a picture of it." He opened a door and came out with a large but poorly done black-and-white picture. Two men were running along in the snow looking upward. A big white four-story building was across from them on the open field. Overhead, filling the photograph, was a monstrous aircraft with skids instead of wheels. Much of it was unclear, but one thing stood out. Two men were standing on a deck midway back to the tail section wearing heavy overcoats. It was as if they were walking on a promenade deck at Brighton!

"I can't believe a contraption this big would fly! What's it good for?"

"Good enough to drop bombs, but I'm not afraid of that. The Russians will never fight with the Germans. They've got a treaty with too many of Germany's potential enemies."

"I don't understand it all," Noelle said sadly. "Why does there have to be a war?"

"That's the big question that men of goodwill and good sense are asking themselves all over the world." Lance leaned back in his chair and pulled her over in his lap. She leaned against him and placed her head down on his shoulder and listened as he spoke quietly.

"For some reason people throw themselves into making preparations no matter how foolish it appears. For example, if we decided to make a trip to the Himalayan Mountains, we'd spend several years getting ready for it, gathering clothing, equipment, and studying routes to the summit. Eventually we'd do it no matter how silly or dangerous it was. Well, that's what's happened in Europe. Kaiser Wilhelm has been building ships, dreadnoughts, and amassing a huge military force of infantry. Austria's doing the same thing. Every little country is. France is the worst of all, I suppose. Well, we have all of these armies, and what's an army to do except fight? And that's what will happen."

"How foolish men are," Noelle murmured. Somehow the fighting felt very real to her at that moment. She could hear the strong heartbeat thudding through Lance's chest, and suddenly a vision came to her. She seemed to see him in the air shot through by enemy bullets, his body bleeding, dead and lifeless. She held to him tightly and prayed that God would not let that happen. *Let him live, Lord,* she prayed fervently. *I need him so much, and so does Gabby. . . .*

★ ★ ★ ★

On June 28, far away from where Lance and Noelle sat, the dawn had already outlined the small city of Sarajevo. The town itself was very old, and in the narrow streets lamplight gleamed feebly, competing with the oncoming light.

Soon the muezzin unlocked a door and climbed to the top of a minaret, where he called out the ancient prayer, "Here, old faithful, there is no God but the one God, and Mohammed is his prophet."

Sarajevo began to stir sluggishly, but soon the sound of hammers broke the morning's silence, the marketplace began to fill up, and the narrow streets were filled with peasants and women veiled in black. The country people came in from the outlying districts and set up their little stalls to sell their wares: vegetables, fruits, strawberries, eggs, and a cheese known as *kajmak*.

It seemed no different from any other day, but the coffeehouses did a business more brisk than usual. The open market was soon filled with the aroma of grilled lamb patties thickly laced with garlic.

It was, on the whole, a peaceful scene, and no one in that small Austrian city had any idea that before the sun went down, an event would take place that would have horrific repercussions throughout the world.

The day grew hotter, and soon the balconies began to be draped with gaily colored banners, for this day the Archduke Francis Ferdinand, heir to the Austro-Hungarian throne, would appear. Early in the morning the crowds had already begun to gather along the streets. Very few of the Muslims paid any heed, but the old men sat sipping coffee and *slivovitz*, a liquor made from the juicy plums that grew in the area. And so Sarajevo nodded and dozed, and time went on as it always had.

Around the world the giant nations of Europe wallowed in some sort of somnambulant insanity. In Russia the court was greatly influenced by a madman named Grigori Efimovich Rasputin, a self-styled holy man and confidential advisor to the czar and especially to the czarina. Rasputin was a drunken, unwashed, lecherous man who had somehow hypnotized the czarina. He had taken advantage of the highest strata of women in Russia, and the czarina would hear no evil of him. She wrote to him, "I wish just one thing, to fall asleep, to fall asleep on your shoulder and what happiness to feel your presence near me."

The czar himself was not suited for the complex duties of ruling a vast empire. He was not a leader by upbringing or temperament. He met the people's unrest with police repression, which paved the way for the Russian revolution. But on this day in June, the czar had no inkling that his doom was already being set in motion in far-off Sarajevo.

Wilhelm II, the leader of Germany, was a shrewd, treacherous, hysterical, chronic bully, and a bluster, which masked his painful inner life. He had the uncertainty of a small man called upon to do big things, and without knowledge or wisdom, he simply rushed ahead. He was determined to be a warrior that befitted his German ancestry and epitomized the spirit that was going on in Germany. He had a lust for violence and a belief for death, as the German chief of staff said, "Without war the world would quickly sink into materialism." Germany would get her fill of war before the next few years were over.

In Paris and all over France, little boys in sailor suits and straw hats played on beaches. Picasso and Matisse painted, Debussy and Ravel wrote music, and writers gathered by the hundreds to pen their literary works.

England, still dwelling in the afterglow of the Victorian age and at the very height of her power, seemed to be straddling the world. The sun never seemed to set on the British empire, but that glory was being challenged by the huge armies of Germany and France. Though there was still safety, it was fragile. Across the sea America did not understand in the least what was happening in Europe. Three thousand miles away, the United States was prospering, and these were the good years, a time of innocence and a time of fervent national patriotism. They were getting ready for the American League Pennant, the New York Yankees against the Cleveland Indians. The fact that a rookie named Babe Ruth pitched his first game with the Boston Red Sox seemed more important than what could possibly happen in a small town in Austria. A race driver named Eddie Rickenbacker drove a Dusenberg to win the big race against Barney Oldfield in Sioux City. Rickenbacker had no idea that one day instead of driving racing cars he would fly a plane, meting out death to the enemies of his country.

And so the day began, and, as always, the earth turned so that the morning sun crept and caused the darkness to flee and awoke all to their last day of real peace on the earth.

At ten o'clock, the Archduke Francis Ferdinand stepped into his waiting car, and he and his wife began the journey that would end not only in their death, but eventually in the death of millions of human beings. A man called Leon Trotsky later said, "History had already poised its gigantic soldier's boot over the ant heap."

★ ★ ★ ★

The sermon had been rather harsh, Noelle thought. She liked

Reverend Denton very much and had entertained him and his wife twice in their home. But as she left the church and muttered an automatic phrase, "Fine sermon," somehow she felt defeated. She tried to cheer up, for they had planned a picnic following the Sunday service. Gabby was chattering at her side and pulling at her.

"Come on, Mama, let's go. I want to go to the beach."

"All right, dear. I'm hurrying." Getting into the car, she settled Gabby firmly down on the seat between herself and Lance. As he started the engine and pulled away from the church, dodging worshipers, she said, "I didn't care for that sermon much."

Surprised, Lance glanced at Noelle. "Why, I thought it was all right. Why didn't you like it?"

"Oh, I don't know. It just seemed sort of depressing."

The sermon had been taken from a text that said, "Love not the world, neither the things that are in the world. If any man loves the world the love of the Father is not in him." Reverend Denton had taken the position that it was a very dangerous thing to become attached to any object or any person. Indeed, to anything at all, including an idea. "An idol," the minister had stated firmly, "is not a bit of stone somewhere off in India or Africa. An idolater is an individual who puts *anything* before his love for God." He had gone on to enumerate how it was the inherent nature of most human beings to learn to love possessions. "Many a man and woman have chosen to make a house made out of stone into an idol. They may not bow down on their knees and lift their voices of praise to it, but in their hearts that home made of sticks and bricks and mortar and glass has become their God. They live for it and put their hearts into it, and it brings a joy into their hearts that they have never known when thinking of God."

Lance steered carefully, making for the beach on the coast of Hastings. It was only a short distance from the church. As they drove down the hill, he was pleased again with the sight, for he had learned to love this small village. "I thought he made some good points. It is easy to get too caught up with things like houses."

"Oh, I know that," Noelle said quickly. "I'm afraid I'm guilty." She laughed slightly and shook her head. "I love our little apartment. It may not be Windsor Castle, but it's ours."

Gabby interrupted by saying, "What are you and Papa fussing about?"

"Why, we're not arguing, dear."

"Yes, you are, but I don't know what you're talking about."

Very carefully Noelle explained what the sermon had been about and then watched as the inquisitive and very active mind of her daughter seemed to mull it over. She had seen this in the child before and had perceived that Gabby was one of the most sensitive children she had ever seen. She and Lance had to be very careful, for a rebuke from them, no matter how mild, seemingly would crush her and bring her to tears. Now Noelle said quickly, "It's not something you have to think about right now, sweetheart. Let's just have a good time at the beach."

"That's a good idea," Lance nodded, and soon he brought the car to a stop. The three descended upon the beach, and for the next two hours, Lance enjoyed playing with Gabby. He had often said, "Gabby's dolls aren't made out of stuffing and china for faces. I'm her big doll. She plays with me just like I was her private, personal toy."

Noelle laughed as she saw Gabby giving commands, and soon Lieutenant Lance Winslow was down on his hands and knees with Gabby astride his back and screaming with pleasure, "Get up! Get up, horsy!" Noelle's heart warmed at the sight. Lance loved Gabby, she was certain of that, but his work kept him late at nights. Days like this were especially precious to her and Gabby. *I mustn't be selfish,* she thought. *His job is important.*

Finally, seeing that Gabby was growing fretful and very dirty, Noelle said, "It's time to go home, Gabby."

"No, Mama, not yet!"

"Yes, it is. We can come back another time. Come now." She looked over at Lance. "Lance, you're a mess. You're as dirty as a pig."

"Well, you try being her play partner sometime. See what it gets you." Lance was wet up to the knees and his hair was full of sand. His face was filled with pleasure, and suddenly he swooped Gabby up and tossed her into the air. He caught her expertly and hugged her, saying, "We'll come again, sweetheart. Don't you worry."

By the time they had gotten back home, even though it was a short journey, Gabby had fallen asleep. "I'll clean her up if you'll carry her upstairs to her room," Noelle said. She followed, and when Lance went downstairs to make tea, she cleaned Gabby off as best she could and put her to bed.

"It was fun with Papa, wasn't it Mama?" she whispered when Noelle leaned over to kiss her.

"Yes, it was. Now, go to sleep just for a little nap."

She left the room and went downstairs to find Lance talking with one of the neighbors, a tall retired soldier named Melton. "Hello, Mr. Melton," she said.

"Bad afternoon, I'm afraid, Mrs. Winslow."

Alarm ran through Noelle. "What's the matter?"

"Oh, it's a political thing," Lance said quickly. He caught Melton's eye and shook his head, and Melton, being very quick, said no more.

After he left, Noelle came at once and said, "What is it, Lance?"

"There's some trouble over in Austria. The Archduke Ferdinand has been assassinated by a Serbian. It probably won't mean anything."

"But you're worried, aren't you?"

"The Serbs and the Austrians are always trouble. You know how it is. It just takes one spark to set off some powder." Then he forced himself to smile. "Nothing will come of it."

★ ★ ★ ★

Lance Winslow had said a tiny spark could set off a charge of powder, and that is exactly what happened. The death of the archduke triggered a series of events with worldwide repercussions. All eager to make some gesture of war in order not to waste their tremendous preparations, the leaders of the European nations began to move. The Austrians saw a chance to snatch up more of Serbia. Even though the Serbs offered to meet all of Austria's terms, still that was not enough. The Serbs were allied to Russia, and Russia felt obliged to come to their aid. The French were allied by treaty to the Russians, which brought them into it. It was at this moment when Sir Edward Gray looked out over London and said the words that would always be associated with the beginning of what would eventually be called World War I, "The lights are going out all over Europe. We shall not see them lit again in our lifetime."

All of the countries involved had made long-range plans for winning the war. For the most part, they trusted in the old military strategies. The war on the horizon would be one of infantry flanked by long lines of proud cavalry backed up, somewhat, by artillery. The country with the most men would obviously have the advantage. Almost none of them, except a few visionaries, expected anything out of the fledgling air forces. Germany, France, and even England saw that airplanes could be used for scouting out the enemy and getting vital information back to the generals. They hinted, perhaps, that it would be best if the air forces stayed out of the way of the real business of war that would be fought on the ground by men with rifles and bayonets. After all, these airplanes were flimsy affairs held together by wire and covered with fabric. They were viewed as a rich man's toy but not at all suitable for such a serious matter as a war. Most Englishmen still cherished their tradition of the British soldier, bayonets held high by men in a thin red line, or a gallant charge of horsemen with their sabers raised high to the sky. Many leaders considered that such disciplined soldiers could never be replaced by anything, much less a contraption that seemed to fly only by a miracle.

But a few men saw the matter differently. The Royal Flying Corps had been established in 1912. It still depended on a de Haviland F–2. This plane could carry two men and a camera at seventy-five miles an hour and stay aloft for a little less than three hours. They also had the Avro 504, the Bristol Scout, and the Sopwith Tabloid, all ninety-mile-an-hour single-seaters.

Germany planned to attack France by driving straight through Belgium, which inevitably would draw Britain into the war, for Britain was allied by treaty to Belgium. Throughout July and into August, the crescendo of war increased every day across Europe. When German troops invaded Belgium's neutrality, Britain had little choice but to respond. On August 3, the British issued an ultimatum to Germany—either Germany halt its invasions of Belgium, or Britain would be at war with her by midnight. It did not avail. Perhaps Germany did not believe Britain would endanger herself, but she was mistaken. On August 4, 1914, Great Britain declared war on Germany.

The day after the declaration of war, Lieutenant Lance Winslow stood before Brigadier General Thomas Summers. Summers was too old for command, but he still had fire, and he said, "You're probably wondering why I sent for you, Lieutenant?"

"Yes, sir. I suppose it's orders."

"Yes." Summers hesitated. "You are hereby promoted to captain, and you will organize Fighter Squadron Number 24. As soon as possible, you will fly your squadron across the Channel and attack the Bosche."

Summers' words sounded like a death knell to Lance Winslow. He knew it meant the end of all things as he had known them, but he said quietly, "Yes, sir. It is for this reason I joined the army. To fight for my country."

Summers dropped his eyes for a moment. He had seen war before. This young man who stood before him had no idea of what death meant. *But he will know,* Summers thought, and his heart seemed to grow dark. *They will all find out what death means.*

CHAPTER SIX

DEATH RAINS FROM THE SKIES

★ ★ ★ ★

As the guns of August began to roar in the fateful year of 1914, all of Europe stirred with the tramp of marching feet. The war was now launched, and like a mighty juggernaut, it could not be stopped. All the nations involved had plans for quick victories. The kaiser had shouted to his men with the spiked helmets, "Home before Christmas!" This call was echoed by other nations, and the thought of a long, drawn-out war was unthinkable. The war was to be fought, as almost everyone saw it, with masses of infantry, aided by cavalry, and artillery playing an important part. Almost no one on either side saw the airplane as playing a significant role in the struggle that lay before them.

It was, perhaps, the last time in the history of the world that a war would be seen in a romantic light. In the harder and more cynical times that would follow, it would be much more difficult to stir young men to go to war singing cheerful songs. Songs such as "Smiles," "Pack Up Your Troubles in Your Old Kit Bag," and "There Are Smiles That Make You Happy" revealed a joy and an innocent mood. Most of this carefree, gay, romantic mood would disappear with the sight of the first casualties, but at the beginning of the war, there was a carnival-like atmosphere that pervaded Germany, France, and most of the other nations that sent their young men out to die.

As for the air force, there were only a few planes, most of which were as much a threat to their own pilots as to the men who flew for the other side. The military use of aircraft had begun in 1905 when the Wright brothers had offered their new invention to the U.S. War Department. Three times they were rejected, and America lost out in the race that followed to produce attack planes. Not a single American-made airplane was engaged in the Great War.

This left it up primarily to the French, who were very much interested in developing an air force. They began earnestly building planes that could be used for military purposes, and when the *Daily Mail* offered a thousand pounds to any man who could fly the English Channel, the race was on to build aircraft with more stamina than the early kitelike affairs. By 1910 the British were also building planes on a more modest scale, but when the archduke was assassinated in Sarajevo, Germany had 1,200 combat machines, while France and Britain combined only had 1,000, and only a portion of these were ready for action. In August 1914, on the Western Front, France and Great Britain were able to muster 220 planes actually ready for flight, while the Germans had 260. England, to be sure, had little confidence in these. The secretary of war said, "We do not consider that airplanes will be of any possible use for war purposes." Nevertheless, in 1912 the British had organized the Royal Flying Corps. When the war started, they began sending this flotilla across the Channel to France. Lance Winslow watched the first squadron sent to France with impatience. He himself wanted to join them, but he had been ordered to organize his own squadron, using more efficient machines and better battle tactics.

Day after day he read of the early pilots who flew a motley collection of planes, none of them equipped with machine guns. He himself knew, as did a few others in the RFC, that until this happened, the airplane would be resigned to simply observing the action that took place.

The value of observation planes became obvious almost at once. General Sir John French walked blindly into the teeth of a German advance in late August of 1914. He was an old-line, stiff-upper-lip type who ran his troops with strict military discipline. However, when warned by his fliers that the Germans' First Army was about to trap him, he managed to scramble back in a retreat from Mans just seven days after the first British plane set down on French soil. There are those who claim that this rescue, by means of scout planes, saved the Allies from losing the war in the first few weeks.

The Germans were better prepared for war and began bombing their targets immediately. By September the German armies were only two dozen miles from Paris, and a group called the Pigeon Unit, which was a cover-up for its real purpose of bombing France, began their work. This group included Manfred von Richthofen, later to be known as the Red Baron, Ernst Udet, one of the finest pilots on either side of the whole war, and Hermann Goering, who would become Adolf Hitler's number two man in the rise and fall of the Third Reich and commander of the Luftwaffe, which would try to crush England in the Battle of Britain in a later war.

The early fliers carried pistols, shotguns, and even Very pistols, but some of them even carried slingshots and the French steel darts called *fléchettes*. Grappling hooks were even tried to tear at the surfaces of the enemies' aircraft.

But in April 1915, the whole picture changed when a French pilot named Roland Garros proved the deadly effectiveness of a well-armed airplane. He mounted a machine gun directly in front of the cockpit. Ordinarily, it would shoot the propeller off, but a French engineer had devised the idea of putting steel plates inside of the propeller itself. Therefore, any bullets striking it would be deflected. Roland Garros became the terror of the German airmen. He shot down plane after plane, and if it had not been for an accident, the French and English would have controlled the skies during the entire war. However, on April 19, Garros's engine failed, and he was forced to land behind German lines. The airplane was captured intact and handed over to a young man only twenty-four years of age by the name of Anthony Fokker. Fokker was intrigued by the device but proceeded to invent a much more effective one. Mounting a machine gun to the engine hood, he invented a cam system that worked a push rod connected by wire to the hammer of the machine gun. In effect, this stopped the hammer from hitting the firing pin every time the blade passed the gun. As Fokker put it, the propeller controlled the gun. Oswald Boelcke, who became the leading German Ace, took it up in a Fokker E–11 and shot down a French plane with ease. From that time on Germany ruled the skies. French and English planes could not stand up against the deadly new weapon, and there was talk in high places that the Fokker invention would win the war. The Allied pilots began to call themselves "Fokker fodder" as man after man went down in flames under the guns of the German pilots.

The German pilots were ordered not to fly over enemy lines so that none of their planes could be captured, but, in an irony that often comes in wartime, a German pilot caught in a thick fog landed at a French airfield. His plane and the secret of the Fokker gun invention were all captured, drawings were made, reports were written, and then all was filed away. Not a member of the military personnel did anything about getting the invention to men such as Lance Winslow, who so desperately needed it.

★ ★ ★ ★

Immediately after the war had started, a strange message had been widely spread across Europe. "England will be destroyed by fire." Some said this was simply an attempt on the part of Germany to intimidate its enemy. The belief that Germany wanted spread was that the United Kingdom would be brought to its knees by the Zeppelin, a powerful airship of destruction that had been invented by the influential German Count von Zeppelin.

For ten years the Zeppelin had proved its worth as a potentially great mode of transportation. It had been the target of a great deal of military investigation, and one year before the beginning of the war, a young naval officer entered a German naval headquarters in Berlin. He drew himself up before the senior officer, who said without any preliminaries, "Lieutenant Strasser, we have lost the commanding officer of our naval airship division. He went down in the crash of Zeppelin L–1 in the North Sea."

"Yes, sir. I heard she had gone down with all hands."

"Lieutenant, I am placing you in command of Naval Zeppelins."

Lieutenant Peter Strasser stared in disbelief. "But, sir, I have no experience in lighter-than-air craft!"

"We know that, Lieutenant, but we know you have the technical ability and flexibility to transfer your talents to this arm of our forces. We must bring England down, and you will be the man in charge of accomplishing it."

Lieutenant Peter Strasser threw himself into learning his craft. For one year he drove himself like a demon possessed to learn everything there was to know about airships. He became a walking encyclopedia in his field, and soon he found himself in charge of a fleet of mighty and enormous Zeppelins with which to institute bombing raids against Britain's targets, especially London. He did face one obstacle. Kaiser Wilhelm II had blood ties to the British Royal Family and cringed at the reputation he would achieve as a murderer within his own family if German bombs killed women and children and other British civilians. Finally, however, he relented, and on New Year's Day 1915, a telegram informed Strasser that the kaiser had authorized raids on London. The raids were limited to docks, military facilities, and troop encampments. No bombs would be dropped, the order read, on the heart of London.

Peter Strasser was ready and his men were eager. On January 19, 1915, the historic first Zeppelin raid on England took place. Three new ships, L–3, L–4, and L–6, lifted off at eleven A.M. Strasser himself led the raid, but engine trouble forced him to turn back. The raid itself was not much. Two Zeppelins reached their target and each one dropped six 110-pound bombs in the Norfolk region. The bombs damaged the town square, destroyed several buildings, killed four people, and injured sixteen others.

Strasser was not discouraged. He saw the Zeppelin as the means of bringing England to its knees and threw all his efforts into the task. All Germany needed was one big, successful raid to launch its basic objective, which was to paralyze its enemy and force it quickly into submission.

★ ★ ★ ★

"Papa, take me out to look through the telescope."

Gabby pulled at her father's shirt, her eyes turned upward. "Please, Papa. Before I go to bed I want to look at the stars."

Lance had just informed Gabby that it was time for bed, but, as usual, she began a crusade to put off such a move as long as possible. He shook his head and smiled, saying, "It's too late, Gabby. Tomorrow night I'll take you out to look at the stars." Looking over, he smiled at Noelle, who was seated across the room reading. "She knows the names of more stars than I do."

Noelle looked up and smiled. "I'm glad you're teaching her things like this. She likes the telescope so well, don't you, Gabby?"

Lance had bought a powerful telescope, which Gabby had learned to love. Lance had become an amateur astronomer and had bought several books on the subject. Nothing relaxed him more than getting out after dark and studying the night skies. Now that May 1915 had come, he had the spring skies to gaze at with a new set of constellations.

Gabby pulled at his shirt again. "Please, Papa! Just for a little while."

"Will that be all right, Noelle? It's not too late?" Lance inquired.

"Well, just for thirty minutes, perhaps."

"I think we'll go down the street where there are fewer lights.

Easier to see that way. Come along." Lance went over and, bending down, took Noelle's face between his hands. Tilting it upward, he kissed her and winked. "You wait right here, Mrs. Winslow. I have a few things to say to you tonight."

Noelle's eyes twinkled mischievously. "Very well, Mr. Winslow. Your obedient wife will be waiting for you. You put Gabby to bed and come right along." There was a warm promise in her eyes, and she pulled his head down and kissed him, then put her lips close to his ear. "I'm glad you're still romantic even after we're just an old married couple."

Lance held her for a moment. "You'll never be old," he whispered. Then he straightened up and said, "Come along, Gabby." Picking up the telescope, the two left the flat and made their way down the street. The stars overhead were bright and sparkling, and he pointed upward, saying, "Do you know that constellation, Gabby?"

"Of course I do, Papa. That's the Big Dipper. Everybody knows that!"

"And can you find the North Star for me?"

"Yes. That's it right there. See?" She pointed upward and chatted incessantly until they reached their position. He set up the telescope, and soon the two were deeply engrossed in looking at the glittering stars overhead. It was a mild night with very little wind blowing, and their part of the city lay quietly under the night skies.

Abruptly the silence was broken by a shattering roar that brought Lance upright in a stiff position.

"What was *that?*"

"That was a bomb, sweetheart." He grabbed the telescope, his heart beating fast. "Come along. We've got to get back to your mother."

Even as the two ran back, another explosion took place and then a series of them.

"Zeppelin raids!"

Lance had not been concerned about an air raid, for they had been rare, but now ahead of him he saw flames shooting up and the earth rumble as more bombs struck. He glanced upward and thought he saw a shadowy form high overhead, but he did not stop to think.

God, keep Noelle safe, he prayed as he moved along as swiftly as possible. His pace was impeded by Gabby, who began to cry. He picked her up in his arms, and then as he turned the corner, what he saw drew him up still, and fear shot through him.

Their flat was burning, and the one next to their place was completely obliterated. Flying debris was in the air, and already he heard the screams of the wounded. He wanted to rush ahead, but he had Gabby in his arms. Looking wildly around, he saw Mrs. Williams, who lived down the street, standing dazed, staring at the rising flames.

"Mrs. Williams, keep Gabby. I've got to see to my wife." Without waiting for a reply, he rushed ahead, but as he crossed the street, his heart seemed to stop. There was nothing but rubble all about. He began tearing through it like a madman, crying out, "Noelle! Noelle!" He tore his fingernails and his hands were bloody. All the world seemed to stop. He was aware that other bombs were falling farther down the street, but his only thought was of his wife.

He lost track of time as he wildly pulled at boards and fallen plaster until finally he felt a hand on his arms. He looked around, his face black with soot and his hands bleeding.

"Sir, come along. It's no use, I'm afraid."

Lance turned and saw a fire engine that had drawn up, and firemen were piling out. He tried to think but no thoughts came. The fireman, a short man with a strong face illuminated now by the light of a fire that still burned down the street, said, "You had your family inside?"

"My wife—she's in here! You've got to get her out!"

Compassion filled the fireman's face, but he looked at the rubbish and knew how little hope there was. "Let us get at it, sir."

Lance started to argue, but then the firemen moved in and began shuffling through the debris. He stood there, his mind paralyzed, and then he heard a voice—"Papa! Papa!"

Turning, Lance saw that Mrs. Williams had advanced, holding Gabby, whose face was streaked with tears. He moved stiffly toward her, scarcely able to think, and saw the fear in her eyes.

"Is Mama all right?"

The question pierced Lance Winslow's heart. He knew there was no hope. Holding his daughter closely, he turned away sick and nauseated. The sounds of the bombs had ceased, but he knew, somehow, that life would never be the same for him again.

★ ★ ★ ★

General Montague Trenchard was known throughout the Royal

Flying Corps as "Boom." This nickname came from the manner he had of speaking. General Trenchard had one philosophy, which he called strategic offense. He had one aim in life, and that was to win the skies over France for the Allies. Now, however, General Trenchard sat staring in his London office after he had come back from a quick visit to France. The walnut desk before him was littered with papers, and the clock on the wall kept a solemn ticking sound that reminded him of how much sleep he had lost and how tired he was. His was a job that brought incessant pressure, and now as a lieutenant came in, he looked up out of bloodshot eyes and asked wearily, "What is it, Lieutenant?"

"I'm sorry to bother you, sir, but Captain Winslow is here."

Trenchard sat still for a moment, then nodded wearily. "Have you talked to him, Townsend?"

"Yes, sir. I have."

"He's not taking it well, his wife's death, is he?"

"No, sir. They were very close."

"I forget. Does he have children?"

"One child, sir. A little girl about five, I believe."

The general felt a flash of anger as he always did when he heard of Zeppelin raids. He shook his head, muttered something, and then pulled his shoulders together. "Send him in, Lieutenant Townsend."

"Yes, sir."

Trenchard got to his feet and stood waiting. He had close ties with most of the men under his command and had great confidence in Lance Winslow. Squadron 24, which was being formed under Winslow's hands, was to be a crack squadron, and Trenchard put great hopes in it. "Poor blighter," he said sadly. "I know how I'd feel if I lost Heather." He straightened up and stepped forward as the door opened. Going at once, he put out his hand, then changed his mind and put an arm around Winslow's shoulder. "I'm sorry, Winslow," he said quietly. "Nothing to say at a time like this."

"No, sir. Nothing to say."

This was not the same Winslow that Trenchard remembered. The man he knew had had sparkling eyes and had been full of life and vigor. Lance Winslow's eyes now seemed cold and distant. He kept himself pulled up at attention, and there was a hardness that surrounded him that had not been there before.

"Sit down. I'll have Townsend make some tea."

It was just a ploy to take some of the tension off of the meeting, but it did not succeed. Winslow went through the motions, speaking when spoken to and drinking his tea, but a fiery light lay behind the surface of his eyes. For a time, Trenchard talked about what was happening and then shook his head. "I'm so sorry about your wife."

"Yes, sir."

The words were clipped and revealed nothing of the pain Winslow felt, but Trenchard was certain that if he could have looked inside, he would have seen an inferno of grief. He had met Mrs. Winslow once and had been impressed with her youth and beauty, and now she was gone.

"Sir?"

"Yes. What is it, Lance?"

"I wish to leave England."

"But the squadron isn't ready."

"It's almost, sir. We can finish when we get there."

Trenchard hesitated for only a moment. "As a matter of fact, we do need you rather desperately. I was thinking of next month, but if you say you're ready now—"

"Yes, sir. We're ready, and I have a request."

"Of course. Anything."

"This may be impossible, General, but as you know I have a daughter. She's only five. I have little family myself, but my wife—" When Lance said these words for the first time, some of the pain was manifest. He could not say the word "wife" without nearly breaking. "My wife's parents live in Belleville."

"Why, that's where one of our bases is."

"Yes, sir. That's what I would like to ask. If there is any possibility of having the squadron stationed there, at first at least, so I could get my daughter settled with her grandparents?"

"Why, certainly. I had not made up my mind which base for Squadron 24 to operate from, but that will do very well."

Relief washed across Lance's face. "That's very kind of you, sir."

"Why, not at all. Not at all." Trenchard shook his head vigorously. "When would you be ready to leave?"

"Immediately, sir. As soon as possible."

"Very well. I'll draw up the orders. Is there . . . anything else I can do?"

A flash of bitterness then escaped from Lance Winslow's lips. "No, sir," he said. "There's nothing anyone can do."

★ ★ ★ ★

"There it is, Gabby. This is where you'll be staying with your grandfather and grandmother." Lance got out of the car and went around to open the door. When Gabby got out, she took his hand and looked up fearfully.

"Will you be here, Papa?"

It was a question Gabby had often asked since the death of her mother. Lance had obtained an apartment across from the location of their old place. Everything had been destroyed, so Gabby had none of the old familiar things that might have given her comfort. After the funeral Lance had spent as much time as possible with her. When it came time to transfer the squadron across the Channel, he had put his second-in-command in charge of the flight. When the two of them had crossed the Channel, Gabby had clung to him almost desperately. "Why, I'll be right out at the airfield. Just on the edge of town. I'll be home every night, and your grandparents will be so glad to see you. Come along."

Gabby held her father's hand tightly as they went up the steps, but before they could enter, the door opened and Danielle Laurent came out quickly. "Oh, you're here!" She ran forward at once and stooped beside Gabby. "Gabby!" she said. "I'm so glad you've come. We've been fixing up your room, but you'll have to help me decorate it just like you want it."

A wash of gratitude came to Lance then, and when Danielle stood, he said huskily, "Thank you, Danielle." He looked down at Gabby and could not speak for a moment. He wanted to say more, but at that moment Katherine came out and put her arms around him.

"I'm glad to see you, son," she whispered.

"I don't know what I would have done if it hadn't been for you and Pierre," Lance said.

"Come in," Katherine said. "Pierre will be home soon."

Pierre came home in less than an hour and greeted Lance warmly. Sadness and grief filled his eyes, and he said only, "We will miss her, will we not, my son?"

Lance could not even answer. He found himself unable to speak about Noelle's death, and later when he was alone with Danielle he tried to explain this. They were out in the garden, and inside they could hear Katherine singing and talking with Gabby. "I don't say things like this very well, Danielle," Lance said, "but this place is like a haven to me."

"It's been very hard on you, Lance. You loved her so much. We all did."

"Yes, I did."

The words seemed stark and bare, and Lance, realizing the inadequacy of them, turned to face Danielle. She was wearing a simple dress of light blue, and her hair was fixed differently than he remembered in a chignon at the back of her neck. He said simply, "I can't talk about her. I don't know why."

"It hasn't been that long since her death, but as soon as you can, you should try. Gabby needs to hear about her mother always."

"I'll try." Lance swallowed hard, then said, "It's asking a lot, just dumping Gabby off on you."

"Not at all. This is her home. She will be all right. We will all love her. She will miss her mother, but we will do the best we can."

Lance impulsively reached out and did something he had never done. He put his arms around Danielle and held her tightly. "I can't tell you how much . . ." he started to say and then could say no more. She was pressed against him and he could not see her face.

For Danielle Laurent this was what had been in her mind when she had been a fourteen-year-old girl falling in love with a tall Englishman. Now he was holding her in his arms, and she could not speak. She knew that it was not love that had made him embrace her, but for that one moment she did not care. That brief fulfillment of a dream was hers, and she knew the memory of it would linger in her thoughts for weeks to come.

"Sorry about that. I guess I lost myself."

"It's all right."

Lance took a deep breath and tried to smile. "Still no wedding bells for you?"

"No. Not for me."

Lance could not understand why she had never found a suitor to marry, but he was not thinking clearly. He could only say, as he gave her an affectionate look, "Fellows around here must be blind and stupid as well. They're missing something very beautiful."

Danielle turned away at once, for she felt tears rising to her eyes. Her throat seemed to thicken, and she managed to say, "I think I'll go see if Gabby would like to go for a walk."

★ ★ ★ ★

Squadron 24 had been with Lance Winslow for a long time. They had all learned to trust him and were in awe of his superb flying skills and his encyclopedic knowledge of every wire and strut on the planes they flew.

But the Lance Winslow that stood before them now was a stranger. His light blue eyes had little life about them, but at the same time they had a glint of cold blue fire. He had called them together for their first meeting in France, and now as the fliers sat nervously, they were meeting a new Lance Winslow.

They were accustomed to a man of quick wit and humor, but there was none of that in Captain Lance Winslow now. His eyes fixed on them, he said harshly, "We're here to kill Germans! Put everything else out of your minds! If a German plane goes down, follow him. If he lands safely, kill him in his cockpit before he can get out. If one of the Huns parachutes out, shoot him as he's falling."

"That's not very sporting, sir," said Pug Hardeston. He was the youngest man in the group, so called because of his low brow and a nose that had been spread over his face by many opponents in the ring. He was still enamored that he had made the squadron. Hardeston had been accustomed to a Winslow who would listen, but he quickly discovered his mistake.

"Lieutenant, you are here to kill Germans. This is not a game of cricket. Your orders are to kill Germans! Every German you see! If you do not kill them, they will kill you or one of your fellow pilots."

A silence reigned over the room, and then Winslow said, "All right. The first patrol will take off in half an hour. I will lead it, along with Lewis, Bentley, and Hartley. You will get a taste of what this war is all about."

After Winslow had left the room abruptly, Hardeston said, "Well, he didn't have to bite my head off!"

Both Lewis and Bentley gave him a stern look, and it was Lewis who said, "There's no joy in him since he lost his wife. I don't think there'll be much in this squadron either."

"Kill Germans . . ." Lewis nodded. He got up and said thoughtfully, "Come along. I've got a feeling if we see any Germans, our commanding officer is going to go right for them. That's the kind of man he's become!"

"I never thought of it that way," Bentley nodded, looking down at the other two from his great height, "but that's what he's become. A killer, and a shame it is, too."

PART TWO

Jo

★ ★ ★ ★

CHAPTER SEVEN

JO MEETS A COWBOY

★ ★ ★ ★

Josephine Hellinger stared at the huge German shepherd that had positioned himself exactly on top of the skirt and jacket she had laid out on the bed. With exasperation she reached out and grabbed him by the scruff, tugging at him. "Bedford, will you get off of my clothes! You're going to ruin them!"

Bedford growled deep in his throat, came reluctantly to his feet, then suddenly leaned forward and licked the face that had come within his reach.

"Now stop that!"

With another tug Jo pulled the huge animal to the floor and stood there in her chemise, shaking her finger in his face. "Bad dog! You ought to be ashamed!" She studied the face of the sleek animal, then grinned. "I can see you're not broken out with repentance. You don't know the difference between right and wrong." Turning from Bedford, who sat down and yawned hugely, she proceeded to put on the clothing she had laid out. She slipped on a pair of white hose and shoes, then donned the two-piece jacket dress of pongee. Finally she picked up a straw picture hat that had a full crown covered with multicolored silk flowers. Whirling, she moved over to the full-length mirror that hung across from her bed and studied herself carefully. "Not bad," she said. "This ought to impress Mr. Ed Kovak." The dress was a light green with darker green stripes along the edge of the skirt, which came six inches above the ankle. The green set off the color of Jo Hellinger's eyes and her red hair, which fell in long ringlets down her back, catching the morning sun. It was an odd shade of red that had a golden tint to it when the sun struck it just right. The face she saw as she leaned forward was rather square with a determined chin, high cheekbones, and thick lashes that overshadowed the green eyes.

As she studied her reflection in the mirror, she began singing a tune unconsciously, " 'When you wore a tulip, a big yellow tulip, and I wore a big red rose—' " Suddenly she broke off with annoyance. "Why do I sing that dumb song?"

Preferring opera to popular songs, Jo had developed an abhorrence for tunes that everyone was singing—"Peg of My Heart" and "You Made Me Love You." She had remarked once to a friend that they were nothing but sugar-coated nonsense. The friend had grinned back. "I like sugar-coated things. You could use a little sugar yourself, Jo."

Finally satisfied with her dress, Jo moved to a large table that was piled high with photographic equipment. She picked up a large box camera with a sling and draped it over her shoulders, then grabbed up an enormous brown leather purse that contained extra flashbulbs. Moving toward the door, she said, "Come on, Bedford." When she opened the door and stepped outside, the big dog accompanied her. She turned the key in the lock, dropped it into her purse, then said briskly, "Time to go beard the lion in his den."

"Wuff!" Bedford barked.

"That's right. *Wuff!* If Ed Kovak doesn't give me a better assignment, I'm going to let you bite him. Now come on."

Leaving the brownstone apartment house, Jo looked up toward the blue-gray sky dotted with hard-edged clouds. Somehow, she knew it would be another hot June day. The spring of 1914 had been unseasonably warm, and the summers in New York could be unbearable. She stood on the street corner with Bedford pressing himself against her left leg. She had trained him to heel without using a leash, and now when a taxicab pulled over, she said, "Now be nice, Bedford."

"Lady, you can't get that dog in here. He's dangerous!" The cabdriver had rolled down the window of the Buick and was staring at Bedford apprehensively.

"He's just a pup. Don't be silly. Are you afraid of a puppy?" Without ado Jo opened the back door and motioned for Bedford to get in. The big dog scrambled inside, positioning himself right behind the driver. He sat up straight, and the driver shot a frightened glance at Jo, who settled down beside the big dog.

"Don't let that animal get at me! I'll sue you if he bites me!" He scrunched his head down as if he were afraid the big dog would clamp his enormous jaws on the back of his neck.

"If he bites you, you won't be able to sue anybody! Now, take me to the *Times* building."

He was an expert, as all New York cabdrivers were, at threading his way through the steady stream that headed to the downtown section. He did not relax until he pulled up in front of a towering building with the single word *Times* ensconced on the very apex. "That'll be a dollar twenty-five, miss."

Fumbling inside her large purse, Jo came up with a handful of bills, took two of them, and said, "Keep the change."

"Hey, thanks, lady. If you want that monster hauled anywhere else, just give me a call."

Ignoring his invitation, Jo got out of the car and spoke to Bedford, who jumped out immediately. She walked with determination toward the entrance, ignoring the stares that several apprehensive citizens gave to the large dog beside her. *He's got to give me something more to do than covering golden wedding anniversaries, and I'm sick and tired of the fashion page!* she thought as she entered the door.

When she got to the elevator, Mose Johnson grinned at her. "Mornin', Miss Josephine."

"Good morning, Mose. How are you today?"

"I'm finer than frog hair. Hello, Bedford. Are you fine, too?" He laughed when the dog sat down and stared at him and barked sharply. "I guess he's fine."

Mose moved the lever in front of him and stopped the car at the fifth floor. "You're all dressed up this morning, Miss Josephine. You must be gonna ask for a raise."

"Something like that, Mose. When I see you next time, I'll either have a better job or I won't have one at all."

"Hey"—Jo left, making Mose crane his neck around the corner—"you'd better be careful about that. Jobs ain't easy to come by these days."

Waving carelessly at the diminutive operator, Jo entered through a set of opaque glass doors and stepped into another world. It was an enormous room crammed with desks as close together as possible. Typewriters were making a staccato sound, people were calling shrilly across the room, and copyboys ran from desk to desk, snatching sheets of papers out of some wire baskets and slamming others into them. Threading her way down the narrow passageway that went the complete length of the room, Jo spoke to several people who greeted her, but her mind was not on them. When she reached the end of the room, she paused for one moment before a door marked "Managing Editor." Taking a deep breath, she said, "Well, Lord, here I go. Thrill me or kill me." She opened the door and marched in with Bedford pressed close to her side. She shut the door loudly behind her, then positioned herself squarely in front of an enormous desk, the top of which was completely obscured with papers, photographs, documents, and ashtrays.

Ed Kovak stared up at her angrily. He was a large, strongly built man with a square face, piercing brown eyes, and black hair that was thinning on the crown. The cigar he was chewing on sent up clouds of purple smoke. He placed both thick hands flat on the papers before him and snarled, "Don't bother to knock, Hellinger! Just barge right in!"

"I've got to see you, Mr. Kovak."

Kovak stared at the huge dog. "I told you not to bring that animal here again! Have you got a hearing problem?"

Jo Hellinger had decided earlier when she first came to work for the *Times* that Ed Kovak had no use for anyone without a backbone. She had stood up to him from the first day of her employment, and the assistant managing editor had told her later, "You won't last long. Nobody ever goes head to head with Kovak and comes out on top."

But Jo Hellinger had come out on top, and she had won a grudging acceptance from the burly editor by being faster, more innovative, and tougher than any woman, at least, that he had ever allowed to work under him. He had given her the most dreary assignments, and she had never complained. True, they never met on a social plane, but then Kovak never fraternized with any of the hundreds of people that worked for him. *"Business is business, home is home,"* he said, and most of the time he spent with his five children and his very pretty wife.

"What do you want, Jo? I'm busy. The Panama Canal's going to be completed, and I've got to come up with a feature story on it."

"Let me do it, Mr. Kovak."

Kovak leaned back, and his dark eyes flickered over the young woman. *Good-looking babe,* he thought. *Tough too. Too bad she's a woman. She's smart enough and tough enough to be a man.* "I already gave it to Simmons." He pulled the cigar out, stared at it, then jammed it back in his mouth. Chewing on it, he repeated the question. "What do you want? I haven't got time for chitchat."

"You've got to give me a different assignment. I've done everything you've ever asked me to do, Mr. Kovak, but I'm sick of weddings and anniversaries, the society page, and even the cooking page. I've done them all, and I've never complained, have I?"

"No you never have." Kovak leaned back, locked his hands behind his head, and grunted, "Well, what do you want?"

"Anything! Let me cover a prizefight."

"That's a joke! Women can't cover prizefights."

"How do you know? Have you ever let one try?"

Kovak studied the young woman more carefully and realized, to his surprise, that he not only respected Jo Hellinger, he even liked her. Not that he would ever show it, for that would be favoritism. He was aware, however, of his fondness for her, and now he said roughly to cover his own feelings, "Why don't you get married, stay home, and change diapers like other women?"

"It's not time for that yet, Mr. Kovak. One of these days I will, but now I've got to do something I've always wanted. While other girls were primping and going to parties, I was learning photography. While they were getting engaged and getting married, I was learning journalism. And I want to do something exciting!"

"Like what?"

"Anything except what I've been doing!"

Kovak felt a sudden pang of pity tinged with admiration. He leaned back in his chair, then said thoughtfully, "Women haven't made it yet in this world, kid."

"Then I'll be the first."

Kovak came to an instant decision. It was what made him a great editor. He could think quickly, and most of the decisions were excellent. "I'll tell you what. You're due a vacation, aren't you?"

"Yes, sir."

"Then make it a working vacation. Go somewhere, do a feature story complete with photos, come back, and give it to me. If you do a good job, we'll talk about putting you on something a little bit more exciting than the society pages.

"I don't blame you for not wanting them. They bore me to death. Well, start tomorrow." He removed the cigar again, got up, came around the desk, and awkwardly patted her shoulder. "Good luck, kid. I'd like to see you make it. I really would." He heard a low growl and, startled, turned to see that Bedford had risen and stood with his eyes fixed on his jugular vein. "Hey, I was just kidding, Bedford!"

Kovak said nervously. He shot a glance at Jo, who was smiling, and asked, "He wouldn't really bite me, would he?"

"Not unless I told him to, Mr. Kovak." Jo laughed suddenly, and reached out and patted Ed Kovak's cheek, something no reporter had ever done in the *Times* building. "I was going to have him tear your throat out if you didn't give me a chance, but now you can pet him if you want to. Be nice, Bedford."

"I'll take your word for it," Kovak grinned. "Go on. Come back with something good. We'll see where it goes."

★ ★ ★ ★

The field seemed to be alive with the green grass as it swayed back and forth in the gentle breeze. Low rolling hills broken by gullies lay off to Jo's left, while at her feet a small and insignificant stream purled and murmured, making a sibilant sound—a counterpoint to the breeze that stirred over the prairie.

"And this is where it happened, Mr. Price?"

"Yes, ma'am. This is the place." The speaker was a slight man with dusty gray eyes that peered out under heavy, bushy eyebrows. He wore a pair of faded brown pants and a white shirt buttoned at the sleeves in spite of the sweltering heat. A dark brown Stetson, which looked the worse for wear, having apparently survived many winters of rain and summers of blistering Montana sunshine, was pushed back on his forehead, allowing crisp, gray curly hair to be exposed over a bronzed forehead. He lifted his hand and pointed to the east. "Right over there was where I was with Major Reno, and right there"—he shifted his arm—"is where Custer and all of his men died."

Overhead a trio of buzzards circled lazily, and the old man's eyes followed their motions. "I remember," he said quietly, "three days after the battle the sky was full of buzzards. They had plenty to eat. Most of the Seventh Cavalry and quite a few Indians."

"What was it really like, Mr. Price?"

"Most folks just call me Nels. Short for Nelson, ma'am." The dusty gray eyes came to rest on the young woman Price had driven all the way from Billings to the site of the Little Bighorn battlefield. He had expected her to complain about the heat, but she had not, and now he saw that her gray dress was soaked and she was sunburned pretty badly.

"Better get back in the car. This sun's going to cook you, Miss Hellinger."

"Why, it's all right. I want to get a few more pictures if I can. But tell me about the battle."

Jo spent the next few hours taking pictures of the battlefield, although there was nothing much to see. The grass had come and covered all the scars made when Custer and most of his beloved Seventh Cavalry had died in a pitched battle with the largest collection of hostile Indians ever gathered on the open plain. She found it much more interesting to talk to Nels Price, who had actually been in the battle. She had been shocked, somehow, to realize that there were still men alive who had fought alongside Custer. When she had found him at Billings, she retained him as a guide to take her to the battlefield. Price had been glad to get away from his small store and leave his older son to run it. He had been reticent at first, saying little, but when he discovered that the young woman from the East was actually interested in the truth of the battle and not in the romantic myths and legends that had grown up, he became more loquacious.

Finally, as the sun was going down, he paused at a certain spot and said, "That's the hill right there where I climbed up with what was left of us."

"That was Major Reno's force."

"That's right. We split off from Custer, and thank God we did. If we had gone with him, we'd have been killed along with all of his men."

"None of them made it?"

"Not a man made it back alive. Of course, we couldn't see any of it. We had fought our way back up on top of that hill."

The wind keened around the pair as they stood on the slight rise fifty yards away from where the car was parked. There were no other visitors that day, and a loneliness seemed to fill the open prairie. Price was silent for so long that Jo thought he had forgotten, but finally he shook his head, took his hat off, and wiped his forehead.

"We fought our way up the hill and stayed there out of ammunition. Finally Major Benteen came back with one ammunition train, and the next day all the Indians pulled out. We knew Custer was dead, and that's when the buzzards began gathering."

"It's still a little hard for you to talk about, isn't it, Nels?"

"Yes, miss. It is. I lost some good friends that day. Never have forgot them." The old man stood hipshot in place for a moment, jammed his hat back on, and then twisted his head to one side. "What you want to know all this fer, Miss Hellinger? It's old news, and nobody's interested in General Custer anymore."

"I am," Jo said quickly. "I've always been interested in the military. My father was a soldier, and he taught me a lot about it, but all I've done is read about it in books, and now, out here, you've made it all seem so real."

"It was bloody that day. Men were dying everywhere you looked. What are you going to do with all them pictures you made?"

Jo hesitated. "My editor told me to go get a story and take pictures. I couldn't think of anything to write a story about that interests me much, then I got to wondering about the West. Of course, I've read about it all my life, but I realize that most of it's gone. But I decided there might be a little of it left, and so I came out West to see what I could find."

"Mostly all gone now, miss," Nels said. "Them was better times, as far as I'm concerned."

"Well, I thank you for bringing me out here and for telling me about your experiences. You must be very proud of the part you played."

"Well, I don't know. Feel kind of sorry for them Indians." Price bowed his head, stared at the ground, then traced a design in the thin soil at his feet. Finally he looked up and shook his head. "I hated them then, but now I've been thinking, as I get on myself in years, they was just tryin' to make it like I was tryin' to do. Don't see how as we gave 'em a fair shake." He shook his shoulders together and then made a grimace. "Well, we'd better get back to Billings."

The two piled Jo's photographic equipment in the back of the big Packard that Nels drove. On the way back, he said, "When will you be going back East?"

"I've got to get back pretty soon. My time's about up and I'm about broke, too."

"You find anything for your story?"

"Oh yes. Quite a bit. Yours will be in there. Be sure and give me your address, Nels, and I'll send a copy to you. You don't mind my using it, do you?"

"Why, I reckon not. I'd be proud to see it." He suddenly swerved to miss a jackrabbit that darted out in front of the car and laughed. "That fella's not long for this world. He's not used to these newfangled automobiles."

"Is there anything else I ought to see while I'm here before I go home?"

"Well, have you been to any of the rodeos?"

"No, I haven't."

"You ort to take in one of them. There's one right now outside of town at the stock arena. Of course, it ain't one of the big rodeos like they have in Cheyenne or down in Fort Worth, but it's big enough." He hesitated, then said, "Be proud to take you, ma'am, if you wouldn't be ashamed to be seen with an old soldier."

Jo leaned over and squeezed the thin arm. "I'd be happy if you'd escort me, Nels. What time should we go?"

"Let's go about six o'clock. I'll take you around and introduce you to some of the bronc riders."

"That would be very nice."

"Better watch out for them cowboys, ma'am. They're pretty bad medicine when it comes to pretty young gals like you."

"You'll be there to protect me, Nels."

"Well, dog my cat! Maybe I'd better strap on my forty-four just in case any of them long-legged galoots get the wrong ideas about you."

★ ★ ★ ★

Nels Price had understated the problem a pretty girl might have with cowboys. From the moment Nels led her back under the stands where the horses were constantly being shifted, they were besieged by lanky men, mostly undersized and wiry. Nels seemed to know them all, and finally he had to push several of them away who crowded around, saying, "Git back thar, you ugly galoots! Ain't you hairpins never seen a lady before?"

"Never one this pretty!" A tall, gangly cowboy with a face like a dried apple grinned. He had no teeth at all, but that didn't seem to bother him. "Why don't you come with me, Miss Jo. I'll show you what a real cowboy's like."

"Legs, you get away or I'll salivate you!" Nels threatened. He had, indeed, put a forty-four in his belt, and now he pulled back his vest to expose it. "See that? It's just for birds like you who don't know how to treat a lady decent like."

Legs Moreland grinned but did not seem alarmed. "You watch me when I'm up on Dynamite, Miss Jo, and you be sure and write me up in that story of yours. You want to get my picture?"

"Yes." Once Jo had taken one picture, she found herself overwhelmed by cowboys who offered to pose.

Finally Nels shooed them all away, saying, "You birds get going! You got hosses to ride."

"They're all so small. I thought they'd be bigger," Jo said.

"Ain't no man, no matter how big he is, gonna manhandle a three-thousand-pound Brahma bull. But I tell you one thing—" Suddenly he broke off and said, "Hey, there's the fellow I want you to meet." Grabbing Jo by the arm, he pulled her toward a cowboy who had just entered with a light gray, flat-crowned hat pushed back on his head. He was wearing, as most of the others were, a pair of blue jeans and a red-and-white checkered shirt. "Hey, Logan! Got somebody for you to meet here!" Nels said. "This here's Miss Josephine Hellinger. Come all the way up from New York just to see what the Wild West was like. This here's Logan Smith. Fancies himself a bronc rider, Miss Jo."

"I'm happy to know you," Jo said and on impulse put her hand out. It was grasped at once in a powerful grip, and she received a nod and a smile.

"Glad to know you, Miss Hellinger. Don't believe a word this fellow says. He's the father of all liars."

Logan Smith was no more than five ten, but he was all smooth muscles, and there was an electricity about him. His skin was olive with a deep sunburn and he had crisp brown hair that was slightly curly. The strangest thing was his eyes, which were a shade of blue Jo had never seen before. They were close to indigo and as direct as she had ever seen in a man.

"You've been to many rodeos, Miss Hellinger?"

"No. This is my first. I don't know a thing about them."

"Well, I'll be ridin' first. If you care to watch, I'd sure be glad to have you."

"Oh yes!" Jo said quickly. Logan Smith nodded, then turned around and walked away.

"Come on. We'll get a good view from here. Let me explain something about horse riding," Nels said. "This here's the bareback riding. The horses don't wear no saddles, and the cowboy has to hang on to a leather handhold. You look there in that chute. That's some hoss that Logan's gettin' up on. Ain't many ever ridden him for the full ten seconds."

"Is that how long they have to stay on?"

"It's a mighty long time on top of a pile of dynamite like that! That horse's name is Man Killer. Now you watch. When they turn him loose, Logan will have to touch the spurs to the horse's shoulders. He's got to spur that horse through eight seconds of that ride."

"How do they know who wins?" Jo asked.

"Why, each cowboy's judged on how well he rides, how well he spurs, and then, of course, how well the horse bucks. Now, look out. There he comes!"

Jo heard the announcer's voice say, "And now one of our own, Logan Smith, comin' out of chute number six on Man Killer! Watch him go!"

Jo leaned forward, her eyes wide as the gate swung open and the horse seemed to explode. He was a dark brown horse and hit the dirt kicking up a fury. Smith's head, she saw, was whipped back and forth by the jolt. She found herself holding her breath, wondering how anybody could stay on. It seemed to last a long time, and finally she saw Smith step off the horse and land on his feet, his knees bent. He picked up his hat, which had fallen off, beat it against his leg, then walked back toward them.

"That was a good ride, Logan," Nels said. "Ort to be at least an eighty-five."

"Don't ever try to outguess the judges." The cowboy turned to Jo and said, "You know, these horses have an easy time. They don't make 'em buck very often so they'll stay fresh, then they only have to be on for ten seconds. Wish I had a job that only lasted ten seconds a week and got paid for it."

"Will you ride any more?"

"Oh sure. Next thing will be the bull riding, if you'd like to wait around."

Jo did wait around, and if the bareback riding had been rough, the bull riding was worse. The bulls were monstrous Brahmas, and she watched as Logan Smith settled himself and got a grip on the rope that was looped around the animal's middle like a noose.

"It's braided flat and has a handhold like the flat handle of a duffel bag," Nels said. "See there? Then he wraps the free end of the rope across his palm."

"Those things are awful! They're so big."

"They like to stomp a fellow, too. Ain't no job for weaklings. I tried it myself when I was a younger man, but only once."

The bull came out of the chute spinning around, and Jo had only time to notice that it was perfect balance that kept Logan on the bull's back. She found herself counting off the seconds. She gasped when Logan Smith suddenly flew over the bull's shoulders, did a complete somersault, and landed on his heels. The bull charged him, but two clowns came out waving red cloths in front and distracted the bull as Logan jumped up on the railing. She drew a sigh of relief. When

Logan came back, she said, "Do you ever get hurt doing that?"

"Everybody gets hurt in this line of work, Miss Hellinger."

"Do you ride anything else?"

"Gonna ride the saddle bronc competition. That's all for today."

Jo hesitated. "I wonder if you'd mind coming out with me and Nels and having supper. I'd like to interview you."

"Sure," Logan smiled. He winked at Nels and said, "Don't let her get away. I never missed a free meal."

Two hours later Nels left the two alone at the restaurant, saying, "It's gettin' late for an old man." He reached over and smacked Logan on the shoulder. "You mind your manners with Miss Jo, you hear me?"

"You bet, Nels. Don't worry about a thing."

After the old man had left, Jo said, "He's a fine man, isn't he?"

"Sure is. I've known him since I can remember. He and my dad are good friends."

They were eating steaks and had almost finished by this time. Logan studied the young woman, then said, "So, you're a writer?"

"That's right, and a photographer. I'm getting a story together on the Old West along with pictures. If I do a good job, my editor will take me off those boring society stories. I'm so sick of brides and wedding dresses, I could scream."

Logan grinned and finished the glass of iced tea. "Well, I hope you make it." He hesitated, then said, "You know, you ought to talk to my dad if you are writing a story on the Old West."

"Why's that?"

"Well, he's part of it. He was an outlaw for a while, almost."

"You don't mean it!"

"He doesn't talk much about it, but he could have gone that way. For a time he was a marshall, though, under Isaac Parker down in Fort Smith. That was before he married and came up here to Montana to become a rancher. But if you want to know the Old West, you ought to come and talk to Dad."

"I'd love to, but where does he live?"

"Oh, our ranch isn't more than thirty miles outside of Billings. No trip at all."

"I usually don't push myself on people, but if you don't mind, Mr. Smith, I'd really like to meet your father."

"Logan's fine. Why, sure. I'm going back first thing in the morning. Be glad to have you come with me."

"Oh, you'd have to tell your relatives."

"No, we got a big old place. Just Mom and Dad and my brother, Frank. He's seventeen. We've got a big old ramblin' ranch house, and Ma's starved for female company. Where are you staying?"

"At the Palace Hotel."

"I'll pick you up at seven. We'll get home in time for some of Ma's good biscuits. They can't cook anything in these restaurants." He smiled at her and said, "I'm afraid most of the Wild West is gone, but you'll like my folks anyhow."

"I'm sure I will, Logan."

★ ★ ★ ★

Jo took an instant liking to Mr. and Mrs. Lafayette Smith. But she soon discovered that no one called Logan's father anything but Lobo. He had carried the name since early manhood. When she had been introduced to him, she thought, *Why, that's what a western outlaw should look like*. Lobo Smith, now fifty, was not large, but he still had the strength of a younger man. He had a black patch over his left eye, and the other was the same indigo color of those of his son. His wife, Lanie, was an attractive woman a few years younger, and their other son, Frank, seventeen, two years younger than Logan, had eyes exactly the same color.

For two days Jo enjoyed the Smiths' hospitality. She particularly delighted in Lobo's interesting tales of when he served as a marshall for Judge Isaac Parker, the hanging judge. She liked Frank very much, who yearned to be the world's champion bronc rider. He often complained, "Don't see why I couldn't have been born first. Then I could have beat Logan."

It was on the third day of her visit that Jo discovered another side to Logan Smith. He approached her that morning and said, "I'm going over to do a little tinkering on my airplane. Care to come?"

"You have an airplane?"

"Well, a friend of mine does. We're sort of partners in it."

"I'd love to go," Jo said instantly. "I have to go home tomorrow, but I've always been interested in the Wrights and their airplanes."

After breakfast the two climbed into Logan's Rio and drove twelve miles over to a small shack that was overshadowed by a large, flat-roofed barn. "We keep the plane in the barn to keep it from blowing away," Logan said as he brought the Rio to a stop. He jumped out of the car and hollered, "Hey, Rev, come out of there! You've got company!"

As Jo got out of the car, she saw the door to the small, weather-beaten shack open. She blinked, for the man who came out was one of the most extraordinary figures she had ever seen. He was six feet, at least, but appeared to be all legs and arms. The first thought that jumped into Jo's mind was, *Why, he's like a spider!* The tall man's face was very homely. She could only think of his face as being somehow squelched down with a chin very close to the nose, but a pair of merry blue eyes twinkled out at her as he ambled over and nodded.

"Howdy, Logan. Who's this pretty lady?"

"I'd like for you to meet Miss Josephine Hellinger. She's a writer from New York. Came to write about the Old West. And this is my friend, Mr. Rev Brown."

Jo put out her hand and smiled, saying, "I'm very happy to know you." Her hand was completely swallowed by the enormous paw that seemed to dangle on the end of the long arm of the man. He was very careful, she noticed, not to exert his strength, which must have been considerable considering the size of the hand. She noticed it was hard with calluses and seemed to have endured some hard usage along the way. "I didn't quite catch your first name. Is it Rev?"

"Well, my full handle is Revelation." Brown grinned and said, "That's right, ma'am. My dad was a nonconformist preacher back in England, where I come from. My father loved the Book of Revelation, so he named me after it."

"I bet you never run into anybody with a name like yours," Jo smiled.

"Nope. Had two brothers, though. One named Dedication and one Incarnation."

Jo laughed out loud. "You're making that up!"

"No, he's not! I've seen the letters they write," Logan grinned. "And his sisters. Tell Miss Jo their names, Rev."

"Incense, Praise, and Blessing. How's that for a trio?"

"I think it's delightful. I wish I had a name like that. Incense Hellinger! That beats Josephine all to pieces, doesn't it?"

"You two come in the house. I'm just brewing some tea."

Jo stepped inside and was surprised at how neat the inside of the house was. Actually it was much neater than the outside. She sat down and soon had a cup of tea in front of her as Rev Brown sat down across the table from her.

"Have you ever been born again, Miss Hellinger?" he inquired in an interested fashion.

"Why—" Jo broke off, for she had never been asked that question exactly.

"I should have warned you about Rev. He asks everybody the same thing. Rev, I wish you wouldn't spring your religion on people until they've gotten used to you."

"Well, I'm sorry. I don't mean to be offensive."

"Oh, it's all right, Mr. Brown. Or can I call you Rev? Well, yes, I am a Christian."

"Well, praise God! Here we are, three Christians all together."

"Rev can quote the whole Book of Revelation by heart, but don't ask him to do it," Logan said hastily. "He might just do it."

Jo found Revelation Brown quite extraordinary. He had been born in England but had left there when he was only a boy. At the age of thirty-six, he appeared to have traveled all over the world. When she asked him about the airplane, she could tell by his smile it was one of his favorite subjects.

"Well, I worked for the Wrights for a little while. I figured I might make my own plane someday, and then when I got out here just about broke, Logan here came up with the cash. So together we've been putting together a plane that's going to make us right proud."

"I'd love to see it."

Instantly Revelation Brown stood up. "Come along. We'll give you a full display."

They went outside and soon Revelation and Logan had pulled their craft out of the barn. It looked very flimsy to Jo.

"I appreciate Rev's ability to quote Revelation, but let me tell you, in addition to that, he's the finest mechanic I've ever seen," Logan said. "He can make any engine run like a watch. Would you like to go up?" he asked abruptly.

"Oh, you mean now?"

"Now is as good a time as any."

Jo had a sudden idea. "Can I take my camera with me and take some pictures from the air?"

"Take anything you want, lady," Logan Smith grinned. "It's a little dangerous, you understand. I've piled her up twice already."

Jo Hellinger shook her hair back. "I wouldn't get on the Brahma bull, but I'll get in this airplane."

"Well, come along, Miss Jo. We'll give you your first airplane ride, then you'll have something to write about for that editor back in New York City."

CHAPTER EIGHT

"A War Is No Place for a Woman!"

★ ★ ★ ★

Restlessly Jo paced back and forth, her head down and her eyes unseeing for the most part. Across from her on the couch, Bedford lay watching her with an alert expression. Finally, however, he sensed there would be no walk forthcoming for a time, so he put his chin down on his paws and watched her through half-hooded eyes.

The afternoon sun was laying pale bars of light across the multicolored carpet of Jo's living room. Finally, she became aware that the day was almost gone. "I've got to do something besides pace the floor," she muttered. Turning toward the window, she advanced and stared out at the late afternoon traffic. Idly, she named many of the cars that passed by, Maxwells, Studebakers, Packards, Stanleys, and wondered if she ought not to buy one. They were still expensive affairs, rich men's toys rather than anything else, and she put the idea out of her mind.

With a gesture of impatience, she walked over to the desk backed against the wall and moved books, papers, and photographic chemicals aside and removed the newspaper from the center drawer. Laying it down, she read it avidly, noting the heading, " 'The Old West Lives,' a story by Josephine Hellinger." Her eyes followed the text she had practically memorized, and she seemed to gloat over the words.

"Well, Ed Kovak can't say that story wasn't good! A lot of people called the paper, telling how much they enjoyed it, and some wrote letters, too!"

The thought of letters caused a shift of mind, and she fumbled in the right-hand drawer, extracting an envelope from which she removed a single sheet of paper. She had heard from Logan Smith twice since she had returned, and this letter she had received yesterday intrigued her. Her eyes ran over the text. She noted that his handwriting was strong and masculine in a heavy block style.

Dear Jo,

I received your letter yesterday afternoon and shared it with Revelation. We both appreciated the story you wrote and the part you gave us. You made me out to be quite a hero riding dragons rather than broncs, but it was a good story. Not many writers get the details of rodeoing right, but you did a fine job.

Rev and I have been flying quite a bit, that is I have. It seems he has no talent at all for flying an airplane. As a matter of fact, he's a terrible automobile driver too. I think there's something about balance that makes a person able to fly. I've always had good balance. I think I could have been a wire walker if I had set my mind to it. In any case, Rev keeps the plane going, and I keep flying it. My folks think it's a foolish notion, but, Jo, somehow I think it's more important than just a toy.

I've been reading the stories about what's happening in Europe, and it seems to me that Germany and France are on a collision course. I get the picture of two trains on a single track running with open throttles and the brakes gone. Sooner or later they're going to collide, and there's going to be a terrible explosion. When that time comes, I think it's not going to be confined to Europe. Sooner or later it will come to this country as well. When it does, every able-bodied man will have to decide what he's going to do about it.

I've talked to my dad about this, and he doesn't understand. He says that America is concerned only about America and not what's happening in Europe, but one day not too far off that won't be so. Not that I expect to have the Germans knocking on our door anytime soon, but the cause is what's important, isn't it? I know that sounds idealistic. Even my mother says I've always been a little bit that way. I've always liked stories of King Arthur and his court. To tell the truth, which I never have to any living soul, I always saw myself as Sir Galahad rescuing a maiden in distress. That's something for a hard-headed cowboy to dream about, isn't it?

Jo read the letter through twice and then put it back in the envelope slowly. A thoughtful look had come into her eyes, and she ran over in her mind the enjoyable times she had spent with Logan Smith. She was accustomed to the hard spirit of New Yorkers, and there was something open about this young man that had impressed her. Replacing the envelope, she slowly rose and went over and sat down on the bed beside Bedford, stroking his head. When she stopped he poked her with his muzzle, and she murmured, "All right. All right. Don't you ever get enough petting?" She thought for some time of what Logan had said and agreed with it. She herself was not a political analyst, but it didn't take one of those to know that grave trouble lay ahead for the world. Finally she rose and said, "Do you want to go for a walk?"

"Wuff!"

"Well, come on. We might as well do that and I'll write Logan when I get back."

★ ★ ★ ★

The assassination of the archduke in Sarajevo triggered a series of events that echoed like a small explosion, each one a little louder than the other. Americans had difficulty comprehending what was going on, for the United States at that time was an impossibly happy nation. People were prospering, and the common man, at least, was almost totally uninformed about Europe. During the month of July, the New York Yankees and the Cleveland Indians struggled to win the American League pennant, although the Athletics from Philadelphia finally won it. In the prizefighting world, Jack Johnson, the first black champion, had pointed Frank Moran. Eggs were twenty-one cents a dozen, and a good cigar cost a man six cents. And thus America and the world moved ahead, but the sinister forces that were to shake the earth itself could not be withheld. After the assassination of the duke, nations began lining up. Russia, Germany, France, Austria, all were talking of mobilization. None of these nations had any idea what lay ahead of them, for war cannot be tested ahead of time. There had been war since man had first disagreed with other men, but the scale of operations during August 1914 was almost beyond belief. It was incomparably so much greater than any nation had expected. The nations were like small boys with machines who sat behind the controls of a powerful locomotive with no knowledge of how to operate one and no comprehension of the destructive power about to be unleashed.

And so finally in July, Germany carried out the act that was to draw other nations into a world conflict. They demanded passage through Belgium so that they might attack France. There were meetings, and desperate statesmen struggled to do something to stop the juggernaut of war, but on August 3, Germany declared war against France and the die was cast.

★ ★ ★ ★

"I tell you, you can't do it, Jo!" Ed Kovak shouted. For ten minutes he had been listening with growing impatience to the woman who stood before him, and now he seemed to explode. "You must have lost your mind! In the history of the newspaper business, there has never been a female war correspondent!"

"Then I'll be the first!"

As soon as the news of the declaration of war came over the radio, Jo had made up her mind. She had slept little the previous night but had walked the floor, thinking of arguments that would persuade her boss to send her to Europe to cover the coming conflict. She had known beforehand there would be a battle, but now she saw it was going to be even more difficult than she thought.

"Look, Ed," she said in a pleading tone of voice. "I know I can do this thing, and you don't have any other reporter who can take pictures like I can."

"That's beside the point!" Kovak shook his head stubbornly. He was a stocky individual, and someone had said of him, *"He looks like he's about to lower his head and run it through an oak door."* His stubbornness was now at full tide, and he chomped on his cigar while shaking his head with an angry motion. "I absolutely, positively refuse even to consider the idea! War is no place for a woman!"

"They used to say a newspaper room was no place for a woman, but I'm here, and so are other women. Somebody's going to get great stories out of this war, and it might as well be the *Times,* and I might as well be the one to do it!"

"Look, Jo. In the first place, this isn't our war. In the second place, some of the experts are saying it'll be over before Christmas."

"Then they're nincompoops! Idiots!" Jo snapped. "You ought to know better than that! It's not going to be a quick war! There's too much at stake. France and Germany, Russia and Austria will fight till the last man before they'll give up." She pleaded impassioned for some time and finally saw she was getting nowhere.

"Look, just give me a chance. Let me go for a month. If it doesn't work out, I'll come back."

"No. You could get killed, and I'm not going to be the one writing a letter to your family saying how sorry I am. Fat lot of good that would do." Kovak maneuvered his stub of a cigar from one corner of his mouth to the other, then leaned forward. "I'm sorry, Jo, and I'll make it up to you. You did a good job on that story about the West. You've got a good future here. Why, I might even let you cover the World Series this year. That'd be something a woman has never done before."

Ordinarily an assignment like that would have been a great victory for Jo, but somehow she had set her sights on bigger things. She was well aware that the big news in the future was going to be the European war, not the World Series, except in those cities where it was played. She saw, however, that it was useless to plead anymore, so she sighed and her shoulders drooped. "I think you're making a big mistake."

"I may be, but at least this mistake won't get you killed. Now, go on to work, Hellinger. You've got a bright future. You're sharp, you're tough, and one of these days you may be sitting right here in my seat."

The rest of the day Jo went about her work in a mechanical fashion. She had been assigned to cover a meeting of the legislature, which proved to be intensely boring. She took pictures of some of the politicians, who smiled and smirked like Hollywood movie stars in front of the camera, and finally at the end of the day made her way home. When she stepped inside she was greeted, as always, by enthusiastic advances from Bedford. He insisted on rearing up on her no matter how many times she stepped on his feet to convince him that such an action was wrong. Shoving him down, she moved over to the table, dumped her camera and purse, then went to the bed and threw herself on it. She felt the bed creak as Bedford leaped up beside her and began nuzzling her. "All right, Bedford. We'll go for a walk in a minute. Let me rest, can't you?"

But Bedford was in no mood for resting. As always, his energy built up so that by the time she got home, he was ready for his exercise. Jo arose and left the apartment, and for the next forty-five minutes, Bedford romped through Central Park. He chased squirrels but never seemed to catch any. "Don't you ever learn anything, Bedford?" Jo asked crossly. "You're never going to catch one of those things."

Finally, when it was time to go, Jo said, "Come on. I'll stop by and get you a treat at the grocery store."

The two arrived home, and as soon as Jo had given Bedford the huge bone the butcher had saved for him, the phone rang. Moving across the room, she picked up the receiver. "Hello?"

"Hi, is this you, Jo?"

"Yes. Logan?"

"Yeah, it's me."

"Where are you? In Montana?"

"Montana? No. I'm right here in New York City."

For a moment Jo could not answer, her surprise was so great. "In New York! Well, where are you? I want to see you."

"That's why I called. I'm lost in this place. I've got your address, but I don't have any idea how to find it."

"Just get in a taxicab and give him my address. He'll bring you here. Come as quick as you can. We'll go out and eat."

"I've got Revelation with me."

"Bring him. We'll all three go out to eat."

Jo waited impatiently until finally she heard a knock at the door. Bedford at once came to full attention and positioned himself, waiting to see who was invading his territory. Opening the door, Jo saw the grinning face of Logan Smith and immediately behind him Revelation Brown.

"Hi, Josephine," Logan said. He impulsively reached forward and caught her up and squeezed her so hard she lost her breath.

At that instant a low-pitched, frightening snarl suddenly penetrated the room, and Logan got a glimpse of the white fangs of the huge dog that now faced him. He saw the hair rising on the back, and the teeth looked like those of a great white shark.

"Be quiet!" Jo commanded. She reached down and petted the dog, and said apologetically, "He's a little bit possessive. He's kind of my antiburglar device." She turned at once and hugged Revelation, which gave that gentleman quite a surprise.

"Well," he said, grinning broadly, "I ain't been welcomed like that in quite a spell. Is that there animal safe?"

It took a few moments to introduce Logan and Revelation to Bedford, but the big dog, finally satisfied that all was well, proceeded to give the two a good going-over, sniffing them carefully and finally sitting down on Revelation's feet to show his approval.

"Let's go out and eat. I'm starved to death."

"We're not interrupting anything, are we, Jo?"

"No. Just a lonely evening at home. Come on. Let's go."

The three left the apartment accompanied by Bedford, and Logan asked, "Does he go eat with you?"

"He goes pretty much anywhere I go. Some restaurants won't have us, but I've found out those who will. What do you want? Chinese food, Mexican, American?"

"If the hair and hide's off of it and the horns have been removed, I'll eat it," Revelation said, then added, "Well, as the Good Book tells us, 'Whatsoever parteth the hoof, and is clovenfooted, and cheweth the cud, among the beasts, that shall ye eat.' That's in Leviticus chapter eleven verse three. So as long as it fits them qualifications, lady, lead me to it."

Jo laughed and said, "Well, I expect a cow fits that. So how about a first-class steak?"

"I feel strongly led to eat one, Miss Hellinger," Logan said. "And I'll even buy one for your dog there. What's his name?"

"Bedford."

"Odd name for a dog," Logan observed.

"He's named after General Nathan Bedford Forrest, the finest cavalry commander the world ever saw."

"I know. Sherman said about him, 'We've got to get rid of that devil Forrest before we can win this war.' "

"You know your history, Logan. Come on. Let's go eat."

Two hours later the three two-legged guests were at the Elite Café, and the four-legged one had done his best to annihilate the steaks that the owner, George Grierson, had provided for them. Jo Hellinger was a favorite of his, and he liked dogs, so he had provided a juicy hamburger patty for Bedford. He had eaten it in two swift gulps and watched every bite that went down the throats of the other guests.

As they ate, Jo listened avidly as the two men, between bites, told the story of their odyssey to New York.

"As soon as the news of the war came, which we both knew it would," Logan said, chewing on a morsel of his rib eye and swallowing it, "we decided we had to get in on it."

"Get in on the war?" Jo asked blankly. "What do you mean?"

"Why, I mean we're joining up. We're going to fight for the French."

"That's right," Revelation said. For such a lean man, he had put away an inordinate amount of food, and now he was working on his second piece of pie. "It was Logan here that brought it up, but I prayed over it, and I'm convinced that it's the thing to do."

"How did you come to that conclusion, Revelation?"

"Don't know, but sometimes I hear a voice, and it's the Lord, and when He says go, I goeth. When He says come, I cometh." He grinned at her, finished off his pie, and then picked up the huge coffee mug and washed it down thirstily. He wiped his lips with his sleeve and then said, "In any case, it's all written down."

"What do you mean all written down?" Jo asked uncertainly.

"Well, I mean before this here earth was ever created, God had plans for all of us. Didn't you know that, Miss Jo? I'm plum surprised at you."

"Oh, I see, then you're a Calvinist."

"Sure am! That feller Calvin had it figured out right. Whatever God decides, it's going to be."

"Why, Rev even parks the car on the railroad tracks." Logan smiled fondly at his ungainly friend. "He believes it's going to happen whether it does or not."

"You go on and make fun of me, Cowboy, but you're going to find out that I'm right. And God meant for us to go to this here war, and we're both going. Before it's over this cowboy is going to fly them airplanes, and I'm going to fix 'em and keep 'em to where they're fit to fly. You wait and see if it don't happen like that."

Jo was somewhat confused. She had never imagined such a thing. "Aren't you being a little bit idealistic?" she asked.

"I don't know about that, but I know we're doing the right thing." A worried frown swept across Logan's face. "Had trouble with Mom and Dad, and then Frank, of course, wanted to come, too. But I talked him out of it."

The three sat there talking until finally the manager came and said apologetically, "Got to close up, Miss Jo."

"Oh, I'm sorry, George! I didn't realize we were here so long."

As she fumbled in her purse, Logan said quickly, "We don't ever let a lady pay."

"That's right. We don't," Revelation nodded. He plunged his hand into his pocket, but Logan beat him to it, handing several bills to the waiting manager. "Fine steak," Revelation said. "Are you saved, brother?"

George Grierson stared at the gangly, long-legged, long-armed man with the apple-pinched face. "Am I what?"

"Are you saved? Are you under the blood? Have you been redeemed by the Lamb?"

Jo stood there watching the bewilderment on George's face. She knew he was a devout Catholic, but all of this would mean nothing to him. Finally Revelation reached into his pocket, pulled out a handful of tracts, and handed one to him. "Read this. Wrote 'em myself and had 'em printed up in Billings. It will show you the way to the throne room, brother. God bless you, and may I see you when we cross the River Jordan."

Jo patted George on the arm and said, "It's all right, George. Don't worry about it."

"What is he? Some kind of a preacher?"

"I think so," Jo said. She smiled at Revelation, who beamed back at her. "Come along. You can preach at me, Revelation." When they were outside, she said, "Where are you staying?"

"We got us a hotel room, but tomorrow we're gonna sign up."

"I don't think it'll be that easy. You'd better meet me down at the newspaper office. We'll talk to some of the men there. My boss, Ed Kovak, might know about things like this."

"All right. We'll be there." Logan Smith reached over suddenly and hugged Jo. "I'm glad you're here. I need me a big sister to guide me through the world, and you're elected."

"And I guess I'm not quite old enough to be your pa, but I'm old enough to be your big brother," Revelation said. He took Jo's hand and squeezed it carefully. "We'll be there in the morning."

★ ★ ★ ★

As soon as the two cowboys from Montana arrived at the newspaper office, Jo introduced them to Ed Kovak, who stared at them blankly as Jo explained why they had come to New York.

"Going to join the French army? Do I hear you right?"

"Yes, sir, Mr. Kovak. That's what we're both going to do," Logan smiled.

Revelation nodded cheerfully. "Yes, the Lord's done spoken. Are you saved, brother?"

Jo had known this would happen, for she had discovered that Revelation Brown's evangelism was boundless. He put the question to almost everyone he met. He was not obnoxious about it in the least, always cheerful, and when he encountered resistance, he never grew bellicose or seemed upset. She hurried on to prevent Rev from going on by saying, "Where could they go enlist, Mr. Kovak?"

"Why, in France, of course," Kovak said. "You don't think France has an enlistment office down on Thirty-first Street, do you?"

When they realized it wasn't possible to enlist in America, the three left the office quite deflated.

"I never thought of such a thing as this," Logan said. "I don't know where the French Embassy is, but we'll find out."

That began two days of hard searching, but at the end of that time all three were convinced there was no way to join the French army in New York City.

They went back to George Grierson's Elite Café for another meal. George greeted them warmly, although he eyed Revelation warily. Revelation, however, seemed to feel that he had done his duty as far as the stubby owner of the Elite was concerned.

They ordered, and midway through the meal Jo asked, "What are you going to do?"

"Well, we're going to France, of course," Revelation said. " 'Whatsoever thy hand findeth to do, do it with all thy might.' "

"Why, you can't do that!" Jo said.

"Why can't we?" Logan asked.

"Why, it takes a passport for one thing, and then you'd have to pay your way on a ship."

"The Lord's going to take care of those things, Miss Jo," Revelation said firmly. "Everything's under God's hands. He owns all the steamships. Didn't you know that? He can sure get two cowboys a place on one of them."

Jo was stunned by what she heard. She listened as the two excitedly made plans to go to Europe, but that night when she went home, she stayed up for a long time. Bedford watched her from his accustomed position on the bed, but finally even he dozed off.

Jo sat down in the chair beside her bed and thought of how her own plans to get to Europe had failed. Somehow seeing the determination and excitement of Logan and Revelation did something to her. She was not at all sure of their proclamation that God was sending them, but she was very certain of her own determination to get there.

She went to bed, slept fitfully, and rose the next morning with her mind made up. When she arrived at the office, she knocked on Mr. Kovak's door, and when a gruff "Come in!" sounded, she entered.

"Well, you've learned to knock on doors, I see. Where did the two cowboys go?"

"They're getting passports this morning."

"You mean those two clowns are going to France?"

"That's right."

Kovak pulled a match from his shirt pocket, struck it on his desk, and lit a fresh cigar. When he had it going, he gave her an odd glance. "Do you believe all that religion stuff that the tall one was spouting about God sending him and all that?"

"I . . . I'm not sure about all that, Ed. But I am sure of one thing."

"What's that, Jo?"

"I'm going to France myself. I know you can't send me—" Here she interrupted Ed by raising her hand and lifting her voice. "So I'm quitting today. You've been good to me and taught me a lot, but I've got to go, Ed."

Ed Kovak stared at the young woman before him with mixed feelings. He had developed a great affection for her, which he took great care not to show, but now that she had made this announcement, he was disturbed. "It's dangerous over there, Jo. I'd hate to see anything happen to you."

"I'm going, Ed. That's all there is to it. I'm going to be a free-lance writer. I'll send you some stories. If you like them, you can use them. If not, I'll send them to other newspapers. And I'm going to write a book, too, and take lots of pictures. I'm going to this war, Ed, and that's all there is to it!"

CHAPTER NINE

PARIS!

★ ★ ★ ★

The *Lusitania* seemed enormous to the three passengers who stood looking up from the docks. Revelation Brown shook his head and said, "There ain't no such ship this big!"

Both Logan and Jo laughed, and then the three started up the gangplank. The hour was late, after ten o'clock in the evening, and it had been a struggle to find any accommodations on an Atlantic ship. The *Lusitania* had been the only one they could obtain passage on.

When they reached the top of the gangplank, they were met by a steward in white, who said, "Yes. May I see your tickets?" After glancing at them casually, he said, "You are on the second deck, miss. And you two gentlemen are on the fourth deck. And the dog will have to be kept in the kennel. Come. I will show you."

Finding their way on the monstrous vessel would have been difficult, for, as Revelation said, "It's about twice as big as the little town where I was born, in Shropshire."

After dropping Bedford off in the kennel—which was one of the finest accommodations Jo had ever seen for a dog—the steward led them to Jo's cabin. It was in the first-class section, that being all that was available. She found the cabin more exotic and luxurious than any room she had ever had. As soon as she stepped inside, agreeing to meet her friends for what dinner could be had at that late hour, she walked around, studying the cabin. It was a large stateroom done in Queen Anne style and consisted of two small suites and a private bath. She moved to the wall, ran her fingers over the polished oak, and murmured, "I had to spend too much for this, but I will admit it is really impressive." She unpacked her suitcase, then went at once to find the dining room. She found it without too much trouble on the second deck.

Standing off to one side of the main door, Revelation and Logan greeted her. "How is your room?" Logan asked.

"Luxurious! Far too nice for me. And yours?"

"Well, it's better than the one I've got at home."

"Better than that shack I was living in, too," Rev said. "But I've learned in whatsoever state I'm in to be content. Now, let's eat."

Acting on Revelation's suggestion, they moved into the dining salon, which was at least sixty feet long and decorated with Colonial furniture. Ornately carved sycamore paneling outlined the entire dining area. They were seated by a maître d' in a white coat, who said, "Your waiter will be here promptly."

As soon as he left, a short, swarthy man with a spiked black mustache and dancing black eyes said, "Yes, indeed! May I bring you something to drink?"

"I'd appreciate a glass of water, and let me ask you a question, brother. Have you been washed in the blood of the Lamb?"

"Sir?"

Without lowering his voice one decibel, Revelation started inquiring into the waiter's spiritual condition but was interrupted at once by Logan, who said, "You can do your preaching later, Rev. Let's order."

The waiter stared at the two men quite askance, for both were still wearing jeans and checkered shirts and had placed their Stetsons on the table. Neither wore spurs, but both wore high-heeled cowboy boots. The waiter smiled, "You are from the American West, I take it?"

"Montana, partner," Logan grinned. "Now, let's talk about something to eat."

"Yes, of course. We have lobster. Here is our menu."

The three took the menus, and at once Revelation exclaimed, "Why, this here ain't English!"

"No, sir. It is French."

Shrugging his narrow shoulders, Revelation put his finger on one line and said, "I'll have some of this."

The waiter's glance followed his finger, and he sniffed. "That is not something to eat, sir. That is the motto of our line. *The finest ship afloat.*"

"I guess we'd better learn to read French if that's where we're going. I had a year of it in high school," Jo smiled. "Let's see if I can figure it out."

The meal turned out to be quite an event. They had lobster with mayonnaise and spiced round of beef, and Revelation insisted on trying ox tongue.

He pronounced it to be not as good as jerky but passable. They also consumed huge salads dosed with Cheshire cheese and sliced apples. For dessert they had rice custard pudding and coffee.

The coffee did not suit either Logan or Revelation, for it came in small china cups.

"Hey, buddy," Logan said. "Have you got any big white mugs back in there?"

"I'm sorry, sir. These are the largest cups we have."

"Why, I spill more than this, fella!" Revelation protested.

"You'll just have to drink more cups to make up for the size," Jo smiled. "Now, stop tormenting the poor man." She turned to the waiter and said, "Merci beaucoup."

The waiter beamed. "Certainement, mademoiselle."

The trio sat there drinking coffee, and Jo said, "Are you sure we've done the right thing? It seems so . . . impulsive."

"When the Lord moves, He moves all of a sudden," Revelation nodded firmly. "It's what God planned for us before the world was even built."

"I wish," Jo said quietly, "that I were as sure of everything I do as you are."

"Why, you ought to be," Revelation said with surprise. "You don't think the Lord wants to keep things a secret from you, do you?"

"I think He does sometimes," Jo murmured.

"Well, I guess I've got to work on your theology a little bit, Miss Jo. But we've got a long trip to do it in. Why don't we meet every morning for a little Bible study?"

"That would be fine, but you'll have to go slow. I'm not as advanced as you are."

"How about if I go get that soup hound of yours and take him for a walk?" The officer in charge had been firm that Bedford could not be kept in Jo's cabin. The three had gone down to inspect the quarters and found that there was a well-designed kennel, clean and airy and yet well heated when necessary. Bedford had whined when put into the cage, but it was large with a thick rug on the deck. The attendant had assured her that he would be watered and fed regularly.

"I wish you would, Revelation," Jo said. "He gets lonely."

As soon as Revelation left the dining room, Jo smiled fondly in his direction. "I like him very much, but he's very unusual, isn't he?"

"I'll say," Logan nodded. "I never met anyone like him."

Logan leaned back in his chair, his legs out in front of him as he studied Jo. Finally he asked without warning, "How come you're not married?"

"Never found a man I wanted."

"You must be pretty picky."

"I am."

"Plenty of men in New York, though."

"Plenty of squirrels, too. It's not the same thing, is it, Logan?"

"I don't know. I've never been in love but six or seven times myself."

Laughing, Jo sipped her coffee. "I bet you've had lots of romances."

"Nary a one. Not serious, that is. Hard to believe, isn't it? A good-looking galoot like me."

"Yes, it is. But you're only nineteen."

"Well, my best friend was only eighteen when he got married last year. I feel like maybe I'm missing something."

"But if you were married, you couldn't just jump up and run off to France, could you?"

Logan's lips turned upward in a smile. His tanned skin caught a gleam of the light, and he looked hard and tough and fit as he sat there. A lot of riding had slimmed him down, molded his muscles, and he had an eagerness about him that had never been quenched. "This all may amount to nothing, this war, I mean. They may settle it even before we get to France."

"No. I don't think so, Logan," Jo said quietly. "It's gone too far for that." She hesitated, then said, "Have you thought about the fact that you might be killed?"

"Oh sure. Always possible. Every time I got on a bull I thought that, too. A man can get killed crossing the street."

"It's not the same thing, is it?"

Logan sobered then and put his hands together in front of him. They were tough hands, strong, with flexible fingers, scarred by rope and hard work. He clenched them together tightly for a moment, then shrugged. "It's just something I have to do."

The two sat there for some time, and finally the dining room was almost empty. They were about ready to leave when a man next to them suddenly turned.

"I didn't mean to eavesdrop," he said, "but I couldn't help overhearing some of your conversation."

Both Logan and Jo turned to look at the man. He was a handsome man with blond hair and bright blue eyes and very fair skin. "Did I understand you to say you're going to France to enlist in the French army?"

"That's right."

"It will do you no good, I'm afraid," the man said.

"Why's that, partner?" Logan asked. He was studying the stranger carefully, trying to make out what his purpose was in addressing them. "I figure I'll be doing a good thing."

"My name is Mueller. Kurt Mueller. I am also leaving the States to enlist in the army." He hesitated, then his mouth grew tense. "But it will be the army of Kaiser Wilhelm."

A silence then seemed to implode around the three. Jo's eyes were fixed on the German's face, and she glanced once at Logan. *This is it in miniature. The Germans versus the rest of the world. Anyone that stands in their way. Americans, French, Russians.* She said quietly, "I'm afraid we do not agree with your politics, Mr. Mueller."

"No. I think not. I believe it will be a very short war, and that all of us will be home by Christmas."

"I doubt that," Logan said. Then a curious thought came into his mind, *What if I meet this man on the battlefield? We'd each have a rifle and we'd try to kill each other*. He saw the health blooming in Mueller, could even see the pulse beating in his throat. He was full of life, and Logan asked himself the question, *Could I aim a gun at this man's heart? At this man's brain and pull the trigger? Or could I drive a bayonet into his body?* For some reason the war seemed to be closer, and he said quietly, "I hope you're right, but I have doubts."

"I wish you well," Mueller said. He bowed slightly, then turned and walked away.

"How about that?" Logan said. "Good-looking man, isn't he? And strong. I think he would make a good soldier."

"Germans make good soldiers, but their cause isn't always right."

The two rose then and went to their cabins, and when Logan told Revelation about the incident, the face of the other twisted up into a grimace. "That's the trouble with wars. You have to kill nice folks sometimes."

★ ★ ★ ★

From the time the trio descended the gangplank and traveled by train to the city of Paris, they were stunned by all they saw.

The worst of all for the three of them was, of course, the language. Except for a smattering of French possessed by Jo, they were helpless before cabdrivers, waiters, officials, and anyone else. They finally managed to get to a hotel with the help of a cabdriver who spoke something Logan thought was English but resembled it only slightly. The man demanded full fare for Bedford, and that only after Jo pled with him.

Fortunately, the clerk at the hotel spoke excellent English and greeted them warmly. "Ah, welcome to Paris. Your first trip?"

"Yes, our first trip. We need two rooms please," Logan said. "One for me and this gent, and one for the lady and the dog."

"The dog?"

"Yes, I have to have him with me," Jo said quickly. "I'll pay extra, of course."

"In that case, it will be all right."

They found their rooms comfortable enough, but at Logan's insistence they left at once. "We need to find an enlistment office," he said.

"But this is Sunday! They won't be open!" Jo protested.

"Well, we can find out where it is."

"None of that. We're going to church," Revelation said firmly. " 'Six days shalt thou do all thy labor,' as the Scripture says. This day belongs to the Lord, so we're going to find a church."

Finding a church proved to be somewhat difficult, but after a few attempts they got instructions from a policeman who spoke some English. "Ah, church. L'église." He gave some garbled instructions, then said, "Big building—cathedral."

"Come on. We can't miss a cathedral," Logan grinned.

As they strolled down the street, Revelation seemed to be in deep thought. Finally he said, "You know what I think?"

"What's that, Rev?"

"I think if you woke any of these people up in the middle of the night—"

"What about it, Revelation?" Jo questioned.

"Why, if you did that, I think they'd talk just like we do. Just like everybody else does."

Both Logan and Jo found this amusing, but Revelation saw nothing odd about it. Soon they found their way into a large cathedral. When Revelation saw the worshipers stopping to dip their hands into the holy water and cross themselves, he proceeded to do the same.

"Why, you're not a Catholic!" Logan protested.

"It must be the way these folks do it. When they come to my church, they can do like I do. When I'm in their church, I'll do like they do."

They went in and took their seats, and all three were stunned by the enormous size of the building. Looking up at the ceiling so far above them, Logan murmured, "I've never seen such a building."

"Neither have I," Jo whispered.

Revelation said nothing. He sat through the Mass not understanding a word of it, but when the service was finished, he leaned over and asked a tall, distinguished looking Frenchman, "What time does the preaching start, brother?"

The Frenchman, startled, twisted his head around. "Pardon, monsieur?"

"I say, what time does the exhorting begin?"

"The service. It is over," the tall man protested.

"Well, if that's it, I suppose I'll have to be satisfied. Are you saved, dear friend?"

It took both Logan and Jo to pry Revelation loose from the object of his quest, who understood absolutely nothing of what he was talking about. "He wouldn't have understood you even if you were speaking in French," Logan said. "These people don't know what you mean when you say, 'Are you saved?' "

"Well, haven't they ever read the Bible?"

"Most of them haven't," Jo murmured. "The French believe, for the most part, that the priests read the Bible, and then they explain it."

"Well, I wouldn't like that. Not at all. I don't guess I'll ever be a Catholic."

After the service was over, they had lunch out on a sidewalk café.

Revelation inquired as to the waiter's spiritual condition, and upon being met with a blank stare, he looked around and said, "I guess they couldn't afford to build a building."

"No. They just like this, I think," Jo said. "It is kind of nice, isn't it?" The sun was shining, and the café was soon filled up. Once again Jo ordered from the menu, but not recognizing many of the selections, they had a light lunch.

Afterward they strolled the streets of Paris and finally retired to their hotel rooms. After a brief nap, Jo took Bedford out and noticed that most of the strollers kept a good distance between her and the great dog. As she passed by a large fountain, she sat down and watched the water shooting up high into the air and falling back. It made a tremendous roaring sound, and she studied the greenish bronze figures of nymphs and mermaids and gargoyles. Somehow a feeling of fear came to her. "What am I doing here?" she said. "I must have lost my mind. Those two are obviously crazy, but I think I'm as crazy as they are." She reached over and hugged Bedford and said, "You've got to be a crazy dog, because you've got a crazy lady for an owner." Taking a deep breath, she got up and walked back, thinking, *I'll have to get somebody's permission to get to the battlefields, and I haven't the slightest idea where to start.*

★ ★ ★ ★

"What do you mean we can't enlist?" Logan said loudly and indignantly. "Why, my friend and I have come all the way from America to fight your war."

The French officer was a lean, sallow-faced individual with sad-looking eyes. He did speak passable English but had to do so slowly. "I am sorry, but it is against the law."

"Against the law! Well, that can't be!" Revelation said. "God's told us to come over here and fight. He wouldn't tell us to do anything that's against the law."

The lips of the Frenchman suddenly twisted upward into a thin smile. "If that is the case, you must take it up with Him. God's regulations sometimes differ from ours, you understand."

Jo stood to one side studying the officer. The recruiting office had not been difficult to find, and they had discovered that many were signing up to fight. None of them were Americans, however, that she could detect.

Finally after a long argument, Logan said, "I really came over, sir, to fly for France. I am a pilot, and this man is my mechanic, the best in the United States."

"I'm sure your services would be appreciated," the officer said, "but it is impossible."

"Why is it impossible?"

"Because in order to enlist in our army, you must renounce your American citizenship and become a citizen of France."

Logan stared at him blankly. "Why, I can't do that!" he exclaimed.

"Me either," Rev spoke up. "I'm an American. Always will be."

"Then it is clearly impossible."

The argument went on for some time until finally the officer threw up his hands. "You will have to talk to the captain. I have other men to enlist. He will tell you the same as I, but he might do it more clearly."

Captain Renard was a short, heavyset man with an olive complexion and tired gray eyes. He listened as Logan told his story, and then said, "Lieutenant Moreau has informed you of the obstacles. All who enlist in our army must be French citizens."

"But there must be *something* you can do, Captain."

For a moment the officer stared at Logan, then sighed and spread his hands out in a gesture that was completely French. "There is one way, but I do not recommend it."

"What's that?" Logan demanded quickly, seeing some hope.

"The Foreign Legion enlists men from other nations without requiring French citizenship. If you enlist in the Legion, you can fight in the war."

"But I want to fly."

"I cannot guarantee that. I cannot guarantee anything, and I must tell you the Legion is a hard bunch of men. I would not think of it if I were you."

They could get no more information out of the captain, so they left the building. For the rest of the day they walked around watching and listening to all the sights and sounds of the city. Not understanding the language was a difficulty, but it was obvious the nation was in an uproar. The streets were full of young men who had come in from the provinces to sign up. Young women were there too to put flowers in the lapels of the volunteers. Once a new troop came down the street, and the young women ran out to put flowers down the muzzles of the rifles and to kiss the long mustaches of the soldiers, who enjoyed it all.

Later that night, after supper in a café, they sat talking until late. "There's nothing more to be done. As the Lord says, 'The lot is cast into the lap, but the vision thereof is of the Lord,'" Revelation announced.

"What does that mean?"

"It means you can cast dice or draw cards to try to find out what to do, but when all that's done, then God makes a decision. He didn't bring us over here to pick daisies, and if the only way we can fight is to join the Foreign Legion, that's what I plan to do."

"All right. I'll do the same," Logan said firmly.

"But you don't know anything about the Legion. I've heard terrible things about them. They treat their men like dogs," Jo countered.

The argument went on for some time, mostly with Jo protesting that it was too rash an act. But the two men settled down into a defiant resolution, and finally just before midnight, Jo said wearily, "I'm tired, but I hope you won't do it."

"Don't you worry about us, Miss Jo," Revelation said. "The Lord's brought us over here, and the Lord's going to take care of us. He gives His angels charge over us. That's one advantage we'll have."

The three returned to the hotel, and the next day they went out to locate the office of the Foreign Legion. To their surprise, they were met by a muscular lieutenant who smiled sourly. "So many of you Americans are coming in, we'll have to have a special swearing in. It will take until the twenty-first to get the paper work done."

"That's all right," Logan said quickly. He and Revelation filled out the preliminary paper work, and when they left, Logan threw back his shoulders. "Well, now we're getting somewhere."

Not happy with their decision to enlist, Jo said, "I don't think it's the right thing to do." But turning to Revelation she smiled. "I'll be praying that you're right that God will give His angels charge over you."

"We've got to get you started taking pictures and getting stories about this war," Logan said. "Why don't we find a French airfield? Go out and meet the officers."

"Why, we couldn't do that!" Jo protested.

"Yes, we can," Revelation nodded firmly. "Let's go get your camera and a pocket full of them little bulbs, and they'll be plum glad to see us."

★ ★ ★ ★

They hired a taxi to take them fifteen miles outside of Paris, where they found a haphazard collection of tents and mobile homes. They got out of the car and stared at the scene, and Jo said quietly,

"It's not much, is it?" The aerodrome, as it was called, was a disappointment to all three of the American visitors.

"Look at that field," Logan said. "I don't see how they can land anything on it." The airstrip was nothing but a pasture and meadow that had been grated and rolled, but the heavy rain had washed craters into it. "I guess that's what they use for lighting, those oil flares over there. But it's not much," Logan said.

"Look on the bright side of it. These fellows are just getting started," Revelation said cheerfully. " 'Do all things without murmuring and complaining,' so the Scriptures say. Come on. Let's find us a general and tell him we've come to save him from the Huns."

After a few attempts, Rev found a man who could speak some English, and he pointed them to the sturdiest building near the airstrip, which was the operational headquarters. When the three made their way inside, they were greeted by a French officer whose English was very poor. He turned them over finally to another officer, this time a captain, who listened carefully as Jo explained rather awkwardly what she had come to do.

"So my friends are hoping that one day they'll be in your flying service."

"Ah, but they must go through the Legion, I understand. It is a difficult way. I wish you success, my friends. And you, mademoiselle, what is your purpose?"

"I have come over to write the story of the war so that Americans can understand it." Jo was wearing a green dress that narrowed down from knee level to ankle. It had yellow trim, and she wore a hat of dark crimson velvet. Her eyes were bright with excitement as she explained quickly, "My countrymen need to know why France is fighting. One day Americans will come by the thousands, not just a few such as my friends."

The officer, who had given his name as Captain Clairmont, said quickly, "That would be most helpful to our cause, but what is it exactly you would like to do?"

"I would like to take pictures of your men and of the planes they fly, then I will write a story, which I would send back to America."

"You understand that such material would have to examined by the authorities?"

"By you, Captain?" Jo smiled.

"Yes, by me, Mademoiselle Hellinger."

"Then you will help me?"

"Of course, I will do what I can. Come. I will show you around."

The next two days Jo collected a tremendous amount of material and used up all of her film. She discovered, as did Logan, that the situation was very bad. The planes were old and not designed for military purposes at all.

Captain Clairmont said, "We will have better planes soon. Even now our factories are going into full production." He smiled then and lifted an eyebrow at the two men. "By the time you do your service and get enough of the ground war, perhaps you may transfer into our service."

"Would you be willing to help them, Captain Clairmont?" Jo asked.

"There's little that I can do, but I am always at the service of those who want to help France."

That night, Jo strolled around the airfield with Logan and Revelation. Logan looked at the planes and said longingly, "I wish I could just get in one now and start flying."

"Be humble. Be clothed with humility, brother. That's what the Scripture says. 'Humble yourself unto the mighty hand of God and he shall exalt you in due season.' "

"You always have a Scripture for everything, don't you, Revelation?" Jo smiled, thinking how much she would miss these two.

"Well, I usually do. One time," he grinned, "I was trying to speak to a church group, but a big bug flew in my mouth. Wasn't nothing to do but swallow him, so I did. One of the deacons came up later, and he asked me, 'What Scripture you got for that, Revelation?' Well, it come to me, and I said, 'He was a stranger and I took him in.' "

"You two be careful," Jo said suddenly after she had stopped laughing at Revelation's story. "I worry about you."

"That's good to know that somebody cares. Look, you've got my folks' address. Write them once in a while, will you? Mail may not get through so well from the Legion. Just don't know about that."

"I'll be praying that both of you will be able to get into the flying service very soon."

"We'll all agree on that," Revelation grinned. " 'And if any two or three of you agree on anything, it will be done.' So the Scripture sayeth." He looked up at the sky and said loudly, "Lord, we agree that we want to come out of this here war alive."

Jo sobered then and said quietly, "Lord, I'll second that. Give your angels charge over Logan and Rev." She felt sad but covered this with a smile, saying, "Let's go eat some snails. I feel like living dangerously!"

CHAPTER TEN

DEATH OF A LOVER

★ ★ ★ ★

Paris held a charm for Jo Hellinger she had found nowhere else. Though the urgency of the moment dulled some of the pleasure she was enjoying, as she sat in a sidewalk café across from Logan and Revelation, she thought, *This city is wonderful! I've never seen one like it anywhere in America.*

The three had roamed around Paris, the men waiting impatiently for the real thing to begin, but for Josephine, Paris *was* the real thing. Somehow the sunlight was different here, brighter, warmer, bringing to life the brilliant colors of the flowers that filled gardens and window boxes all over the city. The colors were richer and deeper, at least to her eyes, and the city had a grandeur that seemed to be missing in the modern cities of Chicago and New York.

She delighted in the age of the city, and as they had crossed the Seine and left the Boulevard St. Germain, they had strolled into neighborhoods that were nothing like what she had seen in America. They were very old, and poverty was evident in many of them, yet the colorful little neighborhoods that were studded throughout the area seemed more delightful to her than anything she had seen in her native country.

She talked excitedly and practically dragged her two companions through narrow cobbled streets lined on either side with rows of gaily painted flats. True enough, some of them were stained with soot washed down from the chimney pots and the tile roofs, but she found even that picturesque. The houses were all jammed side by side, and narrow avenues intersected them. When they explored one of them, they discovered they led to small courtyards in the rear.

As they passed on to other neighborhoods, they came upon shops that sold everything imaginable. In America the department store had become the new rage, but in France, specialty stores were still in vogue. Jo had said to her companions, "It's so much better to go into a shop and talk to the owner than to go into a huge department store and talk to a girl popping her gum who's only waiting for quitting time."

Now as Jo sat at the sidewalk café, she leaned back and observed the crowd that had gathered. The streets were packed with people of all sizes and descriptions, but there was something undeniably Gallic about the scene.

"I wish there were no war," she said dreamily. "It would be wonderful just to stay here and enjoy this place."

"I don't know. It ain't so nice as home, I don't think," Revelation said. He sipped at the glass of water that was before him and took a bite out of the piece of bread he had lathered with butter. "The butter's not as good as it is at home, either," he murmured. " 'But as a bird that wandereth from her nest, so is a man that wandereth from his place.' "

Logan laughed. "Well, we wandereth from our place all right. This doesn't look like anyplace I've ever been. It's so different from Montana."

The three sat there talking and nibbling at the food. Revelation, suspicious of everything he did not know, had finally settled on what was supposed to be a chicken sandwich. But when he tasted it, he said, "Well, it don't taste like no chicken I ever bit into."

"What does it taste like, Rev?" Logan teased, as he winked at Jo.

"Well, kind of like an owl, I guess."

"An owl!" Jo's eyes flew open. "You've eaten *owl?* What do those taste like?"

"Well, somethin' like this." Rev suddenly grinned. "I ain't makin' no complaints. When a fella's away from home, he eats what's set before him."

They sat there enjoying the hum of conversation of which they understood practically nothing. The chairs and tables were packed so close together that a thin man with an olive face listened for some time. Finally he said, "Welcome to Paris. Just from America, I take it?"

"Why, yes!" Josephine said. She introduced the three of them, and the man bowed slightly.

"My name is Pierre Guillon. You're here on business?"

Jo hesitated, not knowing how much to tell.

Logan spoke up and said, "We've come over to join up in this fight."

The man's face changed at once. He had been withdrawn, but now his eyes beamed. "Then I must buy you all a drink, and we will have a toast."

"I guess you'll have to excuse me, partner," Revelation said. "I don't drink any intoxicating liquors."

Guillon laughed suddenly. "You will have difficulty in France, then. Some people haven't tasted water here in years! To be truthful, that's why many people here drink the wine. It's safer than water, especially for foreigners."

"I'll just take my chances. The Bible says if a man eats any deadly thing, it will not harm him."

"Ah, you're a minister?"

"Me?" Rev grinned. "No. Not a bit of it. Just a believer. Are you saved, brother?"

Jo and Logan expected to see the man's face freeze up, but instead he laughed aloud. "But *oui*. I am a believer in the Lord Jesus."

"Well, hallelujah! Praise God and glory to God and the Lamb forever!" Rev shouted. He put his hard hand out and said, "Put 'er there! A fellow believer here in the middle of Paris!"

Guillon found his hand crushed by Revelation Brown's enormous paw. "I'm most pleased to welcome you again the second time. I attend a small Protestant church here in the heart of Paris. Perhaps you could come and attend our services."

"Why, we'd be proud to, brother! You just draw us a map and we'll come. Of course, we don't understand the lingo."

"I would be glad to interpret."

Logan leaned forward and said, "Mr. Guillon, I'm a little confused about what's going on here."

"You mean the war?"

"Yes. We've been trying to listen, but since we don't speak French, it's quite difficult. I can't even make out through the papers what's going on."

"Well, *poof!*" Guillon kissed his fingertips with an inexpressibly French gesture. His eyes rolled back, and he shrugged his shoulders eloquently. "You must not pay any attention to the newspapers. They are, as usual, not accurate."

Rev reached over with his stiff fingers and poked Jo's shoulder. "There you are. You see what Mr. Guillon says about your profession?"

"Ah, you are a journalist! I am sorry. I did not mean to offend. But, on the other hand, one sees few women journalists."

"I'm not offended, Monsieur Guillon, but I've come over to get the truth to send to the newspapers back in America."

"Well, truth is a rare bird. You must catch it quickly before it flies away," Guillon said. He seemed to turn moody then. His olive complexion gave him a rather dour cast, and yet there was an innate cheerfulness in this man. He sat quietly for a moment sipping his wine, then shrugged. "Well, I can tell you what I think."

"We would be glad to hear it, monsieur," Jo said quickly. She whipped out her pad and pencil, which caused the Frenchman to smile. "I'll take notes, if you don't mind."

"I do not mind. You can even use my name. Imagine, Pierre Guillon being printed in an American newspaper!"

"What's going on? We hear all kinds of rumors," Logan said, leaning forward, his eyes intent on Guillon. "One minute we hear that the Germans have retreated. The next we're hearing that we'd better get out of Paris. That they'll be here in thirty minutes."

Guillon made a steeple out of his fingertips and thought for a long moment. Finally he shrugged again, a habitual gesture with him, and began to speak. "The strategy of our army has been well planned," he said quietly. "We have seen for some time that war with Germany was inevitable. So here is what the masterminds at headquarters have decided." He took a pencil out of his pocket and said, "May I borrow a page of your pad, mademoiselle?" Taking the page, he began to draw lines.

"We have mustered three-quarters of a million men here in the eastern corner of France. It is the intention of the general to forge through Alsace and Lorraine."

"I see. And drive on up the Rhine, is that it?" Jo said.

"Ah, you are very quick, mademoiselle! Yes. We will drive up the Rhine and the *Grandquartier Général*—that is general headquarters—feels that we can win using the courage and the dash of the French infantrymen."

"And you do not think, monsieur, that that will work?"

"I do not." Guillon shook his head, and a sadness clouded his dark brown eyes. "Courage is necessary, and French soldiers are noted the world over for their élan, but these qualities will not substitute for heavy guns."

"You do not have enough artillery."

"No. Our general said they were not needed because the courage of the soldiers would be enough."

Logan had listened intently, and now he leaned over and said, "You think your army's going to take a beating."

"Our generals apparently have never heard of machine guns," Guillon said bitterly. "A bayonet was a fearsome weapon back in the day of Napoléon when all one needed was a superior number of men. Each man, for the most part, had only one shot. When that was fired, it was up to the bayonet to win the day."

"I remember studying the Civil War," Jo said. "The leaders on both sides never seemed to learn that the bayonet was useless against entrenched troops."

"Exactly! They were foolish and our leaders are foolish, too! They will be no match for the German machine guns!"

"What is happening, monsieur?"

"What is happening? A slaughter is happening!" Guillon drank his wine and put the glass down with unnecessary force. "The bugles blow, the masses of our infantry charge, there are long bayonets gleaming in the sun. Ah, the courage and the nobility and the honor of it all! They fling themselves against the machine guns with inhuman valor. Divine valor, I might even say. And—"

"And the slaughter, I suppose, is unbelievable?" Jo asked quietly with her eyes on the face of the small Frenchman.

"It is inhuman and unthinkable. Bodies piled high, and still the general sends the men in."

"But they will learn, won't they?" Revelation Brown asked. "I mean, after all, when you send men in and lose them like that, you have to learn *something*."

"You and I might, but we are only ordinary human beings, monsieur. What is your name, sir? Revelation?"

"That's it. It's Revelation."

"A most pleasing name. Well, generals are not ordinary men. They apparently learned nothing. They are still sending mass troops against artillery and emplaced machine guns."

"What are the Germans doing?" Jo asked quickly.

"They are following the plan laid down by Count Alfred von

Schlieffen. I think it is an old plan. Germany has had this war at the back of its mind for a long time."

"What will they do?"

"Well, as you probably know, the German strategy is based on a movement through neutral Belgium. That would carry the army through Paris and pin our country up against the Swiss frontier. And so far their strategy has worked. They have punched their way through our lines, and only by tremendous loss of life have we been able to keep them from Paris itself."

The three Americans sat quietly absorbing all the Frenchman had to say. It was obvious he had lost the hope and the excitement that had swept the country at the beginning of the war.

"We will pray that things will change, monsieur," Jo said.

"Yes. We will pray for that indeed, mademoiselle. God is able, and nothing is impossible with Him."

"Amen, brother," Revelation said and clapped his hand on the shoulder of the diminutive Frenchman. "And just wait until our folks get over here. Why, we'll turn this whole thing around in no time."

Monsieur Pierre Guillon mustered up a smile. "Well, we will hope for that end, my friend, and now I will draw you a map so that you will be able to find our church. With a name like *Revelation*, I would expect you would be able to preach, so I may call upon you."

"But I don't speak your lingo."

"I will be your interpreter if you would trust me."

"Well, I just might do that. I'm no preacher, but I love to tell the glories of the Lord Jesus. I'd be proud to say my piece. Of course, you'll have to clean up my grammar a little bit."

"Grace is more important than grammar," Pierre Guillon said quietly. He rose and shook hands with the three and, after giving them careful instructions, walked away from the café.

"What a sad man," Jo said.

"He is, isn't he?" Logan nodded. "But I'm not going to let it get me down. The French generals will learn, and we'll see what happens when America finally enters this fight."

★ ★ ★ ★

"Hey, get your gear on! We're going to the front!"

Jo had been sitting in her room writing a story to be sent back to the States. She looked up, startled, and saw that Revelation's eyes were beaming. "What do you mean going to the front?"

"You remember that Frenchman, Pierre Guillon?"

"Of course." They had gone to the church Guillon had invited them to, and they had been overwhelmed by the welcome they received. The minister, an older man with a shock of iron gray hair, had insisted that Revelation do the preaching. Revelation had put his heart into it, and had been enthusiastically received. Since then they had seen Pierre Guillon several times, and now Jo stood up at once. "Are you serious?"

"I'm serious as the measles," Revelation grinned. "I've been wanting to see some of this fighting. I know you wanted to get a story for your newspaper back home, so I talked him into taking us up there."

"But does he have any authority?"

"No, but he's got a car, and that's all we need. You're press, aren't you?"

"Well, in a way I am. But I don't have any authority here."

"That doesn't matter. They're so busy fightin' this war they won't pay any attention to three curious Americans. Come on! Grab your coat!"

"And my camera, too! Here, you'll have to help me carry some of my gear."

Jo hastily loaded as much film and flashbulbs as she could get into a large leather bag, which Rev carried down for her slung over his shoulder. She grabbed her camera and purse, and they left the room quickly. When they arrived downstairs, they found Pierre smiling.

"Are you certain you want to go to the front? It's not like a trip to the Louvre, you know. Nice and pleasant."

"We'd be very grateful to you, Pierre, if you could take us. But is it legal?"

"Probably not," Pierre said. "But what can they do? Fine us? Put us in the jail for a night?"

"It would be worth it," Logan said, "if that's all. I want to get a glimpse of this fight close up." His eyes were gleaming, and he added, "Wish we had a rifle. Might take a few potshots at the Huns."

"I do not think that would be possible, Logan," Pierre grinned. He studied the strongly built American before him and then shrugged. "Come. Get in. It will not take long."

The car was small but it started at once. "It is difficult to keep a car these days," Pierre said. "Petrol costs so much."

"You never did tell me. What do you do for a living, Pierre?"

Pierre smiled, his teeth very white against his olive complexion. "I am what you Americans might call a gentleman bum."

"You mean you're rich?"

"My father was. When he died, he left me just enough to survive on without working, which I have managed to do."

"I don't believe that," Jo said, turning to study Guillon's profile. "I think you're painting your character worse than it is."

"Good. I will make the most of that. Actually, I am an art student."

"You're an artist! You paint?"

"Yes. At least I say so. My instructors are somewhat less emphatic." Turning to her, Pierre grinned. "My father always said it was an excuse to stay out of work."

"I'd love to see some of your paintings."

"That can be arranged," Pierre said, "if we do not get blown to kingdom come by the Germans. Hang on now. This will be a little bit tricky."

The trip proved difficult, for the roads were packed with vehicles. They passed lorries, small automobiles, even carts and wagons hauled along by mules. It seemed taxicabs had become a favorite means of conveying material, and Pierre said, "It is, as you see, war on a small scale. We do not even have enough vehicles to haul supplies to the front."

Jo sat tensely in the seat, looking at the stream of men and machines that seemed to be going in both directions. Some troops of soldiers came by headed away from the front, and she noticed that many of them wore bandages, some on their heads, and others had their arms in slings. "They're the wounded from the front, aren't they?"

"Yes, Jo, and there are a great many of them. The hospitals are already overflowing," Pierre said soberly. "These are new recruits. They've moved up to take their places."

As they approached the front line, the roads grew even more dense, and they had to pass through several roadblocks. Without Pierre they would never had made it, for the questions came in French, and he answered them in rapid-fire fashion.

"What are you telling these people, Pierre?" Logan demanded.

"Oh, I think up a different lie for each occasion," Pierre smiled. "This last one, I simply told him that the generals had sent for you to give advice as experts."

"Experts in what?" Jo asked with amazement.

"I did not specify. What does it matter? There are no experts in war anyway."

The trip ended when they were well within range of the sound of guns firing. They were stopped by a hard-faced French sergeant who refused to permit them to go any farther. "No civilians any closer to the front. I am sorry."

A rapid interchange between the sergeant and Pierre Guillon took place. Pierre he turned and said, "Come. Bring your cameras and gear. We can go forward on foot from this point."

The sergeant protested vehemently in French, but Pierre somehow managed to convince him to let them proceed.

"What did you tell him?" Jo asked curiously.

"I told him you had come all the way from America to get pictures that would show the glory of the French army."

The four plunged forward, and the ground soon turned to mud. Jo was grateful she had worn low quarter shoes, for soon she was muddy up to her skirts. The boom of the cannons seemed to be far off in the distance. From time to time, against the darkening afternoon sky, she could see the flickering of the guns themselves.

"How far away are those guns, Pierre?"

"I am no soldier. I cannot say."

"Close enough where they're lobbying those shells in pretty close," Revelation grunted. His eyes narrowed, and he said, "This is going to be a little bit dangerous. Jo, why don't you stay here while we go take a look."

"We're not going to start that, Rev!" Jo snapped. "I'm here to cover this war, and I can't do it from a sidewalk café in Paris!"

As the four of them made their way through the thickening mud, Jo stopped from time to time to take pictures.

Once she was shocked when she saw a soldier with his leg blown off at the knee. The bandages were crimson with blood, and his face was pale. His eyes were open, and he cried out something as he was carried by on his stretcher.

"What did he say, Pierre?"

"He was crying out for his mother."

"Will he make it?" Logan asked.

"I doubt it. He'll probably bleed to death before he gets to the hospital."

Soon they passed many other wounded soldiers retreating from the front line. Some with their eyes bandaged were being led, and others were carried on stretchers.

"So many of them," Jo whispered.

"And these are the lucky ones, Jo," Pierre said quietly.

He did not elaborate, and as they went forward, the sound of rifle fire and then machine gun fire filled the air with crisp, crackling sounds. The overhead sky was now darker, and suddenly a sound caught Logan's ears. His head swiveled up, and he cried, "There's a plane!"

They all stopped dead and looked up. Sure enough, a frail-looking aircraft came winging over. It was a one-man aircraft and obviously was some sort of observation plane.

"Is it German or French?" Jo said.

"I have no idea, but everyone's shooting at it."

Even from where they stood, the spectators could see the French blazing away with their rifles.

"It must be German!" Jo said. "The French wouldn't shoot at their own plane."

"I do not think they know the difference."

Logan stared at the kitelike affair, expecting it to be blown out of the sky, but it finally rose slowly out of the range of the rifles, turned almost majestically, and flew east.

"He's gathering information for somebody. I don't know whether it's for the Huns or for us," Pierre said. "Come along. You must get your pictures, and we must get you out of here, Jo."

The four continued until suddenly a voice said, "Halt!"

They turned to see a French lieutenant coming to stand before them. His uniform was spattered with mud, and his right hand had a blood-soaked bandage. He stopped before them, a slight young man of no more than twenty-two or three with light brown eyes and a youthful face. "Where are you going?" he asked. "What are you doing here?"

"These, Lieutenant, are Americans who have come to join with us. The lady is Miss Josephine Hellinger, a famous American newspaper woman."

"I'm Lieutenant Paul Devries. You cannot go any farther. You must go back at once!"

"But, Lieutenant," Jo said, stepping forward, her eyes fastening on his, "it is important that people back in America know what is happening."

"That is true, Lieutenant," Pierre said quickly. "France needs all the friends she can get, and Miss Hellinger needs the truth."

Devries hesitated and then, with more persuasion by Pierre, he nodded and said, "I will have to take you to my colonel."

Lieutenant Devries led them on a serpentine path through supply dumps and hastily constructed fortifications until finally they were led down into a cavelike bunker, where they were introduced to Colonel Lignon. Lignon was a tall, dark-haired man with a black mustache and equally black eyes. He was a hard-faced individual and shot questions at the group for some time.

Finally Jo smiled at him. "Do you think we're spies, Colonel?"

Lignon stared at her. He had been under fire steadily now for three days, and the humor that was ordinarily his was almost obliterated. "I suspect everyone," he said.

"Then put us under guard, but let me get the truth of this war home to my people. America is against Germany, but we need evidence such as this to convince our politicians."

Lignon stood silently for a minute, and Jo was afraid that he intended to send them back. But finally he waved his hand angrily. "All right. If you get killed, it's your business! Lieutenant Devries, you're responsible for these people."

"Yes, my colonel!"

Leaving the bunker, Lieutenant Devries said, "What would you like to see?"

"As much as you can show us," Jo said.

Revelation said, "I'd like to see some of the fighting. By the way, are you a believer, Lieutenant?"

"A believer in what?"

"Why, in the Lord Jesus Christ."

"Oh yes. I was baptized as a child. I am a believer, of course."

His answer did not satisfy Revelation, but Logan quickly cut him off, saying, "Rev, you'll have to put off your evangelizing for a time. The lieutenant's busy."

Devries grinned and said, "As long as I'm with you and not about to get killed up at the very front, I will show you anything you'd like to see."

Lieutenant Devries proved to be a most worthy guide. He showed them the trenches, and Jo was appalled at the filth and the stench everywhere.

Lieutenant Devries apologized, saying, "Some of the men were killed several days ago. We can't get out to bury them. Some of the Huns are out there, too. No help for it."

"Don't apologize, Lieutenant," Jo said quickly. "It's what we came to see. It's very terrible, isn't it?"

"Oh yes. War is always terrible."

"Have you been a soldier long, Lieutenant?" Logan asked. He found the young man very likable, and now he studied the youthful face with interest.

"Only for a month."

"What were you in civilian life?" Jo asked.

"An accountant." Devries grinned shyly. "I don't know what I'm doing here. I think there's a mistake of some kind."

"I'm sure there wasn't. It must be very hard for you," Jo said.

"Well, it wouldn't be except—"

"Except what?"

"Well, you see, I'm engaged to be married."

"Well, congratulations," Rev said at once. "As the Scripture says, 'He that findeth a wife findeth a good thing and obtaineth favor of the Lord.' "

Devries stared at the gangling form of the American and said confusingly, "I suppose that is true."

"When are you to be married?" Jo said.

"In three days."

"Will you be given leave?"

"Oh yes!" Devries smiled happily. "It is all arranged."

"What's your fiancée's name?"

"Renée."

"That is a beautiful name. Congratulations. I'm sure you'll be very happy."

"Thank you very much, and now you must get your pictures before dark, which will come very soon. You cannot stay here after dark, I'm afraid. It's much too dangerous."

The quartet got a quick view of life in the trenches, and they were all thoroughly horrified by the primitive conditions. Soldiers watched them out of listless eyes as they passed along, and Jo used up all of her film.

"You must go now, I'm afraid," Lieutenant Devries said. "Come. I will escort you back to your vehicle."

They followed a zigzag path until finally they came to an open space. "Come. We must run for it here. There's no cover. Be quick."

Jo felt Logan's hand on her arm, and she flashed him a quick smile of gratitude.

He soon found, however, that she was fleet of foot and gasped, "Well, you don't need my help, but I may need yours."

Even as he spoke, a tremendous explosion shook the earth. The ground under Jo's feet seemed to roll. A huge mountain of mud and dirt flew up over to her left, and she found herself suddenly flung to the ground. She protected her camera as she fell, thinking, *I mustn't break my camera.*

The explosions went off in an earsplitting cadence, five of them equally spaced. Jo lay there with her face against her arm, trying to press herself into the earth. She heard the whistling of shrapnel flying all around her and knew the ugly reality of war.

Finally the explosions rolled away into a dull rumble, and she felt a hand on her arm and found herself rolled over. "Are you all right, Jo?"

Looking up she saw Logan staring down at her, his face tense with anxiety.

"I'm all right," she said. "How about you?"

"No damage. Rev, are you okay?"

"Right. The Lord took care of us in that one, didn't He?"

Pierre was rising from the ground, and he stopped suddenly. "The lieutenant—"

Immediately Jo saw Lieutenant Devries lying still. He looked as if he had fallen from a great height, and she ran at once to him. He was lying on his stomach, and when she rolled him over, she saw that his breast was scarlet with blood. His eyes flickered open, and a scarlet froth came to his lips as he tried to say something.

"We'll get you to a doctor, Lieutenant. Don't try to talk." Jo said.

As she leaned forward she heard the faint whisper.

"Tell Renée . . . that I loved her—!"

Amidst the dirt and the mud of France, Jo Hellinger knew the horror of war. As she held the dead body of Lieutenant Paul Devries in her arms, she also knew that it would never change. Tears came to her eyes, and when she looked up at the three men who were watching her, she could not blink them back. They ran down her cheeks unheeded, and she held the bloody body of the dead lover to her breast.

CHAPTER ELEVEN

THE FOREIGN LEGION

★ ★ ★ ★

Jo stood at the back of a small crowd that had gathered in the courtyard of the Hôtel des Invalides.

The huge golden dome that sheltered the remains of Napoléon Bonaparte overshadowed the white yard that was now filled with uniformed army officers, silk-hatted diplomats, and a variety of others. Jo listened to the patriotic speeches that echoed throughout the courtyard. Everyone defied Germany and promised a quick end to the war. Several had praised the "selfless act of so many foreigners who wished to contribute their part of courage and blood to the history of France."

It was August 21, and after the swearing in of the new Legionnaires, Jo went to congratulate Logan and Revelation. They were still wearing civilian clothes, and both looked quite solemn.

"You know," Logan said slowly, "now that it's all over, I think I'm a little bit shaky."

"It's all right, Logan," Revelation nodded quickly, a smile on his face. "We've done what we came here to do, and now we're going to do it right."

Jo had felt reservations concerning the Foreign Legion. She had heard tales of the horrible and difficult existence the Legionnaires led, but she let none of this show on her face. "Cheer up, Logan," she said. "You'll be all right."

"Sure," Logan grinned, casting away his cares. He was naturally a cheerful young man, and at this point in his life, he had not been bruised enough to be very fearful of what the future might hold for him. He took Jo's arm and squeezed it. "Suppose you take us out and buy us one last meal."

"Hey, that sounds fatal! That's what men get in the death house, ain't it?" Rev complained.

"Well, I didn't mean it like that, but we'll be leaving for Rouen this afternoon."

"Rouen? Where's that?"

"Somewhere east of here. We don't know much about it, but that's where we're going," Logan said.

"Well, come along then. I'll buy you the best meal we can find in this whole city."

They found a café, which was crowded, as all cafés in Paris were at this time, and Jo bought them the best meal they had had yet.

"How are you going to pay for all this?" Revelation inquired after he had put away enough food for three men. "Are you making that much money working for your newspaper?"

"As a matter of fact, I'm not making any money from my newspaper. I'm here on faith."

Logan Smith stared at her. "I didn't know that," he said. "We shouldn't have let you spend your money on this expensive food."

"It's all right. I've got enough to keep me for a while. I've sent some stories back," Jo said. "I really expect that my editor will buy some of them. In any case, don't worry about me. I think you've got enough to worry about."

"Why, we don't have anything to worry about. 'Cast your burden on the Lord.' That's what the Good Book says," Revelation said. He drained his tiny coffee cup for the fifth time and hailed the waiter over. "Say, fella, do you have any bigger cups than this?"

The waiter, who understood little English, took some time to figure out what he meant. He shook his head. "No. This is the only size we have," he said.

"Well, bring the pot then."

The three sat there enjoying one another's company, but Jo felt sad. When they rose to go to the train station, she said, "I don't know when I'll see you again. You can write in care of the hotel. If you're anywhere close to there, I'll come and see you."

"That's good of you, Jo. I don't know how much time we'll have for writing or where we'll be, but let's keep in touch."

The three made their way to the Gare St. Lazare that afternoon. Just before they got on the train, Jo suddenly threw her arms around Logan's neck and kissed him, then did the same for Revelation.

"Take care of yourselves," she whispered. "God be with you."

As the train pulled out, she stood there feeling desolate and alone. A deep sadness arose in her as she realized that all over France, as well as all over Europe, men were getting on trains and being separated from their wives and sweethearts and mothers. Many of them, she knew, would not come back. "God keep them safe," she breathed and then turned and left the station.

★ ★ ★ ★

Logan Smith and Revelation Brown arrived at Rouen, and their dreams of the glory of the Legion were quickly shattered. The place was overrun with a mixture of wounded men from the British armies, stragglers from the Belgium army, refugees, French reservists, and a British army service corp unit—and all seemed to be totally lost and confused. The streets were a teeming mass of men. Some were so drunk they could hardly walk. Others were so angry they were ready for a fight with anyone that would offer it.

"This is your barracks," Sergeant Mitton said. He was a keg-shaped individual with a broad face and a pair of slitted dark blue eyes that peered out at the world with suspicion. He waved his hand around at the building they had entered.

"Rev, this is pretty sorry," Logan whispered.

"I've been in some jails that were better," Revelation said, "but the Bible says to be content in whatever state you are."

The beds consisted of nothing but compressed bales of straw, and the entire floor seemed to be covered with it as well. After the long, rough train ride on which they had been given nothing to eat and only water to drink, most of the men were exhausted. They fell into a deep sleep and were roused at four o'clock by Mitton, who cursed fluently in at least four languages.

"I need two volunteers," he said. "Men who want to serve France."

Rev held up his hand at once. "That's us, Sergeant," he said cheerfully.

"You shouldn't have done that," Logan muttered.

"Why not?"

"I don't know, but I think it's dangerous to volunteer for anything around here."

Sergeant Mitton came over and said, "Ah, your first opportunity to serve France. Come with me."

He led the two of them out of the barracks and into a large shed that contained the filthiest toilets that either man had ever seen.

"Clean these latrines," Mitton commanded. He stood there waiting for them to protest, but both Logan and Rev knew there would be dire consequences for disobeying orders.

"Praise the Lord in all things," Rev said. "Are you saved, Sergeant?"

"I am a sergeant in the Foreign Legion. That is all the salvation I know. Now, get these latrines clean!"

"Well, we're winning the war. Our first military action," Rev said as he began to swab enthusiastically.

Logan was almost gagging over the stench of the latrines. He glared at Rev, saying, "I hope you learned something from this. Never volunteer for anything again."

The two suffered the indignity of cleaning toilets all day, and the next day Mitton chose two more hapless victims.

The next few days seemed to crawl by, and finally Logan managed to get up enough courage to complain to Sergeant Mitton. "I came here to fight. Not clean latrines and sleep in a barn. When does the fighting start?"

Mitton's eyes, which were slits anyway, narrowed even more. "I think you will get all the fighting you wish, American. Have you ever killed a man?"

"No."

"Well, that will be your pleasure very soon now, if they do not kill you first. Let me give you a bit of advice. Never question the orders of generals. It does not pay."

"Or of sergeants either?"

Unexpectedly Mitton grinned. "That is wise also. I've been watching you. You and your friend are tough enough. We have some here so weak they will not make it through the first week." He studied the American carefully and said, "Are you a typical American?"

"I guess so."

"I wish we had a million more just like you. We'll need them to stop the Huns."

"What's happening out in the trenches, Sergeant?"

Mitton cocked his head to one side and was thoughtful for a moment. "The French army is getting ready to fight somewhere on the Marne."

"The Marne? What's that?"

"It is a river. You'd better learn some French geography if you intend to serve."

"How long will we be here?"

"You're leaving tomorrow."

"For where?"

"You're going to Toulouse."

"Where's Toulouse?"

"Three hundred and fifty miles to the south."

"Do we have to march?"

"No. You will go on railroad cars. It will be a luxury."

Somehow Logan knew from the small smile on the face of the sergeant that luxury would not quite define their trip.

The next morning he and Rev, along with the rest of the men, were herded aboard a small wooden railway car that reeked of manure. They were still wearing their civilian clothes, and Rev said, "They sure ruined a good suit here." He fingered his crumpled, filthy coat and shook his head. "I wonder when we get uniforms."

A corporal came along issuing blankets and small canteens. The cars were designed, they discovered, to accommodate either eight horses or forty men. But Rev took a head count after they were underway and counted fifty-six sweating recruits.

Just before the train pulled out they were served rations. Each man was handed a large can.

"What's this?" Rev said.

"It's beef," the sergeant said. "Each can will keep a man alive for four days."

And then the door banged shut, and the train began its long journey.

For a time the men talked about the action soon to come. Most of them were excited at getting out of Rouen, but Logan shook his head. "I doubt if Toulouse will be any better. Here, let's squeeze in so we can back up against the wall of this thing." It took some doing, but the two finally managed to wedge their backs against the wall. As soon as they did, Logan took the lid off of his can and sniffed the meat.

"What's it smell like?"

"Well, I don't guess it matters, since it's all we've got." Taking out his pocket knife, Logan sliced off a bit and chewed it thoughtfully. "Tastes as much like shoe leather as anything else."

The train rattled over the tracks, jolting the men inside until their teeth ached. The heat grew worse, and there was little discipline among the recruits. Most of them drank up their water, and by the morning of the second day, the salted meat had aggravated the men's raging thirst.

"Ain't there no other water on this train?" Rev asked. "I could drink an ocean dry."

"I guess we'd better learn to save what we've got," Logan said. His tongue seemed enlarged, and finally, five hours later when the train stopped, the men piled out and a fight broke out at once. There were not enough water spigots, and the men jostled and shoved and pulled to fill their canteens.

Sergeant Mitton fought and cursed and pulled at them, but their thirst was too great. When they got back on the train, Mitton came into the car and cursed them, saying, "You are children—children! You cannot be trusted to do anything right! I'm going against the order of the day and rationing your meat as if you were babies!"

The ride seemed to last interminably, and, in effect, took ninety hours. Knowing the distance from Rouen to Toulouse, Logan figured out in his head as they arrived how long it had taken. "We've been traveling almost four miles an hour by my calculations."

"That's not as fast as a man could walk," Rev said.

"That's right. I hope the rest of this Legion is a little better organized than this."

Even as he spoke the train pulled to a stop in front of the station, and the men staggered out. As they marched through the streets of Toulouse in full view of the crowds, the sergeant told them to smarten up. "You look like bums!" he shouted.

"I feel like a bum," Rev said. He looked down at his soiled clothing and felt his whiskers, and said, "If this is the best the Legion can do, I don't think much of it."

It was with a sense of relief that they reached the barracks at Toulouse, where Sergeant Mitton informed them that this was the former home of the One Hundred and Eighty-Third Regiment. "You will love it. Only thirty-two of you will share the same room."

As they entered the room to which they were assigned, Logan saw that each man had a low wooden bed with a shelf above on which to stack clothing. They had no time to pick a bunk, for supper was being served right then. Afterward he threw himself onto the straw-filled pallet and fell into a deep sleep. Despite his weariness, he tossed for most of the night. When the bugle jolted him awake early the next morning, he could hardly open his eyes.

He rose up and began clawing at his stomach. Looking over he saw Rev doing the same thing. "I guess we've got visitors."

"Bedbugs like I never saw," Rev nodded. The two of them clawed but it did no good.

After breakfast, Sergeant Mitton said, "Burn the straw and paint the beds with kerosene."

As soon as all the straw had been carried out and burned, each man was issued a uniform, which consisted of a blue greatcoat, coarse white fatigue uniforms, and a white *képi,* along with laced field shoes apparently made out of iron.

The rest of the equipment included wool shirts, a blue sash nine feet long, two blankets, and a suit of long underwear.

After they had put on their uniforms, Sergeant Mitton handed the new recruits, individually, their rifles.

"What kind of a rifle is this, Sergeant?" Rev asked. "Never seen one quite like it."

"An eight-shot eight millimeter bolt action," the sergeant said. "It's called a Lebel."

"Kinda heavy, ain't it?" Rev said, holding it up and taking a sight.

"It weighs nine pounds and is fifty-one inches long. And this," the sergeant said, "is for skewering Germans." He held up a long, thin bayonet, which made the Lebel over six feet long from butt plate to bayonet tip.

Rev and Logan cleaned their rifles and the two leather cartridge boxes, then examined their tin-plated bowl with a cover and a knife and fork.

"What about socks, Sarge?" Rev said.

"There are no socks in the Legion. You can buy muslin and wrap it around your feet."

The two men sat there for some time, but it was understood that they would begin drilling at once. The barracks were noisy enough, and the men seemed happier now that they had donned their uniforms.

"Does this uniform make you feel more like a soldier, Rev?" Logan asked.

"I reckon so. Still, it's not like the good old U.S.A. uniform, is it?"

"No. But there won't be any fellows wearing that uniform for a long time. You still feel like God's put us here, do you?"

"Shore do. What about you?"

Logan Smith looked over the recruits. Most of them looked like villains. None of them had the noble features he had seen on recruiting posters scattered around Paris. "I've got to believe it," he said. "And so do you. It's all we've got to believe in right now."

★ ★ ★ ★

The house that stood back off the street more than was customary in Paris had an air of respectability about it. It was made of brown sandstone, and two white pillars framed the ornate doorway.

Getting out of the cab, Jo waited for the driver to announce the fare, which was ten francs. She paid it without question, even though she was relatively sure she was being cheated. For the most part, taxicab drivers were brigands in Paris, and she knew she would have to learn to bargain. But now she was nervous and had no stomach for it. As the cab roared off, she mounted the stairs and knocked on the door. It had taken her some time to come to the decision to visit the young woman who had been engaged to marry Lieutenant Paul Devries, but with the departure of her only two friends in the country, she had had plenty of time to think about it. For days after coming back from the front line, she had gone over and over in her mind the death of the youthful lieutenant. Finally it became clear to her that she had no other choice but to visit his fiancée. Now she stood there waiting, wondering what she would say and how she would be received.

The door opened and a young woman with enormous black eyes greeted her in French.

"I don't speak French very well. Do you speak any English?"

"Yes. A little."

"I'm looking for Mademoiselle Renée Denys."

"I am Renée Denys."

"I wonder if I might speak with you for a moment."

The young woman hesitated and then nodded. "Come in," she said.

The entryway to the house was dark, for there were no windows in the foyer. However, as Jo followed the young woman down the hallway and then turned right, she found herself in a large, well-lighted room. A large bay window admitted sunlight, and the furniture, she saw, was very fine.

"Will you sit down?"

"I think I might. I hope I'm not taking too much of a liberty."

Renée Denys' face was pale, and there was a sadness in it, but she spoke politely. "I cannot imagine your business. You are American, are you not?"

"Yes, I am." Jo stood there, unable to meet the young woman's gaze for a moment. Now that she was there, she wished she were anywhere else. *I shouldn't have come,* she thought. *No matter what I say, it will not help*. Nevertheless, she knew she had to try. Suddenly, her eyes fell on a portrait on the mantel over the fireplace, and she recognized the youthful features of Lieutenant Paul Devries.

The young woman opposite her noted the direction of her gaze. Her own eyes went to the picture, and she seemed to stiffen. "If you would state your business . . ."

"Yes, Mademoiselle Denys. I am new in Paris. My name is Josephine Hellinger. I am an American newspaper woman." She continued to speak, giving her background, knowing all the time that she was putting off the inevitable. Finally she took a deep breath and stopped. Studying the young woman's face, she said quietly, "I felt I had to come, Mademoiselle Denys. You see, I . . . I was with Lieutenant Devries when he was killed."

A sharp intake of breath and Renée Denys seemed to turn to stone. "You were there when he died?"

"Yes. I had gone to take pictures and to get a story to send back to America."

"You saw him? You talked with him?"

"Yes. He was assigned to be our guide."

"Tell me everything."

And then Jo knew how hard it must be for this young woman whose dreams had been shattered. She must have known that there was nothing pleasant to tell, for death on the battlefield is cruel. Still her enormous eyes seemed to swallow Josephine as she began to speak. She related how she had met the lieutenant and he had taken them to visit the colonel. She expanded as much as she could on how Devries had guided them through a tour of the trenches.

"How did he seem, Mademoiselle Hellinger?"

"He seemed very happy. He . . . spoke of himself. He told us that he was an accountant and that he had only been in the army a short time."

"Did he speak of me?"

"Oh yes. He was very happy about getting married. He was looking forward to it more than anything else."

"Tell me everything," she said. "Please."

Desperately, Jo racked her memory as she tried to remember every detail of their last conversation. This young woman sat there, hanging on to her words as if she were starving for water in an arid desert.

Finally the tears began to flow down the woman's cheeks, and she said, "After he was . . . wounded, did he say anything else?"

"Yes, and that's why I came here, Mademoiselle Denys." She hesitated, then continued. "He was terribly wounded, and when I saw that he would not survive, I held him in my arms. He looked up at me, and with his last breath, he said, 'Tell Renée that I love her.' "

"He said . . . that?" she asked, choking on the words.

"Yes. They were his last words. He loved you very much, Mademoiselle Denys."

The young woman suddenly seemed to crumple. She was falling, and Jo leaped forward and held her. The young woman clung to her, and Jo held her upright. Heart-wrenching sobs racked the young woman's body, and Jo could do nothing but hold her, pat her shoulders, and try to console her.

When the storm of weeping was finally over, Mademoiselle Denys said, "It was good of you to come. Will you have tea?"

"If you wish."

Jo wanted to leave, but she felt that she had to stay. In fact, she stayed so long that Renée's parents came, and she found herself telling the story again. It was an hour and a half before she left the house. The young woman took her hand and suddenly kissed it with an eloquent gesture.

"You have done so much for me. It has been so hard, and I miss him so much. God bless you. Thank you for coming."

Tears filled Jo Hellinger's eyes as she left the house and walked almost blindly down the street. She would never cease to remember the effect of the dying man's words on Renée Denys's enormous eyes as she had listened so intently.

"If I had any thoughts of war being glorious," she said, "I've lost them forever. That poor girl and that poor young man—all blasted by war!"

★ ★ ★ ★

Jo's glimpse of the airfield was disappointing. It consisted of little more than a collection of what appeared to be quickly constructed huts. There were more tents than huts, and the hangars huddled forlornly in an open field. As she was guided down a muddy pathway by a young sergeant, she noticed a large herd of black-and-white cattle grazing undisturbed around the collection of flimsy-looking planes that occupied the field. A whining, buzzing noise caught her attention, and she stopped long enough to watch a biplane with an exceptionally large wingspread as it dropped out of the sky and managed what appeared to be a controlled crash.

"If you will, this way, please, mademoiselle."

"Was that airplane out of control?"

"Certainement. They often are," the sergeant grinned. "Follow me, please." The diminutive sergeant led her by a rather circuitous route to a dilapidated hut somewhat larger than the rest. The sign over the front read, "Seventeenth Esquidrille General Headquarters."

There was no step up to the building, and when the sergeant stepped aside and grinned, Jo knew she was being put to some kind of a test. The threshold was nearly two feet up. Without a change of expression she hiked her skirts up, lifted one foot up to the level, and then, grasping the doorframe, she pulled herself up.

"I will wait outside in case you need an escort back to your automobile," the sergeant said in perfect English.

"How do you speak English so well, Sergeant?"

"I studied at Harvard," he said.

"Really! What did you study?"

"Architecture."

"You're a long way from Harvard, Sergeant."

"Yes, mademoiselle. I wish I were back there now."

"Well, they say the war will be over by Christmas. Perhaps you will be."

"So they say."

Bemused by the deadpan sergeant, Jo turned and found herself facing an officer in a striking uniform. He was of medium height but stood so erect he seemed taller. He was examining her with a pair of bright gray eyes, and she took a moment to examine the uniform, the most colorful she had seen. It was composed of a slate blue tunic with four amber bars just above the cuff of the right sleeve. A set of brass wings gleamed from over the right pocket and a row of brightly colored ribbons were pinned over the left. The most startling part was a pair of crimson red jodhpurs tucked into brown puttees and a pair of laced-up brown shoes. A wide brown belt circled the trim waist with a narrow one going over the right shoulder. A snow-white scarf was tucked inside around the soldier's neck and then into his tunic.

"My name is Josephine Hellinger," she said. "I'm here to see Major Dietrich."

"Major Dietrich at your service, mademoiselle. You have business with me?"

Several lesser officers were standing around, their ears attuned, but Josephine was used to this. Being a woman in a man's war had been a difficult lesson for her at first. During the days since Logan and Revelation had left, she had thrown herself into the fight for news and photographs. "I represent a New York newspaper," she said. "I have a letter here from headquarters in Paris from General Haille."

"Ah, General Haille. May I see it please?"

Major Dietrich took the letter that simply stated Jo's name and asked any officers she approached to show her consideration.

"I am to show you consideration. I'm not sure what that means. Would you like to have dinner with me tonight in Paris?"

"I would like that very much, Major Dietrich, but I very much doubt if my newspapers would be interested in a story about dinner with a dashing French airman. On the other hand," Jo arched her eyebrows, "perhaps they might. Perhaps we could do it this way. If you would allow me to interview some of your pilots and see some of your machines, perhaps we could arrange to have dinner together."

Dietrich suddenly laughed. "I can see that you are a—how do you Americans say it? A go-getter?"

"I prefer to think of myself as *efficient*, Major."

Dietrich had a harried look on his face. He had the expression of a man who had missed too much sleep and had to make too many critical decisions in too short a time. He had a pencil-thin mustache and was really an attractive man. Though he was not physically strong, he seemed to be one of those wiry men who can run on nerves when muscles play out.

"I really would appreciate it if you would give me a little of your time. This is my first visit to one of your advanced airfields, although I've been to those closer to Paris several times."

As it happened, Jo had caught Major Dietrich at a good time for an interview. The pressure of the war was rigid, but for twenty-four hours the Germans appeared to have let up. The nerves of the major were drawn thin, and he now shrugged his shoulders in the Gallic fashion and said, "Come into my office. You may interview me and I promise to tell nothing but lies."

"Of course, Major. What else."

Once Jo stepped inside the office, which was no more than a ten-foot-square room with a desk, two chairs, and a filing cabinet, she took the chair Major Dietrich indicated and pulled out her camera. "May I take your picture?"

"Yes. This is my best side," he smiled, suddenly turning to the left.

The flashbulb popped, and at once Jo began to ask questions in a rapid-fire manner. She had become an expert interviewer and soon had found out the basics of the dapper major.

"Do you think the Americans will come into this war?" he asked.

It was the inevitable question, and she gave her stock answer. "I expect they will, but it will not be soon. Americans are not sensitive to European problems. We're too selfish, and soft, and preoccupied with our own comfort."

"That will change. I expect as soon as the Germans sink some of your ships, you Americans will change your mind."

"I expect you're right. Tell me, would it be possible for me to see some of your machines and to interview some of your pilots?"

"Of course, and then afterward we will have our dinner in Paris."

"But it's forty miles from here, Major."

"I think it is important to keep a good relationship with the press," Dietrich said smoothly, his eyes glinting with humor. "It is my duty to go. Come. You will meet some of my pilots."

It was the beginning of a grueling day. Major Dietrich seemed to take pleasure in showing off his command. He took Jo first of all to a hangar, where a plane was being put together piece by piece.

"All of my men must know how to take their planes apart and put them back together," Dietrich murmured. "It's my theory that a flier needs to know his airplane thoroughly."

They moved out of the busy hangar and into a lane that led to a line of tents. "These are the temporary quarters for my pilots. You must be prepared for men at war. They are not as polite, perhaps, as they are in America."

"I spent some time on a cattle ranch in America. The cowboys there were fairly rough. I doubt if your men are much more undisciplined."

"It's a strange thing about the men who fly airplanes. They do not submit easily to discipline. They are individualists. Not like the soldiers in rank. When you see a battalion of men marching, every man in step, every hand in the same position, every head at the same angle, it seems that all of them are the same man. Not so with the pilots. They all have their . . . idiosyncracies is how you say it, non?"

"How do you account for that, Major?"

"I am not able to account for it. All I know is that the things they do require a skill that lies beyond most men. It attracts men from every walk of life."

"I can see how it would take a special kind of man to get up above the earth and fight to the death with a gunner man."

"Georges Guynemer, whom you perhaps will meet, is one of the finest fliers I have ever seen. I think he will set records. But he's very frail. He appears to have every symptom of tuberculosis."

"Not really!"

"Yes. He once almost fainted at a review held in his honor."

"How strange that such a frail man could lead such a physical existence."

"Well, he's unusual. On the other hand, we have Charles Nungesser."

"I have heard of him already."

"Yes. He's the best French flier in the service. He's an athlete of enormous strength. He can play at any sport. He's a boxer, a champion swimmer, and a cyclist. He's so powerfully built he has trouble squeezing himself into the cockpits."

"Is he on the field?"

"I think he's off on a mission now. Perhaps he'll be back before you leave. You would be impressed. He's a very handsome man."

As the day progressed, Jo did not meet either of these two, but she did meet Adolphe Pegoud. He was sitting outside his tent in a canvas chair as she approached with the major. He came to his feet at once and put his sleepy dark eyes upon her.

"And this is Adolphe Pegoud. Pegoud, this is Miss Hellinger, an American. She wants to make you famous by writing about you in an article for American newspapers."

"I am perfectly willing to be idolized, madame."

"It's mademoiselle."

"Ah, in that case we will have dinner together in Paris, and I will tell you why I am the greatest flier who ever lived."

"I'm sorry, Pegoud. I've already asked mademoiselle to have dinner with me."

"Rank has its privileges."

"But I would like to interview you if you have time," Jo said.

"I have two hours before I go up to kill more Huns. Would you care to come into my tent?"

Something about the invitation sounded off-key, and Jo could not help laughing. Her eyes crinkled up, and she said, "I think I better have the major present during our time."

"A wise move indeed," Major Dietrich grinned. "Now, you ask all the questions you please. Airman Pegoud is known as a man who never tells anything but the exact truth."

It was from Pegoud that Jo got most of her information, yet she sensed the innate sadness of the man. After the interview she asked the major, "Why's he so sad?"

"I don't really know. He's a strange man, but it could be that he's fairly certain that he's going to be killed."

Jo whirled to looked at him in astonishment. "What do you mean by that? I thought he was a fine aviator."

"He is, but when you go up day after day, engaged in combat constantly, no matter how skilled you are, eventually the chances are you will have an off day."

"Do they all feel that way?"

"Most of them do, although they cover it up. Most of us won't last long."

"Do you fly, too, Major?"

"Oh yes. I'm the squadron leader. You'd better enjoy this date we're going to have tonight, for it may be your last chance." His eyes gleamed, and he put forth his hand and touched her shoulder. "Be kind to a soldier who's giving his all to his country, mademoiselle. It's the least you can do to show your love for France."

Jo laughed suddenly. "Is that the line you give all of your ladies?"

"Bien sûr. Every one."

"And do they all fall for it?"

"No one has failed yet to show the proper respect for a hero of France."

"Well, let us understand clearly that all we're having is dinner."

"So you say now, but you have never felt the full effect of my charm. Come. We will be in Paris in less than an hour. I know a little café there. There's a violin player there who will tear your heart out."

"He may tear my heart out, but remember this is strictly business, Major."

It was an enjoyable evening. Major Dietrich was a charming companion, and he talked long into the night, describing the serious plight of the French. He was convinced that air power was the way to win the war, but his superiors would not listen. They were convinced the war would be won by longstanding traditions of massive armies on a battlefield, not in the air.

It was well after midnight when Jo said, "I must go."

"And alone, I suppose." He raised his hand when she protested. "I understand, and I honor you for it. I must get back to my command. Come back in a month and tell me what you think of the war then."

After the major had left and she had made her way back to her hotel, Jo sat on the bed thinking about the major. *A shadow of death is on him. As charming as he is, he seems fatalistic. They all seem to know they're headed for death.*

★ ★ ★ ★

Logan Smith and Revelation Brown found themselves thrown into a cauldron of difficulty. Both of them were in good physical condition, but they had never faced anything as demanding as the training the Legion required. The veterans who fluttered into the camp were baked dark brown by the scorching sun. They came from nearly every nation on earth, and soon the seasoned regulars were divided among the recruits so that there was at least one veteran for every two rookies. These hardened veterans saw to it that there were no stragglers, and soon grueling marches of twenty miles, burdened with a killing load, became the daily agony. The drill field was filled with screaming men plunging their needle-sharp bayonets into yielding bags of straw.

While they were resting in the shade of an old barn one day, Revelation Brown read aloud from the handbook that had been issued to every recruit. "From the moment of action, every soldier must passionately desire the assault by bayonet as a supreme means of imposing his will on the enemy."

Rev had removed his shoes and now scratched the sole of his right foot vigorously. Looking over to where Logan lay flat on his back, his eyes shut, he inquired, "Do you passionately desire to stick a bayonet in the stomach of a Hun?"

"I passionately desire a cup of cold lemonade with ice floating on the top of it," Logan answered.

"Well, you ain't likely to get it."

"You didn't ask me that. You asked me what I wanted."

"Come on," Rev said. "It's time to eat."

"I can hardly wait." Logan struggled to his feet, and the two men went without enthusiasm to the wagons that dealt out the daily rations. Logan took his bowl of soup and stared at the bits of bread and meat, then picked up his coffee and a cup of pinard, the standard army red wine. It was the same meal every day, and they noticed that the loaves of bread were stamped on the top with the date of baking.

"These here bread loaves are just like money with the date and everything on 'em," Revelation said. "I will say that for these Frenchies. They do know how to bake."

At that moment Mitton came up and stared at the two. He had become fond of the Americans, for they had taken their training without complaint and had toughened up admirably. "There's a battle starting on the Marne River."

"What does that mean to us?" Logan asked.

"I think it means we are going to fight. You might as well get ready to move out."

"I've been looking at these armies on the map, the Germans and us," Logan said, sipping his coffee slowly. "They move around like crabs, forward and sideways and backward, and then they stop when they get tired, which is what I am right now."

"You won't have to worry about that. You are moving out."

"Where are we going now?"

"Mailly-le-Camp. Everybody's been wanting a fight, and I think we're going to get one there. We'll leave first thing in the morning."

The process began to answer a call for five hundred veteran Legionnaires and five hundred trainees with previous military experience. They were to form a battalion for immediate transfer to the combat zone. When the call for volunteers was made, everyone wanted to go. Sergeant Mitton inquired about each recruit's previous service.

"You have been in the army?" he asked a tall, weather-beaten American.

"Five years."

"Which army?"

The American grinned. "The Salvation Army."

Many of the men claimed to have fought with the Mexican army, and others claimed service with nonexistent military institutes. Finally Battalion C was formed and was made a part of the Second Regiment. Each man drew a hundred and twenty rounds of ammunition. With barely four weeks of training behind them, they left for the front lines on September 30.

As the battalion, one thousand strong, moved out, they sang loudly the melody known halfway around the world. Legionnaires had sung it on every continent:

> "Nous sommes soldats de la Légion,
> La Légion Étrangère;
> N'ayant pas de Patrie,
> La France est notre mère!"

Mailly-le-Camp occupied nearly thirty thousand acres of rolling hills. It was only eighty-five miles east of Paris and a little less than thirty miles from the front and was the largest staging area in France. The train carrying Logan and Revelation finally stopped after three days and nights.

"It looks like a feller could get on a train, go somewhere, and get off without taking three days," Rev complained.

"I thought you quoted a scripture the other day," Logan said with a grin. "Something like, 'Do all things without murmuring and complaining.' "

"Well, brother, you got that right! Come on. Let's see what we're into now."

As they dismounted from the train, they saw that the station was riddled with shrapnel, and the streets were littered with the signs of battle. There were gaping holes in the walls and the roofs of the buildings from furious shelling during the Battle of the Marne.

"This looks like the real thing," Logan said as they marched to their barracks through an area strewn with the debris of battle. The two men took in the litter of spiked helmets, smashed rifles, and haversacks, whose contents were scattered. As soon as they were settled in, they were sent out to gather dry wood for cooking fires.

They had not gone far when suddenly Rev said, "Look there, Logan."

Logan had bent over to pick up a piece of firewood. Straightening up, he saw what Rev was pointing at. It was a large, swollen corpse lying in an open space. Bluebottle flies swarmed around the body, and Logan's stomach seemed to turn over. "I guess that's not the last dead man we'll see. I wonder why they don't bury him?"

They soon discovered there were many corpses that had not yet been buried, and the two never became accustomed to them as did some of the other Legionnaires.

Their regiment stayed in Mailly until October 18, then marched out on the road to Reimes. They walked until their feet were sore, and the hundred pounds of equipment on their backs dragged them down. Their shoulders were creased by the leather straps that cut into their heavy wool uniforms. Though their neck muscles were tough, they ached unbearably from straining against the brutal load. Without socks, their feet were soon blistered, and once on a break they removed their shoes and tried to rearrange their blood-stiffened linen clothes. They were slow getting started.

Mitton came along and screamed at them, "March! You're Legionnaires now!"

It was two days later when they finally reached what they had left America to find, the front line. They had been marching along a twisted road that turned abruptly into a narrow path. The trees were close together, and the column dissolved out of marching order into a line of lurching, exhausted men advancing forward to try to stop the Germans.

The first thing Logan and Revelation saw was that it was a war of mud. They were accustomed to mud, but this miasma was not like any mud they had ever seen. It was like acres of chewing gum, and it had an odorous stench that turned them nauseous. They hated to put their feet in it, for they were sure that mixed in with the mud were the bodies of those already blown to bits that, unburied and fragmented, had become a part of the putrid landscape.

As they plodded along, suddenly a sharp crack sounded, and a shell screamed through the air, landing almost in the middle of the Legionnaires. Bodies flew into the air, and the survivors threw themselves into the stinking mud to avoid the other shells raining down on them. It soon became a nightmare of death with the shells flying overhead like banshees. By the time it was over, the new recruits knew that they had faced their first encounter with the horror of war.

Logan finally pulled himself out of the mud as Sergeant Mitton shouted orders to the men. He scraped the stinking mud from his face and looked around at the scattered bodies, some of them only fragments. Fourteen men lay dead and thirty more were badly wounded. He looked over at Revelation, who was, for once, silent.

"Well, have you got a verse that fits this, Rev?" Logan asked in a hard voice.

Revelation Brown looked around at the death that surrounded the two and said slowly, "I guess I'm thinking of the Book of Revelation, which I was named after. You remember the part about the four horsemen?"

"I remember it, Rev."

"Well, I guess we found one of them horsemen. The one named *Death.* And it's not a pretty sight!"

CHAPTER TWELVE

OVER THE TOP!

★ ★ ★ ★

Ed Kovak stared with satisfaction at the front page, his eyes focusing on the feature story. The title "Men and Death" was his own artwork, but aside from that, the story had been printed exactly as Jo had sent it. He read through the first few lines and smiled.

> *Men march forward, leaning into the heavy enemy fire like men leaning against a strong wind. With bombs exploding all around, the soldiers drop in their tracks. Some kick and scream in pain, while others simply lie still, their lives given to defend their freedom. It is death on the battlefield, and men have come to terms with that death here in France.*

"I'd like to say I taught her everything I know," Kovak grunted, "but that's not so. She's just got the knack for it."

Chris Harwell, the assistant editor, stared over Kovak's shoulder. "What do you think, boss?"

"About Hellinger's stuff?"

"That's what we're talking about, ain't it?"

"I think it's great. Best war writing since Stephen Crane! No—better than Crane, I say."

"Too bad she's a woman," Chris grinned. "Think how good she'd be if she were a man."

Kovak shifted the stub of his cigar from one side of his mouth to the other. "Lots of men couldn't carry her typewriter, and look at this picture. Did you ever see a better battle photo in all your life?"

The oversized picture printed next to the story showed three

French soldiers glancing over the top of a trench. The background was lit by exploding rockets and shells, and even with the crude, coarse black-and-white picture, the terror of war showed on the men's faces.

"I wonder how she got around in *front* of those guys," Chris mused.

"If I know Jo, she crawled out under fire and waited until the first rank went over the top. I wish she wouldn't do that."

"You're worried about her, aren't you, boss?"

"Yes, I'm worried about her. She takes too many dangerous risks."

"Her stuff's selling good, though. I understand it's going to be syndicated."

"Already is. She took the chance, and now she's the most famous correspondent on the Western Front. Still"—he shifted the cigar again and his brow was a corrugated mass—"I wish she wouldn't put herself in harm's way."

"Why don't you write her and tell her so."

"Why don't you get out of here and go to work," Kovak growled. He waited until the door closed and then shook his head. "Why don't I tell her! I *have* told her a dozen times, but you don't get pictures like this without risking your skin." He studied the photograph again and then picked up the phone. "Janet? Send this wire to Jo Hellinger. 'Your stuff has been syndicated all over the country. Keep the stories coming and the pictures too. You'll get a raise out of this—and maybe a Pulitzer if I have anything to say about it. Respectfully. Kovak.' "

He slammed the phone back into the cradle, then laced his fingers behind his head. Since the war had begun in Europe, he had tried to picture the sounds and the smells and the scenes of the Western Front. These pictures had brought it to life for him, and many of the better shots were from Jo Hellinger. He was a hard, demanding man, this Ed Kovak, but he had a paternal feeling for his star reporter in France. Now he looked up at the ceiling and said, "God, you and I ain't on speakin' terms, but if you'll overlook a sinner like me comin' to you, I'd appreciate it if you'd send an angel or two down to look out for Jo. I ain't much, but that girl's the real goods. I guess you know all about that. Anyway, see what you can do. . . ."

★ ★ ★ ★

Winter had come with all the miseries for those who were out in the cold and mud. Jo Hellinger had endured some of the harsh conditions, but at the moment she was back in Paris. She had run out of photographic supplies and had returned to stock up again. She thought of making another visit to see Renée Denys, who had been robbed of her fiancé, but had finally decided against it.

Now she sat in her hotel room and removed a thick envelope and settled back, tucking her feet under her. Bedford, propped up on the couch, put his head in her lap and demanded some attention.

The letter was from Logan and was the third Jo had received since he had joined the Legion. She opened it eagerly and was pleased to see eight pages, written on front and back. Logan wrote in a strong, sweeping hand, and she had once told him, "You should have been the reporter. You have the gift of describing things." She began to read and was soon lost in his vivid descriptions of what war was like in his part of the world.

Dear Jo,

I hope this letter finds you well. Both Rev and I are alive and kicking. The cold weather makes it harder, but in one sense it isn't so bad. At least the mud is frozen now, so we don't sink into it up to our knees, and it seems to kill some of the foul smell.

One night on patrol, Rev and I were crawling along on our bellies. My hands were numb but, as always, on patrol your mind stays pretty alert. The slightest sound seems to trigger something in you, and more than once the squeak of a rat just about set me off.

Rev and I had crawled as far forward as we thought wise and had stayed there for two hours. A cold rain had been falling, and a dense fog covered the earth. We had expected the Germans to make an advance, so both of us were pretty nervous.

Finally Rev, who was about ten yards away, whispered, "Look out, Logan. Here they come."

A fellow named Ed Stone was on my left. I heard him talking to himself. He sort of fancies himself as a top soldier, and he is a good one.

"Independent firing. That's what the sarge said," Ed whispered. "Keep your shots low until you can pick your target."

Well, what happened next was this. Somebody let off a shot, and it startled me so that I pulled the trigger, although I could only see a vague, hazy outline. It sounded as though every soldier in our battalion was firing, and we could hardly see anything.

At a time like that, Jo, you don't think too much about the man you're shooting. I figure it's better not to see him. So every time I saw something move out there in the fog and the haze, I just pulled down on it and blazed away.

Finally Rev called out, "Hey, I think we got 'em all. Nobody's movin'."

Ed Stone said, "I'm going out to take a look."

"Don't be a fool, Ed," I said. "You don't know that they're dead."

But Stone is a go-getter, and I thought I'd better go with him. We crawled together while Rev and the rest stayed to offer us cover. We hadn't gone more than twenty yards when suddenly I stopped dead still. I had been walking crouched down, and I looked down. There at my feet was not a dead soldier, but a dead cow.

"Hey, Ed, this is a cow!"

"I know," Ed said, his voice muffled. "There's one over here too."

We began to look around, and it became obvious that a small herd of cows had somehow wandered into our line of fire.

"What's going on out there?" Revelation called out.

"We're going to have a good meal tonight, that's what."

A rough voice from the trenches called out, "You going to eat their livers?"

"No, what we've done is killed a bunch of the finest cows I've ever seen. Anyone want barbecue?"

Well, that was it. The cows all went to a good cause. As soon as the men up and down the line heard about it, they came from every direction. It was pretty much like a Western barbecue, all right. We fed on fresh beef, the first we've had since we've gotten here. Put the meat on our bayonets and cooked it over fires. Best meal I've had in quite a while!

Jo paused long enough to reread this incident and then murmured, "He's making light of it all, but I know it's terrible."

She read the rest of the letter and pinpointed one thing. Both Logan and Rev were sick of the trenches already and were ready to fly airplanes, but he ended his letter, saying, *It looks like there's little chance. We're stuck here in these trenches for the rest of the war.*

She put the letter down and stroked Bedford's head, then reread the entire letter. An idea came to her and she straightened up. "Why don't I send this letter back and let it be printed? It'll be a relief from some of the grim stories I've sent. I'll have to change the names, but it's the real article. I'll bet Kovak will like it."

★ ★ ★ ★

Benny Fears was a small man, not over five five. He was thin, almost emaciated, and on many of the long marches, Revelation had helped him carry his pack. He had become attached to the younger man and had preached at him almost constantly. Fears had been christened as a child, but he had no knowledge at all of the Bible.

Benny was sitting now with his back to one of the timbers down inside the trench. He was bundled up to his ears in his heavy overcoat with his woolen hat pulled down over his ears. He had been sitting there shivering in the cold, waiting and listening as Revelation, who was standing down the trench, spoke to five of the Legionnaires. It was a custom of Revelation to preach whenever he got a chance, and it mattered not whether his congregation was one or a hundred.

A burly corporal, who was smoking a cigar, grinned broadly and interrupted Revelation. He had a strong European accent and spat into the frozen mud before saying, "Don't you ever get tired of preaching, man?"

"Why should I get tired of preaching?" Revelation asked with some surprise. His face was red with the cold. His nose made a red dot in the cold morning air, but his eyes were alert and cheerful. "Nothing better to talk about than the Lord Jesus."

"Why don't you leave that to the preachers and the priests," the corporal grunted. "I don't see God out here in all this."

"He's here, Corporal Maluk," Revelation said cheerfully.

"I don't see nothin' but mud and dead men!"

"Do you think God's only to be found in a nice clean church that smells good? No. The Lord God is everywhere. Even right here in this stinking trench."

Maluk gave up and puffed on the cigar until it glowed like a tiny furnace. He said no more but slumped down, staring at his feet.

Revelation cheerfully moved forward with his sermon. His sermons would not have been accepted in any seminary, for he simply spoke of the goodness of God and the grace of Jesus Christ to save sinners. He always identified himself as the worst of sinners, and now he said again, "If Jesus Christ can save me, He can save anybody."

Benny Fears listened as Revelation read from the Bible and illustrated it with stories mostly drawn from his experiences back in the States. Finally Revelation closed the Bible and said, "I guess that's the end of the sermon today. Anybody here want to be saved?"

Benny Fears had been listening to Revelation Brown for some time now. Indeed, there was a longing in his heart to find peace. He woke up every morning trembling with fear and stumbled through the day expecting to be blown to bits at any moment. At night he could not sleep either. For a fear of not only death but what would come after plagued him. Now he longed to speak up to indicate that he did want the kind of peace that Brown had, but he was afraid of the jeers of his fellow Legionnaires.

Revelation said nothing, but he had seen the slight change in the eyes of the young man. Later on he came and sat down beside him. "Well, Benny, I think it's about time for you to give your heart to Jesus."

No one was close enough to hear. Benny looked covertly around and shook his head. "You make it sound so easy, Rev. How can it be so easy?"

"How could it be anything else? Suppose God told you to crawl a hundred miles backward through broken glass and then He'd save you?"

"I guess I'd try it."

"Sure you would, because you're proud."

"Proud? I'm not proud!"

"Yes, you are. God's offering to give you a gift, and you're just too proud to take it. You see, Jesus died to save sinners, not good people. That's what I am, and that's what you are. All the sin comes short of the glory of God."

"You don't have to convince me of that," Fears whispered. He bowed his head, and fear came over him again. "I'm scared of dyin', Rev."

"Well, there are lots of Christians afraid of dyin'. When the time comes, God will give you dying grace."

"What's that?"

"He'll take away the fear. After all, once you're saved, dying is just passing from one room to another. And let me tell you," Rev said gently as he laid his hand on the smaller man's shoulder, "what's in that other room is a whole lot better than anything you've ever had here."

Benny Fears had never had much in his room. His life had been hard. He'd grown up in a brutal orphanage. When he came of age, he had been thrust out into the world. He had drifted from job to job until finally he had ended up in the trenches of France, which had brought him to the point of despair.

"I don't know what to do," he moaned. "Tell me what to do, Rev."

"It's easy. Jesus loves you. Do you believe that?"

"That's what the Bible says, ain't it?"

"Right, and it's true. I never had nobody really love me," Revelation said, "in my whole life until Jesus loved me. That's why I came to Him. I needed somebody to love me. "

"Guess I do, too."

"Well, you can believe it. How do you know it? Because He died for you on the cross."

"But how does that help me?"

"You know that pack you carry every day?"

"Sure. Just about cuts my shoulder off."

"Suppose you're trudging along and that pack's pulling you over backward, cuttin' creases in your shoulders and rubbing blisters, and then all of a sudden somebody just reaches out and takes that pack off. Say like me, and I toted it for you."

"You've done that more than once, Rev."

"Well, it's the same thing with your sins. You're bowed down with sin, knowing you're bound straight for hell and you're miserable. But Jesus reaches down and takes that load off and He puts it on His own back. He died for those sins. That's the way it is. The just for the unjust."

For a long time the two men talked quietly, and finally Benny Fears threw up his hands. "I've got to do something. I'm going crazy. Tell me what to do."

"You just pray this prayer. 'Lord Jesus, I know I'm a sinner. I don't know much about anything else, but I know you died for me. You love me, and you want me to be saved. I turn right now from my sin, and I give you my heart and ask you to save me, oh, God. In the name of Jesus.' "

The thin young man echoed the prayer of Revelation Brown. When it was over, he looked up with tears glimmering in his eyes. "Is that all there is to it?" he whispered.

"No, that's not all there is to it. Did you pray the prayer?"

"Yeah, I did."

"All right. Now you belong to Jesus. From this moment on, whatever He says, do it no matter how hard."

"What do you mean what He says? Is He going to talk to me?"

"He already has, in the Bible. Now, the first thing He says to do is to confess Him before men. So I know it will be hard, Benny, but the next time you get a chance, just tell somebody you're trusting in Jesus."

Benny Fears swallowed hard. "They'll make fun of me."

"They won't crucify you, though. That's what they did to your Lord. Come on. I'm right there with you. Jesus is with both of us."

★ ★ ★ ★

Benny Fears turned out to be more courageous than he thought. It was difficult for him to make his first public profession, but once he did and had endured the jeers and scoffs of his fellow Legionnaires, he found it easier each time to share his faith. Soon they were calling him "Holy Ben," for he read the Bible that Rev shared with him almost constantly and could seemingly talk of nothing else but of what Jesus had done in his life.

"It's great, Rev!" he beamed. "For the first time in my life, I haven't been afraid. Here I could be killed any minute, but I'm not afraid. Ain't it great?"

"That's right, Ben. It's great to be saved."

★ ★ ★ ★

When May came the first offensive of the Allies began to take shape. The French army made a tremendous effort to break the stalemate.

Logan and Rev were at the point of the spear that attempted to pierce the German line. The attack across the red clay was under the command of Marshal Ferdinand Foch. He shoved eighteen divisions into position on May 5. All of the men began digging trenches leading to the German lines that were only a few hundred yards away. Four days later Logan and Rev were crouched in a trench waiting for the command to go over the top. Rev looked around and winked at Benny Fears, who was on his right side. "It looks like we're going for it this time, Benny. Is Jesus walking with you?"

"Praise the Lord. He is," Benny grinned. His face was pale, but he said firmly, "If I don't make it out of here, Rev, I'll see you when you get to heaven."

At that moment whistles began to blow, and the officers and sergeants began screaming orders. The blast from the whistles pierced through the sounds of the guns, and Logan heard the officers shouting, *"En avant!"*

Scrambling up out of the deep trench, Logan joined the long line of Legionnaires that moved forward. The earth seemed to be shaking, and the deafening crashes from exploding shells numbed his eardrums. From everywhere came the rattle of small arms being fired, and then he closed his mind from everything except the blue haze of smoke ahead of him. He threw himself into it, trying to keep up with Rev on his right side. He had not gone more than twenty yards when he tripped over a body. Looking down he saw that it was a dead Legionnaire, his face gleaming whitely. He had been killed the day before. His name was Johnson, but no one had been able to get to him and bury him.

Grabbing the Legionnaire's rifle, he began to fire into the mist in front of him. Only shadows could be seen, but he fired until the bolt clicked uselessly.

Moving forward, he pulled another clip from the dead man's belt and then staggered to his feet.

He moved like a man in a dream. From time to time he heard the whistling of bullets as they sang through the air around his head. Something plucked at his right sleeve as he staggered forward. Once he called out, "Rev, are you okay?" and he heard a vague answer.

Suddenly a voice cried out, *"Du Englischer Schwein!"* and immediately in front of him a dark, bulky shape rose up. He caught the glimpse of cold steel and managed only to get his rifle up and parry the bayonet thrust. He was thrown backward, and before he could move again, something struck him in the side. It did not seem to be a heavy blow, and he thought, *Just a nick.* But within seconds waves of pain came over him as he fell over backward. He tried to raise his rifle, for the German was coming again, this time with his bayonet poised.

This is death! he thought. But then the German stopped dead still. Logan wondered why the tall German was prolonging the kill, then he saw the soldier begin to lean forward. He fell like a large tree, not attempting to catch himself, and when he hit the frozen mud, he did not move.

The fighting went on and Logan drifted into unconsciousness. He came out of it from time to time and could hear wounded men screaming all around him. Finally he heard someone ordering the men to fall back and retreat. He knew he would lie here in no-man's-land and would never see home again.

★ ★ ★ ★

"You're gonna be okay, Logan."

Coming out of the anesthetic, Logan could not think clearly. He saw a face in front of him, but it was in long, wavy lines as if he were underwater. He blinked his eyes and took a deep breath, and the pain ran through his side. Opening his eyes again, he made out the features of Revelation.

"Are you okay, partner?" Revelation said.

"How . . . did I get here?"

"Well, I reckon I carried you. They got you all patched up now. You're gonna be all right."

"How're the rest of our boys?"

"Not good. We lost more than two hundred."

"What about Benny Fears?"

"He's in heaven right now. Thank God he found the Lord before he went over the top."

Logan lay still, trying to focus on the face of his friend. "Where am I?"

"Field hospital. We're waitin' on an ambulance. I'm gonna get 'em to give you another shot of that dope. When you wake up, brother, you'll be in a hospital in Paris."

"Will you be there?"

"No, but I'll come back as soon as I can get the general to give me a pass."

That was the last thing Logan remembered. Revelation's face began to fade, and he tried to speak. Though his lips moved, nothing came out. He heard Revelation whispering in his ear and made out the words, " 'I'm with you always even to the end of the earth.' "

And then Logan Smith drifted gently off into a deep sleep, and the blackness surrounded him like a blanket.

PART THREE

LOGAN

★ ★ ★ ★

CHAPTER THIRTEEN

"All Americans Are Rude!"

★ ★ ★ ★

Logan looked up at the ceiling and counted the flies. They seemed to form some sort of pattern, but he had no idea what it was. There were six of them now, whereas an hour before there had been only five.

"Are you guys having a convention up there?" he muttered. "Why don't you go out and call the rest of the flies in? That way you can have a really big meeting."

The ward in which Logan lay contained ten beds, and all of them were occupied. Since he had regained consciousness, he had rapidly improved enough so that he now was acquainted with all of the men there. He was the only Legionnaire. The rest of the patients were the wounded who had come back from the Western Front in a steady stream. Only two of them spoke understandable English, and the rest he could communicate with only in some sort of laborious sign language. As it happened, both of them were now out of the room, and Logan had no desire to play the linguistic guessing game that communication had become. His French had improved only slightly, but still it was a difficult process.

Overhead the flies shifted their positions slightly, and Logan studied the new pattern. *Now,* he thought, *you look like the Big Dipper.* He lay flat on his back, and when he had to shift his position, he did so very slowly. The wound he had taken was extremely painful, but he had confidence that it was merely a matter of time before he would be completely healed. Cautiously he twisted his body and was rewarded by a sharp spasm of pain that ran along his side. Disgruntled, he put his hands down by his sides and considered turning over. He hated to sleep on his back, but lying on either side brought sharp pains, so he had learned to lie there day and night.

One of his fellow patients, a short man named Benoit from down the ward, got up and hobbled toward him. He was on crutches because his right leg had been amputated just above the knee. He was a short, dumpy man with an unhealthy pallor and a pair of small eyes. "Hello. How are you?"

The words were pronounced very slowly and with great care and constituted almost the entirety of Benoit's English vocabulary.

"I—am—fine," Logan said slowly, pronouncing every syllable carefully. "It—is—a—fine—day."

"Oui. The day is bon."

For some time Benoit stood there, balancing on his crutches, but finally both men gave up trying to hold a conversation. Benoit said something that Logan did not get, then turned and hobbled out of the room.

The silence of the ward flowed over Logan then, and for a while he closed his eyes and tried to sleep. But a man could sleep only so much, and since he had come into the hospital, he had had plenty of rest. He tried to think of the date and could not remember if it was the second or the third. *What does it matter,* he thought, *what day it is? Every day is just alike.* He lay there trying to let his mind go blank, but instead he kept thinking impatiently of how long it would be before he would get out of the hospital. He had never been seriously ill. One time he had taken a bad fall from a horse and had lain in the hospital in Helena with a broken ankle for awhile. Thinking back on it, he remembered he had been just as impatient then as he was now. *Just not made to be a patient, I reckon,* he thought.

He suddenly thought of the letter he had received from Rev and reached over thoughtlessly, rolling onto his side. Pain struck him like a blow, and he caught his breath and lay there until it slowly ebbed away. Carefully he extended his arm and picked up the envelope. Opening it, he began to read the letter that had come three days earlier. It was mostly filled with Scripture, and Logan took in every word. It closed with the words, *The Lord be with you, dear brother. He has kept me safe thus far. He will bring both of us safely home. Put your faith and trust in Jesus as I do. Your friend, Rev.*

He read it again, and then folding it, he put it back in the envelope. He did not feel up to leaning over and putting the envelope on the table, so he simply let it drop on his bed. He closed his eyes and soon dozed off again. He came out of a light sleep when he heard the sound of footsteps. Looking up, he saw two doctors and an orderly moving down the aisles. He watched them as they stopped at each bed, conferring with each other as they examined each patient's wounds. Finally when they got to him, he managed to grin. "Hi, Doc."

"Morning, Smith." Fortunately the doctor spoke excellent English. "How is it today?"

"Same as it was yesterday. When do I get out of this bed?"

"When I say that you are ready." The doctor made a motion, and the orderly came and hauled Logan into an upright position. He grunted involuntarily, and the doctor said sharply, "Be careful there! That's not a bag of oats you're handling!"

"Sorry, Doctor."

The orderly was awkward and hurt Logan considerably as he removed the bandage. Logan winced as the man unwound the strips that went across his stomach and side and all the way around his torso. Logan managed to get a glimpse at the wound and saw that it still looked bad. "No better, is it?"

"Perhaps a little. You're fortunate to be here. If that wound had been a little to the right, you would still be out there in an unmarked grave." The doctor leaned forward and probed at the wound and shook his head. "You must lie still and drink lots of fluids. You'll be all right, but you must take care of yourself. By the way," he said, "you're going to be transferred."

With a grunt, as the orderly reached around him and pulled another bandage tight to hold the compress on, Logan glanced at the physician. "Transferred? Why, and where?"

"As to the *why*, we need the room here for more serious cases. You'll get better, Smith. It'll just take time. As to the *where*, I'm having you transferred to a small hospital about ten miles outside of Paris. It won't be much of a trip. The name of the place is Belleville. A pleasant little village. You'll like it there."

"When will I be going?"

"Probably tomorrow. Now, be a good patient. Soon you'll be back fighting again."

Somehow, Logan did not receive these words of assurance with great pleasure. "Thanks, Doc," he said. He lay there as the doctors moved on and was hardly conscious of them as they visited the other patients. Finally, when they left the ward, he thought, *Well, it can't be any more boring than it is here.* Looking up at the flies, he saw that there were now eight of them. "That's right. Get your whole gang in here. What this hospital needs are more flies."

★ ★ ★ ★

"Well, a visitor. I can't believe it."

Logan was sitting up in bed attempting to read a novel in French. He read better than he spoke or understood, but still it was one of the most boring books he had ever read. He had picked it up in desperation, but now as Jo Hellinger stood over him, a smile spread across his face.

"How are you, Logan?"

"Fine—fine! Hey, it's great to see you, Jo. You look great." She was wearing a peach-colored, loose-fitting tailored day dress, with a bodice jacket that fell to hip level. The sleeves were long and close-fitting, with deep cuffs trimmed with buttons and braid. She looked like life itself to Logan Smith.

Pulling up a hard, unpadded chair, Jo sat down and studied Logan's face. "You've lost weight," she said. "I can tell it here." She pinched her own cheeks with her two fingers. "You've had a hard time, haven't you?"

"Not as hard as some. Where's Bedford?"

"He's outside. They wouldn't let me bring him in. I've got him tied to a lamppost. I hope he doesn't pull it down."

"Tell me what you've been doing. Any more stories accepted back in the States?"

"Yes. My editor shipped me these. I brought them to you. I don't know whether you'll like them or not." Reaching down, she extracted a sheaf of newspapers and handed it to him. "Thought you might like to read some American papers."

"Would I!" Logan grasped at them eagerly. "I've missed out on everything! I don't even know who won the World Series."

"Boston beat Philadelphia. A clean sweep. Four straight games."

"Well, I missed that one," he said with a quick smile. "It's good to see you, Jo," he said. "I know you've been busy."

"Pretty busy. Have you heard from Rev?"

"Yes. Got a letter from him yesterday. Here, you can read it." He sat there watching her face as she read Revelation's short letter. He enjoyed the sight of her. Her red hair brought a dash of color into the bland setting of the ward, and the other patients, he noticed, those who were awake, at least, had their eyes fixed on her.

Looking up, she smiled. "He never gives up, does he? I never saw as much of the Bible packed into one letter."

"That's about all he thinks about, I guess. Not a bad way to be. If it hadn't been for him, I guess I'd be dead."

"I pray for him every day," Jo said.

"So do I. It worries me to think that he might not make it."

She sat there speaking quietly, and after a time he said, "I've got a little news."

"What's that? You won the *Croix de Guerre?*"

"Not quite," he said dryly. "I'm being transferred out of here."

"Transferred! Where to?"

"A little place about ten miles outside Paris. I don't know where. The name of it is Belleville."

"Oh, I know that! There's an aerodrome there. Isn't far at all. A nice little town. You'll like it."

"I didn't think I'd come over all the way to France to spend my time in a hospital. Oh, I'm not complaining," he said, seeing quick compassion sweep across Jo's face. "I'm lucky to even be alive. A lot of the fellows didn't make it, but I'm not a very good patient."

"Neither am I," Jo said. "We're a lot alike in that respect. I'll tell you what! What's the use of having a writer for a friend if you don't use her? I brought my tablet and plenty of pens. Let's write to your folks. You dictate what you want to say, and I'll jot it down."

"Hey, that would be great! I wrote them a short letter, but I'm sure they'd like to hear the details."

Jo pulled a pad and pen out of her purse, crossed her legs, and smiled. "Let's have it."

For the next hour Jo wrote letters steadily, and finally at the end of that time, Logan said, "That's enough. I'll wear you out."

"I'll get them off today. Your folks will be glad to hear from you." She got up and put the pad and pen back in her purse, then came to stand over him. Impulsively she bent over and kissed his cheek. "Get well, Logan. When will you be transferred?"

"Maybe tomorrow."

"I'll come out to see you. You know what I'm riding around in now?"

"A limousine?"

Jo laughed. "Not likely. I've rented a motorcycle with a sidecar." Her laugh suddenly rang out, and her eyes twinkled. "You ought to see us riding around, me driving and Bedford sitting bolt upright in the sidecar. I got him some goggles, and he's gotten to where he likes them."

"He must make quite a sight," Logan grinned.

"Oh, just another crazy American. I'm sure that's what they say of me. Well, I'll see you tomorrow. I won't be making any long trips for a while. I've got a lot of writing to catch up with. Good-bye, Logan."

"Good-bye, and thanks for coming."

★ ★ ★ ★

"Is he here?"

"No, Gabby, he's not here yet." Katherine Laurent shook her head and looked down at the girl, saying, "You've asked me that a dozen times already."

Gabby Winslow knew that her grandmother was put out with her. Moving over, she reached up and took Katherine's hand and said, "I'm sorry, Grandmother. But I'm so anxious to see Papa. He hasn't been here for a week."

"No. It hasn't been that long. Only three days."

"Well, it seems like a week," Gabby pouted. "I don't see why he can't stay here with us."

Katherine Laurent felt the same way. She had been more than happy to take Gabby. Since her daughter's tragic death, there had been an emptiness in her life that the small girl had managed to fill. She and Pierre had been very disappointed that Lance had decided to live at the aerodrome. His reasoning had been that he needed to be with his men night and day to build up the relationship between them. Still, she had been greatly saddened that he had found so little time to come and spend with them. She knew that Gabby was very lonely at this time and needed her father. Now she suddenly leaned down and kissed Gabby on the cheek, saying, "He'll be here soon. It's almost suppertime. Would you like to come in and help me finish cooking?"

"Oh yes! I'd like that very much!"

As the two went into the kitchen, Katherine thought, *She's doing much better. When she first came here she was so quiet. I was really fearful for her*. She glanced over now to where Gabby was cheerfully and enthusiastically mashing potatoes. It had become one of her favorite foods, so she demanded mashed potatoes with every meal. She had asked for them for breakfast, but Katherine had drawn the line at that.

The door opened and Pierre said, "He's here."

With a squeal, Gabby dropped the potato masher and scooted out the door.

"She's excited, isn't she?" Pierre said. He was wearing a dark suit, as usual, with an immaculate white shirt and a wine-colored cravat. He came over to stand beside Katherine, his face thoughtful. "I'm glad Lance is coming tonight."

"Gabby's missed him terribly. He's very busy, I know, but he needs to spend more time with her."

Pierre leaned over and hugged Katherine. He kissed her on the cheek and said with approval, "You've done a fine job. She's settled in very nicely. Does she ever mention Noelle to you?"

"Hardly ever. I'm not sure whether to talk about her or not. It's hard to know with children."

"It's hard to know with anyone," Pierre said quietly. "Such a loss."

The two stood there thinking of the daughter who had been so vibrant, so full of life, and finally Katherine said, "Gabby looks so much like her. It's eerie."

"I know. I was looking through the old pictures of Noelle the other day when she was Gabby's age. It's amazing how much alike they look."

"You know, I think that's bothering Lance."

"What? That Gabby looks like her mother?"

"Yes."

"How could that be?"

"It brings back the memories, and he's suffering pretty badly, Pierre."

"I know he is. I've never seen a man grieve more for a woman. But he ought to be glad that Gabby looks like Noelle."

"One would think so, but I've watched his eyes sometimes when he's watching her. The pain there is almost unendurable, and he has to turn away."

They had no time to speak more of this, for the door swung open and Lance came in under tow by Gabby.

"Look, Papa brought me a present! See?" She held up a package. Her eyes were aglow, and her face seemed to radiate excitement.

"Well, it's not even Christmas or your birthday," Katherine said.

"I asked her if she had been a good girl and deserved a present," Lance said. He looked down at Gabby, who was struggling with the package. "She confessed that she had been very good."

"Well, she has. She deserves a present," Katherine said as she and Pierre watched Gabby tear the paper away and then open the box that was inside.

"Oh, it's beautiful, Papa!"

"What is it? Let me see," Pierre said.

"It's a snowstorm," Gabby cried. She held up a glass ball and turned it upside down. Tiny bits of white fluttered down over what seemed to be a white castle. "Look, isn't it pretty?"

"I had one like it when I was just your age," Lance said. His hand touched the top of Gabby's head, and he suddenly seemed to run out of words. He stared down at her, then cleared his throat and said quickly, "I hope I'm not late."

Both Pierre and Katherine had seen the break in Lance's expression and knew he was thinking of Noelle.

"No. You're just on time. Dani's upstairs getting dressed. Why don't you take Gabby into the parlor, and she can entertain you while I'm putting the meal on the table."

"Yes. Come along, Papa. I know a new song."

"Help me set the table, Pierre. Or go call Dani."

Fifteen minutes later they were all seated at the table, and Gabby spoke with enthusiasm. She showed an excitement that looked good to all the family. Danielle leaned over and smiled. "It's good to have you, Lance. We've missed you."

"I've been very busy at the base," Lance said defensively. "Is that a new dress you have on?"

"No. You've asked me that the last two times I've worn it."

Lance grinned. "I'm not much on women's fashions."

It was, as a matter of fact, a very becoming outfit. It was a dark green side-slit hobble skirt with a short full tunic with three-quarter-length sleeves worn on top. It had a low neckline, and the bodice was decorated with white beads and embroidery. For some reason she looked so mature that it startled Lance.

Dani looked quickly at him, searching his face, and then murmured, "We haven't given up on your coming to live here."

"I'm afraid that won't be possible, Dani. I need every moment I can get with the men."

Dani did not answer, but later on when they were washing dishes, she brought the matter up again. "It would be good for Gabby if you could be here more often, Lance. I don't mean to nag, but she misses you a great deal."

"I know. I'll try to be more regular, but the flights are so irregular.

I come in too late sometimes to see her. She'd be in bed."

They spoke quietly for a time, and when the dishes were done, Lance said, "I guess I'd better get back to the base."

"Go up and say good night to Gabby."

"Why, she'll be asleep."

"Wake her up then. She'll go right back."

"If you say so, Dani."

Danielle watched as he left the kitchen and thought, *He looks so hard. Isn't he ever going to get over Noelle's death?* She waited until he came back downstairs, then went to the door with him. "Will you come tomorrow?"

"I'll try," he said. He suddenly reached out and took her hand. "Thanks for everything," he said. "I couldn't have made it, nor could Gabby, without you and your parents."

She was conscious of his strong hand holding hers. For a moment she started to say something more personal, but then she kept her silence. "Good night. Try to come tomorrow."

★ ★ ★ ★

The trip from Paris to Belleville should have been simple, but Logan had had a bad night previous to leaving. He had not slept at all, and a new influx of badly wounded men had demanded the attention of the doctors and the orderlies. He had been shuffled out of his bed and placed in a larger ward to make room for a seriously wounded man. Then later on he had been shifted from there to a wing hardly ever used.

He was glad to get in the ambulance, but there had been a breakdown, and he had lain helpless along with three other men wedged shoulder to shoulder in the ancient vehicle. The heat and the flies had driven him to distraction, and finally when they pulled up to a stop, he grunted, "I hope this is it. I'm sick of this."

Finally the door to the ambulance opened, and the attendants carried his stretcher inside and up the steps. One of them missed a step and jolted Logan, bringing a searing pain to his side. He gasped and said angrily, "Watch where you're going!" Then he realized that neither man spoke English, so he lay there grimly until they reached the end of a hall. Turning inside, they managed to bump him against the doorframe, which brought the pain racking back, and then they dumped him unceremoniously on the bed. He was wearing dirty pajamas and a ratty-looking gray robe that was also unkempt. His hair had not been combed, and he had not had a shave for three days. He glared at the stretcher bearers, who ignored him and left the room.

"Hello. *Bon matin.*"

Logan looked across at the bed next to his and saw a tall, thin man sitting up reading a magazine, which he lowered. "Do you speak English? My French is rotten."

"Yes. Not very well. You just in from the front?"

"No. I've been in the hospital in Paris."

"You look terrible."

"I feel that way."

"My name is Henri Nane. What outfit?"

"The Legion."

Nane found this interesting. "When did you get hit?" He listened as Logan gave him a brief review, then nodded. "Not a bad place here. You'll like it."

Logan was exhausted. He closed his eyes without answering. It was hot in the ward, but he was accustomed to that. He felt gritty, and his side was giving him a great deal of discomfort. He dropped off to sleep almost at once and then was aroused out of it by a hand on his shoulder and a woman's voice.

"Wake up."

"What? What is it?"

"Wake up. You can't lie there in those filthy clothes on those clean sheets."

Opening his eyes, Logan took in the woman's face. She was wearing a white cap and uniform, so he assumed she was a nurse. "Sorry about that. Next time I'll wear my tuxedo."

"Here. Sit up. We've got to get you clean."

"Come back later. I've just dropped off to sleep."

"No. Now. Sit up."

Logan felt strong hands pulling him upright, and he was irritated. She swung his legs out and jerked at the bandage around his waist. "Where do you come from?"

"Paris. The hospital there." He stared at the woman, who pulled his robe down off of his shoulders and then practically jerked it out from under him. The rough motion hurt him, and he snapped, "Be careful there! What kind of a nurse are you?"

"I'm a clean one, at least. I never saw such filthy pajamas! How long have you had them on?"

Actually Logan was ashamed of his appearance. Just before he was transferred, the orderly had spilled food on the front of his pajamas, and it had dried, though they had not been terribly clean to begin with. But all the new patients had been the priority, so he knew that he was rough looking. "Sorry about that. I'll try to do it proper the next time."

"What is your name?"

"Logan Smith."

"My name is Nurse Laurent. Now, you've got to have a bath, and then we'll have a look at that bandage."

"Is the doctor here?"

"He'll be along later. Don't give me any trouble."

Danielle was not in a good mood. She had had a long and tiring day and a restless night. For what seemed like hours, she had lain awake thinking about Lance and about herself and Gabby. When she finally drifted off to sleep, she had dreamed of Noelle, yet somehow she felt disloyal when she remembered it in the morning, although she could not tell why.

She tore Logan's pajama tops off and then started tugging at the bottoms. "Wait a minute! A man's got a little modesty!"

"There's no time for modesty here." Danielle ceased pulling at the pajamas, for she had seen the filthy bandage. "I never saw such a bandage! Is that the way they treat soldiers in Paris now? You must have gotten a bad doctor."

"He was a very good doctor," Logan said angrily. "But there were men coming in with legs and arms blown off! I guess this little scratch didn't look very important to them."

Danielle began stripping off the bandage, and then she pulled out a pair of surgical scissors and snipped away at it. The pad was stuck to the wound, for it had bled and then dried. "I'll have to soak that off," she said, then left at once to obtain water.

Nane grinned at Logan and said, "She's worse than a sergeant."

"Is she always this rough?"

"No. Not usually. She seems to be in a bad mood today. Make the most of her. She's the best-looking nurse around here."

Logan lay there until Nurse Laurent came back with a pan of water. She carefully put a wet towel over the bandage and let it soak. In the meanwhile she washed his face and upper body. It actually felt very good. The water was tepid, and he grunted with pleasure, but then when she pulled the bandage off, some of it still stuck.

"What are you flinching about? Don't be such a baby."

"Are all of the nurses here as mean as you are?"

"Mean!" Something about his accent caught at Danielle. "What are you, an American?"

"Yes."

"That explains it!"

"Explains what?"

"You're rude! All Americans are rude and selfish!" She was staring at the wound and shook her head. "That's a bad wound you have. I'm going to leave a light bandage on it until the doctor gets here to examine you."

She finished his bath, put a clean sheet over him, and then jammed a thermometer between his teeth. He studied her carefully while she took his pulse and was impressed at the beautiful complexion and the clarity of her eyes. *She's a beauty,* he thought. *Too bad she's so tough.*

"You have a fever. You lie there while I go and get you something for it."

She came back soon and gave him two small pills. He spilled the water down the front of his chest, and she mopped it up with a towel. "Where are you from in the United States?"

"The West."

Her eyes opened. "Are you a cowboy?"

"As a matter of fact, I am—or used to be."

Danielle was interested. He was a fine-looking man, and though she suspected he was below the weight he usually carried, there was strength in his body. His muscles seemed smooth and strong. She guessed his age to be about twenty, close to her own. "Your hair is filthy."

"Sorry about that."

"I wasn't being critical. I was just thinking that it'll have to be washed."

"Can't handle that yet."

"Well, I can." She was brusque and nodded emphatically. "I'll do it this afternoon after the doctor sees to your wound." She hesitated, then said, "I'm sorry I said you were rude."

"That's all right. I am rude. Right now, at least."

Danielle glanced over at Nane, who was taking all this in. "What are you staring at, Henri?"

"I always like to look at rude Americans. They're quite a sight, aren't they?"

Suddenly Danielle smiled, and Logan saw that it changed her completely. She had one of the prettiest smiles he had ever seen. It went away quickly, but he thought, *Well, she's got some humor beneath that rough exterior. And if she can get my hair washed, I'll put up with her.* When she left he lay there savoring the feel of the clean sheets and the bath. *Maybe this place will be all right after all.*

★ ★ ★ ★

As Jo entered the waiting room of the hospital, she was met at once by a nurse dressed in white. "You can't bring that animal in here."

"Well, I can't let him run loose."

"You shouldn't have brought him in the first place."

"But I hated to leave him outside. Wouldn't it be all right if I took him in?"

Danielle stared at the woman but shook her head firmly. "We can't have animals in the hospital."

A soldier leaning on a cane had been standing with his back against the wall. He straightened up and said, "I'll take care of the dog, ma'am, if you'd trust me." He had some sort of odd accent, and Jo thought she recognized it.

"Are you Australian?"

"Yes, mum. Ringer Jones is the name."

"I'm glad to know you, Sergeant." Jo went over and shook his hand with a smile. "If you wouldn't mind taking care of Bedford, I'd appreciate it."

The sergeant leaned over and held his hand out, allowing Bedford to sniff it suspiciously. Bedford seemed to find the soldier agreeable enough, for he lowered his head and let the man pet him.

"I miss my dogs," he said. "I had three of them, all border collies, to take care of the cattle. Come along, boy. I'll take you outside."

"I won't be too long."

"Take your time, ma'am. I'm not going anywhere."

"Now can I make my visit?" she asked the young nurse.

"Who would you like to see?" Danielle asked.

"Logan Smith."

"I might have guessed." The answer leaped to Danielle's lips and she shook her head. "You're American."

"Yes, I am."

"Your friend is down this way. Come along. I'll take you to him."

The two walked down the hall, and as they did, Jo asked, "How is he?"

"He's doing very well. The doctor says he's making good progress. When he came here, he was in bad shape with some infection, but he's much better now."

"My name is Josephine Hellinger, but you can call me Jo. I'll be here often."

"Are you a relative?"

"No. Just a friend. We came over to France together."

Danielle wondered about what sort of relationship that might imply, but she said nothing. Opening the door, she led Jo into the ward, and at once every man in the ward seemed to come to attention.

"Jo, you made it!" Logan was sitting up in bed and his face lit up. He winked at her, saying, "This is my favorite nurse, Nurse Danielle Laurent. Nurse, this is my good friend, Jo Hellinger, the famous American journalist."

The two women nodded at each other, and after Danielle had left the room, Jo came over and put out her hand. "What have you done to her? It looks like you haven't made a friend there."

"We didn't get off on the right foot. Where's Bedford?"

"Outside. An Australian sergeant is taking care of him. They seemed to hit it off."

"Sit down."

"I brought you something to eat. I don't know whether you'll like it or not."

"Well, like Rev says. If its got hide and hair, I'll eat it."

Jo handed him the basket, and he eagerly pulled the cover off. "Fruit! Fresh fruit!" he said. "Hey, Henri, help yourself. This is Henri Nane."

"I'm glad to know you, Henri."

"Thank you, mademoiselle. This fruit looks good."

"Pass it around among the boys," Logan said.

"Anything you like special? I'll bring it the next time I come," Jo said.

"You know how it is in the hospital. Anything's good. Now, sit down and tell me everything."

Jo sat down and began to speak. She had just come back from a long tour of airfields, and finally she said, "I'm not going to be moving around much."

"You're not going back home, are you?"

"No. I've come over to do a job, and I've got to do it, but I'm going to change my focus a little."

"How's that, Jo?" Logan asked as he took a big bite out of an apple.

"Well, I've gotten the big overall look. It's not too bright, I might say, but what I want to do now is put a squadron under a microscope. So I've decided that the Fourteenth Squadron stationed here in Belleville will do as good as any." Her eyes crinkled as she smiled, and she reached over and put her hand on his. "After all, you're here."

Logan felt a warm glow. "That's fine. Have you met any of the fliers out at the field yet?"

"Not yet. Haven't visited that particular field."

The three sat talking for a while, and Logan was cheered by her visit. He was somewhat irritated when he looked up to see Nurse Laurent coming toward them with a basin and a towel over her arm.

"It's time for our bath," Danielle announced firmly.

"For *our* bath?" Logan said, then he looked over and winked at Jo.

Jo laughed and shook her head. "You haven't changed, Logan." She rose then and said, "Be patient with him, Nurse Laurent. He's really a nice fellow."

"When will you be back?" Logan asked.

"Tomorrow. You be sweet now. Maybe I could convince Nurse Laurent to put you in a wheelchair, and I could take you outside."

"I'll have to ask the doctor," Danielle said.

After Jo left, she went outside and found Sergeant Jones, who was sitting down stroking Bedford's head.

"He's a fine dog, ma'am. Anytime you need to leave him, I'll be glad to take care of him."

"Would you really? That would be so nice at times. I hate to leave him cooped up in a hotel room."

Ringer Jones' roughhewn face broke out into a smile. He was very tan from a lifetime outside, and his eyes crinkled as he smiled. "He'll be good company, ma'am. We get along, don't we, Bedford?"

Bedford barked, and Ringer Jones reached out and roughly caressed his head. "I've got nothing else to do, mum. If you want to leave him all day, that's fine."

"That would be most kind of you, Sergeant. I must make it right with you."

★ ★ ★ ★

For the next three days Jo came every afternoon to visit with

Logan, happy that Bedford had a friend to spend the day with. It was on the third day she was sitting beside him when Doctor Pierre Laurent came in for his daily visit. When Logan introduced her and spoke of her work, Doctor Laurent was interested. "I imagine this little village gets a little boring for you after Paris."

"Not a bit of it," Jo said vigorously. "I like little villages. I grew up in a small town in America no larger than this one."

Doctor Laurent hesitated and then said, "Perhaps you would care to come to dinner at my home. My wife would like to meet you. I understand you already know my daughter."

"Your daughter?"

"Yes. Nurse Danielle Laurent."

"Oh, I didn't make the connection! Why didn't you tell me, Logan?"

Logan shrugged his shoulders. "Don't know. I just didn't."

"I'd be happy to come, Doctor. You name the night. I'm open."

"Tonight would be excellent."

"I'll be there. What time?"

"Shall we say seven?"

"I have a dog."

"Bring him along. My granddaughter would love to see him."

★ ★ ★ ★

Gabby heard a roar outside and went to the window to see a motorcycle with a sidecar pull up in front of the house. "Look, a dog is on the motorcycle!"

Katherine went over and saw a tall young woman step off of the motorcycle, remove her helmet, and push her goggles up. An enormous German shepherd was in the sidecar. She saw the woman speak to him and he leaped out.

"I think it's our guest," Katherine said.

"Oh, can I pet the dog?"

"We'll have to ask," Katherine said.

Even as the door opened, before Jo could speak, Gabby flew outside and threw herself at the dog. "Oh, what's his name?"

"His name is Nathan Bedford Forrest," Jo smiled. "But he answers to *Bedford*." She found the young girl to be very beautiful but then looked up at the woman who appeared. "I came in my working clothes," she said. "I've been out to the airfield."

"Have you indeed! My name is Katherine Laurent. This is my

granddaughter, Gabby. Gabrielle, actually."

"And this is Bedford. You two are going to get along, I can see."

"Come in. Pierre is getting cleaned up. Dinner is almost ready."

Gabby could not leave Bedford alone, and finally she was allowed to walk him on a leash with a warning not to go outside the garden.

"Will it be all right?" Pierre asked with a worried look. "He's such a large dog."

"He's very gentle and very well trained," Jo assured him.

The meal had already started when another guest came, a tall man with captain's stars, and Pierre Laurent said, "Miss Hellinger, this is our son-in-law, Captain Lance Winslow."

"Oh, Captain Winslow, I've been trying to see you out at the aerodrome, but you've been flying."

Lance Winslow looked at the tall young woman and nodded. "My sergeant told me that an American lady had been there to see me. I hardly expected to see you here."

"Miss Hellinger has a friend in the hospital," Danielle said quickly.

Lance looked out the window. "Is it safe for Gabby to be with such a large animal?"

"She's very safe with Bedford," Jo said. She was studying Lance Winslow carefully without appearing to do so. She had heard a great deal about this captain who drove his men very hard and had shot down six German planes. She said quickly, "I wanted to talk to you about my friend in the hospital. He's a very fine pilot."

Interest flickered in Lance's eyes. "Is that so?"

"Yes. He enlisted in the Legion, but he hopes to transfer out into the flying service."

Lance Winslow appeared to be rather cold to Jo. "And you would like for me to get him transferred into the Fourteenth Squadron?"

"I would like for you to meet him, at least. The rest, of course, would be your decision."

"I'll be glad to have him in the Fourteenth if he's any good."

"That would be most kind of you."

"Well now, I'll have to go try to separate Gabby from Bedford so we can have our meal. Would he be all right in the dining room, Miss Hellinger?"

"He's very well behaved. Better than I am, I think," Jo smiled. Her mind was on Captain Lance Winslow. He was a handsome man, but she sensed something not *right* about him. He seemed quite cold toward her and acted with tremendous reserve. *It's like he's built a fence around himself,* she thought. *His eyes are hooded. I can't make him out.*

The meal was very pleasant, and when it was time for Jo to leave, Captain Winslow said, "I'll be glad to drop you off at your hotel."

"Oh, I've taken a room in the village. Besides, I travel by motorcycle now. It's much easier to get around."

Jo said her thanks to the Laurents, and Gabby said, "Will you bring Bedford back to play with me?"

"I surely will, honey. Very often."

As she rode back toward the cottage where she had taken a room, Jo reached over and looked at Bedford. His eyes were half closed, and he was enjoying the wind in his face, as always. "I'll have to be a little bit smoother with Captain Winslow. It would be wonderful if he could get Logan and Rev transferred into his squadron." She put her mind to it and formed a resolution. "It can be done," she said. "Logan is a fine flier and Captain Winslow needs experienced men like Logan Smith."

CHAPTER FOURTEEN

"NO MAN CAN SHOP FOR A GIRL!"

★ ★ ★ ★

Far beneath the flight of planes, the emerald earth rose and fell in undulant swells, much like an ocean, but only a brighter green. Lance leaned over the cockpit of the Nieuport and felt a mixture of pleasure and disgust. Below him the Fourteenth Squadron was spread out in three flights. Each flight was an inverted *V* with one plane in front and two behind. The pleasure came from watching them as they kept close formation. "At last they're getting to where they can stay together," he muttered. "It was like trying to drive a herd of bees across the desert when we first started formation flying."

The disgust that followed this pleasure at the sight of the squadron moving along through the blue skies keeping station almost perfectly evaporated, and he looked back, his eyes narrowing, as he studied the squadron. They were all painted a dull olive and had the honor of being the first British squadron to come to full strength in France. But it was a sorry selection that made up the squadron. His eyes went from B.E.2s to Morane-Saulnier Parasols, Blériots, B.E.8s, one Avro 504, a Farman, and only one other Nieuport beside the one that led B-flight.

I wish they were all Nieuports, he thought with longing. Ever since he had been in France, he had tried to mount a squadron with top quality planes. But every squadron in France was screaming for better airplanes, and the excuses for planes Winslow received from England were not enough to fill the gap. He himself had shot down six planes, but the rest of the squadron together only accounted for three. Most of the pilots were all green. None of them had ever seen any real action, and some of them had less than two hundred hours of training. The planes were only a step or two removed from the early experiments of the Wright brothers in America. One of them actually looked like a flying bedstead, which is what the pilots actually called it.

Feeling the eyes of the flight leaders on him, Lance raised his gloved fist, pumped it twice, and then moved the stick so that the Nieuport banked and fell into a dive. There was something comforting about the roar of the nine-cylinder rotary engine. It only produced up to 110 horsepower, and the propeller, which was on a rotary, was bolted directly to the engine crankcase. Everything, including the cylinders, revolved around a stationary crankshaft. There was no carburetor, and the fuel was sucked from a hollow portion of the crankshaft. The smell of castor oil, which was mixed with the gasoline, was sickening even now at full speed with the wind whipping around his head.

There's got to be a better way to build an engine than this, Lance thought. The engine had to be cut in and out with great frequency, and it sounded like an enormous hornet as it sped through the skies.

There were no Germans in sight, but Lance half rose from his seat, reached up, and pulled the .303 Lewis gun into firing position. It was mounted on the top wing, where the bullets would clear the whirling propeller blades. A drum on top held fifty-seven rounds that could be emptied in five seconds of continuous firing. This meant that the pilot had to fly the plane and change drums in flight. It was something only a juggler could do with any ease at all. The pilot had to pull the gun down so that the barrel was pointed straight up, then, half standing and fighting the prop wash, he had to jerk the drum off and replace it with a fresh one. As often as not, the drum would slip from his hand or the plane would shy sideways or even go into a spin from being released from the pressure of the pilot's hand on the stick.

"I'm lucky I haven't been shot down trying to change this fool drum," Lance muttered.

He gave up on the gun, hoping that no Germans would appear. Looking around, he saw that the flight formation had, more or less, disintegrated. This could be accounted for partially by the fact that the engines were all different, and it was almost impossible for three planes to maintain the same speed. There was also a natural tendency at top speed to move away from anything close. Therefore, the distances among the planes of the various flights had become measurably greater.

The wind whipped at Lance Winslow's face and pressed his goggles against his flesh. For a long time he had enjoyed the sheer ecstasy of flying, but that joy had disappeared the day Noelle had died from the bombs of the Germans' Zeppelin raid. Since then flying had become merely a means to put him within reach of those who had murdered his wife. Flying for joy was something for amateurs or for men with nothing to settle, but Lance awoke each morning thinking of how he could get a German plane in his sights and touch the button on top of his control stick. He kept this focus for himself all day long, and he kept it before the pilots, as well, who were constantly harangued, "You're here to kill Germans. Nothing else matters. Kill Germans! That's why you're in these airplanes."

The fields below laid off in neat, multicolored, checkered squares, according to the crops that were growing, seemed to rise up to meet him. Knowing that some of the planes in his squadron had a tendency to shed the lower wing in a dive, Lance signaled for a pullout. He felt the Nieuport shudder under him, but obediently the nose rose, and he was relieved to see that there had been no midair collisions. Fully half of the deaths in the British squadrons, and he suspected with the French as well, were due not to the bullets of German fighters but to accidents. The planes they flew were so flimsy and behaved so erratically that men counted themselves fortunate each time they came back to earth without being chewed up and spat out of the planes with their canvas-covered bodies and wings.

Glancing down at a gauge, Lance saw that his fuel was low. He signaled again and led the squadron back over the field. He came in for a smooth landing, but by the time he had rolled his machine up and killed the engine, he looked over and saw that Holmes was headed straight for the hedge that marked the barrier between the hangars and the field. "Pull up, you idiot! Pull up!" The flier crashed into the hedge, and the engine died abruptly. "Hope he hasn't killed himself!" Lance muttered in disgust. Stepping out of the cockpit, he glanced at his mechanic, Tom Morrison, and nodded briefly. "Check her over, Morrison."

"She handle all right today, Captain?" Morrison was a thin, rangy man with hazel eyes and a hook nose. He ran his hand lovingly over the side of the Nieuport, and when he received only a nod from his officer, he said, "No sign of the Huns today?"

"No, and it's a good thing. They would have knocked us all out of the air."

"You'll get there, Captain. The boys are a bit green, but they've got a good teacher."

Grunting at the compliment, Lance said, "Better check everything. We'll be going on another flight in an hour."

"Yes, sir. She'll be humming like a sewing machine." Tom Morrison had a touch with engines that few men possessed. He not only kept the captain's plane in tip-top shape but, in effect, instructed the other mechanics as well. Some of them were none too expert, but under the tutelage of Morrison, a capable crew of mechanics had begun to be pulled together.

Walking slowly with his head down, Lance moved until he stood in front of the hut. Overhead the June sun was bright, but he had no eye for the rolling green of the hills or the fleecy white clouds that dotted the azure heavens overhead. He stood waiting until the pilots all tumbled out of their ships and had a word with their mechanics, then he raised his hand and called, "Inside for a briefing!"

The men moved slowly, and Pug Hardeston, a short, muscular man, turned to mutter to the strongly built man beside him. "Hey, sailor, what do you reckon the cap's got up his sleeve this time?"

Sailor Malone was aptly named, for he had been a sailor. He still had the swinging, weaving walk of a sailor off the ship for the first time. He ran his hand through his brown hair and grunted, "Who cares?"

"You don't, do you?" Pug Hardeston grinned. He studied his companion as the two made their way to the headquarters building. "You're gonna get yourself killed if you keep on takin' chances like you did in that brush with the Jerries yesterday."

"So what? When you're dead you can rest," Malone said.

Hardeston muttered, "Well, don't get yourself killed, mate. That's all I've got to say."

As the two reached the steps, a tall, aristocratic-looking man nodded to them. Clive Bentley was only twenty-two, but he had all of the fine blood of the Twenty-fourth Squadron. His father was a member of Parliament, Sir Claude Bentley, and Clive himself had all the smooth good looks of a matinee idol. Bentley let Hardeston and Malone go up and stopped long enough to say, "What do you think, Cecil?"

Cecil Lewis, tall, blond, and lanky, with blue eyes and a scholarly look, did not answer. He was, in fact, a professor of English at Balliol.

As usual he had a tag end of poetry, which he quoted as he responded to Bentley's question. "We all so serve who only stand and wait."

"Don't see what that's got to do with it," Bentley grinned. "We haven't got to stand and wait in a long time. I'll bet you a fiver we'll be up again in an hour."

"No takers."

The two entered and soon two more men came wandering in. One of them, Harold Holmes, had a wild look in his eye. He was only eighteen, the youngest of the squadron, and was more timid than any fighter pilot had a reason to be. He was the only son of a shopkeeper and had led a sheltered life with his three sisters and his mother. Now he kept his head down and refused to look up.

Pete Jennings, called *Copper* because he had been a policeman in a small village, grinned and said, "Don't worry about it. If you can walk away, it's a good landing."

"The captain's going to kill me!" Holmes said.

"No, he won't, Harold. He needs pilots too bad. If he gives you any trouble, just stand and look at him, and he'll let you alone."

A man with very pale blue eyes and tow-colored hair had come in and heard him. He was a small man, small enough to be a steeplechase jockey. Some of those riders reached as high as five ten, and Jerold Spencer had the tough look that most jockeys accumulate over a period of years of wrestling with animals weighing twenty times their own weight or more. "Wonderful landing, Harold! You must have spent a lot of time practicing it."

"Oh, leave him alone!" Copper said. "I've done worse."

"So have I," Spencer said. He saw that Harold Holmes was upset and said, "When you fall off, get right back on. That's the first rule of riding a horse. I think the same thing's true of flying a plane. If you crack up, go right back at it."

"Attention!" Captain Lance Winslow stepped out of his inner office and now stood surveying the pilots. They had all come trooping in now, and he thought again of what a motley crew they were. *Nobody would ever pick some of them out to be pilots,* he thought. But he put that behind him. "I have a few remarks to make about your flying."

"I'll bet he does," Sailor Malone whispered under his breath.

"Did you say something, Lieutenant Malone?"

"No, sir. Just clearing my throat."

Lance stared at him until the burly man dropped his eyes and then continued for ten minutes to explain how they were quite possibly the worst pilots in the entire world. Finally he grudgingly said, "I will give you this, though. Your formation flying is a little bit better."

"When are we gonna get new planes, Captain?" Cecil Lewis asked. He had pulled a pipe out and was puffing on it, the blue smoke rising in large featherlike plumes. "That Farman of mine is going to fall out of the skies at any time."

"We'll talk about that later. In the meanwhile I do have one bit of good news."

From somewhere among the men the whisper came, "About time," but Lance ignored it.

"Any of you ever hear of a pilot called Roland Garros?"

"I have," Sailor Malone spoke up. "We flew together back a few years ago."

"I've heard of him," Clive Bentley said. "He's got five kills. That makes him an Ace according to the new method of scoring things." This much was true, for only recently had the word *Ace* been used to identify a pilot's number of kills. At the present time, anyone who had shot down five planes was automatically considered an Ace, at least in the British service. The French and Germans scored somewhat differently.

"Well, I've never met Garros, but he's evidently a pretty sharp fellow."

"What's he done, Captain?" Sailor asked.

"He got tired of standing up in his seat," Lance said, "and trying to fire that gun balancing on one foot and changing drums with the wind whipping around you."

"Who doesn't?" Pug Hardeston said. "You don't mean to say he did something about it?"

"That's just what I mean." Lance waited for a moment and then shook his head. "I don't know why no one thought of this before, but Garros decided to shoot right through the propeller."

"Through the propeller! Why, my dear sir!" Clive Bentley said, looking down his aristocratic nose. "Impossible! He'd shoot his propeller off!"

"Well, that's what one would think, but Garros had one of those ideas that come along once in a great while. He put steel plates on the back of his propeller shafts."

Instantly Cecil Lewis, the deepest thinker of the group, narrowed his eyes. He took the pipe out of his mouth. "My sainted aunt!" he breathed. "And did it work?"

"It worked like a charm. He had a Hotchkiss that fired twenty-five rounds, and most of those missed the propeller. Those that didn't were ricocheted off."

"Has he tried it in combat?" Lewis demanded quickly.

"Yes. That's how he shot down five planes. The Germans just can't believe it, I would think."

"As Shakespeare would say, 'There's a divinity that shapes our ends.' It looks like the good Lord has given Mr. Garros a great idea."

A clamor went up, and it was Sailor Malone who demanded, "Are we gonna try it, Captain?"

"Yes. We'll try it on the ground first so we'll be sure we've got the right plates. I've already had them made up. We'll attach them to our propellers, and if they work, the Germans are in for a shock."

Lance let the talk run around the room, and then finally he said, "That's not the only good thing." When he got their attention he smiled again.

Sailor Malone thought, *Two smiles in one day. That's used up Captain Winslow's smiles for a year.*

"The good news is that the whole squadron's going to be fitted with Nieuports."

Excitement spread around the room, and Lance made no attempt to stop them from cheering loudly. He waited until they quieted down, and then he said, "These will be factory fresh. Any man that gets shot down will incur my displeasure."

As all the men laughed, Lance happened to glance over to the door, which was to his left, and a shock ran through him as he saw Jo Hellinger standing there.

"That's all for now. We take off in an hour."

The pilots trooped out, all of them taking a good look at Jo. She met their gaze with a friendly smile, and when they were all gone, she came over and said, "I didn't mean to interrupt, Captain."

"I'd appreciate it if you wouldn't do that again, Miss Hellinger. Really, it's not too good to interrupt one of our briefings."

"I am sorry, and it won't happen again. You're going up again?"

"Yes. In an hour, as you heard."

"I wonder if I could have a little of your time after you get back."

"It will be fairly late."

"That's all right. I don't mind waiting. I'd like to talk to some of the mechanics, if you don't mind, while you're gone. With your permission, of course."

For some reason, Lance was irritated with Jo Hellinger, but he could find no way to bar her. Rather curtly, he said, "Certainly. Now if you'll excuse me."

Jo watched Lance as he left headquarters. She stepped outside the door and watched him walk straight to where his mechanic was working on a plane. The two men engaged in quite a long conversation, and finally she said to herself, "Well, he's a hard nut, Mr. Lance Winslow. I wonder if he's as hard on the inside as he is on the outside."

★ ★ ★ ★

"I would like to spend more time with you, but I'm afraid I don't have it to spare."

"Could you spare time for a cup of tea?" Jo smiled at him demurely. "After all, I have waited four hours."

It was two o'clock in the afternoon, and Jo had spent the entire time speaking to the mechanics. She had found them a fascinating group of men, and they had fallen for her head over heels. Jo had done wonders for their morale.

"No one ever pays any attention to us," one of them said. "It's always the pilots that get all the glory. But they wouldn't be up there if we didn't keep those planes humming."

After Lance agreed and they had gone to a small tea room in the center of town, Jo told him what she had found out. She spoke glowingly of the mechanics. "I don't know how good they are at their trade, but they are very possessive. They speak of the planes as if they belonged to *them*. They all say when *my* plane gets back."

Lance nodded. "It's good they feel that way. And they're right about one thing. They are the ones that keep the planes up. I'm sorry there's not more credit given to them." He stirred his tea, sipped it, and said, "Are you actually going to write about the mechanics?"

"Certainly!"

"But people wouldn't be interested in that."

"Oh, I think you're wrong, Captain Winslow. Everyone's heard about the pilots. I've written a dozen stories about them, but people are interested in those stories that go unnoticed as well."

"I never thought of it that way. But I'm all for you if you can get any credit to those men. They're hard workers. And quite frankly, I wouldn't take my plane up if I didn't know my mechanic had done a thorough look-over before."

Jo noticed that he was tense and she waited, making small talk mostly about the mechanics and the aerodrome. He was interested in what she had to say about the other aerodromes she had visited. He began to ask many questions about how many planes they had and what she had found interesting about the pilots. Jo spoke quietly but with knowledge, and was not afraid to say from time to time, "I just don't know, Captain. I'm just an amateur. But it might be good if you could make a tour of these other places. You could see what they're doing."

"I'd like to, but I just don't have time." Lance took a sip of tea, then fell silent.

"You look very worried. But I suppose that goes with your job."

"You saw the pilots. Did you notice the youngest one out there?"

"The small baby-faced pilot? He didn't look over sixteen."

"That's Harold Holmes. He's only eighteen. He's had only a hundred hours flying time, and here he is flying in combat." Putting the cup down, Lance shut his eyes and rubbed them with the heels of his hand. "Can you imagine writing a letter to his mother and sisters?"

"How big a family does he have?"

"Just the three sisters and his mother. His father's dead now. Of course, all their hopes are with Harold."

"How terrible!"

Surprised, Lance looked at her. "Yes. It is terrible, but it happens over and over again. I've had to write more letters than one for pilots who are no more than boys, just like Harold."

"I'm sorry," she said. She was wearing a light gray dress with a green scarf around her neck, and as she leaned back, she noted, with interest, that for once Captain Lance Winslow was looking at her as a woman instead of a journalist. It encouraged her, and although she was not flirting, she was glad to see that he did let down his guard from time to time.

"If you have time, I'd be glad to take you by the hospital to meet Logan Smith."

"Oh yes! The pilot. How long will he be in the hospital?"

"They'll be releasing him in two days. He'll have to go back to the Legion if you can't arrange to have him transferred."

"I'll give him a try. If he can fly, I don't think it will be a problem. We've done it before."

"I'd be so grateful."

Lance studied Jo curiously. "You two are very close?"

"I met him out on the ranch his family owns out west. He's a very fine young man. A rodeo competitor."

"Rodeo? Riding horses and bucking horses? They do that sort of thing?"

"Oh yes. It's very popular, especially in the West."

"Looks like a rather dangerous occupation to me."

Jo suddenly laughed. "Dangerous! After what you do every day, and you call that dangerous?"

"People are afraid of different things, I suppose."

"I've noticed that. The bravest man I ever knew was scared to death of rats. I think he would have picked up an eight-foot rattlesnake with his bare hands, but the sight of a rat turned him to jelly."

"We all have our secret places."

"Secret places? It sounds like something from a poem."

Lance smiled. "I don't think so. It just popped out."

As he sipped his tea again, Jo noticed how his fingers were long and tapered. They looked like a surgeon's hands or perhaps those of a violinist or a pianist. She wondered if he played, but she was still thinking of what he had said. *"Our secret places."* "I think one of mine might be snakes. If anyone threatened me with a snake, I believe I'd die."

"You know what one of mine was when I was younger?"

"No. What?"

"High places."

"You're kidding me!"

"That's a fact. When I was young I took a fall off of a barn. For a couple of years after that, I could hardly stand up on the curb."

"Well," Jo smiled and sipped from her cup, then put it down. "You've certainly gotten over *that* secret place. Any more?"

"I guess we don't talk about those things. Anyway, I have to pick up my daughter, but we'll go by the hospital and meet your cowboy first."

★ ★ ★ ★

"Let me give it to you straight, Mr. Smith," Lance said. "I don't know how much flying you've done, but there's a lot of men who can get a plane up in the air but can't make it as a combat pilot."

Logan had stood up when the two had entered, and as soon as Jo had introduced Captain Winslow, he had been excited. He briefly told Winslow about his experience flying and nodded. "I wouldn't ask for anything but a fair chance."

"When will you get out of here?"

"Day after tomorrow. Maybe even tomorrow, if I beg."

"No, you don't," Jo said. "You'll do what the doctor tells you to do. His doctor's your father-in-law, so I think your word might carry a little weight, Captain."

"He's an excellent doctor, Smith. You were lucky to get him. That's who I'd want if I got shot."

"I think he would be a wise choice," Smith agreed.

Lance suddenly smiled. It seemed to be his day for smiling, he thought. "Have you heard the song about the dying aviator?" When they shook their heads, he sang in a pleasant baritone.

> "The young aviator lay dying,
> Beneath the wreck he lay.
> These last parting words
> He did say:
> Take the cylinder out of my kidney,
> The connecting rod out of my brain—
> From my backside remove the crankshaft,
> Assemble the blasted
> Engine again."

"I didn't know you were musical, Captain," Jo said.

"I'm not. The boys sing it all the time." He straightened up, looked at Smith, and said, "I'll give you a try, Smith. You may find combat a little more exacting than riding wild horses."

"I'll do my best, Captain Winslow. And I thank you very much for the opportunity. Oh, and by the way. This may be premature," Logan said, "but if you decide to take me on—or even if you don't—I can give you the name of the best mechanic in France."

"You mean Rev?" Jo said.

"Exactly! Even if I don't make the squadron, I'll guarantee he can take any plane you've got, wing it out, and make it fly like you've never seen it fly before."

"Leave his name with me. You understand I'm not making any promises."

"Of course not, Captain."

"You know," Logan began, "my mother's maiden name is Winslow. I wonder if we could be related somehow."

"Well, I did have an ancestor who was born in America before moving to England to be a minister," Lance replied. "Actually, he was born in the American colonies. The revolution had not happened yet.

His name was William Winslow. I believe, if I remember correctly, that his father's name was Miles Winslow."

Logan answered excitedly, "My grandfather, Zach Winslow, used to speak of the early family stories, and I remember him telling about a great-great-great-grandfather Miles!" He stretched out his hand. "Well, how do you do, cousin."

Lance smiled as he took his hand. "It's wonderful to meet one of my American cousins. We'll have to spend time talking about our family connections. But now I really must be going. Have a good day."

Lance and Jo left at once, and Lance glanced sideways at Jo. "I haven't sung that song in a long time. I don't sing much anyway."

"You have a fine voice. Were you in a choir as a boy?"

"Yes. It was a long time ago. But I still remember all those songs I sang in church."

"I do too. I wonder if we sang the same ones? Did you sing 'The Old Rugged Cross'?"

"Oh yes," Lance said. They went on discussing the songs they had grown up with, and when they reached the car, he said, "I've got a chore to do. I have to take my daughter, Gabby, shopping."

"Well, that doesn't sound like a chore."

"It is for me. Did you ever know a man who knew how to shop?"

"No man can shop for a girl," Jo smiled. Then, on impulse, she asked, "If I wouldn't be in the way, perhaps I could help."

"Would you really do that? You're not busy?"

"Not a bit. Come along. Let's get her."

"She'll be happy," Lance said.

"I'm not sure about that. She probably wants all the time she can get with her father."

Lance shook his head but did not answer. He opened the door, closed it, then went around and got in beside her. "Gabby talks about you and that motorcycle a lot. She says you promised to take her for a ride."

"With your permission."

"You'll tie her in good, won't you?"

"Oh yes, and I'll go very slowly. Bedford likes it."

"Where is that dog? I usually see him with you."

"One of the patients out at the hospital is keeping him. An Australian, Ringer Jones."

They picked up Gabby from the house, and the rest of the afternoon was a delight, at least to two of the party. Gabby was delighted to see Jo, but, of course, she clung to her father.

"Papa," she said, "are we going to eat at a restaurant?"

"Certainly! First-class style for my best girl."

Lance had not exaggerated when he said he knew nothing of shopping. Jo suspected that his wife had done this chore, and as tactfully as she could, she made herself available. Lance finally wound up tagging along behind the two as they went from shop to shop. His eyes fell often on Gabby, and Jo couldn't help but notice the sadness that filled them.

They ate at a restaurant Jo had already discovered, and both Lance and Jo were delighted at how bright Gabby was.

There was a light in the child's eyes as she looked at her father, but Jo was quick to notice how Lance Winslow found it difficult to keep his eyes on Gabby. She could tell that his smiles were forced, and his conversation with her was stiff. Jo quickly surmised that it was the resemblance between Gabby and her dead mother that created the tension.

Finally the evening ended and they dropped Gabby off. As they got back in the car, Winslow said, "I'll drop you off."

"It's such a nice night I could almost walk."

Winslow did not answer. His mind, apparently, was still on the child. When he did not speak but drove slowly down the narrow streets toward the house where Jo had taken a room, she said, "She's such a beautiful child. You must be very proud of her."

"Yes, I am."

"Is she very like her mother, Captain?"

"Almost unbearably."

It was a revealing statement, and the tone was clipped and short. "No admittance," Jo said, and she suddenly thought of what he had said about how everybody had a secret place or a secret fear. She knew that, somehow, Gabby was part of that for Lance Winslow. "You're fortunate to have the Laurents to help you with her."

"I thank God for them every day," Lance said fervently. He would have said more, but he was in front of her house. He stopped the engine and turned to face her. The moonlight flooded in through the front windshield and bathed her face with warm, silver moonbeams. Though his thoughts were on Gabby and the problems that he had, he felt a stirring of memory as he looked at Jo. *A strong woman*. Inevitably he thought, *like Noelle*, and then was shocked, for he had not thought this of any other woman since his wife's death. The thought troubled him, and his hands twisted the steering wheel restlessly.

"Well, good night, Captain. It's been a lovely evening."

"Good night." He would have gotten out to open the door for her, but she said, "Don't bother. Thanks for the ride."

"We'll do it again sometime. Go shopping for Gabby, if you don't mind," Lance said.

"Any time, but I'll spoil her. I promise you."

"She can use all that she can get." He hesitated, then grinned ruefully. "So can I, I guess."

Jo did not know what to make of that, but for that moment, he seemed more vulnerable than she had ever seen him. She tried to think of something to say, but everything that came to her mind sounded trite. Finally she smiled and said, "Good night, Captain. Thank you for giving Logan a chance," she said as she got out of the car.

"Good night." Lance started the engine and drove away. As he drove back to the aerodrome, he enjoyed the quietness of the town. Tomorrow, he knew, would be filled with roaring engines, machine gun fire, and, perhaps, death for him. But now, at this moment, he felt complete and relaxed in a way he had not since he had come to France. A sudden thought came to him, *Something about that woman. She's tough enough, but she's so feminine, and she made the shopping trip a lot easier*. He thought again of what she had said, *No man can shop for a girl*, and his lips curled up in a smile. *Well, we'll do it again sometime.* The thought pleased him, and he gunned the engine slightly as he sped toward the aerodrome.

CHAPTER FIFTEEN

LOGAN AND HIS NURSE

★ ★ ★ ★

"I suppose you'll be glad to get out of the hospital?"

Logan had been moving about restlessly all day, leaving his room, from time to time, to go out into the warm sunshine. It was hot, for July had come with a blistering dry heat that had warmed the land, sending up heat spirals toward the slate blue skies overhead. He had been sitting on a bench talking with the Australian sergeant, Ringer Jones, whom he had often seen walking the large German shepherd. He liked this ex-stock rider very much, and now he nodded at the rangy man's question. "Yes, but I don't look forward to going back into the trenches."

Ringer Jones answered quickly. "No man would look forward to that, but I thought you had a chance to get out."

"So I do. If I can impress Captain Winslow with my flying, I can transfer from the Legion to the air arms."

"Be much better, I would think, although I've never been up myself."

As the two men talked idly, Danielle Laurent emerged from the hospital. "Here comes your nurse," Ringer said. "You two get along like cats and dogs."

Logan was watching Danielle, who was wearing, as usual, her white uniform, complete with white stockings and high-top black shoes. "I don't know what there is about me that gets her back up."

"Why don't you turn on the charm, old boy? You Americans are fairly rough like us Australians. These Frenchmen have all the manners."

Suddenly Logan nodded. "You know, Ringer, I think I'll just give it a try."

"Tallyho and good luck. All that sort of rot," Ringer grinned. He watched as Logan Smith moved across the yard to intercept the young woman and murmured, "Good-looking woman, that nurse, but she's got a hard streak in her for Americans, I think."

"Good morning, Nurse Laurent," Logan said.

Danielle looked up with surprise. "Oh," she said, "I didn't know you were out here!"

"Have to start getting my exercise. Your father says that I'm fit to take part in the world again."

"You had a quick recovery."

"Yes. I just get a twinge now and then."

A silence fell on the pair, both feeling somewhat embarrassed. In all truth, they had gotten off to a bad start. Danielle had noticed that the American got along with almost everybody else. He was well liked, not only by his fellow patients, but by the staff. He was a true diplomat, she had noted, and had been interested enough in the woman who cleaned his room to find out that she was trying to put two children through school and had an aging mother who was not in good health. Danielle had come upon them once when he was talking earnestly to her, telling her that she was doing a good thing and that he admired her for it.

"I understand from Miss Hellinger that you're going to try to get into the flying forces."

"I'm going to try. That's what I came to France for."

"Well, I hope you succeed," Danielle said. She hesitated, then said, "What are you doing for dinner tonight?"

"The same thing I do every night. Eating what they put before me here."

An impulse took Danielle. "Why don't you join us for dinner? Miss Hellinger's coming."

"Jo will be there? Well, I'd like that very much, if you're sure it won't put you out."

"Put me out? What does that mean?"

Logan grinned crookedly. He had a most attractive smile, and now that the pain lines were erased by good health, he looked rather fit. "Just an American saying. I don't know where it comes from. I suppose you French have sayings like that, too."

"Oh yes. I suppose so. Well, you'll come, then?"
"What time?"
"Come at seven. Nothing fancy, you understand."
"It will be a treat. I'll see you then."

★ ★ ★ ★

As Logan entered the large parlor of the Laurent household, he stopped abruptly. Leaning on the mantel was Captain Lance Winslow. "Oh," Logan said lamely, "I didn't know you'd be here, Captain."

"I took a night off to be with my family." Winslow came over and shook hands with the young man who was wearing his Legion uniform. It was the only clothing Logan had, and he felt out of place in it. He tugged at the fabric, saying, "I'm not dressed for much formal entertainment."

Lance himself was wearing his light olive uniform and looked very sharp. He was the kind of man who could put on anything off the rack and make it look expensive. There was a strength in his lean body and yet at the same time a grace that Logan Smith admired. He was made of rougher material, and his years on the range had put a toughness in him that nothing could disguise. When he moved there was strength in his movements, and the two men made an interesting contrast. Jo had been talking to Danielle, and now she smiled.

"I'm glad you could come, Logan."

"Good to see you, Jo. I got a letter from Rev today. He asked to be remembered."

"Is he all right?"

"Oh yes. You know Rev. He never worries about anything."

"You'd find our friend Revelation Brown quite interesting, Captain," Jo smiled. "He's a hypercalvinist."

"Yes, and as I've told you, sir, he's the best mechanic I've ever seen in my life. He could have made a fortune in the States working for any of the automobile plants, but he preferred to tinker with airplanes. Built one from the ground up. Knows engines inside and out."

"We could always use a man like that," Lance nodded. "I've already sent the papers to get him transferred."

"Oh, that's great!" Logan's face glowed. "Whether I make it with your squadron or not, you'll find Rev a good man."

"What is his name? Rev?"

"Well, his real name is Revelation."

"Revelation? What a strange name!"

"Well, if you think that's strange," Jo laughed, "you ought to hear the names of his brothers and sisters."

"What are they?" Danielle asked.

"Well, he has two brothers. One is named Dedication and one is named Incarnation."

"I can't believe that!" Doctor Laurent said. "Who would name a baby Incarnation?"

"What did they ever call him? *In* or *carn* or *nation?*" Katherine Laurent exclaimed.

"Well, his sisters did a little better," Jo smiled.

"What are they called, pray tell?" Doctor Laurent asked. He was amused by the Americans. "I hope they are a little bit more feminine."

"I don't know about feminine. His sisters are named Incense, Praise, and Blessing."

A laugh went around the room, and Lance said, "I don't care what his name is if he can make an airplane fly."

"How are things going with your squadron now that you have the new planes, Lance?" Doctor Laurent asked.

"Much better. We can actually meet the Germans on their own terms now."

"I understand that fellow Fokker is quite a prize for the Germans."

"Yes," Lance nodded. "He's a Dutchman, really. Mechanical genius, apparently. At least he turns out planes that are probably as good as anything in the air today. Doesn't seem to care about honor or anything like that. I think he'd just as soon be making planes for the French or the British, but the Germans offered him more and got to him first."

"What are the new Fokkers like, sir?" Logan asked.

"Oh, fast, maneuverable. They can do anything ours can do except dive. They can't follow us in a hard dive."

The talk went around for some time, and finally they moved into the dining room. Logan found himself seated beside Danielle, and after her father had asked a blessing, she began to urge him, saying, "Better make the most of this home cooking."

"I will. It reminds me of my home."

"Do you live on a ranch?"

"Yes. I grew up out on the range."

"Herding cattle and all that sort of thing?"

"Sure. Our home was nothing like this, though. You would find it pretty primitive. Big heavy beams overhead. We lived in a log house. My grandfather built it himself."

"What's your family like?"

Logan had discovered that the Europeans were tremendously interested in the American West. He tasted some of the soup that was steaming in front of him and said, "This is good." Then he turned to her and said, "Well, this sounds like something out of a Wild West book, but my father was an outlaw—for a time, at least."

"You don't mean it!"

Danielle's eyes were enormous as she turned to look at him. She had beautiful eyes, clear and a golden brown, and he found himself admiring the satiny sheen of her cheeks. There was an inner beauty to this girl to match the outer attractiveness, and he found himself drawn to her more than ever. "Well, he was on the borderline. For a while it wasn't clear whether he'd be an outlaw or a marshal, but he finally took a badge and became a law enforcement officer."

"Did he carry a gun and all that?"

"Oh sure. Back in those days everyone did. This was in Oklahoma Territory. The wildest part of the Wild West, I suppose."

"Did he ever meet Buffalo Bill?"

"I think he did."

"What about Wild Bill Hickok?"

"He said he met him once. Said he was the windiest old bore he ever saw in his life."

Everyone had been listening to this conversation, and now Doctor Laurent said, "They make him out quite a hero. Lightning fast with his guns, as all the novels say."

"Dad told me once that all of that business about two men meeting and waiting on the other one to pull their guns was a creation of novelists."

"What did he say it was like?" Lance asked. He found himself making mental notes about Logan Smith as he did with all prospective pilots. He had no idea about the man's skill in the air, but he wanted to know more about the man himself.

"Well, Dad said that those old-time desperadoes didn't fool around with courtly duels." He grinned at Lance and said, "They'd wait in a dark alley some night until their enemy went by, then step out and shoot them in the back of the head."

"Not very noble, I'm afraid," Doctor Laurent said.

"Well, perhaps not, and there may have been exceptions. But mostly they were a pretty motley crew." Logan went on to describe some of the outlaws of the early West that his father had known. "I met Frank James once."

"You mean the outlaw, Frank James? The brother of Jesse?" Danielle exclaimed. "That's like something out of a storybook!"

"He was a tall fellow, big mustache, not too exciting. I think he shot a few people when they weren't looking, too. The James boys have been pretty well romanticized, but they were just criminals."

Suddenly Lance asked, "Would you shoot anyone in the back? If you were flying, I mean?"

Somehow Logan knew instantly that this was a test for him. Carefully he answered, "I have had no combat experience, Captain Winslow, but I've talked to one of the pilots who was in the hospital, Mark Jamison."

"Yes. I know Jamison. A good man. Has two kills."

"Jamison said," Logan spoke carefully, "that the point of flying an airplane is to shoot down the enemy, and the best way to do that is to come at him from out of the sun on his tail. He said he didn't see much point in being polite and saying, 'I beg your pardon,' before firing."

"So it's not really much different from the desperadoes in the Old West, stepping out of the alley."

"Maybe a little bit different. Those men who were shot like that were not expecting it, but isn't it true, sir, that every time you climb into an airplane you know you're putting your life at risk? And the enemy knows the same thing. So it isn't quite the same."

"That's a good way of looking at it, Smith. You'll find out, if you join us, that we're out to shoot down as many Germans as we can. If three of us can get on one of theirs, then so much the better. This isn't a courtly duel that you read about in the medieval romances."

"I always loved those stories," Jo said. "Two men on big chargers with lances and shields rushing toward each other. One of them winning, one of them losing."

"I've noticed some of your fellow writers make out our patrols to be the same way. Sort of a nightly duel among noble adversaries." Lance nodded with approval. "I've been reading your stories, some of them, and I noticed that you don't put out that kind of nonsense. I commend you for it."

"I'm glad you like what I write, Captain Winslow."

"Oh, call me Lance!"

"All right, Lance. I'm glad you like what I write. Is there anything you didn't like?" Jo asked.

"You want me to critique your writing here at the table?"

"I'd like to know what you think."

"I think you're too easy on the Germans. We've got to kill them before they kill us."

It was a raw, hard statement that did not seem to fit in with the beautiful white tablecloth, the crystal goblets, and the gleaming china. The war was something happening far away in a trench, or high in the air, where death could come instantly. Here in this beautiful dining room, with polite conversation, it seemed to be a jarring note. Lance noticed it and said, "This is no place to talk about that. Tell us some more about your American desperadoes."

Logan spoke at length about his family, and when the conversation turned to a different subject, Danielle said, "You miss your family, don't you?"

"Yes, I do. Quite a bit."

"Do you have any brothers and sisters?"

"Only one brother, Frank. Two years younger than I am."

"Do you think he'll come and join as you have?"

"I hope not. One of us is enough, and besides, America will come into the war sooner or later."

The meal went off smoothly enough, and afterward, in the parlor, Danielle found herself sitting beside Logan and showing him family photographs mounted in an album. Across the room Gabby was monopolizing the attention of Lance and Jo.

"Is this you?"

"No," Danielle said quickly in a whisper. "That's my sister. You know she was killed in a Zeppelin raid. Lance is desolate. They were very much in love."

"What was she like? Like you?"

"Oh no. She was much better than I am."

"Good you think so," Logan grinned. He studied the picture for a time and said, "She's a very beautiful woman. You must miss her a great deal."

"Lance misses her more than anyone." She continued to speak for some time about Lance and about her dead sister, Noelle. Something in her tone and in the way she looked across the room at Lance Winslow set off a small alarm in Logan's mind. *She seems very interested in her brother-in-law,* he thought. He watched as her eyes went to him again and again and wondered what it meant.

Finally the evening came to an end, and Jo took Logan back to the hospital in her sidecar. She dropped him off and said, "Good luck tomorrow. I hope you impress the captain."

"So do I. It was a fine evening, wasn't it?"

"You and Dani seemed to hit it off. I thought you two were mortal enemies."

"Well, we gave each other a hard time when I first got to the hospital." He stood beside the motorcycle on one foot looking down at her. "But she's a fine girl." He hesitated, then said, "I noticed that she likes Captain Winslow a great deal."

Jo did not answer, for she had observed the same thing and had her own ideas on the subject. "They're a very close family. Lance is very fortunate to have them to take care of Gabby."

"That girl's a sweetheart, isn't she?"

"They say she looks just like her mother, and she's bright as a new penny. Well, as I said, good luck tomorrow. What do they say in the theater? 'Break a leg'?"

"I don't want to break anything tomorrow. I'm going to be on my best behavior. Good night, Jo."

"Good night. It will be good to see Rev again."

"Yes, it will. I can hardly wait."

He turned and walked into the hospital, and Jo revved the engine of the motorcycle up and made her way back to her quarters. When she went inside, as usual, Bedford reared up on her and nearly knocked her to the floor. She got him calmed down, took a bath, and then sat for a long time propped up in bed writing. Finally she put her writing materials away and began to pray, as she usually did. She found herself praying, "Lord, I pray that you'd give Logan grace in your sight. He wants so badly to get out of the ground war and into the air, so I don't know how to pray about these things, but I trust you to do what's best for him."

★ ★ ★ ★

"Well, here it is. We'll just go up and try some very fundamental maneuvers."

"She's a beautiful plane. Looks like a delight to fly," Logan said.

Logan had arrived at the airport just after dawn and had waited until Captain Winslow had approached him. The two had gone out to the airfield, and now they were standing looking at the Nieuport

17. It was painted white except for a target of blue, white, and red on the upper sections of the top wing, and the rudder had the same colors. The fixed undercarriage seemed sturdy, and for the next hour, Logan sat in the cockpit while Winslow instructed him on the peculiarities of the Nieuport. "You'll notice that we've installed the steel plates on the propellers."

"It must have been terrible trying to stand up and fire a gun placed over the wing."

"It was no fun," Winslow said. "Someday someone will invent an even better system. As for now, it gives us an edge."

"You like this particular machine gun, Captain?" He touched the handle of the Vickers machine gun and turned to face his instructor.

"It's a little bit too lightweight, I think, but better ones are coming."

"What do the Germans use?"

"A Spandau. A very fine gun."

"But this one will do well enough. It fires very rapidly, and you won't have any trouble with it. Are you ready now?"

"Yes, sir."

"Fine. Just follow me, and when we get up, after we've flown through the simple maneuvers, I'll hold my hand up. That means I want you to follow every maneuver I make. You won't be able to, of course, since you haven't flown a machine this powerful, but do the best you can. I'll be able to tell something about what kind of flier you are."

"Yes, Captain."

An hour later Winslow looked with approval at the mirror he had had installed. It was something he had come up with himself. On long patrols a man was apt to get a neck ache trying to look over his shoulder constantly, and if an enemy got on your tail, one glance into the mirror was much quicker than trying to swivel your head.

He's really quite exceptional. I'm surprised, Lance thought. *But now let's give him something really tough.*

He held his hand up, and a glance in the mirror showed Smith nodding at him. Instantly he hauled back on the stick and sent his Nieuport into a steep climb. He had done it very quickly and was pleased to see that Smith was right with him. *Good reaction time,* he thought. *Now, let's see if he can follow me in a roll.*

For the next ten minutes Lance put the Nieuport through every tricky maneuver he could think of. He was shocked and pleased to find out that Logan Smith stayed with him practically all the time.

He managed to lose him only twice, and that was by using techniques that he himself had perfected for losing enemy fighters.

Finally he signaled toward the ground, and the two sailed back toward earth.

Logan scrambled out of his plane and came over at once to stand before Winslow. "She's a marvelous airplane, sir!"

"Well, I'm very happy that you like her because you'll be flying it from now on."

"You mean I'm accepted?"

"There are a lot of things I don't know about you, Smith, but one thing I know, you're a good pilot."

Logan flushed. "Thank you, sir. I'll do my very best for you."

"I don't want any heroes in my squadron. You'll take it slow and easy and learn how to fight as a team. We were talking last night about knights roaming out on adventures and taking on dragons and that sort of rot. We do not do that in my squadron. We fight as a team. You will protect your fellow fighters, and they will protect you. Get that one thing in your head. No heroes, no knightly quests."

"Yes, sir!"

"Now, come along. You'll meet the men that make up the Twenty-fourth Squadron."

The rest of the squadron was gathered in the hut that had been set apart for recreation. It was merely a large room with a few tables, chairs, and lamps. All of them were drinking, and one sat over in a corner playing a violin.

"Knock off that violin playing, Harold. I want you to meet our new pilot. This is Logan Smith. You'll be able to tell as soon as he opens his mouth that he's an American."

The vein of humor that ran under Lance Winslow's strict exterior surfaced then. "He comes from a family of outlaws, I understand, from the Wild West. So be careful. He's not carrying his two guns today, as is his custom."

A laugh went up and at once the fliers began to give Logan a hard time. Sailor Malone came to stand before him. He had a tough face and was strongly built. "An outlaw American, eh? Well, I always wanted to meet one. How many buffalos do you usually shoot before breakfast?"

"Not more than I can eat at one time," Logan grinned. He was prepared for such rough handling as this, for he had received it all of his life. He had been with men who were accustomed to facing danger for a long time now, men in the rodeo and then, of course, in the Legion. Now his eyes went around as the men introduced themselves. These would be the men in whose hands he would put his life, and they were entirely different from what he had expected.

Cecil Lewis was sitting in a chair tilted back against the wall. He had a book in his hand, as usual, and he said, "Do you read, old boy?"

"Words of one syllable."

Lewis's eyes gleamed with humor. "I'll read you some poetry from time to time. You Americans need some more culture."

"Thank you. I'll be glad to receive whatever you have for me."

"Do you play the piano?" Harold Holmes asked.

"No. I'm afraid not."

"Too bad. I thought we could play a duet."

"If you don't lay off of that violin, I'm going to shove it in your ear, Harold! It's the most mournful sound I ever heard!" Copper Jennings said as he came and sized up the American with a pair of knowing eyes. "How much flying experience have you had?"

"Not enough."

"That's a good answer, and it applies to some of the rest of you," Lance said. "Now, he'll be in your flight, Copper, so take care of him. Teach him what he needs to know."

As Lance left the room, he noticed that whatever other abilities his new recruit might or might not have, he had the ability to assimilate himself into a group. *He seems to be a pretty tough fellow,* Lance thought as he stopped outside and moved toward the headquarters building. *I hope he lasts longer than some of the others did.*

★ ★ ★ ★

"No, this is not my favorite baby. This is Helen."

Jo took the doll that Gabby handed her and smoothed the hair back. "She's very pretty. She's not your favorite?"

"No. My favorite is Frances."

"Well, may I see her?"

"Yes." Gabby dashed across the room, opened a chest, and pulled a doll out. It was an old doll, not particularly attractive, but the child held it very carefully. "This is Frances."

"Oh, and she's your favorite?"

"Yes. My mother gave her to me when I was just a baby." She held the plain and not so attractive doll very tightly.

"She's a very beautiful baby. I know you love her very much."

"Yes. She's my very special baby." She looked up and said, "Did you have dolls when you were a girl, mademoiselle?"

"Oh yes. I suppose all girls have dolls."

"What were their names?"

Jo had discovered that Gabby had an inquiring mind and wanted to know every little detail about everything, which made it easy to entertain her. Now she sat in the room that belonged to Gabby on the single bed surrounded by dolls. It brought her childhood back to her, and she smiled and reached over and passed her hand over Gabby's shining hair. "I had a favorite doll, too, and my mother gave her to me when I was about your age."

"What was her name?"

"Her name was Miss Cordelia."

"That's a funny name," Gabby giggled.

"Yes, it is. I don't even know where it came from now."

"Do you still have her?"

"Packed away somewhere back at my parents' house. I suppose I'll give her to my little girl when I have one someday."

"Miss Cordelia. That's a funny name. What did she look like?"

Gabby listened intensely as Jo described her doll, and finally she said, "Could we have a tea party?"

"Yes. Grandpère's home. Can he come too?"

"I think so, and maybe Aunt Dani would like to join us."

The tea party turned out to be quite exciting for Gabby. She was a lonely child, Jo had discovered, and to have her grandfather join in the tea party was very special for her. She asked more than once when her father would be coming back, and each time either Danielle or Doctor Laurent would give her an evasive answer.

Somehow this troubled Jo, and when she got Danielle alone, she said, "She's very lonely for her father."

"Yes. Ever since her mother died, she clings to him."

"He's very busy. I don't suppose he comes as often as he would like."

A shadow passed across Danielle's face. "No. He doesn't, but as you say, he's very busy."

They went back into the tea party, and Doctor Laurent, who loved Gabby quite fiercely, was holding her on his lap. "We have decided that you are to marry Logan Smith, Dani."

Danielle gave her father a surprised glance and laughed. "You're always making matches for me. Last time it was the son of that manufacturer, the one with the slick black hair."

"He was a nice fellow."

"His hair was so slick a fly would fall down and break his leg if he landed on it," Danielle said.

Gabby found this frightfully funny and giggled. "I'd like to see that," she said.

"You wouldn't like him, Gabby," Danielle smiled. "He was too full of himself."

"What does that mean? Full of himself?" Gabby asked with a puzzled expression.

"Well," Danielle smiled. "He was in love with himself. He couldn't think of anyone else."

"In any case, I've decided you shall marry the cowboy. Then we can all go live on his ranch in the American West." Doctor Laurent was feeling particularly good that day. "I could get me some woolly chaps and some high-heeled boots and a huge sombrero."

"Not a sombrero. A Stetson," Jo said.

The amiable talk went on for some time, and finally Doctor Laurent left. It had been a long day, and Gabby finally took her favorite doll, Frances, and crawled up into Danielle's lap and listened as the two women talked.

Jo smiled. "Your father is quite a matchmaker."

"Oh, he's always saying things like that. I'm about as likely to marry the prime minister as I am Logan Smith."

"He's a very fine young man and comes from a good family."

"He's an American."

Jo was amused. "You sound like you just said he's a criminal."

"Oh, I don't mean that, but Americans are so different. I don't mean to be insulting."

"Well, we think the same of you French," Jo smiled. "But I hope you get to know Logan better. He's very idealistic, you know."

"Is he? I wouldn't have thought that. He seems so—well, so practical."

"Well, he's that too. Whatever he sets out to do, he puts his whole heart into it. But he's idealistic, too. I'll tell you a secret."

"Yes?"

"You know Lance was talking about knights and things like that and how he didn't want his fliers to think of themselves in that way?"

"I remember."

"I think sometimes Logan does think of himself that way. Sort of a flying cavalier."

"That is romantic. I would never have suspected it. You don't think of men as being idealistic or romantic or artistic."

"Some of them aren't, of course," Jo shrugged. "But it's something I've seen in Logan ever since I've known him."

This information seemed to interest Danielle, and the women spoke of him for some time.

Suddenly, without warning, Gabby began to sniffle. Startled, Jo looked down and saw tears running down her face.

"I'll put her to bed. When she gets tired she gets upset like this. Wait for me in the parlor. I'll be right back."

Jo went at once to the parlor, and ten minutes later Danielle joined her. "Is she ill?"

"Oh no. She has these times of depression. She misses her mother so much."

"Your family is all she has then, I suppose."

"Yes. That is true." Danielle's eyes went up to one of the pictures on the mantel. It was a picture of Noelle Winslow, Lance's deceased wife. Danielle said, "Lance loved her so much, and when he sees Gabby, he sees her."

"It's very sad. You were very young when they married, I suppose."

Startled, Danielle looked at her. "Yes . . . yes, I was."

Something about Danielle's attitude confirmed what Jo had thought, and she wondered about the relationship between the two. Finally she said, "Does she know what kind of thing he does? Flying? I mean, every time he goes up, there's a chance he may not come back."

A look of pain flickered briefly in Danielle Laurent's eyes. "She doesn't realize what it means." There was a silence and she bowed her head. "But I know. We all know."

Jo said no more, but after she left the house, she thought for a long time about the Laurent family. She knew that the lives of fliers were notoriously brief. Some of the new men, she had found out, lasted an average of no more than three or four weeks. Only experts survived this test.

As she rode her motorcycle home, she thought of Lance being shot out of the skies by German bullets, and a grief settled on her. "He's had so much sorrow already, and he has a daughter to care for." Compassion filled her heart, and she knew she would not be able to set it aside.

CHAPTER SIXTEEN

A COWBOY IN FRANCE

★ ★ ★ ★

To Logan Smith the aerodrome had become his universe. It was not an ornate world. It consisted primarily of crude huts and tents, and the hangars rested on the mud when the spring rains came. Everything was makeshift, and there was nothing particularly attractive about any of it.

Logan had taken his place in the sleeping quarters, which had plenty of dogs and cats and reeked of wet, smelly clothes. The walls were furnished with relics of the war, shattered propellers, patches of enemy insignias, and group photographs of fliers, many of whom were already dead. Logan often felt a shiver when he looked at them. Men with arms around one another staring into the camera, and where were they now? Blown to bits by enemy fire, burned to a crisp, or shattered by an engine explosion.

He had learned his trade well and quickly. He had not flown any combat yet, but he knew that challenge was coming soon. The war was grinding on as huge armies met each other in the fields with steel bayonets. The trenches now stretched all the way from Switzerland near Basel to the North Sea. On both sides the enemies lined up to their knees in mud, and men died like flies of disease, quicker even than from the enemy's bullets.

This particular aerodrome, like most of the others, was in a semipermanent condition. It was set down near the town with one or two major roads passing through it. Recently, the flying field had been covered with tarmac, a mixture of tar and macadam. Such strips were easily patched when they were bombed by the enemy. The hangars were scattered randomly over the landscape, plain, homely wooden structures with corrugated iron roofs. Each hangar had room for a dozen machines, and each was a beehive of activity.

Three mechanics were usually assigned to each plane, and they worked over them as grooms worked over fine thoroughbreds. Mechanics were filthy with oil stains, their hands black with grime. The squadron had from twenty to twenty-four planes, depending on how many were shot down or had been damaged in a battle.

The living quarters were primitive, and even such a thing as a hot shower or bath became a luxury. Most of the officers spent their spare hours on the base at a lounge, drinking themselves past good sense. They fled the aerodrome whenever possible, vying over passes to Paris, and came back, as often as not, half carried in, for drunkenness was a common problem among the pilots. Whether legally obtained or otherwise, brandy and whiskey were always available. Many of the men were suffering from battle fatigue, although no one called it that, and the alcohol made it worse.

Things turned for the better for Logan when on August 15 Revelation Brown showed up. He suddenly appeared in the hangar where Logan was talking with several of the mechanics about a problem he had encountered with the ailerons. The first Logan sensed of him was when he heard Rev's voice, saying, "Hey, partner, I'm here! We can get on with the war now!"

"Rev!" Logan ran toward him, and dropping his bags, Rev engaged in a wrestling bear hug, and the two men waltzed over the greasy floor of the hangar. The other mechanics looked on with a grin, for officers did not greet their mechanics with such enthusiasm.

"Fellas, I want you to meet Revelation Brown. Better known as Rev. I want you to make him feel at home."

Rev went around to half a dozen mechanics getting their names and inquiring as to the spiritual condition of each one. After the first "Are you saved?" the others tried to shy away, but Rev was outgoing and obviously delighted to find out about each man's spiritual condition.

"Actually," Logan said, "I doubt if any of them's got any religion at all except working on airplanes and drinking all the French wine they can get a hold of."

"Ah now, Lieutenant. Don't give us that," Max Sutherland said. He was a fine mechanic in his own right and worked primarily on Copper Jennings' Nieuport. "You can come to church with me. We've got a good one. The preacher's a hot number."

"Sounds good to me, partner," Rev said. Then they all turned, for Captain Lance Winslow had entered the room.

"Captain, this is Private Revelation Brown. I've told you all about him."

"How do you do, Brown?" Lance nodded. "If you're half as good as the lieutenant says, I'll love you like a brother. Have you worked on Nieuports before?"

"No, but I know rotary engines pretty good, Captain," Revelation said. "Give me a day or two to take one apart, and I'll see what I can do." He added without a breath, "Are you washed in the blood of the Lamb, Captain?"

Lance could not restrain the smile that came to his lips. He had already been warned by Logan of Rev's peculiar methods of evangelism.

"As a matter of fact, I am," he said. "Sometimes I don't live like it, but I've been a Christian for quite a while."

"First rate, sir! Now, give me one of these planes to work on, and I'll get acquainted with it."

"Well, of course, you'll be Lieutenant Smith's master mechanic. After all, you two are old friends."

A few days later Sutherland told the captain, "He's a wizard, sir. I never saw anything like it." He shook his head in admiration. "It's almost like he just waves his hand, and those engines just open up to him. Never saw anything like it in my life."

"Good! We need all the help we can get."

★ ★ ★ ★

By the time Revelation had settled down and ascertained the spiritual condition of every man on the base, he had also mastered the engines of the Nieuports and every other part of the aircraft. He seemed perfectly happy, and he and Logan had many long talks about the States and what was happening there and the men and planes of the Fourteenth Squadron.

"What do you think of the captain, Logan?" Rev asked. He had pulled an engine apart and now was oiling all of the segments, holding them lovingly in his enormous hands. "Is he a pretty hot pilot?"

"Yes, he is. About the best I've ever seen," Logan said.

"He seems like kind of a hard case. Why is that?"

Logan shifted. He did not like to talk about his superior officer, but after all, Rev was his old friend. "He's got problems, Rev. He lost his wife in a bombing raid, and he's got a burning hatred for Germans. That's all he thinks about, killing Germans."

"Well, that's one way to look at it. That's what he's here for, isn't it?"

"I know, but it controls his whole life. He's got a fine daughter, but he hardly ever goes to see her. His wife's family lives in town. They think a lot of the captain, but I think he's got such a bug about revenge that he doesn't treat his in-laws squarely."

"That's pretty bad news. Do the men like him?" Rev asked as he reached for a wrench.

"I think they're afraid of him in a way. He's cold to them. Doesn't have any real friends. Of course, maybe that's the way it should be with a squadron commander."

"Well, I'll pray for the captain and for you, too. Have you shot at any Germans yet?"

"I haven't got a sniff of one. Captain Winslow's been keeping me pretty close to the base here doing maneuvers. He's strong on formation flying." Logan shifted uncomfortably and stared at Revelation. "I think it's foolishness."

"Well, planes have to stay together, don't they?"

"Well, this is different from just staying together. He wants us to fly so that our wing tips are practically touching. You know what that means?"

"Have to pay pretty close attention to what you're doing or you'll smash up with your buddy."

"Exactly right. So I'm busy looking at Copper on my left and Pug Hardeston on my right. How can I watch for Jerries overhead and do that at the same time?"

"What does the captain say about it?"

"He says the squadron leader will look for the enemy, but that doesn't make sense. Better that twelve men look than just one set of eyes."

"You talk to the captain about this?"

"Who me? I'm the new kid on the block. He wouldn't listen to anything I had to say. Anyway, it seems foolish to me."

"How would you do it?"

"Spread out where there's no danger of crashing into one another. That way all three men in our flight could be looking for the Jerries to pounce down on us."

The very next day Logan was once again frustrated as the squadron was practicing flying in formation. His flight leader, Copper Jennings, was on his left, while Pug Hardeston was on his right. They had left for a somewhat longer reconnaissance flight than was necessary, and Copper had said, "I'll look out for the Jerries. You fellas keep an eye down on the ground. See if you can make anything out of the troop movements."

The sun was high in the air, and as his engine roared and wind whipped past his ears, Logan had all he could do to keep formation with his two comrades. They had been flying for thirty minutes when suddenly, without warning, he saw a hole suddenly appear in his windshield. It spattered in front of him, and without thinking, he hauled back on the stick. Then he heard the sound of gunfire. As he rolled upward and over, he saw three German fighter planes had come out of the sun and attacked his flight from the rear. Desperately he tried to remember the instructions, but his mind seemed to be a blank. Every movement was by instinct. He did remember one bit of advice that Hardeston had given him. "If you're going to take evasive action, turn left, not right. The Germans will be expecting you to turn right, which is the way a right-handed man will turn."

Wrenching his stick and kicking at the pedals, he twisted the Nieuport into the tightest left turn possible. He saw the German Fokker as it shot past him, and as he completed his turn, he suddenly was on the tail of the plane that was going for Hardeston. He quickly aimed the plane and loosed a stream of bullets, the first time he had fired in combat. The tracers fell in behind the plane and he made an adjustment, watching the white streamers as they hit the tail of the Fokker. He saw the bullets go up the fuselage. The pilot suddenly lunged forward, then slumped down. The Fokker nose-dived, and with a yell he did not know he was uttering, Logan followed him down. He loosed more shots and saw some hit the engine, which burst into flame immediately.

Suddenly reason came back to him. He looked around and saw that the other two Germans had fled. He did not see Pug Hardeston or Copper Jennings for a moment, and then he saw them coming back. They had taken evasive action. He wiggled his wings, and Hardeston and Jennings motioned toward the base.

As they flew along, Logan found himself trembling. He had been in some fistfights before, but now he had seen his bullets tear into the enemy, and then a sickening feeling came over him as he watched the plane crash and burst into a fiery inferno far below.

I've killed a man.

The thought shook him, and he could not control the trembling of his hands.

Even when he landed, he was unsteady. He got out of the plane and found himself suddenly picked up off the ground by Pug, who was a muscular man.

"You got him! You got him!" Pug yelled.

"You sure did!" Copper grinned. "That one's confirmed. You done for that Jerry."

The three went hurriedly into the headquarters, where they excitedly gave the report of their mission to Captain Winslow.

"And you all saw the plane go down?"

"Yes, sir!" Copper and Pug said enthusiastically.

"You know, sometimes we think we've shot somebody down. They go down low and then they limp on in. I've done the same thing myself. I'm sure I've been claimed as a victory by some of the Germans."

"Not this one, sir." Copper shook his head definitely. "We saw him plow right into the ground. It blew up like an oil tank. It's a kill, all right."

"Well then," Winslow said. "Congratulations. That's your first." He studied Logan's face and found something there that troubled him. "Feeling a little bit queasy?"

"Well, yes, sir. I guess I am."

"Natural enough. You'll get over it. By the time you've done it twenty times, it'll just be another job."

Logan did not answer. He was still seeing the German's body slump as his bullets tore into it. "It wasn't like I thought it would be," he said.

"It never is, but you've been blooded now. There's one less of the Huns to kill."

As always, the squadron was excited when anyone made a kill, and Logan had been accepted by all of the men. Jerold Spencer, the ex-steeplechase jockey, said, "I got a poem I learned."

A groan went up, but Logan said, "I'd like to hear it."

Clearing his throat, Spencer quoted, amid much laughter, a well-known poem.

> "Beneath a busted Camel, its former pilot lay:
> His throat was cut by the bracing wire, the tank had hit his head,
> And coughing a shower of dental work, these parting words he said:

Oh I'm going to a better land, they binge there every night,
The cocktails grow on bushes, so everyone stays tight,
They've torn up all the calendars, they busted all the clocks,
And little drops of whiskey come tinkling down the rocks,
The pilot breathed these last few gasps before he passed away;
I'll tell you how it happened, my flippers didn't stay,
The motor wouldn't hit at all, the struts were far too few,
A shot went through the petrol tank and let it all leak through.
Oh I'm going to a better land, where motors always run,
Where the eggnog grows on the eggplant, and the pilots grow.
They've got no Sops, they got no Spads, they got DH–4s,
And the little frosted juleps are served at all the stores."

Laughter went up, and Logan said, "My heart is really touched, Spencer."

The celebration went on, and finally Cecil Lewis came to stand beside Logan. He had not taken much of a part in the celebration, and he had seen that Logan was forcing his laughter.

"Not feeling so good," he said. "Well, that's natural. I remember when I got my first one. I threw up everything I had."

"It's what we're here for," Logan said quietly, "but I keep thinking about what he looked like."

"Yes. And you keep thinking it might be you."

Surprise washed across Logan's face. "Do we all feel the same way?"

"We'd be fools if we didn't."

"How am I going to get over it?" Logan said. "You think it'll have any effect when I go back up again? Will I back off? Chicken out?"

"You can't do that," Lewis said. "We've all got to do our job, and that's what our job happens to be. The captain was pleased, I suppose."

"Well, yes. Of course he was."

"You know, after the war's over, I don't know what Captain Winslow will do. He's got one passion now, and that's killing Germans. That'll be against the law after the war. What will he do then?"

"Well, I guess he'll do like the rest of us. He'll go back to business."

Lewis shook his head slowly. "I hope so, but some men take it harder than others." He was smoking a pipe, and now he sent a purple wreath of smoke into the air. "I'm worried about the captain. A man needs something besides killing Germans in his heart."

* * * *

That night at the Laurents' for dinner, Lance spoke of Logan's victory. "He got his first German today, a Fokker. From what I understand from his flight commander, he has reactions like nothing human."

"Did he get hurt?" Danielle asked quickly.

"No. A bullet went right past his head and out his windshield. Hardeston said he never saw anyone react so quickly, and that's good. It probably saved his life. Maybe the other two men, too. They got caught napping." He sat there thinking about it for a while, then said, "It was a near miss, but he made it all right this time."

Later on, after Gabby had been put to bed despite her many protests, Lance had come downstairs to stand silently in the center of the parlor. He thought he was alone and suddenly started when he saw Danielle sitting in the shadows in a winged chair. "Oh, I didn't know you were here, Dani."

"Did she go to sleep?"

"Oh yes. She was very tired."

"Did you tell her a story?"

"She asked for one, but I couldn't think of any except 'The Three Little Pigs.' Not a very exciting story."

Danielle rose from the chair and came over to stand beside him. The room was semidark with only one small lamp lit. The rest of the family had gone to bed, and the silence seemed to hang over the room.

"It's not what story it is. It's just hearing one. I'm glad you told her that one."

Lance felt uncomfortable. He often did with Danielle and did not know why. Now he stood looking down at her and saw that she seemed troubled. "What's the matter?" he asked. "Something wrong?"

"No. Why do you ask?"

She was wearing a light green dress, and her hair was done up in a different fashion he had never seen before, a twist at the back that gave her a fashionable look. She was not usually one, he thought, to experiment with new fashions. Now he grew more concerned. "There is something wrong. I can see it in your eyes."

"It's nothing."

"Come. You can tell me." He reached out suddenly and took one of her hands and held it in both of his. It was warm and soft and felt very strong. "Come on. Just think of me as your older brother."

"You're *not* my brother!" she snapped.

The vehemence of Danielle's reply caused Lance to blink. "Well, of course not, actually, but I've always felt that way. Anyway, you have problems I might not be able to fix, but I can listen."

He was still holding her hand, and Danielle was very conscious of it. His hands were beautifully shaped. She had always thought so and loved them, and now he held her hand tightly, unaware, perhaps, of the pressure he was putting on her. Suddenly without meaning to, she reached up and put her hand on his cheek. It was a gesture of trust and something she had often longed to do. She leaned closer to him and whispered, "Oh, Lance, I'm so mixed up!" She suddenly leaned over against him.

Taken completely by surprise, Lance put his free arm around her and felt her begin to tremble. "Why, Dani!" he stammered. "What is it?"

But she could not answer. The pressure of his arms about her, light as it was, had stirred her, for it was something she had often dreamed about. Now his hand was holding hers, his other arm around her, and held in a half embrace. She suddenly felt herself unable to control her emotions. This was unusual, for Danielle Laurent was a strong woman. All the feelings she had tried to ignore suddenly loosed in her, and as she looked up at him tears brimmed in her eyes. She tried to speak, and her lips were soft and vulnerable and trembled.

Lance Winslow was completely nonplussed. He was not good, or so he thought, at comforting people, especially lovely young women who were on the verge of tears. If it had been Noelle, he would have known what to say, but for this moment he had forgotten Noelle. Now he was conscious of the lilac perfume that Danielle wore. It was subtle and yet somehow potent. He had smelled so much gasoline and castor oil in the stench of battle that the gentle fragrance was half intoxicating to him. Her eyes seemed to be pleading with him, and he saw that her lips were trembling. He tightened his grasp, and with what he thought was a brotherly gesture, he leaned over and kissed her cheek, which was damp with tears.

"Don't cry, Dani," he said. "It can't be that bad." At that moment he realized that she was not Dani Laurent, the fourteen-year-old girl he had somehow always kept in his mind. No, this was a lovely young woman, fully mature. With a quick motion he stepped back and released her awkwardly. He was tremendously embarrassed. "I'm so sorry, Dani. Perhaps you'd rather be alone."

She did not answer, and the sense of being ill at ease came over him even stronger. "I've got to get back to the base. Good night."

"Good night, Lance."

As soon as the door closed, Danielle moved shakily to a chair and slumped down. She put her face in her hands, and sobs began to rack her shoulders. It was the first sign of weakness she had shown in years. "I thought I was getting over him, but I'm not. It's worse," she sobbed.

★ ★ ★ ★

"These French sure know how to cook," Rev said as he bit an enormous chunk out of the bread he had layered with yellow butter. He chewed thoroughly and raised his eyebrows. "I will admit they cook some things better than we do, but I bet they can't make barbecue."

Logan grinned. "They wouldn't know what barbecue was, Rev."

Jo laughed, saying, "Don't tell them. We need something American in the kitchen."

The three had gone out to a restaurant after Logan had returned from a mission. Jo had been waiting for several hours, during which time she had talked with Rev. The two had become very close. Most of their conversation had to do with the pilots, and Rev had become an expert on each man. He knew all of their weaknesses as a good servant will know the weaknesses of his master. He had shared all this with Jo, knowing she was genuinely interested.

As the meal progressed, Revelation eventually steered the conversation to theology. He said, "You know that German flier that bailed out and got captured? I talked to him quite a bit."

"I bet I know the first thing you said to him, Rev," Jo smiled. "You said, 'Are you saved?' Come on. Isn't that true?"

"Well, he didn't speak much English, and I don't speak any German at all. But I got me an interpreter, and, sure enough, that's what I asked him. You know what he said?" Rev looked surprised. "He said he's been a Christian since he was thirteen years old, and he feels like he's serving God and his country in what he's doing."

"The same thing we say," Logan said. "I guess it's always that way in a war. Both sides feel like God is on their side."

"That's right," Jo said, who had studied the history of wars thoroughly.

"Well, I think you can't look at it like that. There's only been one Holy War," Rev said dogmatically.

"One Holy War? Which one is that, Rev?"

"It's the one in the Old Testament when God told Joshua and his boys to clean up on the Philistines. You know, those heathens. Now that's the kind of war I'd like to be in, when God just comes out and admits whose side He's on." His eyes grew thoughtful, and he nibbled at a piece of beef. "It was funny. He wasn't no more than twenty years old. You know, Logan, he kind of reminded me of some of the boys we grew up with back home. I bet you knew some just like him. He seemed like a good kid. No harm in him, but there he was trying to kill you, and you were trying to kill him."

"What do you make of it, Rev?"

"Can't make anything out of it. All I know is God's put you here, and He's put me here, and we're gonna do the best we can. 'Whatsoever thy hand finds to do, do it with all thy might.' "

Shortly after this Rev rose up and said, "I've got to get back to the field. I ain't satisfied with the way your engine's runnin'."

"It sounded all right to me."

"What would you know about it? You do the fightin' and I'll do the fixin'."

After Rev had left, Jo shook her head. "He's one of a kind, isn't he? I bet if he met a general, he'd ask him if he were saved."

"I bet he would, too."

Logan lounged back in his seat and sipped at the tea that remained in his cup. "You've become pretty close to the Laurents, haven't you, Jo?"

"Yes. They're a fine family. All of them."

"What do you make of Dani?"

Jo stared at him. "What do you mean?"

"Well, to tell the truth, I kind of like her."

Jo fastened her eyes on Logan. He was wearing a fresh uniform, he had showered, and now he looked very handsome as he sat there leaning back. His hands were big and square and brown and looked very strong. The teacup looked very small in them. He was thoughtful now but insistent.

"I'm not much of a ladies' man, and I've taken my best shot, but she just doesn't seem interested. I wonder if she's got a boyfriend tucked away that I haven't heard about."

"I think," Jo said slowly, "there may be someone else."

Logan looked at her quickly. "Who do you think?"

"I can't say, but I have a feeling that he may be somehow unobtainable."

"Well, I may not be too smart, but I'm stubborn. You'll have to give me that. I'll have to turn on the charm."

"You do that. She's a fine girl. Strong minded, though. What would you do with her back in the States after the war is over?"

"Oh, I might stay over here and become a Frenchman."

"I can't see that," Jo jeered. "You'll be back flying airplanes, or riding wild horses, or something like that."

They sat for a long time talking, and finally they went outside, where Bedford was tied to the motorcycle. He came whining, then when he got into the seat at a signal from Jo, Logan laughed. "That's the funniest thing I've ever seen! You and that dog riding around. Why don't you teach him to drive, and you can ride in the sidecar."

"He's smart enough," Jo said. She rubbed Bedford's head, then gave Logan a strange look. "I know you're serious about Danielle, and I want you to be. She deserves a good man."

"You know something about this fellow she likes, don't you?"

"Nothing I can really put my finger on. But you're a good man, Logan Smith. Put yourself into it."

"I'll do that. Good night, Jo."

"Good night, Logan."

★ ★ ★ ★

Three days later Logan shot down two planes in less than thirty seconds. He had been flying in close formation and had glimpsed two bombers off to the right. Without thinking he peeled off out of the formation and threw his Nieuport into a steep dive. He had completely forgotten that Captain Winslow was in another formation above him. Indeed, he had forgotten everything. He took the first bomber from above and saw it burst into flames as the tracers hit the engine.

The second took evasive action, but it was a slow-moving affair, and Logan managed to come up and get a belly shot. He was no more than fifty yards away when he racked the entire plane from rudder to nose. The bullets seemed to have no effect, and the pilot veered away sharply again. Making a tight turn, Logan shot ahead of the bomber and wheeled to take him head on. He poured his bullets into the nose of the bomber, saw the windshield disintegrate, and pulled up just in time to escape the explosion. Parts of the bomber flew all over the sky, and Logan let out an excited cry.

When he got back to the ground, though, expecting to be commended, he found Lance Winslow livid with anger.

"Look, they may call you *cowboy* around here, but you're not a cowboy! You're an officer in the Royal Flying Corps, and you deliberately disobeyed orders!"

"No, sir! I didn't do that," Logan stammered.

"You broke formation! Do you not know that your orders were to stay in that formation?"

"Yes, sir, but I saw them down below. Two fat bombers. I couldn't miss."

But Lance Winslow was not through. For ten minutes he tore into Logan and finally wound up grounding him from flying any mission for two days.

"You're going to learn to obey orders, or you'll get out of this squadron!" Winslow said.

Later, when Logan tried to explain it to Jo, he said, "I just don't understand him."

"I don't think he understands himself, but it has something to do with the death of his wife."

Jo wrote the story up and sent it home, disguising the names. She did so with apprehension but trusted that Lance would never see it. She thought a great deal about Lance Winslow at this time and found herself wondering what her interest was.

He'll never love any woman but his wife, I don't think. And she's dead. Somehow this thought troubled her. She hated to see a life wasted, and as far as she could see, Lance Winslow had two focuses, to idolize his dead wife and to kill Germans.

"That's not a good mixture," she said. "He needs to snap out of it. None of us can live on hate. . . ."

CHAPTER SEVENTEEN

"You'll Always Love Her, Lance!"

★ ★ ★ ★

October had come to France with cold showers. Jo had almost forgotten what the sun was like and found herself dreaming of being back in America, where, at least, there was still warmth even during the fall. The rain on the Continent was a cold, soaking variety that saturated the clothes and seemed to go down into the bone.

Nevertheless, she felt obligated to see that Bedford got his daily exercise. It was on the third day of that month when she put on her raincoat and galoshes, and took down the large black umbrella that had become standard equipment with her. Bedford, as usual, followed her with his eyes, and when she said, "Walk?" immediately he barked and made a dive at the door.

"Well, you'll have to let me out, you silly creature," Jo grumbled. She pulled the door back, and Bedford dashed out in a flash. Locking the door behind her, Jo opened the umbrella and began walking down the rain-soaked street. Everything seemed to be monochromatic. In the summer every house was a bright flash of flowers, every color imaginable, and the grass itself was green beyond anything she had known in the States. Now, however, the houses seemed to lean against each other with a gray indifference, and the trees wept as a slow, steady rain poured down out of the somber, gray-colored sky.

"Just the thing to cheer me up," Jo muttered. "Nothing like a beautiful day to go for a walk."

She was tired, almost exhausted even, for she had conceived the idea a few weeks back of writing a book. It was to be concerned with the psychology of men at war, and Ed Kovak, her editor back in the States, was excited about the idea. He had promptly offered to market the book for her if she could get it written and would grant him permission to print sections of it as a long-running serial.

The fact that her name was well known in America had not sunk in to Jo Hellinger. She was far away from her home, and although she got copies of her stories printed in the newspapers, somehow it seemed to have nothing to do with her. The book, however, had turned out to be more difficult than she had thought. It had meant becoming involved with the men of the Fourteenth Squadron and others in the area, which had proved to be somewhat depressing. She knew now that her gray mood had something to do with the fact that a young pilot named Benny St. James had gone down over Germany. She had interviewed him several times and had loved his cheerful, bright approach to the deadly life that he led. He had epitomized for her the strength of Britain, and she had watched him go up on his last mission cheerful, smiling, and laughing. He had even yelled at her over the roar of his engine, "I'll bring back the kaiser's helmet for you, Miss Hellinger!"

She had smiled and waved back, but Benny had not returned. She had been shocked beyond measure when Lance had landed and given her the bad news.

"Benny didn't make it," he said quietly. He had seen the pain and grief in her eyes and had turned away, saying quietly, "He was a good man. Just something else to chalk up against the Germans."

Now as Jo walked along the streets, the sound of water rushing down the gutters, she thought of Benny, and the grief seemed to close her throat. She tried to write a story about him, but that had proved impossible. She had obtained the address of his family and had written several letters, tearing up each of them until finally in despair she had written half a page expressing her sorrow and grief. It had seemed so inappropriate. Just a few words on paper was all she could find to say about a man whose life had been crushed, wiped out, obliterated. He had such a bright future, and now there was nothing left of him except a shallow, hurriedly scratched-out grave somewhere in Germany.

The rain began to fall in larger drops now, each one of them making a bull's-eye as it slapped down against the glossy surface that the sidewalk had become. A low rumble of thunder sounded in the distance, and then a flash of lightning flickered across the sky. She shivered and drew her coat closer up under her chin and wondered at Bedford, who was running ahead as if the sun were shining and there were not a drop of rain falling from the sky. She watched as he leaped over a low wall, stopped to sniff a low plant, and then went on down the street ahead of her.

She walked for over an hour, her mind filled with thoughts of war, and discovered that fear had come to be her constant companion. She had expected that as the war went on and she grew more in touch with it, she would somehow become hardened. But this was not the case. Almost every day she looked in the faces of the pilots, she found herself cringing, wondering as she touched one's hand, *Will this hand be cold and still forever tomorrow?* When Harold Holmes sang a song, rollicking and weaving as he played his violin, she watched his eyes and wondered if this would be the last song he would ever play. Immediately after the song was finished, the squadron had left, and she stood watching them until their planes became tiny dots in the sky.

Day after day she became more sensitized to the war. The news that fifty thousand men had died in some battle on the Western Front did not mean as much to her as the loss of someone she knew well like Benny. War had become very personalized, and she did not eat well or sleep well these days.

Finally, she arrived opposite the hospital and on a whim went inside. She went looking for Ringer Jones and found him playing a game of draughts, which is what the English call checkers, with another soldier.

"Bit of a drop outside, eh?" he said as he got up.

"Yes, it is, but I have to walk Bedford."

"How about tea? I can badger a little from the cook."

"That sounds marvelous!" Jo said as she took her wet coat off.

The two found their way to the kitchen, where the cook, a large woman with huge forearms and a pair of merry blue eyes, greeted them. "Well, what are you doing out on a day like this?"

"Have to take Bedford for a walk, Martha. He's worse than a husband to take care of."

"I doubt that. At least not as much trouble as Oscar."

"Has Oscar been giving you trouble again?"

Martha's troubles with her husband, Oscar, were legendary. Jo had seen him only once, a slight, diminutive man with an ineffective chin and a pair of washed-out blue eyes. He apparently had some appeal, for he was constantly giving Martha trouble with one woman after another. He seemed a most unlikely ladies' man, but to Martha he was the handsomest man in the world, a fact that puzzled everyone who knew Oscar.

"Sit down here. I just made a pound cake. Still hot from the oven."

"Oh, I love you forever, Martha!"

Soon Ringer and Jo were eating huge slices of pound cake and washing it down with drafts of scalding hot tea.

"I wonder if they have pound cake and tea like this in heaven," Ringer smiled. He had a very nice smile, and though he was not handsome, there was an honesty in his steady blue eyes that made everyone trust him.

"Ah, something that good or at least better. Milk and honey, I suppose."

"Maybe manna. I always wondered what that tasted like."

"When will you be getting out of here, Ringer?"

"Next week, so Doctor Laurent says."

"Will you be going back to the front?"

"No. I'm going home. Can't get around well enough on this leg of mine to do any good." Ringer had taken a terrible wound just over his knee. It had healed, but it had left the joint so stiff that he could not move with much grace.

"I'm glad for you," she said. "Do you have family there?"

"I did have. My wife died three months ago."

"Oh, Ringer, I'm so sorry! You never told me."

"No. I guess I didn't."

"Do you have children?"

"One boy. He's six. Here, I've got a picture of him."

Jo studied the faded photograph and said, "He's a handsome lad. He'll be glad to see you, but Bedford will miss you terribly."

"And I'll miss him, too."

"Will you be going back to stock riding?"

"Can't do that with a bum leg like this. No. I'll have to find something else to do." A worry crept into his eyes, and he said, "I've been thinking about it. Stock riding's all I know. I don't know what I'll do for a living."

Impulsively Jo reached over and covered his hand with hers. "You'll find something. The Lord will find a way."

Jones looked down at her hand covering his. "That's a kind heart speaking," he said quietly. "I'll think of you when I'm in Australia."

"And you must write me, too. Write in care of the hospital here. I'll have it forwarded to me wherever I might be."

"I'll write you back as soon as I hear from you."

Somehow the thought of Ringer leaving was both good news and bad. She had grown to depend on him to take care of Bedford and now knew she would have difficulty finding someone to watch Bedford.

Ringer must have read her thoughts, for he said, "That lad I was playing draughts with? His name is Farley. Comes from somewhere around the north of England. He'll be here another couple of months. He's told me several times he'd like to help you with Bedford. He loves dogs."

"Oh, that would be wonderful! I'll speak to him before I go."

They finished their pound cake and then went to find James Farley. He was a shy twenty-five-year-old who agreed at once to keep Bedford as Ringer Jones had done. "He's a lot of company, mum," he said, smiling at her with a crooked grin. "I've got a dog myself back home. Not so big as Bedford, but I miss him a lot."

"It would be a great help to me, Farley," Jo said.

Jo left the two men, whistled for Bedford, who was roaming the grounds, and started down the steps. The rain was still coming down, and she fumbled with the umbrella, trying to get it opened. It resisted her stubbornly, and engaged in this, she caught her heel on the top of a step. She was pitched forward, and as she fell, she threw the umbrella wide and cartwheeled her arms. She came down hard on her left wrist and left elbow and cried out with pain. She had fallen into a puddle of water and was struggling to get up. Bedford was no help at all as he came to her and nudged her.

"Oh, I say, Miss Jo! That was a bad one!" She felt strong hands under her and looked up to see that Farley and Ringer had come to her assistance.

"We seen you take a header. Are you all right?"

"Just my left arm. I popped my elbow, I think."

"Better come inside and let Doctor Laurent take a look at it."

"Oh, it'll be all right if I get home."

"None of that now," Ringer said. "They teach us here to pay attention to the nurses and the doctors, so come now, and no protests."

Twenty minutes later Jo was sitting in Doctor Laurent's room with her coat off. He had examined her elbow and said, "Not broken, of course, but it's going to be very stiff for a few days. I'm going to give you something for the pain. Otherwise you won't sleep tonight. And I want you to wear it in a sling."

"Thank you, Doctor. I feel like such a fool," Jo grinned wryly. "Falling down. It always makes you feel so silly."

"I guess it could happen to anyone."

Jo tested her elbow and winced with the pain. "You know the first thing anyone does when they fall down like that?"

"Why, no. I don't think I do."

"No matter how bad it hurts, you look around to see if anybody saw you." Jo managed a smile and said, "You feel like such a clumsy oaf."

"Well, I see that you need to get home, and you can't walk through this deluge."

"Oh, I'll be all right. I can hold the umbrella with this arm."

"Now, no argument. Danielle's going off duty in thirty minutes. It won't hurt her to take off a little bit early."

Jo protested, but Doctor Laurent insisted. She sat there waiting until Danielle came in.

"Well, I heard you had a fall."

"Yes. It's a wonder I didn't break my neck." Getting to her feet, Jo said, "You really don't have to take me home."

"Don't be silly! And I'm not taking you home. I'm taking you to our house."

"But I can't do that."

"Of course you can. Gabby thinks you've been neglecting her. Come along now."

Dani was a strong-minded woman, and thirty minutes later Jo was sitting in an overstuffed chair in the Laurents' parlor with Katherine Laurent fussing over her. Gabby was right up in her face, her eyes anxious.

"Did you hurt yourself bad, Miss Jo?"

"Not bad at all. Just popped my elbow a little. It'll be all right in a day or two."

"Do you feel like playing with me?"

"Why, Miss Jo can't play with you! She's been hurt!" Katherine Laurent exclaimed.

"Well, I'll tell you what. Why don't you be the nurse, and I'll be the patient. You can wait on me, and I'll be crabby and fuss like a real bad patient."

Jo had discovered she had a gift for making up games like this that Gabby loved, and so the game began at once. Gabby threw herself into it and even made herself a uniform, of sorts, out of an old dress. Dani fixed a headpiece for her that could pass for a nurse's cap.

The day went pleasantly, and Jo was glad she had not had to go home to her apartment. Bedford was glad too, because he was permitted in the kitchen, where he dozed by the warm stove happily.

She stayed for supper, and it was one of those rare nights when Lance Winslow came back. He seemed concerned to hear about her elbow and after supper had insisted on driving her and Bedford back to her place. Gabby wanted to go too, but he said, "It's raining too hard. You'll have to make it another time."

"I'll tell you what. I'll come back tomorrow, and we can play patient and nurse some more. Will that be all right, Gabby?" Jo smiled at the girl.

"Oh yes! That was fun! Papa, you could come and be the doctor."

As usual Lance looked uncomfortable whenever Gabby urged him to come. He managed a smile and said, "I'm afraid I wouldn't be a very good doctor."

Lance's car was small, and Bedford took up most of the backseat. Lance drove carefully, and when they got to her place, he said, "I'd better see you in."

They went inside, and as soon as they did, Bedford went to examine his food bowl.

"You'd think that dog was starved to death! He thinks he has to eat every half hour."

"Sounds like me when I was a boy."

"Will you stay and have tea?"

"No. I'd better get back." He hesitated, then said, "That was good the way you made up that game with Gabby. I wish I could do things like that."

"Oh, I think you could if you just had time."

Lance seemed wistful. "I used to do things like that before her mother died, before the war. Another thing that's lost." He was standing beside the door. His uniform was wet, but he seemed oblivious to it. "Is there going to be anything left by the time this war is over?"

Jo moved closer. Her arm was paining her considerably, but she ignored it. "What are you going to do when you go back tonight to the station?"

"Go over reports and think about the mission tomorrow."

"Don't do that," Jo said. "I'm lonely. Would you mind staying and talking to me?"

Lance stared at her with surprise. "I wouldn't think you'd be the lonely type."

"Why should you think that? I get lonely like anyone else. You forget I'm far away from home just like you are."

"You mean it?" Actually Lance had dreaded going back to the station, and the invitation came as an unexpected relief. "If you wouldn't mind, I will stay for a while."

"You'll have to help me make tea. A one-armed cook isn't much good in the kitchen, and I think we have some sweets to go with it."

It was a pleasant time for both of them. The rain outside was falling gently, and Lance built a fire in the fireplace, and they sat on a couch facing it.

"Nothing like a fire on a cold, wet evening," Jo said sleepily.

Watching the yellow flames lick upward and pleased with the sight of the sparks that ascended up the chimney, Lance said, "I've always loved a fire. I was always glad to see winter come because we could have a fire in the fireplace."

"I felt the same way at home. We had this big old house with a huge fireplace. My father would take me out with him to cut wood, and we'd haul it back in an old truck. It was such hard work, but I loved it."

"Tell me more about what you were like when you were a girl."

Surprised, Jo looked up. "Why would you want to know that?"

Lance studied her face. She seemed to be such a strong woman, and yet there was a clear, classic beauty about her that attracted him. She had an inner stillness he did not find in many women, and now as her green eyes caught the reflection of the fire, he thought with a shock, *Why, she's beautiful!* With the shadows flickering over her face, he saw the clear running lines of her jaw, the smooth sweep of her cheek, and the high, smooth forehead. Her red hair gave off glints from the reflections of the fire, and he found himself admiring her as he had never admired any woman—except Noelle. "You're a very beautiful woman, Jo," he said suddenly, not meaning to do so.

Jo was stunned. "I'm not really, but I'm glad you think so."

"Didn't mean to come out with that," Lance said, somewhat astonished at himself. "I don't go around tossing out compliments like that."

"No. I've noticed that."

Lance gave her a quick look. "What does that mean?"

"You're too serious. You're so busy killing Germans, you don't have time to pass along compliments to women—or to your pilots."

The fire popped and sent a spark out on the rug in front. Lance reached out and covered it with his foot. He ground it into a cinder and then sat back. "I suppose you're right," he said quietly. "I'd be a better commander if I wasn't so hard on them."

"I think you're a wonderful commander, but men like to be encouraged." She smiled then and laughed. "So do women."

The clock on the mantel ticked slowly as the two sat there talking, and he said again, "Tell me what you were like when you were a girl."

"Like all other girls, I suppose. I grew up being very unhappy with the way I looked. When I was fourteen, I was certain I was going to be all legs and arms with no body at all. Like a huge spider."

"Well, it didn't turn out that way."

"But I didn't know that. Girls are very sensitive. My complexion got bad when I was fifteen, and so the world ended again. When I was sixteen, I fell in love with my science teacher who was thirty and happily married."

"Not really!"

"Oh, not really, of course, but I thought I was," Jo said. She smiled now at the memory and leaned back, cuddling her arm. She had taken a pain pill, and it had made her rather dreamy. She murmured, "Poor Mr. Shelton. I embarrassed him so much."

"You mean you actually *told* him you loved him?"

"Oh yes! I had no shame. I wanted him to leave his wife, and we'd run off together to Hawaii or somewhere."

"That must have come as quite a shock to the fellow."

Jo laughed aloud. "I've never seen anybody so shook up. He fled as if I'd waved a gun in his face and spent the next year dodging me. I don't think he ever looked straight at me again."

"Did you ever go tell him that it wasn't all that serious?"

"No. You don't understand young girls very much. I couldn't face him. I felt so rejected."

"Tell me some more about your aborted romances."

The fire was soaking into Lance now, and the dinner had been excellent at the Laurents'. Outside a wind was blowing, and the rain was still pattering on the windows, but inside, the room was warm and the lights were low. He listened as Jo continued to speak of her childhood.

Finally she exclaimed, "Here I am talking all about my silly self when I was a girl! Surely you don't want to hear more of that."

Lance was silent for a moment. "It's good to hear about things like that. That's like another world, isn't it, Jo? You can't go back there, and I can't go back to being the boy I was. Where is that boy, I wonder?" He half closed his eyes. "I came across an old photograph of myself not long ago. I was skinny and too tall and not very good at sports. Back then I didn't have the foggiest idea what to do with myself. You know, I think it's all a myth about the golden childhood. Most of my childhood I spent being embarrassed."

Jo suddenly reached over and held his arm. "You're the first one I ever heard say that, Lance, and I feel exactly the same way. I went from one disaster, or so I thought, to another."

Lance was very conscious of her grasp on his arm. He said quietly, "I guess everyone has to lose that time of life and go on to something else."

"I suppose so."

"But that's the way life is."

The two sat there, and finally Jo got up, saying, "I've got some records and a new machine. Like to hear some music?"

"Yes."

She played several records, and Lance seemed to enjoy it, but then she put on a record of "Clair de Lune." Immediately Lance got to his feet. "Well," he said, his face tight with strain, "I've got to go. Thanks for taking my mind off of things."

"It's early yet. Do you have to go now?"

"Yes. I do."

His jaw was tight and suddenly Jo understood. "That song. It must have been one of your wife's favorites."

"Yes, it was. She loved it."

He stood there for a moment, and the pain in his eyes was so cruel that Jo could have cried for him. "I'm sorry, Lance. I wish I'd known."

"There's no way you could have known. It's just that it brings back old memories, and they're like knives going through me, Jo." His voice rose a little, and he shut his eyes suddenly, his lips forming a tight line.

Jo moved over to him, reached up, and put her hand on his neck. She let it rest there, and when his eyes opened with surprise, she said quietly, "You loved your wife. That's a rare and beautiful gift."

"She was a rare and beautiful woman." Lance's voice was hoarse. He stood there with grief etched into his face, and then suddenly he reached out and pulled her toward him. It had been a strange evening for him, and for this one moment, he released the bondage he had kept himself under.

As for Jo, she knew he was going to kiss her. She lifted her face as his lips touched hers. She sensed the regret, the pain, the loss, and the loneliness that lay in this man and knew he had burst forth from the prison he had kept himself in for a long time. She did not turn away. She lifted her good hand and placed it on his shoulder.

Lance knew this woman had fire and spirit and a soft depth, and he had not been stirred so powerfully since his wife had died. With that brief kiss, Lance realized he could not live alone the rest of his life. But when he stepped back and looked at her, he found that he could not speak steadily. "You've got the power to stir a man, Jo. I'm sorry. I didn't mean to do that."

"I guess," Jo said quietly, "we're entitled to one mistake. But I'm not sure it was a mistake."

"You're not? You mean you're not angry?"

"Of course not. Why would I be? You're lonely and so am I."

"You're different from most women." He shook his head and said, "I'd better go. It might be dangerous for me to stay here."

"No. I don't think so."

Her words halted him, and he turned to her. Lance knew there *was* danger for them, no matter what Jo said. He said quietly, "You've been a comfort, Jo."

As he turned and left, Jo stood still for a long moment, thinking of what a strange man he was. She knew she would think of his kiss for weeks.

CHAPTER EIGHTEEN

"I Believe in Love"

★ ★ ★ ★

As usual, on Sunday morning Revelation Brown was busily recruiting every man he could from the aerodrome to attend church. He went into the enlisted men's barracks and in a loud voice began to cheerfully encourage them. "Come on, fellas. It's the Sabbath Day, the day that the Lord hath made. Let us rejoice and be glad in it."

From some a groan of protest went up, and Tom Morrison peered at him sourly. "Go away, Rev! This is the only morning we have to sleep."

"You'll have plenty of time to sleep. Come along now, Tom. There's a good fellow. The Lord may have a message for you this morning, and you need it."

Tom Morrison stared at Rev Brown, whose bright, cheerful face, ugly as it was, seemed to be filled with joy. With a groan he got out of bed and began pulling his clothes on. "I suppose I might as well," he complained. "You're not going to leave me alone unless I do."

"The Lord's going to bless you today, Tom. I feel it." Rev slapped his companion mechanic on the back and then proceeded down the line of cots. He did receive a few curses on the way, which he took in good spirit, winking and appearing not to be touched at all by the language. When he left the barracks, he had five men who had grudgingly agreed to go with him to the service. Rev piled them all into a truck and headed into the center of town. As they unloaded, he saw Logan standing beside Doctor Laurent and his family, preparing to go in. "Hello, Lieutenant!" he said cheerfully. "Ready to get a blessing from God? The manna's going to fall this morning."

Logan, as usual, could not help smiling. "I need it, Rev. Good morning, men." He received several sleepy greetings from the mechanics, and as he turned to go inside, he said to Danielle, "That fellow is a wonder."

"I've never known anyone like him. Every time I see him, he has a good word about the Lord."

"Well, he gets on some people's nerves," Logan said, "but he means business with his faith. I'll say that for him."

The two walked side by side, following Doctor Laurent and his wife. Looking across the church, Logan saw Lance sitting toward the back beside Gabby. "I'm glad to see the captain spending time with that daughter of his."

"So am I. I think he feels guilty about it. Lately he's been different, though."

The two took their seat, and soon the service began. The song leader was a tall, powerful man with a voice to match. Most of the songs Logan did not know, but a few he did. He admired Danielle's clear contralto voice, and once, between hymns, he murmured, "My folks would enjoy this church. It's got a good spirit."

"Yes, we do have the Lord's blessing. It's been the best church I've ever attended," Danielle whispered back.

Finally the minister got up and welcomed them all into the service. There were so many Englishmen there from the aerodrome that the pastor said, "For those of you who are not yet fluent in French, I have decided to use an interpreter this morning." He nodded toward a small young man with a bright, cheerful face. "This brother will attempt to put my feeble sermon into the best English he can." The minister, Reverend Devoe, smiled suddenly. "I hope he will not attempt to correct the theology, although I'm sure I need such correction."

He looked down at his Bible and said, "This morning we will look at one verse in the Old Testament for our meditation. It is found in the seventy-eighth Psalm, verse nineteen." He waited and the room was filled with the sound of rustling pages as those who had Bibles found their place.

" 'Can God furnish a table in the wilderness?' " Reverend Devoe said. "This is the question I would like to put before you. You know, of course, the circumstances, but I will remind you of them again." He quickly reviewed the history of the children of Israel as God led them out of Egypt. He was a fine speaker and graphically portrayed the plagues that fell on Egypt and the miraculous journey of the Israelites through the Red Sea.

Finally he said, "And so now the children of Israel have been delivered from all of their bondage. They are free because God himself set them free. They are on their way to a land flowing with milk and honey, but I would like to remind you and to point out this morning that they were a long way from home. They had been delivered, but they had not reached their final destination."

A silence had fallen over the church. Beams of light came in yellow bars down from the windows, illuminating the pulpit and seemingly lighting the face of the minister. He was one of those who took great delight in proclaiming the Gospel, Logan saw, and he was glad he was there.

"Is this not our own situation?" Reverend Devoe said. "We have been delivered, but we are not home. As I have repeatedly told you, it is very easy to become a Christian. But being the Christian that we want to become is very difficult at times. Because between our point of departure and our final destination is a pathway beset with many difficulties. The Scripture mentions a wilderness, and I would have you think of what the children of Israel had to contend with. Those of you who have been in Israel know how barren that part of the world is. Rocks and heat and sand, wild beasts at every turn. There were no grocery stores or doctors' offices. They had no help in that wilderness through which they had to travel. So on they walked. They had left the comfort of their homes and all they had ever known and held precious, and now they were in a burning furnace of a wilderness with the sun beating down upon them. They only had the food they had brought with them, and soon that was all gone."

For some time Reverend Devoe went on speaking of the difficulties of the children of Israel and what a terrible time it was for them and for their young ones. And finally he said, "So they were brought out of their homes into a wilderness, and that is what we must all understand." He paused quietly and looked out over the congregation.

As his eyes moved from face to face, Logan thought for a moment that the minister's eyes met his and seemed to look deep inside of him.

"Right now you are in a wilderness"—he paused and then shook his head slightly—"or you will be in a wilderness in the future. That is the nature of our lives. Job said, 'Man is born to trouble as the sparks fly upward.' The New Testament says in the book of First Peter, 'Think it not strange concerning the fiery trial which is to envelop you.' Over and over again the Old Testament and the New warn us that we will be entering into our wilderness, and we must not be unprepared. There are those who think that once they become a Christian, life will be nothing but smooth sailing and all their troubles will be taken away. But we know that this is not true, and they must soon come to realize this. God does not take us out of the wilderness." He smiled then and nodded. "He walks with us through the wilderness.

"Do not ask God to take you out of whatever wilderness you happen to be in. You remember the three Hebrew children? The fiery furnace was before them, and if they had been like many of us, they might have cried out, 'Oh, God, deliver us from the fiery furnace.' But they did not. They answered the king straightforwardly. Do you remember? They said, 'Oh, King, we are not careful to answer thee in this matter. God is able to deliver us. If not . . .' That is what I would have you remember. God is able to deliver you from any tribulation, from any trouble, or any pain, but sometimes He chooses not to do this. And like the three Hebrew children, we must cry out, 'God is able to deliver us, but if not'—then we must simply expect Him to be with us. He was with the three Hebrews, and as the king looked in, he said, 'Did we not cast three men bound into the midst of the fire? I see four men loose, walking in the midst of the fire, and the form of the fourth is like the Son of God.'

"The Son of God will be with you in the wilderness. This is His promise, and He is a gentleman who has never lied. He said, 'I will be with you always, even to the end of the world.' Isn't that comforting to you?"

For some time the preacher went on encouraging those who were faint of heart and were experiencing trials. Over and over he quoted the great promises of God's presence from the Old Testament and the New.

"I must point out also that there is more than one kind of wilderness. There is a physical wilderness when we are tried. Some of you here today are ill of body. Some of you may have faced a doctor who has said, 'I am sorry. There is nothing I can do for you.' For those of you who are enduring physical pain or for those of you men who face the danger of death almost daily, let me say that this wilderness is not without its comforts. The question was, 'Can God furnish a table in the wilderness?' You might translate that to say, 'Can God deliver me from physical sickness?' 'Can God deliver me from death in battle?' The answer the New Testament gives, in a resounding voice, is yes. He can deliver you.

"The wilderness may also be spiritual or emotional. Are you suffering grief over loss? Oh, what a wilderness that is! When we lose that which we love, how we grieve and how we feel lost and alone. And how we cry out to God as the psalmist did. 'Oh, God, do not cast us off forever!' And in the twenty-first verse of the seventy-third Psalm, the psalmist cried out, 'My heart was grieved and I was pierced in all of my thoughts.' "

As the preacher spoke about enduring loss, Lance Winslow was sitting with his hand lightly resting on Gabby's shoulder. She had moved to sit very close beside him, and her hand rested on his leg. She seemed to need his touch, and she continually reached out to touch him. Now as the preacher continued to speak of loss, Lance listened carefully. He knew that the preacher was right, for all of his life he had been taught that God was able to give comfort. But he had not yet come to that point where he could find it. The grief that overwhelmed him over the loss of Noelle was so sharp and bitter that he could barely endure it. *Oh, God,* he prayed, *I know this preacher is right. You can give comfort, but I have not found it. Why, oh, Lord? Why have I not found peace?*

The sermon went on and finally the preacher said, "The most important question in life is, 'Can God furnish a table in the wilderness?' Is God able to provide in my life what I cannot provide for myself? Your table may be empty. I'm sure many of the Israelites looked around, and as the Scripture says, 'They were stubborn of heart.' They saw the burning desert and the barren rocks. They began to thirst, there were no water fountains in the desert. The only water they had was what they had brought with them, and surely that water ran out very soon. So they began to complain to Moses. 'Were there no graves in Egypt?' they cried out. 'Thou hast brought us out into this wilderness to die.' The Scripture says they tempted God in their hearts. They spoke against God, saying, 'Can God furnish a table in the wilderness?'

"I say to you this morning, God is able to furnish the table that you need to be filled. I know some of you are grieved and have suffered terrible loss. Some of you do not know how to face tomorrow, but God is faithful. The Lord Jesus Christ is the source of every blessing. He is now at the right hand of God making intercession for sinners such as us. And I encourage you this morning to look unto

Jesus. You may look around you at your circumstances and say you are in the middle of a wilderness and there's no way out. But there is a way out. Call upon the Lord and He will answer you. This is His promise, and His promises are always true."

The service ended shortly, and as they filed out of the church, Logan was greeted by Doctor Laurent. "We're expecting you for lunch today, and if it is not inappropriate, we would like to have your mechanic, Mr. Brown, join us."

"I'm sure he'd be happy to come."

"It won't be awkward having an officer and an enlisted man eating together?"

Logan grinned. "Revelation and I are old friends. I think we can put aside the formalities. I don't know about the captain, though."

Doctor Laurent went at once to Lance, who was just emerging from the church holding Gabby's hand. "Lance, I have invited Lieutenant Smith to come to lunch."

"That's fine," Lance said.

"Ah, but I have also asked his mechanic, an enlisted man. Will that create difficulties?"

"No. I think not. It wouldn't do in a public place, but in your home it will be all right."

The doctor went to Revelation and issued his invitation. Revelation said, "Why, Doctor, I'd be glad to come."

As soon as they arrived at the house, Lance said, "We'll have to be a little bit informal, Brown."

"Yes, sir! I'll be on my best behavior."

Rev went to Gabby, who at first was apprehensive. The big man was rather homely, and even she saw that his long arms and legs made him look like a spider. But his face was bright with a smile, and she saw something in his eyes she trusted.

"I'll bet you have some dolls. I've got a niece at home, and she lets me play with her dolls sometimes."

"You play with dolls?" Gabby stared up at the tall man wearing the olive uniform of an enlisted man.

"Susie and I played dolls by the hour. Nothing like it, I always say. Maybe you and I could have a tea party. Susie and I always did that."

Twenty minutes later Lance was standing at the door to the parlor looking in. Gabby was sitting on the floor, and across from her sat Private Revelation Brown cross-legged. They were surrounded by dolls and having a splendid tea party. Revelation was speaking with great excitement, it seemed, and Gabby laughed more than once at his remarks.

"He does well with children," Lance said to Danielle, who had come to stand beside him.

"Yes. It's amazing. Not many men have that gift."

"I don't have it," Lance said under his breath. "I'd give anything if I could just do what Brown is doing right now."

"You could, Lance. I'm sure you could." Danielle reached out and put her hand on Lance's arm. He turned to meet her eyes, and she saw the pain that was in them. "Gabby loves you, Lance. And you love her. When two people love each other, that's all that's necessary."

"Do you really believe that, Dani?"

Danielle faltered for a moment, and then she met his eyes and said, "I believe in love." She turned and would have left, but he took her arm. "Wait. Don't go away. Talk to me awhile."

His remark took Danielle off guard, but she was happy to have the time together.

"Come. Let's go out in the garden. I don't want to interrupt the tea party. They're having such a good time."

The two went out into the garden and sat down on a bench. Logan looked out the window and saw them, and he was troubled. He could see how Danielle looked up at Lance and thought, *She's in love with him, and he doesn't really see her as a woman. But he will someday.* The thought brought a pang to him, for he knew that he had fallen in love with Danielle Laurent.

During the meal, Logan could see that Danielle could not seem to remove her eyes from Lance Winslow. Logan excused himself shortly after lunch and went back to the base. All afternoon he walked around aimlessly, his mind troubled. *What's the matter with me?* he thought, but he knew the answer. He was in love with Danielle Laurent, and she did not care for him. It was a hard thing for Logan Smith to accept. Ordinarily he would have been able to think it out, but somehow he could not. He grew morose and lost the cheerful spirit that was customary with him.

When Revelation came back to the aerodrome, he found Logan sitting in the cockpit of his Nieuport. "What are you doing up there, Logan? There's no mission today."

"Nothing."

Something about Logan's tone caught Rev's attention. He moved closer and stared up, saying, "You shouldn't have left so early.

Everyone was wondering why you didn't stay."

"Didn't feel like it."

"Something wrong, Logan?"

"Nothing's wrong."

Rev hesitated. He knew something was bothering his friend, but he also knew that when Logan Smith got into a black mood like this, nothing would shake him. Rev went out of the hangar and shook his head. "Something's the matter with Logan, Lord. I don't know what it is, but he needs his wits about him." Revelation was not an educated man, but he was what some called *country smart*. Without formal education he had a sharp, keen mind. He was analytical and able to pull things apart. It was not just engines he understood, but people as well, and as he pondered on Logan, it suddenly came to him. *Why, it's that Miss Dani,* he thought. *He's talked about her a lot, and today she spent all of her time smiling at Captain Winslow.* The more he thought about it, the more certain he was that this was what was troubling Logan.

"Never knew Logan to have woman trouble before. He never seemed to care, but I believe he's shot down now. She's a fine young woman. Pretty as a picture, but you don't have to be around her long when the captain's there to see where her heart is. Too bad. Logan will have to learn to swallow his medicine with less fuss."

★ ★ ★ ★

"I say, the captain is in a rage, isn't he?" Cecil Lewis was leaning back with a volume of Shakespeare held loosely in his hands. The pilots had gathered into headquarters waiting to give a report after their last mission, but Lewis could not pay attention to the words before him.

"He's really tearing a strip off of Cowboy this time, isn't he?" Copper Jennings said. He took a drink of whiskey, shuddered as it hit his stomach, and squeezed his eyes together, then he turned back to listen to the sound of Winslow's voice. None of them could distinguish the words as they came, but there was no question about the fiery anger that blazed in their commanding officer.

"I can't believe he's taking off on Logan like that," Clive Bentley said quietly. His face was lined with fatigue. The last mission had been hard, and he had barely managed to limp home with his Nieuport full of holes, expecting any moment for it to burst into flames. "After all, he shot down two of the Jerries, didn't he? That makes five."

"Yep, that makes the Cowboy an Ace, all right," Jerold Spencer said. He was straddling a chair, and his eyes were dreamy. He had been thinking of riding in a steeplechase, but now Winslow's voice rose to a crescendo, and he shook his head. "If he's tearing Smith apart after having shot down two planes and becoming an Ace, I'd hate to think what he'll have to say to the rest of us."

"Oh, I don't think he'll have much to say," Lewis said. His eyes fell back on the page, his lips moving silently as he read. Then he looked up and shook his head. "It's breaking formation. That's what drives Captain Winslow up the wall."

"Well, I'm beginning to think the Cowboy's right," Pug Hardeston said. "After all, he's doing a whole lot better than the rest of us." He got up and walked back and forth, his muscular body anxious for action. The long hours of forced confinement in the cockpit of the plane often drove him to excesses when he was on the ground. "I go crazy trying to keep in formation, and what's the use of it?"

"Better not let the captain hear you say that," Sailor Malone grunted. He was standing at the window looking outside and now turned and said, "Lewis, you're a professor. What are we supposed to do anyhow?"

Surprised, Cecil Lewis looked at the burly Malone. "Do about what?"

"I been wondering about what this crazy war's all about, and something came to me. I'm not much of a one for thinking ahead, but what'll we do after the war's over?"

"Go back to work at a factory or a bank, I suppose. What did you do before the war, Sailor?"

"I was a sailor! Why do you think they call me that?" Malone said. He turned and looked back out the window, dissatisfied and angry. "So we spend years of our lives doing nothing but killing people, and then we're supposed to go back and sell shoes. Is that it?"

Cecil Lewis knew that the pressures on Malone were great, as they were on all of them. He also knew that Malone appeared to be suicidal. He took abysmal chances and did not seem to care whether he lived or died. Now he looked down at the page and said, "You know, there's a lot of boring stuff in Shakespeare, but every once in a while he comes up with a good one. I think that's why people continue to read him. Just for a few things he said that strike home."

"Like what? What did he ever say about what I just told you?" Malone growled.

"Well, right here in *Henry V*. Listen to this."

"Once more into the breech, dear friends, once more;
Or close the wall up with our English dead!
In peace there's nothing so becomes a man
As modest stillness and humility:
But when the blast of war blows in our ears,
Then imitate the action of the tiger;
Stiffen the sinews, summon up the blood,
Disguise fair nature with hard-favoure'd rage."

Lewis had a thoughtful look in his eyes as he closed the book with his finger, marking the place. "That's about the best advice I can think of."

"What does all that mean, Professor?" Malone asked. "I'm a dolt. You'll have to explain it to me."

"Well, it says there are two kinds of behavior. In peace a man should be still and quiet, but," he added, "when he goes to war, according to Shakespeare, he imitates the action of the tiger."

"I get that one," Pug Hardeston grinned. "Throw all our nice manners out. I never heard of a tiger begging the pardon of a lamb before he ate it."

"That's about what Shakespeare says, Pug," Lewis nodded. "That last line, 'We disguise fair nature with hard-favoure'd rage,' means we have to put aside the politeness of civilization. As you put it, you can't kill someone in a nice way."

At that moment the door opened, and Logan Smith came out. His face was pale, and he said nothing but walked out of the building with stiff-legged steps.

All the pilots turned to look as Lance Winslow came out. His face was stern, and he said, "Lieutenant Smith is grounded for three days, and I want what he's done to be a lesson to all of you! He broke formation."

Although their commanding officer was obviously angered, Clive Bentley uttered a mild protest. "But, Captain, he shot down two planes. Doesn't that count for something?"

"He shot down two planes, and you all might have gotten shot down because of his recklessness! Can't I get it across to you that our safety lies in close formation flying!"

Bentley closed his lips. He disagreed thoroughly with close formation flying, as did most of the other pilots, but that was the policy of the squadron, and Captain Lance Winslow made the policy. He shrugged and listened as Winslow outlined the next mission. But he was thinking, *I wish Winslow were a little more flexible. He thinks he's right, but I'm not sure about it. The least we could do is give Cowboy's idea an honest try.*

★ ★ ★ ★

Logan was angry to the bone. He said nothing to anyone, not even to Rev, who tried halfheartedly to console him by saying, "Well, you need a few days off, Logan. Maybe we can work out a few things on the mechanical side of the plane."

Logan had not answered. He had said practically nothing to anyone all that day or the next. When the mission flew away, he stood watching them, his face hard and his eyes unforgiving.

The next day was much the same. Copper Jennings took the liberty of saying to Lance, "You know, Captain, I think it wouldn't be out of order to give in a little bit on Smith."

"In what way?"

"Well, after all, he is a fine pilot. Maybe the best in the squadron except for you, sir."

"And I want to keep him that way. I want to keep him alive," Lance said tightly. "I want to keep all of you alive, Copper. Can't you understand that?"

"Sure, I can understand that, Captain. But some of us are going to die. After all, he's proved something, hasn't he?"

"He's proved he's a great pilot. I'm not convinced he's got the right battle tactics. He's new at this. I'll tell you what, Copper. He has the fastest reactions of any man I've ever seen. That's what's saved him so far. When he got jumped by those two Jerries, they should have shot him out of the sky. If they had come for any of the rest of us, I don't think we'd be here to talk about it."

"But doesn't that count for something?"

"It means he has to march with the rest of us. We can't have half a squadron flying according to one battle tactic, the other half flying to another," Lance snapped. "You should see that, Copper! You see the need for discipline! You've been a policeman. You know it better than anyone—or should."

"Yes, sir. I can see that. And I'll give you this. It's his quickness that saved him. But he's turning sour. I'd hate to see that happen."

"He'll just have to accept that he's one of a squadron, not some knight on a white horse." The image had stayed with Lance Winslow. He thought of it often. "He's a flying cavalier, or thinks he is. Riding off to meet the enemy, but it's not like it was in those days of chivalry.

It's not man on man anymore. It's squadron against squadron, army against army. We have to fight as a team."

"Yes, sir. As you say."

★ ★ ★ ★

"Hey, Cowboy, look at this!"

Lieutenant Harold Holmes, his baby face alive with excitement and eyes wide open, rushed into the recreation room, where most of the pilots were gathered. Holmes stood in front of them holding a piece of paper. "Did you hear that plane fly over?"

"Yeah, we heard it," Pug Hardeston said. "What about it?"

"Well, it was a Jerry." Holmes saw instantly that he had their attention. "And he dropped this out of the plane right onto the field. It was in this can and had a red streamer tied to it so we couldn't miss it. It's a letter for you, Cowboy."

Logan had never learned to like the name Cowboy, but it was a term of affection, so he accepted it. He was startled by what Holmes had said. Taking the paper, he opened it and read the message written in a bold hand.

> "This letter is to the pilot who shot down two of my comrades yesterday. I do not know his name, but I trust that this letter will be passed to him.
>
> You are a fine pilot, but I think I am a better one. The deaths of my comrades have grieved me exceedingly.
>
> I propose to meet you in single combat tomorrow at dawn. I will be flying over Sector G alone and challenge you to meet me.
>
> You cannot win this war, and I fight for the honor of my fatherland. If you have any courage at all, you will be at Sector G tomorrow at dawn.
>
> Lieutenant Hans Macher"

As the exclamations ran around the room, Copper stepped forward, saying, "Let me see that, Cowboy." He read it and said, "Hans Macher. He's shot down thirty of our fellows the last I heard." He handed the letter back and shook his head. "What does he think this is, some kind of a game?"

"What are you going to do?" Sailor Malone asked.

Logan stared at Sailor and said, "I'm grounded."

"Well, I'm not," Sailor said. "Let me go meet him."

"Now wait a minute! None of you are going to meet anybody." The pilots all looked up to see Lance, who had stepped into the rec room in time to hear the message read. "Copper's right. This is not some kind of a game."

"But, Captain," Logan said. "He'll think I'm a coward."

"Let him think what he wants! You know more about your courage than he does. No one is to have a rendezvous with Hans Macher. They say he is as good a flier as Richthofen, or Boelcke. Those are orders. No one-on-one combat."

The pilots all had to see the message, and it was Pug Hardeston who shook his head. "I'll tell you what we ought to do. We ought to send the whole flight up there. Get high in the sun, and when this Hun comes along, we ought to blast him out of the sky."

"Well, that wouldn't be fair," Harold Holmes said. He was shocked at the idea. "That wouldn't be our style at all!"

"Our style," Pug grunted, "is to kill Germans! It wouldn't bother me a bit."

"Me neither," Malone said. "What about you, Professor?"

"Well, I must admit that it goes against the grain for an Englishman to take unfair advantage, but the Germans started this war. Several times my flight has caught a bomber limping along at low speed. We didn't have any compunction then. We just lit on him and blew him out of the sky."

"But this is a little different, isn't it, Professor?" Harold Holmes insisted. "I mean it's like a man-to-man challenge."

Logan listened as the men talked and finally left the room. He was aware they were watching him closely, and he thought, *They'll think I'm a coward if I don't go*. He went to the hangar and showed the challenge to Rev, who studied it and then looked up at Logan.

"What did the captain say?"

"He ordered me not to go, or anybody else."

"The captain's pretty sharp. I've heard of this Hans Macher. The Germans think he's going to be the biggest Ace in the war."

Logan leaned over and stroked the side of the Nieuport with an odd expression on his face.

"You're not thinking about meeting this Macher, are you?"

Logan still did not answer. He turned and walked away without saying a word.

Why, he means to do it! Rev thought with astonishment. The thought disturbed him greatly, and he spent the rest of the day hoping against hope that it would not happen.

Rev wasn't the only one wondering what his friend was going to do. The pilots were making bets as to whether Cowboy Smith would disobey Lance Winslow's orders and go out to meet the German in combat. The day passed slowly, and at dawn the next morning the rest of the men took off on a mission.

Before he left, Lance came to stand before Logan, saying, "You know your orders, Logan."

"Yes, sir."

Lance bit his lip. "I don't want to be hard about this, but all other considerations aside, it would be suicide. That fellow's a killer. Probably the best flier the Germans have." He waited for a reply, but Logan said nothing. "Well, we'll talk about it when I get back. I know we disagree on tactics, but we're in the same squadron. I'd like to learn to walk a little bit closer."

"Yes, sir," Logan said quietly. Winslow ran to his plane and climbed in. Logan stood and watched as the planes took off and disappeared into the east.

Walking slowly back toward the hangar, he knew what he was going to do. He had made up his mind from the moment he saw that challenge that somehow he was going to meet Hans Macher. He knew also that disobeying Winslow's orders might get him thrown out of the RFC, but Logan Smith was a stubborn young man. He had been thrown by the same horse four times running in rodeos. The horse's name had been Dynamite, and he had been a wild bronc. Dynamite had broken up more than one rider, and Logan's dad, Lobo Smith, had said, "This may be the one you have to give up on, son. We all have to give up once in a while."

But Logan had not given up and had finally succeeded in riding Dynamite to a standstill. As he walked along the edge of the field, he remembered how he had felt when he had come off Dynamite's back, having beaten him at last.

He was thinking about meeting Macher and what tactic he might use when he heard a voice calling his name. He turned to see Danielle and was shocked. When she came up to him, he saw that she was wearing her nurse's uniform under a light jacket. "What are you doing out here?" he said.

"I came by to tell Lance that Gabby's not feeling well. We had to have the doctor come see her."

"Is it serious?"

"No. Just a cold." Danielle looked up at Logan and studied his face for a moment. She saw the tension written there and said, "I just heard from Revelation about the challenge from Macher."

"He's pretty sure of himself."

"You're not going to do it, are you, Logan?"

"Yes, I am."

"But you could be killed!"

"That's a chance I take every time I go up."

"No. It's not like that! You know he's there!" Danielle cried. She found herself shaken by the emotion that swept through her, and now without thinking, she put her hand on his chest and struck him slightly. "Don't do it, Logan. Please don't do it!"

Logan was shocked at the intensity of her emotions. She was watching him closely, her eyes wide spaced, and there was a fire in them. He knew she had a temper, for he had seen it, swinging from one extreme to the other. He also knew she had a capacity for emotion he had never found in any other woman. He felt drawn to her beauty and strength as she pleaded with him not to go.

"I've got to do it."

"Even if I ask you not to?"

"I have to do it, Dani." He saw an expression on her face he could not understand, and then asked, "Would you care if I went?"

"Yes. I would care." She suddenly threw her arms around him and put her head down on his chest.

Stunned, Logan held her. He felt her trembling and said nothing.

Finally she drew back and studied his face for a moment. "You're going to do it anyway, aren't you?"

"It's something I have to do." He leaned forward and kissed her, and she did not resist. Her lips were soft and tremulous beneath his own. Then he stepped back and said. "I've got to go."

Dani watched him as he turned and half ran to the hangar. She seemed to be paralyzed, and she could not understand her own emotions. What she was feeling for Logan was something that shook her to the very center of her being. She had put her hopes in Lance Winslow for so long, and now somehow this American had come out of nowhere. She had not known the depth of her feelings for Logan until Revelation had told her what was going to happen, and she had suddenly found herself trembling and afraid. She stood there until she saw Logan climb into his Nieuport as Revelation threw the propeller. Then she watched as the Nieuport bumped across the ground and rose into the early morning sky.

★ ★ ★ ★

The roar of the engine always thrilled Logan. He eased the Nieuport along, his eyes searching the horizon. Somehow he thought that Hans Macher would come flying from the east. He looked in that direction constantly. It was an hour past dawn now, and his lips were tight as he considered what he was doing.

Macher is not going to be like the others I shot down, he thought. *He's got to be quick and smart, and he's flying a better plane than I have.* He started to pray and then suddenly discovered he could not. This disturbed him, but he had no time to think, for at that very moment he suddenly heard the sound of machine gun fire. Startled, he saw a line of holes appear in his right wing. Twisting around he saw a flight of five Fokkers that had come out of the sun, all headed for him at full speed.

He lied! He said he'd be here alone!

But he had no time to think otherwise, for now they were on him like a pack of wolves upon a wounded deer. He knew he had been hit. Suddenly his engine began to cough, and he smelled the fumes. He threw the plane into the steepest dive he could, dodging and weaving while he still had power. He went down so low that he could see the startled expression on the face of a farmer. He pulled out just in time and glanced up to see the formation of Fokkers circling over him, watching him.

And then his engine quit dead. He saw the fumes gather and knew what that meant.

"She's going to blow up! It always happens that way, they say." As soon as the gasoline fumes begin to flow, the next moment the plane would explode into a fireball.

Logan had made up his mind before that if his plane ever caught on fire he would jump. Better to strike the ground than to be burned alive. He had a normal fear of fire, and now he knew there was no choice as he saw the flames licking ahead of him at the engine. The explosion could come at any moment.

He removed his safety belt. None of the pilots carried parachutes. Some idiot had decided that it would make them less courageous and that they wouldn't fight until the last bullet.

He moved his feet up to the seat and crouched there, keeping one hand on the stick, although it did little good. Suddenly ahead of him he spotted blue water.

A lake, he thought. *My only chance!* It was a small lake, and he timed it as best as he could as he came down low over the water. As the Nieuport suddenly began to burst into flames, he leaped over the side. As he plummeted through space, he thought, *It's death. I've had it.* Then he struck the water feet first. It stunned him and the force of his fall drove him under water some fifteen feet. He struggled and came to the top just in time to see the Nieuport burst into a thousand pieces. A red explosion seared his eyeballs, and he knew he had barely escaped death this time.

★ ★ ★ ★

When Lance returned from his flight, he discovered at once what had happened. He was shocked at first, and then disappointed. He saw Danielle with her head down and her shoulders slumped, and he went to her at once.

Danielle had not left the field after Logan had taken off. She could not bring herself to go to the hospital for work. She was still there when the flight came back.

"Did you know about this, Dani?" he asked, trying hard to control his temper.

"I tried to keep him from going."

"He was foolish! Macher is deadly."

Danielle could not answer. "Are you going to send someone out for him?" she asked.

"No," Lance said. "He'll either come back or he'll be dead."

It was two hours later that a message came over the radio. Lance went to Danielle at once, saying, "His plane went down. It burst into flames."

"Is there any hope, Lance?"

He saw the pain in her eyes and shook his head. "Not much, I'm afraid. He didn't have a parachute, of course. If he was unable to make a safe landing, he's gone, Dani. I'm sorry."

Tears filled Danielle's eyes, and suddenly Lance was startled by the intensity of her emotions. "I didn't know you cared that much about him."

"Neither did I."

★ ★ ★ ★

The pilots were subdued at the news of Logan's crash. They had all learned to like Cowboy Smith, and they kept casting glances at Danielle, who was walking alongside the field staring off at the horizon. She had been there all morning and all afternoon awaiting some kind of word.

"She might as well go home. He's had it," Sailor said. "I hate to hear it. He was a good kid for an American."

"Yes, he was," Cecil Lewis said sadly.

Lance watched out of his office window for some time. He was grieved over the loss of Logan Smith. *He had great potential,* he thought. Even as he was thinking this and watching Danielle out the window, he suddenly saw a farmer's truck approaching. He paid little attention, for the farmers often brought produce in, but then the truck stopped at the edge of the airfield, and he stiffened.

"My soul, it's Logan!" he exclaimed.

Danielle had seen the truck stop, and as soon as she saw the pilot get out, she let out a cry and ran to him. Logan caught sight of her and ran forward.

The two met, and all the pilots of the squadron piled outside and started for him. It was Cecil Lewis who said, "Wait a minute, you fellas! Don't you have any romance in your souls? Give 'em a minute, can't you?"

At that moment Danielle had thrown herself into Logan's arms. She felt faint and could only whisper, "You're safe. You're not dead."

"Not this time." He held her for a moment and said, "I should be, though." He leaned back and looked into her eyes and said, "I guess it was worth getting killed to get a welcome like this. Did you think I was dead?"

"That's what all the reports said."

"I nearly was. Come along. I've got to report to the captain. He'll probably chuck me out."

"No. He won't do that."

Lance, indeed, was in a quandary about what to do. He had come up to join the pilots. They all watched him, waiting for him to tear into Logan. Finally, Copper Jennings said, "Are you going to chuck him out, Captain?"

"I can't do that," Lance said. He saw the look of relief wash across Jennings' face.

"He's a great pilot, Captain."

"I know," he said as he waited for the two to approach. He was aware that Danielle was looking at him with a plea in her eyes. He knew she thought he was going to make an example of Logan Smith in front of the whole squadron.

"Well, Smith. What do you have to say for yourself?"

Logan had expected to be thrown out at once, but he saw something in Lance Winslow's eyes that he had not seen before. "Well,

Captain. I found out exactly how much we can trust the word of Hans Macher. I won't try that again."

"Well, you learned something, and you didn't get killed. You're not grounded anymore. Everybody has liberty."

A cry of exultation ran up, and then the pilots came over to surround the one they called Cowboy.

Dani moved over to stand by Lance, who asked her quietly, "Are you all right?"

Dani looked up at Lance and then over at Logan. "Yes," she said quietly. "I'm all right, Lance. For the first time in my life, I'm really all right!"

PART FOUR

DANIELLE

★ ★ ★ ★

CHAPTER NINETEEN

SOME THINGS CAN'T BE DREAMED

★ ★ ★ ★

A feeble light filtered through the window of the small room where Jo sat writing. Her eyes were gritty with fatigue, and the sound of cannons booming from afar were, to her mind, like the somber drums of a funeral march. From time to time a shell would fly by screaming like a banshee, then there would be a silence, followed by a tremendous explosion.

Jo had learned to live under fire, for during the past month, she had divided her time between the aerodrome at Belleville with visits to the trenches at the front. As she leaned back and read what she had written, she braced herself as a shell whined overhead. The brief moment of silence followed and then the inevitable explosion shook the earth again. Dust filtered down from the beams overhead, and the light swung in a concentric circle. It dimmed and she feared it was going out, but then it brightened again.

"Missed me that time," she said without fear. Fear could not be sustained, she had discovered. After hours of bombarding, one simply learned to accept it.

Looking down at what she had written, Jo had to force herself to stay awake.

> During the first months of the war, a mad race began in Switzerland. Deep trenches with underground dugouts big enough for men and horses were built all the way to the North Sea. This new method of fighting brought about the death to

the mobility of calvary charges that European armies had known for centuries. The charges made by both the Allies and the Central Powers usually were measured in feet rather than in furlongs or miles.

And so the race to the sea ended, and during 1915 the two forces faced each other over mud, barbed wire, and bodies that could not be buried. France seemed to be under the curse of God.

Battles came and men were piled up like cordwood. In the Battle of Ypres, Germany lost one hundred and thirty thousand first-line soldiers. British casualties were over eighty thousand, and together with French losses, the blood toll was nearly a quarter of a million lives snuffed out. General Kishner was appalled and cried out, "This isn't war! This is slaughter!"

Along a four-hundred-mile trench death reigns. Young men who should be studying at school or learning trades, getting married, having children, are mowed down by the hundreds and even by the thousands by the killing machine gun fire. The generals are unable to see that flesh and blood cannot stand up to implanted machine guns. Whether they are stupid or blind, it is impossible to say.

And so the war continues to consume the finest of the young men of the world.

And as if this were not enough, on a lovely day at Ypres, with the sun shining bright, and a fine breeze blowing, for a change, a fine mist seemed to pass over the land, and a new horror was added—chlorine gas. It lasted only fifteen minutes, but men died drowning in the gas cloud as if they were underwater. They were blinded, and their lungs burned and seared as if they had swallowed fire.

Nothing seemed to succeed for either side. At Gallipoli, Sir Ivan Hamilton threw a force against the guns of the Turks, and once again nothing but death came of it. Half a million Allied soldiers were sent to Gallipoli, and more than half of them either died or were terribly shattered by the war in that part of the world.

On August of 1916 the powers are at a deadlock. The battles of 1915 on the Western Front did not end with a great clash of glory but simply petered out into miserable failures.

Other battles took place, but there was no glory, and those who had joined or been conscripted into the army had ceased to expect any. There was no strategy, no tactics, only the dull wearing down of the human spirit. Exchanging lives for lives.

> It is a dreary, terrible war, and the Battle of Verdun seems the capstone of the idiocy and the maniac quality that the world lives in. On February 21, six months ago, two million shells were thrown toward the enemy at Verdun. These included fires, mixed shrapnel, high explosives, and poison gas. The shells fell at the rate of one hundred thousand pounds an hour, and the French forward trenches were obliterated. The survivors crawled out only to die amidst the splintered trees.
>
> The German offensive contained every bit of strength the fatherland could command, and yet it was not successful. The German offensive still goes on, and there seems no end to it. The cost of human life in Verdun stuns the imagination. France has lost over half a million soldiers and Germany four hundred fifty thousand. What sort of insanity has fallen on the world to throw away the lives of nearly a million men in a cause that no one believes in anymore?

Jo stared at the writing and knew she could never send it to the papers as it was. It was too gloomy, too pessimistic, so wearily she stuffed it into a briefcase and left the shelter. She dodged through the trenches, guided by a nervous English second lieutenant named Soames, who had been her guardian and guide during this siege.

When they were back behind the lines, she turned and smiled at him. "Thank you so much, Lieutenant Soames. I know I was a bother."

"No bother at all, Miss Hellinger." The lieutenant's eyes seemed hollow, and fatigue had so worn him down that there seemed to be little life left in him. It was like looking into the eyes of a dead man. His cheeks were hollowed, his skin was sallow and pale, and his uniform was dogged with the mud of the trenches. Summoning up a smile, he said, "Come back anytime. We never close."

Impulsively Jo put out her hand. "I wish you well. May God be with you, Lieutenant."

Going back to her motorcycle, she started the engine and made her way back down the rutted roads that led away from the front toward Paris. Her heart was sickened by the slaughter she had seen, and she felt unclean at the staggering number of casualties. Still the thought came to her, *No matter how many baths I take, I can't wash away what's happened. . . .*

★ ★ ★ ★

"Well, Jo, you're back from the front!" Rev was practically standing on his head as he worked on the Nieuport's engine. He jumped off the ship and came wiping his hands with an oily rag. He stared at one and said, "Too greasy to shake with a lady."

"Not at all." Jo took Rev's hand and shook it. "It's good to see you again."

"How about a cup of tea while you tell me all of your adventures."

"I wanted to see Logan."

"He's out on patrol. Ought to be back in a few hours. You haven't heard about him?"

"No. What's happened?"

"He's got twelve kills now. That's two more than the captain has."

Jo stared at the long-legged mechanic. "I hadn't heard about that."

"Oh, he doesn't say much about it."

Jo listened as Revelation spoke of the victories Logan had won. "They call him Cowboy Smith all the time now. I think they got that from one of the stories you wrote."

"I wish I hadn't put that in," Jo said, a worried look furrowing her brow. "Nicknames aren't always welcome."

"Well, Richthofen doesn't mind being called the Red Baron. So I guess Cowboy Smith is kind of an honorary title."

"How is Captain Winslow?"

"Well, I'm a little concerned about the captain. He's wearing himself down. Still trying to kill every German in the Luftwaffe."

"Have you seen his family?"

"As a matter of fact, I have. Mrs. Laurent invited me out to dinner, and I had a splendid time." A worried look came fleetingly across the homely face of the mechanic. He shook his head. "I wish the captain would spend more time with that daughter of his."

"So do I. He doesn't visit often?"

"No." Revelation looked down at the ground, and then a troubled look came into his eyes. "He's got to let go of that dead wife of his, Jo." He shook his head and added, "A man needs a flesh-and-blood woman, not a memory."

Jo agreed wholeheartedly with Rev but said no more. She changed the subject quickly. "Have there been any losses in the squadron?"

"Afraid so. We've lost three men. None of the old hands. They come in so young with so little experience. It bothers me. I can't remember their faces sometimes."

At that moment Sailor Malone suddenly entered. His curly brown hair was falling over his forehead, and he was more than a little drunk. "Well, if it's not our lady reporter. How are you, Miss Hellinger?"

"Fine, Sailor." Jo shook hands with him and smelled the alcohol. It was not unusual, however, for Sailor and many of the others stayed drunk as much as possible. She had heard it said by the other pilots that Malone didn't care if he lived or died.

"Got time for a cup of tea, Sailor?" Rev said.

"If you don't preach at me, I have."

"Can't promise that," Rev said. "Come along. I've got some special tea brewin', and I got a half a cake left over that I swiped from the kitchen."

The three went to the rec room, which was empty now except for two pilots who sat morosely playing checkers. They looked up and then went back to their game.

"Those two are Polish. Can't speak enough English to comment on," Sailor said.

Jo sat down and listened as Malone described his last patrol. Finally she said, "What's it really like? I mean going up and facing the German who's trying to kill you."

Sailor pulled a small flask out of his inner pocket, filled his half cup of tea with it, then held it up, saying, "Here's to you!" He drank it off and then considered her question. "Don't think I can answer that." He grinned suddenly, saying, "It's like being married, Jo. You can read books about it and have people talk to you about it, but until you go through it, you don't know what it's really like."

Jo sat for some time and Sailor drank steadily. She knew that Lance was aware of the drinking problem of Malone and others, but there seemed to be little he could do about it.

Finally Malone left, and Revelation said, "I've got to do some more work. Can we go out and eat somewhere tonight?"

"Of course. Maybe Logan can go with us."

Jo left the hangar and spent the next few hours talking to various mechanics and trying to carry on a conversation with the Polish pilots. They stared at her with a lack of comprehension, and Jo finally gave up.

She went and sat down on a cane-bottomed chair outside of headquarters. It was a hot day as the August sun beat down on the tarmac runway. Having missed a great deal of sleep lately, she dozed off quickly.

The sound of buzzing motors far overhead came to her, and she awoke groggily. Staring up, she saw the dots in the sky.

"Squadron's coming in!" Rev called to her as he ran out toward the strip.

Jo remained where she was and watched the Nieuports land.

The men piled out and, as usual, headed for headquarters. Jo knew they would be having a debriefing, so she kept out of the way. After that was over she walked along looking at the planes as the mechanics swarmed over them and saw many bullet holes and tears.

"Well, we didn't lose any this time. Just shot all to pieces," Tom Morrison said. "Look at the captain's plane. Another few bullets and he would have lost this wing."

Jo walked along studying the damage, and she thought suddenly of what Sailor Malone had said, *You have to be there.*

Abruptly she stopped and spoke aloud. "That's what I need, to go on a mission!" The thought seemed ridiculous to her, but the more she pondered it, the more it intrigued her. She played with the idea and then determined to pursue it. "Well, I can ask. All Lance can do is say no."

Jo went back to the rec room and said, without much preamble, "Lance, I want to go on some sort of flight over the lines." He just stared at her, for once unable to speak for a moment.

"Well, that's out of the question! Whatever made you think of such a fool thing, Jo? You know I couldn't permit that."

"I don't mean actually get into a dogfight. I mean just on an observer's flight. I can't write about what you do until I've tasted it."

Lance was exhausted from the fight. It had been a mean battle in the skies with damage to his own squadron and to the Germans, though no planes were shot down. He was irritated, and anger at his failure to shoot down any of the German ships edged his voice.

"I've already said no, and I don't want to hear any more about it."

End of conversation! Jo thought. She changed the subject at once but saw that Lance was not in a talking mood, so she went home and spent part of the day with Bedford. After writing some, she decided to go to the hospital and visit several of the wounded she had gotten to know quite well writing letters for them. As usual, the men were happy to see her.

After her visit at the hospital, Jo put Bedford in the sidecar and drove around. It was a beautiful day, and Bedford loved it, his eyes half closed, his tongue lolling as she sped along. He had a habit of barking at every car they passed, and several accidents nearly occurred when drivers turned to stare at the big dog.

Jo never knew how she got her ideas for her stories. People often asked her, "How do you think of the things you write about?" She never had an answer. Sometimes she would say, "How do you not think of them?" Ideas flowed through her mind constantly. She had come to believe that the one criteria of a writer was that ideas had to flow.

As she was rounding a pond, enjoying the sunlight on the blue water, an idea came to her. She continued her ride but finally made up her mind that she might as well try it.

Reaching the airfield, she parked the motorcycle. She and Bedford made their way to the pilots' quarters, where she knocked. Cecil Lewis opened the door, and his homely face lit up. "Well, I expected an ugly, hairy-legged enlisted man to come bringing the mail. You're quite an improvement."

Jo liked Cecil Lewis and said, "Do you have a quotation to fit this occasion from Shakespeare?"

> "Haply I think on thee, and then my state,
> Like to the lark at break of day arising
> From sullen earth, sings hymns at heaven's gate."

Jo laughed. "I think you're full of baloney, Cecil! All of you English professors are."

"Quite true. What can I do for you?"

"Is Sailor here?"

"Yes, he is. You sure I won't do?"

"No. You're too fine a company for me. I'm the earthy type."

Sailor suddenly appeared and shouldered Lewis aside. "Stand aside, mate! The lady prefers sailors."

Stepping outside, Sailor closed the door. "What can I do for you, Jo?"

"Something probably that will get you into a lot of trouble."

At her words, Sailor grinned. "Just what I like, trouble. Let's have it." He listened as Jo outlined the idea that had come to her.

"It's probably impossible, and I know it's wrong."

"But it'll be a lot of fun." He winked at her. "I'm taking off on an observation flight in one of the two-seaters at two o'clock. You be here and keep out of sight. We'll put this one over on the Cap. He doesn't have to know everything!"

★ ★ ★ ★

Lance stared blankly at Jerold Spencer. He could not believe what he had just heard. "You're wrong about that! It's impossible!"

Jerold shook his head and cleared his throat nervously. "I didn't know what to do about it, Captain, but I saw what I saw." He shifted his feet nervously and shook his head. "Miss Hellinger got in the two-seater with Sailor and he took off."

"When was this?"

"About twenty minutes ago."

Blind anger swept over Lance. He remembered Jo's request to go on a mission, and now he thought, *That fool Malone, he'll get her killed! He doesn't care whether he lives or dies and Jo could go down with him!*

"You did right to tell me. I only wish you'd come sooner."

"Well, I thought maybe you had given permission."

"No one likes to be an informer, Spencer, but Malone's a fool. Now I'll have to go after them."

"Can you find them, sir?"

"I know what sector he's supposed to patrol."

"Let me go with you, sir. You might need help."

"No. You stay here."

Quickly Lance donned his flying gear and ran out, pulling his helmet on. When he got to the hangar, Tom Morrison looked up with a startled expression. "What's wrong, Captain?"

"Is she gassed up?"

"Yes, sir."

"Engine all right, Tom?"

"Why, yes, sir. All ready to go. The guns are loaded."

Without another word Lance climbed into the Nieuport. He went through the drill of starting the engine, and when it burst into a roar, he opened the throttle. He knew there was not a second to waste, and the anger he felt toward Malone's foolishness burned in him.

Tom Morrison watched and Revelation came over. "What's eatin' the captain?"

"Don't know. Took off like the devil was after him."

Revelation shaded his eyes with his hand. The two men were standing there watching when Jerold Spencer came over. He had a hangdog look. "Well, I guess he went after them."

"Went after who, Lieutenant?"

"Why, Miss Hellinger. She took off with Sailor on his patrol."

Revelation's jaw dropped. He could not speak for a moment, then he looked heavenward and said, "Good Lord, defend them! Bring them back safe!"

Tom Morrison was as shocked as his friend. "Sailor's got a death wish, Rev. I hope he doesn't get his way this time. Not with Miss Jo up there with him."

★ ★ ★ ★

Lance glanced at his gas gauge and saw that he had, perhaps, enough fuel to get back to the base—perhaps not. He had criss-crossed Sector J where Malone was supposed to be, and even as he looked up and started to turn back, he caught a flicker of movement down below. He stiffened when he saw Malone's plane being attacked by three Fokkers!

At once he put his plane into a steep dive and prayed for skill to drive the Fokkers off. He caught them unaware, sweeping down on the first one like a hawk. The pilot was so busy pumping lead into Malone, who was taking evasive action, that he never saw the Nieuport as the bullets crashed into his back, killing him instantly.

The other two planes immediately stopped firing on Malone's plane, which was already smoking as the engine sputtered.

Lance had no time to see what was happening to Malone and Jo. The Germans were expert and fought as a team. He felt the plane shudder under his hand as bullets ripped through it, and no matter how many sharp turns he made, the Fokkers stayed right on his tail. The duel went on for some time until finally he had no ammunition left. He glanced down to see Malone's plane headed toward a green field. Lance knew that the Fokkers would knock him out of the sky, and he did something then he had never done before. They had divided and were coming at him head on, when Lance shifted his stick sharply and headed straight for the one on his right. He could see the startled expression on the face of the German pilot as he tried to avoid the crash.

Lance was shaken as the two planes met. The undercarriage of his Nieuport racked right across the top of the Fokker, crashing through the windshield and shattering the pilot's face. The undercarriage took off the rudder, and the Fokker began to flutter to the ground like a broken toy.

Lance had no ammunition left, and the remaining Fokker racked him fore and aft with tracers. Without warning, his engine began to sputter, and he went into a steep dive.

Lance managed to land the Nieuport, but the wheels tore off. He was thrown forward against the straps, which broke, and his head smashed into the control panel. He felt blood flow over his face and was blinded momentarily as the plane suddenly rose in the air.

Lance felt himself falling as the plane continued to cartwheel past him. He hit the ground, rolling over, as his plane landed on its back behind him.

Staggering to his feet, Lance yanked out his handkerchief and wiped the blood from his eyes. Staring wildly around he saw the observer plane with its tail sticking upright into the air. He stumbled forward and saw that it had nosed into a ditch.

"Jo, are you all right?"

"Yes. Yes, I think so. But Malone is hurt."

Clambering up on the wing, Lance reached in and saw that Jo had suffered a few bruises and a small cut on her arm.

When she saw the blood all over his face, she cried, "Lance, you're hurt!"

"Never mind me. You've got to get out of this thing. It might blow up any minute." He had seen the streamers of vapor and then turned to Malone, but he saw at once that it was useless. A bullet had taken Malone directly in the back and another in the neck. He had died moments after the plane landed.

He pulled Jo out of the cockpit, and the two fell to the ground. "Run!" he shouted.

"But what about Sailor?"

"He's dead. Come on, we've got to get out of here!"

The two staggered away, and when they were a hundred yards from the plane, it burst into a ball of yellow and white fire. The force of the explosion knocked them down. As they fell, Jo cried out, "Sailor! Oh, Sailor!"

CHAPTER TWENTY

"I'VE FORGOTTEN GOD. . . !"

★ ★ ★ ★

Danielle was sitting on the floor with Gabby surrounded by dolls. The late afternoon sun poured through the window, and as the light struck Gabby's face, Danielle thought, *She looks so much like Noelle!* She missed her sister desperately, and time seemed not to have done much toward healing the wound.

"Why don't we pretend there's a wedding, and we can dress Helen up like a bride?"

"But what will we use for a bridegroom? You don't have any male dolls."

"We'll fix a costume for Jennifer. She's sort of ugly anyway. She can be the groom."

Fascinated by the vivid imagination of the child, Danielle entered into the world of make-believe. She watched as Gabby acted out the roles of minister, bride and groom, and even the bridesmaids. A tender smile came to Danielle's lips, and she thought how she had come to love this child as if she were her own daughter.

"Dani, Logan is here," Katherine Laurent said.

Getting to her feet, Danielle shot a questioning look at her mother. "Were you expecting him?"

"No. He looks troubled, but he wanted to talk to both of us."

"You wait here, Gabby."

"But I want to see Logan."

"You can see him after we have our grown-up talk," Danielle said. "You go ahead and have the wedding reception."

Leaving Gabby in the midst of the dolls, Danielle followed her mother to the formal dining room, where Logan stood waiting. There was a stiffness in his expression that alerted Danielle, and she said quickly, "Something's wrong! What is it, Logan?"

"It's Lance—and Jo."

Both women had been expecting some sort of news about Lance, but the way Logan put the statement puzzled both of them. "Has there been some sort of accident? Were they together?"

Clearing his throat, Logan said, "Jo got in an observer plane with Lieutenant Malone. It was just a routine flight, but some of it was over German territory. When Captain Winslow heard about it, he jumped into his plane and took off."

"You think something's wrong?"

Logan hesitated for a moment, then said in a strained voice, "I think so. They've been gone longer than their fuel would keep them aloft. I'm afraid they're down."

Danielle could not take it in for a moment. She glanced up at her mother and saw the fear that she herself felt in her mother's eyes. Quickly she said, "But it's not certain, is it? Do you think they've been shot down?"

"I think we have to face that possibility. They should have been back long ago. Of course, there could have been engine trouble," Logan said.

"But you don't think that's likely, do you?" Katherine Laurent spoke slowly. "You think they're in trouble."

"I thought I ought to come out and tell you," Logan said. "I'm very worried about both of them."

"What will you do? What can be done?" Danielle asked.

"I'm going back to the field now, and we'll have every plane that can get in the air doing a search. I have hopes that we'll find them. It may be they just simply ran out of fuel." Logan knew that this was not very likely, but it was all he could think of to give a shred of comfort to the two women.

"I want to go to the field with you," Danielle said.

"There's nothing you can do, Dani."

"I'm going, and don't try to stop me."

Logan shrugged his shoulders. "All right, but it'll be a lonely wait."

"I'd rather be there than here. Mother, you can take care of Gabby, can't you?"

"Yes, but send word as soon as you find out anything."

Logan waited until Danielle got her things. The two went out and got into the car he had commandeered from the base. He started the engine and stepped on the gas forcefully. He said no more for a time, but finally glancing over, he saw that Danielle was sitting bolt upright. She clasped a handkerchief in her hands, and she was straining at it, pulling at its corners. He said quietly, "I knew this would be a hard knock for you, Dani."

Danielle turned around toward him and saw the muscles in his cheek were tight. "Yes, it's very hard," she admitted. "Of course we're always worried about Lance, but we never thought about Jo. What possessed her to do such a thing?"

"She's just that kind of woman. The way I understand it, she felt that she couldn't write about the air war unless she had actually been involved in it. She asked Captain Winslow to go up, and he refused permission, so she talked Malone into it. I wish it were anyone except him."

"Why are you worried about Malone?"

"He's a wild man and he's crazy. He shouldn't have taken her." Logan's jaw tightened and he shook his head. "I like Sailor, but he's just not reliable."

When they pulled up in front of the aerodrome, Logan turned to say, "I know how you feel about Lance."

Startled, Danielle could not speak for a moment. She felt a surge of guilt, for she had kept her feelings for Lance hidden, or so she thought. Now she saw that Logan Smith's eyes were fixed on her, and she could not meet them. Dropping her gaze, she whispered, "I don't know, Logan."

"I think you do, Dani. I think you've been in love with Lance for a long time."

Danielle tried to answer but faltered, "It's . . . it's been a strange sort of thing. Everyone thought it was just an infatuation when I was just a girl, but . . ."

When she said no more, Logan said heavily, "Well, I hope he's all right, for your sake." He said nothing of his own feelings, but he closed the door in his mind to any hope. *She loves him and that's it.* He got out of the car and was aware that Danielle was following him. He ignored her as he met with the flight leaders, who all went to the hangar and began making their preparations for a search.

"We'll put every plane in the air we can, won't we?"

Cecil Lewis nodded. "We'd better do it quick. Headquarters would never permit it if they catch wind of it."

Clive Bentley smiled faintly. "I'll let my father take it up with the House of Lords if they give us any static. I say let's go find them."

Thirty minutes later the runway was filled with the sound of roaring engines, and Danielle watched as they flew off toward the front. They disappeared finally, and she turned and started to walk back with her head down to wait in the rec room.

Revelation Brown watched her and finally came over and said, "We've got to have faith, Miss Dani. God's able to do all things."

"I know, but it's so hard—"

"Sure it's hard, but God never offered us a bed of roses. Jesus had to go to the cross, and every one of us is called to be a soldier. Come now. Let's believe God."

★ ★ ★ ★

"Lance, you can't go any farther! You can scarcely walk."

"We can get a little way. We've got to find some kind of shelter." The pain was half blinding Lance, for his head had been split badly by the crash against the cockpit. He knew he needed stitches, but for now Jo had tied his scarf around his head, making a bandage that staunched the flow of blood. He stumbled suddenly and murmured, "Not seeing too well, Jo—seems to be two of everything."

Jo had never been in a situation like this. She knew they had gone down in German territory, or very close to it. The lines changed from day to day, and she was terrified that a patrol of German soldiers would suddenly appear and capture them.

"We've got to get away from here," she murmured. She turned and said, "Lance, lean on me."

"Sorry to be such . . . a bother."

"No. Don't say that." She started to apologize, to say how wrong she had been, but she knew this was not the time. She put his arm across her shoulders, and he put his weight on her and started walking toward a line of trees near the field.

Ten minutes later she stopped. Lance was panting and barely able to keep on his feet. "Look!" she said. "There's a barn over there."

"Is there a house?"

"I think there was. Yes, there's a chimney, but the house has been burned."

"We'd better get inside. I'd about as soon be shot as be captured. Of course *you'd* be all right. You're a civilian, but I'd spend the rest of the war in a prison camp."

"Come. Let's get inside."

She helped him, and they crossed the field that was still muddy from the rain that had fallen two days earlier. The barn had only one door, and it was sagging badly. Moving inside, she smelled the rank odor of old straw but turned to him and said, "This will do until you feel better."

"Guess I'd better . . . sit down."

Jo felt him lurching and led him to a pile of straw. "Here, lie down," she said, "and close your eyes."

Lance sank down on the straw and, to Jo's alarm, went completely limp. "Lance!" she whispered. She bent over and asked, "Are you all right?" When he did not move, she became afraid and thought, perhaps, that he had died. But leaning closer, she put her ear almost on his lips and felt his breathing. Relief washed over her, and she sat beside him.

"I'm glad it's not winter," she said. She sat there for thirty minutes, and then all that had happened overwhelmed her. The horrible reality of Sailor's death flooded her mind. She began to tremble and had a ridiculous and absurd impulse to scream at the top of her lungs and pull her hair.

She closed her eyes and drew her knees up, hugging them, and placed her face against them. She seemed to hear again the thudding of the bullets as they tore into Sailor Malone, and waves of guilt came crashing down on her.

Finally she heard the sound of crickets and a bullfrog croaking somewhere, and the nervous tremors ceased to go through her. She lay back and turned to face Lance. Reaching out, she held his arm, and then, after a time, she went to sleep.

She awoke some time later and had no idea of the time. Outside the sky was black with stars sprinkled over it. She felt Lance stir, and she sat up and tried to brush the straw out of her hair. She could see almost nothing, just a vague outline, but Lance was trying to sit up.

"Don't try to sit up, Lance."

"What time is it?"

"I have no idea. I've been asleep."

"So have I."

Leaning over she touched his head and said, "We've got to get you to a doctor."

"That's not very likely if we're in German territory. I have no desire to see a German doctor. Here, I want to sit up awhile."

Jo helped him sit up, and he scooted back until his shoulders touched the wall. Pain ran through his head like a burning knife, and he could not think clearly. His breathing was erratic, and he did not try to talk for a while.

"Lance, I think I ought to leave you."

Her words came as a shock to Lance. "Leave me and do what?"

"I could make my way back through the lines and find some of our troops. Then I could bring them to help you."

"That won't do," Lance said. He had to summon his strength to speak and said, "There'll be a search party out for us. Already has been, I suppose, but there wasn't much light. But they'll be out again in the morning."

"Do they know where we are?"

"They know what Malone's patrol area was. Yes, they'll know the general area."

"But they can't see us."

"They'll be flying low. If we hear them, we'll just have to go out and wave. If we had a pistol or fire signals, it would help. But we don't have either."

"It's bad, isn't it, Lance? We don't have much chance."

"Not much."

The air was full of the busy singing of crickets, and neither of them spoke for a while. Finally Jo said in a tight voice, "It's all my fault, Lance. I've been a fool."

"You and Sailor should have known better."

"I don't know if I can live with it. It's my fault that he's dead."

"No. Don't say that. He was jumped by three Fokkers. They would have got him no matter whether you were there or not."

"Do you really mean that, or are you just saying it to make me feel better?"

"It's true enough, but I feel sorry for the man. He had some kind of a demon driving him along. I think he was so fed up with this war that he wanted to die."

The time ran on, and a great wave of loneliness and fear came over Jo. She moved closer and said, "I hate to be a silly, frightened woman, but I've got to tell you, Lance, I'm scared spitless."

Lance suddenly found this amusing. Even in as much trouble as they were in, he found this woman sitting beside him infinitely interesting. "You've got a right to be. We're not out of this yet. We could be shot for spies, or you could. I guess you're the civilian."

"Don't say things like that! Somehow we've got to make it back. We've got too much to live for."

"I imagine every man that got killed today thought he had too much to live for."

Jo did not answer for a while but let the silence run on. She thought he had fallen asleep again and was startled when he spoke.

"I've been thinking about Gabby," he said.

"She's such a beautiful child. Her mind's as full as a mind can be and very bright!"

"I've been a bad father to her."

"Don't say that, Lance. You've got a hard job. I'm sure you do the best you can."

Lance moved his shoulders impatiently. He shook his head too, but the movement sent fresh waves of pain through his head. "No," he muttered, "I haven't done the best I can. I've made a mess out of my life, Jo. Ever since Noelle died, I've been living in some kind of horrible nightmare."

Jo listened as Lance continued to talk. Sympathy and pity rose in her for this strong man who had lost so much. As she sat there, she realized, to an even greater degree, the great love he had had for his wife. She had not seen love like that often, and now she felt humbled by it.

"Lance, not many men love their wives as you loved Noelle. Most men get over it because their love isn't so great. But you're different."

"I'm . . . glad you think that, Jo. But it doesn't change things."

Once again they listened to the sounds of the crickets, and suddenly a shadowy form appeared and flew through the barn. Jo let out a small cry and grabbed at Lance, moving closer to him.

"It's all right. It's just an owl hunting for his supper." Lance reached over and put his arm around Jo. As she leaned against him, he was aware, even through the pain, what a desirable woman she was. It was something he had tried to deny, and now he simply held her, saying nothing.

Jo was aware of the pressure of Lance's arm. She had never been in love, although she had had several romances. Amid the musty smells of the barn with the stars sparkling outside the door, she suddenly knew that she loved Lance Winslow. She also knew that it was a one-sided love. *He's still in love with Noelle,* she thought. Wanting the comfort of his arm, she did not move away. She was a strong woman, but at that moment all her strength seemed to have left her. Perhaps it was the violence she had gone through. Perhaps, for longer than she had known, there had been a longing in her to depend on the strength of a man. Now as she felt the warmth of his body as she pressed against him, tears filled her eyes. She was confused, lonely, and frightened, but there was nothing else she could say. Deep down she suspected that Lance Winslow would never love anyone except his dead wife, Noelle, and she was not willing to share a man's love in this fashion.

"Jo—?"

"Yes. What is it, Lance?"

"I've got to tell you this."

His voice was no more than a whisper, and she waited until finally, after a struggle, he continued.

"I've forgotten God, Jo. I used to know Him and love Him, but since Noelle died, that's all gone."

Jo knew then what was in Lance Winslow's heart. "You blame God for her death, don't you?"

"Yes! I do, and it's killing me. I can't live like this, Jo. I can't!"

And then Jo Hellinger knew what to do. Her own heart was filled with pain for a love she could never share with Lance Winslow, but she wanted to reach out and help him. She took his hand, which was around her, and held it tightly. "God is waiting for you, Lance."

"Do you really think so?"

"He's always waiting. He's full of tender mercies and loving compassion. Would you mind if I pray for you?" In the silence that followed, Jo was afraid that Lance was about to refuse her request.

Then he whispered, "Yes. Pray for me, Jo."

There in the silence of that barn in enemy territory with death perhaps lurking a few hours away, Jo prayed, and Lance began to pray as well.

The pungent barn became a sanctuary of healing for Lance Winslow as he began to pour out his heart to God. He relinquished the bitterness for having lost his wife that had kept him bound up with anger toward God all those years. And in its place, a silent peace and strength settled upon him. Tears of joy streaked his bloodied face, for he had finally come back to the God he thought he had lost.

CHAPTER TWENTY-ONE

THE SEARCH

★ ★ ★ ★

A silence seemed to hang over the aerodrome as Rev and Dani stood in the shadow of the hangar. They had watched all available planes leave, including four two-seater observer planes that had been brought in for repairs. Rev and the other mechanics had hastily given them a quick check, and they had joined the Nieuports in the search for Lance Winslow and Jo Hellinger.

Turning to scan the skies, although he knew it was too soon for anyone to come back, Rev automatically calculated the weather. "Well," he said, as cheerfully as he could, "at least they've got good, clear weather for it."

Danielle had not been looking upward. Leaning back against the hangar, she had been staring at the ground blindly. She looked up at the bright blue sky and the fleecy clouds that looked like large balls of cotton. "I suppose if it were bad weather, it would be impossible."

"That's right," Rev nodded quickly. "So you see, the Lord's on our side."

"I wish I had your faith, Rev."

"My faith! Well, I don't reckon I've ever been noted as having big faith. Now you take some of those giants of the faith mentioned in the book of Hebrews. Now *they* had big faith." He felt it was important to talk to Danielle to keep her spirits up, although his own were rather dampened. "Take that fellow Abraham, for example. There he was nigh onto a hundred years old, and the Lord tells him,

'Abe, you're gonna have a baby boy.' Well, that right there would set a fellow back, wouldn't it?"

"I suppose so."

"Sure it would, but Abraham believed God, and it was counted him for righteousness. The way I see it, Miss Dani, that's about all we have to do. You remember back over in the Gospel of John, Jesus taught His disciples something about that. In chapter six, verse twenty-eight, 'Then said they unto him, What shall we do, that we might work the works of God?' Do you remember that?"

"Not really. What did Jesus say?"

"Why, the next verse Jesus said, 'This is the work of God, that ye believe on him whom he hath sent.' Now that's plain and simple, isn't it? The only work we can do, really, is to believe. That's why, I think, in Hebrews eleven and the sixth verse, the Lord says, 'But without faith it is impossible to please him: for he that cometh to God must believe that he is, and that he is a rewarder of them that diligently seek him.' Now, what I want to do most of all is to please God, but there's no way I can do that according to Hebrews except by having faith in Him. I must believe what He says and hang on to His Word. Praise the Lord, those promises are good and true, and they never fail."

Danielle listened as Rev spoke enthusiastically about believing in God, and finally she said, "But, Rev, I really don't understand you sometimes. I've heard you say that the things that happen to us are already planned out, that there's nothing we can do to change them. If that's so, why do we need to pray? I mean, if it's already settled what God's going to do with Lance and Jo, why bother to pray?"

"Because it's God's *will* for us to pray. We don't know what's going to happen, but God has commanded us to pray. We can't look into the future and tell much of anything about that. God has commanded us to bring all things to Him in prayer. That's why in Philippians the fourth chapter there's a pair of verses that I've just about made my life, Miss Dani. You might not believe it, but there was a time in my life when I worried about everything."

Amazed at this statement, Danielle looked up into the homely face of Revelation Brown. "I can't believe that, Rev. You never seem to worry about anything."

"Wasn't always that way, though. Before I learned what the Bible said, I worried about everything. Why, I spent so much time worrying about what was going to happen next week or next month, I didn't have time to handle the trouble that was going on right at the moment. Then, I found these two verses, and I just cabbaged on to them, Miss Dani, and I'm telling you they work. You can take 'em to the bank—the bank of heaven, that is."

"What are they, Rev?"

" 'Be careful for nothing; but in everything by prayer and supplication with thanksgiving let your requests be made known unto God.' That's the first verse," Rev said. "What does it say to do? First, it says don't be careful. That means anxious. Don't worry, in other words. And what else? It says we are to do three things. We are to pray, and we're to make supplication, and we're to give thanks, and if we do this the next verse kicks in." He smiled and put his hand on her shoulder. "You might like this part. It says if we do what's in verse six, God will do what's in verse seven. It says, 'And the peace of God, which passeth all understanding, shall keep your hearts and minds through Christ Jesus.' "

Danielle stood there, and the words of promise started to sink into her. "That sounds so simple. Is it really that simple, Rev?"

"It has to be simple because we're ignorant, foolish sheep. But I've lived in that verse, Miss Dani. I've let God know my requests. I've prayed, and I've given thanks for everything, and God always does His part. That's why the peace of God is always in my heart."

The two stood there leaning against the hangar wall, and Revelation spoke with such confidence that Danielle felt her heart lift. It had been as though a dark cloud had settled over her spirit. Fear had almost destroyed her, but now as Rev quoted the words of the Bible, promise after promise, always giving the chapter and verse, the cloud seemed to lift. Finally she reached out and took Rev's hand, saying quietly, "Thank you, Rev. I feel much better."

"Why, the Scripture says, 'The entrance of his word giveth light.' And that doesn't say the understanding of it either. That just says the entrance of it. That's why I try to fill myself up with the Word of God. I need all the life, and all the peace, and all the joy I can get in this old world. So I just let the Lord do it through His Word."

★ ★ ★ ★

At the same moment Rev and Danielle were leaning against the hangar wall looking up into the sky, Logan Smith was banking his Nieuport and searching the ground desperately. There was no formation flying now. He had divided a section of the area where Sailor Malone had been assigned, telling all the pilots, "Fly low and keep your eyes open for anything. Especially for the planes. They're down somewhere."

Every few minutes, Logan automatically glanced in the mirror and sometimes twisted his head. He knew he would be easy prey for any German that caught him down this low, but he did not give that a second thought.

"They've got to be somewhere! Lord, just guide me to the place where they are."

As he continued to scan the checkerboard country beneath him, much of it scarred by the battles that had taken place since the beginning of the war, he thought of Jo and the friendship the two had struck up. He had not realized how close they had been, but ever since they had left for France, the war itself had drawn them closer together. He had watched her carefully and had been aware that she was falling in love with Lance Winslow. She never mentioned it, but there was something special in her eyes whenever Winslow was near, and something changed in her voice when she spoke to him.

The earth flew under him, and he pulled back on the stick to gain a little more altitude. Feverishly he searched the green earth and found himself praying as he never had before.

"Lord, I know I haven't been close to you lately, but I'm praying that you will help us to find the captain and Jo. I know they're down there somewhere, and my heart tells me they're not dead. There's so much ground to search that there's no hope, except you give your help, so I'm asking you, Lord, to guide us. Help one of us to find them."

The time droned on, and Logan had to turn back. His fuel gauge was perilously close to empty. He fretted as he made his way back to the aerodrome and landed. As the plane rolled up to a stop, he cut the engine and leaped out.

As he hit the ground, he saw Danielle and Rev rushing up to him.

"Did you find them?" Danielle cried. She came up and involuntarily put her hand on his chest as if to draw strength from him. Her face was drawn and her eyes were filled with concern.

"No. I got low on gas and had to come back. Fill it up, will you, Rev?"

"Sure. Right now. You see any Germans?"

"No. I hope none of the rest of them did either. They'll all be coming back soon. They must be about out of gas, too."

"Five of them already came back and gassed up. They're out looking again. So far nobody's shot up."

"Well, that's a miracle."

Danielle took Logan's arm, and said, "Come and take something to eat."

"Not hungry."

"Well, at least have something to drink. Try to eat a little."

Logan allowed himself to be led into the rec room, where Danielle fixed him a sandwich, which he ate absentmindedly. He drank three cups of scalding tea and said almost nothing.

Danielle was aware of his silence, and when he rose, saying, "I've got to get back," she approached him.

Her heart seemed to be strangely moved, and since the pilot's room was empty, she felt she could speak, although it was difficult. "Rev and I have been praying for you all the time you've been gone."

"Dani, I know it's hard for you, but I'll find him if I can." He hesitated, and then said, "I know he means everything to you."

"That's not true," Danielle said. And even as she spoke, she had a sudden thought that frightened her. "Logan, I can't lose you. Please be careful!"

Her words seemed to strike against Logan Smith with a force. He was convinced that she could have no room in her heart for another man. Staring into her face, he could not answer her for a moment. Then suddenly she reached up and pulled his head down. Her lips were soft beneath his, and the kiss was brief. Then she threw her arms around his neck and hugged him as hard as she could. As he wrapped his arms around her, his mind filled with wonder.

And then she turned and walked away. He saw tears running down her cheeks.

She looked back once and said, sobbing, "Come back, Logan. Come back to me!"

Logan Smith was stunned by her sudden display of affection. He turned almost blindly and made his way back to the Nieuport. The engine was already running, but before he climbed in, Rev grabbed him and said, "Brother, God's going to guide you. Me and the Lord have been having a special time together, and I've got faith."

"He'll have to guide me. It's a big area out there, Rev."

"He will. Don't be afraid."

Climbing back into the cockpit, Logan took off at once. As he flew back toward Sector J, he could think of nothing but what had transpired between him and Danielle. He was confused now, for he had known for some time that he was in love with this young Frenchwoman, but he had seen that her heart belonged to another, or so he had thought. Now, however, he remembered the touch of her lips and knew this was not the kind of caress that Danielle Laurent gave easily.

"What's going on?" he muttered. "I don't understand it."

He had no time to think of women, however, although the remembrance of her came floating into his mind as he crisscrossed the area. He saw three of the planes from his own squadron from time to time and waved to them, but then they separated.

His gas was getting dangerously low again when suddenly he saw one of the observers, a two-seater, flown by Cecil Lewis. Lewis saw him and waved frantically, pointing toward the ground to the east. Logan pulled his Nieuport up alongside, and he could read Lewis's lips as he was shouting, "They're down there!"

A great exultation came to Logan Smith then, and he knew, somehow, that God had answered his prayers.

He motioned with his hand, and Lewis turned and headed downward. Logan followed him, and ten minutes later he spotted the downed plane. It was in the middle of a field and was nothing but a wreck. Only the burnt fuselage was left, and Logan suddenly felt himself plunge into depression.

He circled above the wreck in the plane, knowing that nobody could be alive, yet he remembered the words of Rev. *God is going to lead you to them.*

God wouldn't lead me to this, he thought. Quickly he made a decision. He made a circle with his hands toward Lewis, who was doing the same as he, and the two spread out and began searching the ground.

It seemed futile. Farmers out in their fields looked up at the Nieuport as it flew overhead. He saw no troops or signs of patrols, for which he was grateful.

If they got out alive, they'd be hiding, Logan thought. *Maybe in trees, or in an old abandoned shed, or in a ditch.*

Doubt kept creeping in on him, and he had to put away the thought of Jo being burned to a crisp in the wreck.

And then he saw the old barn, with the roof half gone. It sat alone in a field next to the wreckage of a house that had been burned. Only the chimney pointed upward, and he thought it seemed like the finger of God.

Suddenly out of the old barn he saw a figure emerge, and his heart leaped.

"Jo! It's Jo!" he cried aloud. He throttled back on the engine, turned, and went as low as possible. There was no mistake. It was Jo, all right, and she was waving frantically.

"I wonder where Lance is?" Logan murmured. And then she pointed back in the barn, pantomiming, and Logan thought, *He's in the barn. Probably hurt.*

He pulled the plane up and saw that Lewis had brought his two-seater to fly beside him. He also had seen Jo and was using his hands, clasping them like a fighter in a victory.

"We've got to get down. There could be patrols anytime. That field will have to do," he said to himself.

It was a short field and not really long enough for a landing, but they had no choice. The two-seater had the ability to land in a shorter space and could make it fine. He motioned for Cecil to go down and Lewis nodded.

Logan watched as the two-seater went down and almost reached the end of the field but managed to stop. Then he brought the Nieuport down, cutting the engine and breathing a prayer. The wheels touched at the very first clearing, and he wished for brakes as the plane bounced over the rough field. He saw the trees rushing up and thought, *I've blown it this time!* But miraculously the plane stopped, and he cried out, "Thank you, Lord!" He left the engine running, and by the time he hit the ground, he saw that Cecil was out too. He ran toward the barn, and Jo threw her arms around him and held him for a moment.

"Thank God," she sobbed, "you're here!"

"Where's Lance?"

"He's in the barn. He's hurt."

"How bad?"

"He just needs a few stitches on his head."

"Come on, Cecil. We'll have to put both of them in your plane."

Lance had come to the door, and, although his mind was not clear, he recognized his two pilots. He tried to speak but could not for a moment, then when Logan came up, he said, "Well, I'm glad to see you."

"Are you all right, sir?"

"My head's banged up a bit, but I'll be all right. How did you find us?"

"God led us here," Logan said simply.

Lance Winslow smiled then. "I believe He did. Well, get me out of here if you can, Logan."

Cecil and Logan helped Lance to the plane and then practically lifted him and put him in the backseat.

"You'll have to sit with him, Jo. There's not enough room in my plane."

"It's all right. I don't mind a bit."

Jo scrambled up and got into the seat, and the two squeezed together. "A little bit tight, Lance."

"That's all right," Lance said. A peace had come over him, and he whispered, "I don't think I'll ever doubt God again. Not after this."

★ ★ ★ ★

Most of the pilots were back when the two planes approached the aerodrome. It was Rev who said, "It's them! It's the captain and Miss Jo!"

Every pilot and every mechanic on the base ran out to meet the two-seater. As soon as it stopped, Revelation Brown and Pug Hardeston pulled Lance out carefully. Jo was also lifted out by eager hands, protesting to Copper Jennings, "Copper, I'm all right. The captain is the one that's hurt."

"You're going to the hospital, and I don't want any argument about it!"

Danielle stood back for a moment, but when the two came to the edge of the field, she went to them with tears in her eyes, but they were tears of joy. "Lance, you're all right!" She put her arms around him and he held her.

"I'm all right. Just banged up a little."

Revelation Brown had watched them and had seen the expression that came across Logan's face. Logan had come up just in time to see Danielle put her arms around the captain, and now Rev saw something change in his face. The smile that had been there disappeared instantly.

Rev saw Logan suddenly turn and walk away. Two of the pilots tried to talk to him, but he answered them in short replies.

Something's wrong with that boy, Rev thought. He made his way to Logan and fell into step. "Well, you found them, I see."

"Yes."

"What's wrong with you? You ought to be happy."

"I'm glad they're all right," Logan said curtly.

"You ought to go say something to Miss Dani. She's been worried sick about you."

Actually that had been in Logan's mind, but when he had seen her throw her arms around Lance Winslow, all of his old feelings came back. He had thought, *She's still in love with him, no matter what she said to me.*

"What's wrong with you, Logan? Go to Miss Dani. She's worried about you."

"I guess she was worried about Lance Winslow. He's the one she cares about."

Suddenly Rev seized Logan's arm with a strong hand and turned him around almost as if he were a child. The strength of Rev Brown was well known, and Logan could not shake it off.

"Let go of me, Rev!" he said angrily.

"You're actin' like a fool!"

"I said let go of me!"

Rev shook his head slowly. "That girl cares for you, Logan."

"No, she doesn't! She'd care for anybody that was in trouble. It's the captain she's in love with!"

Rev Brown saw the futility of arguing. He released his grip and then shook his head, sadness sweeping across his face. "For a smart fellow, Logan Smith," he said evenly, "you ain't got much sense!" He turned abruptly and walked away.

Logan stood there, confused. He almost called out to Rev, then his pride rose, and he said, "I saw how she went to him! She still loves him. I can see that much even if I'm not smart." His shoulders slumped as he walked quickly away. He had no desire to be a part of the celebration that was taking place at the edge of the airfield, where Lance and Jo were surrounded by the happy, excited pilots and mechanics. A darkness had come to his heart, and he thought, *At least I can kill Germans.* He did not realize how close this was to the same bitter spirit that had been in Lance Winslow. The sight of Danielle throwing her arms around Lance had taken all the spirit out of him.

CHAPTER TWENTY-TWO

A DIFFERENT LOGAN

★ ★ ★ ★

"And this is Elaine—and this is Helen—and this is Marlene."

Lance sat on the floor cross-legged across from Gabby. The two of them were practically buried in dolls, and Lance was trying desperately to keep them separated.

"So this is Elaine?" he asked, holding up one doll with blond hair and shiny blue eyes.

"No, Papa, that's Helen. Don't you know anything?"

"I guess not, sweetheart. Okay, this is Elaine."

"No, no, Papa. That's not Elaine. Elaine has red hair. *This* is Elaine."

"Oh, I see. Of course. Why can't I remember that?"

Standing in the doorway, Katherine Laurent was watching with a fond look in her eyes. Ever since Lance had been wounded, he had lived with them, and both she and Pierre had been astonished at the change that had taken place in their son-in-law.

This is the Lance I remember before Noelle died, Katherine thought. *There's a gentleness in him now, and the love for Gabby just flows out of him.*

Looking up from the floor, Lance grinned at his mother-in-law. "Why is it I can remember the names of a hundred different pilots, but I can't remember the names of half a dozen dolls?"

"You've had more practice remembering the names of pilots. How do you feel today?"

"Like a million," Lance grinned cheerfully. "Of course, I've got a good nurse here." He reached over suddenly, picked Gabby up, and squeezed her until she squealed. He kissed her on the cheek and said, "Why don't you and I go out and fly your kite for a while this afternoon?"

"Oh, Papa, that would be so much fun!"

"And after that we'll go buy you a new dress or something."

"Papa, you don't know how to buy dresses," Gabby said reproachfully. "We'll have to get Miss Jo to go with us."

"I guess we will. What do you want to do now?"

Gabby did not have to think about that. "Let's have a tea party."

"You always like tea parties. All right, I think that would be fine."

"Lunch will be ready in an hour, so you'll have to finish your tea party by then," Katherine said.

Gabby became very busy then. Lance had bought her a table with four chairs just her size. The chairs were too fragile for him, and he had to sit on the floor. Gabby occupied one, but the others were filled with dolls.

"You know your mother had tea parties when she was a little girl."

"Did she really, Papa?"

"Don't you remember her telling you about it?"

Gabby's face grew very serious. "I think I do. It's hard for me to remember sometimes. Tell me more about her, Papa."

Lance had discovered that he could never tell Gabby enough about Noelle. The child's mind seemed to be a sponge, and he realized how important it was for her to have all the knowledge she could of her mother. He had talked with her for hours about the things that he and Noelle and Gabby had done as a family. The fond memories had stirred him and brought about a healing to his soul. He discovered also that this seemed to give Gabby a great deal of peace.

Lance was in the middle of a story, relating how he had taken Gabby and her mother to the zoo, when Danielle came in. "Oh, Mother says lunch is almost ready," she smiled. "But I missed the party."

"Here, you can play for a while, Aunt Dani," Gabby said quickly.

Danielle awkwardly sat down cross-legged next to Gabby and smiled at Lance. "This is easier than flying airplanes, isn't it?"

"I don't know, Dani," Lance smiled. "I'm enjoying it more. As a matter of fact, I'm enjoying everything more."

"Something happened to you, besides being hurt, I mean, didn't it?"

"Yes, it did." Lance spoke briefly, telling how when he had been so badly wounded and he and Jo were alone in the barn expecting capture or death, he had prayed. "And Jo prayed with me," he said. "It was like a load rolled off my back. You remember in *Pilgrim's Progress*?"

"I remember that," Danielle said. "Mama used to read it to me. A pilgrim was going along with a huge load of sin. When he saw the cross, it rolled off his back and fell into an empty tomb. She read it to me over and over again. It was my favorite story and hers, too."

Danielle watched as Lance and Gabby continued to play and thought, *I've never seen such a change in a man, and it's done wonders for Gabby.*

Afterward, Katherine came to the door, saying, "Come along, Gabby. You've got to wash before lunch." She laughed and said, "I suppose you two can wash yourselves."

"I think we can handle that, Katherine," Lance grinned. He got up to his feet and, groaning, said, "I'm stiff. I think about how easy it was to do this when I was eighteen."

"I can remember how easy when I was six, I think. We stiffen up as we get older." Danielle took his hand, and he pulled her to her feet. Her eyes went to his forehead, and she reached up and touched the scar. "It's healing well. It'll always be there, though."

"I don't mind."

"It'll always be a mark of the time you found how to trust God."

"Yes." Lance touched the scar and then said abruptly, "God's given me a second chance, Dani. That's something not many people get."

"I'm so glad." Danielle's eyes glowed, and then she looked troubled. "But I'm worried about Logan."

At the mention of Logan, Lance sobered. "I am too. He hasn't been the same. He's behaving almost like Sailor Malone, acting as if he doesn't care whether he lives or dies. He's shot down twenty-two planes now, and his name's in all the newspapers. He's become almost an idol, but he's so unhappy."

Danielle looked troubled. She bit her lower lip and said, "Lance, I've always meant to tell you that when I was a girl I behaved very foolishly."

"What young person doesn't? I know I made a fool out of myself regularly. Once a month at least."

"No. I'm serious, Lance." Taking a deep breath, Danielle said, "I had a tremendous crush on you. I think that's what the Americans call it."

Lance looked embarrassed. "Well, I don't think that's too unusual. I was pretty infatuated with a twenty-two-year-old woman when I was only sixteen. It went away, though."

Danielle shook her head. "But it got worse than that. I think God tried to tell me it was wrong. I know my parents did, but it's taken me a long time to get over it. There were times when I almost hated Noelle for having you when I didn't." She said quickly, "Of course, that didn't last long, but I was a very unhappy woman."

Lance suddenly blinked with surprise. "Don't tell me this has something to do with why you turned down two or three suitors over the years!"

"I don't know, Lance. Maybe it does, maybe not. I've never found anyone I really cared for. And now looking back, I see how foolish I was, and it makes me ashamed."

Lance reached out and put his hands on Danielle's shoulders. "Don't do that, Danielle. You're a sweet, precious girl. You always have been. And God has something fine in store for you."

Danielle looked up and said, "I was beginning to care for Logan, but he's turned away from me. I don't know what I've done."

"I'll have a talk with him."

"No. Don't do that. It wouldn't help."

Lance felt helpless. "Well, God has brought me out of my foolishness, and He's given me a new lease on life."

"Do you care for Jo, Lance?"

"You're pretty quick, aren't you?" Lance said with an admiring glance. "Yes, I do. It may still be too soon for me, but I do care for Jo in a very special way."

"Lance, don't let your love for Noelle spoil the rest of your life."

"What do you mean, Dani?"

"I mean you had such great love for Noelle, and she for you, but suppose it were the other way around," Danielle said. "Suppose you had been the one who died. What would you want for Noelle?"

"Why, I'd want her to have a happy life the best she could."

"And does it disturb you to think that she might have found love with another man?"

"Not a bit!" Lance protested. The thought had never occurred to him, and he grew solemn for a moment. "She had such love to give. And if I had died and she had found a man that would be good to her and would give her comfort and happiness, why, nothing could have pleased me more."

"And don't you think that that's the way she might feel about you?"

Lance stood there silently. He had never thought in these terms, but since he had come back to God and had seen his responsibility to Gabby, he had begun to think about the future. He had thought about his feelings for Jo Hellinger, and now as he stood there, suddenly he realized that what Danielle was saying had the ring of truth. "I believe you're right." Another thought came to him. "Do you think Gabby would be able to accept Jo? As a mother, I mean."

"I think she would be the happiest girl in the world," Danielle said quickly.

"She needs a mother. She's young enough now that Jo could fill that role, and she loves Gabby dearly. I know she does. She's said so many times."

"Are you two going to come and eat or stand there talking all day?" Katherine had come to the door and said impatiently, "Come along. The food's going to get cold."

"Don't say anything to Logan about the way I feel, Lance," Danielle whispered.

"I won't, but I think you should."

"I'm just not sure what to do yet. I need a little more time."

Lance smiled at Danielle, "Just don't wait too long."

* * * *

"I say, old boy, you scared the pants off me going after those two Germans!" Cecil Lewis had sat down across from Logan and sipped at the tea he had brought with him in a large white mug. "Please don't do that again. After all, you're our Ace around here, and the Twenty-fourth wouldn't get in the papers so often if you bought it."

Logan had been reading a book listlessly. He looked up and stared into Lewis's face. The ex-professor seemed to have a special concern for him, he had noticed. Now, taking in the tall, lanky figure of the man, he said, "That's what we get paid for. Taking chances."

"But I say, Cowboy, it's not right the way you throw yourself into the most dangerous situations! I mean, after all, it's your duty to live. The captain said it's not your duty to die for your country but to make the Jerries die for theirs."

The two were alone, for it was a Sunday afternoon, and the rest of the squadron had gone into Paris for a weekend leave. They sat there sipping their tea, and finally Cecil said, "Have you noticed how different Captain Winslow is lately?"

"Yes. He's not the same man, is he?"

"I guess going down and nearly getting killed made a change in him. Does it make you happy that he's adopted your method of spreading our formations out?"

"It's the right thing to do, Cecil. Gives us more of a chance that way."

Cecil Lewis stared across the table at his friend. Lewis was an astute man with an analytical mind, and he had spent long hours puzzling over the change that had come over the pilot the papers called Cowboy. Up until the point when the captain had been shot down, Logan Smith had been a cheerful, happy-go-lucky young man, the best flier in the squadron, and a good companion. Something had happened, however, that changed him. He was withdrawn, seldom smiled, and flew every mission he could with a determination to shoot down as many of the Huns as possible.

Logan suddenly looked up and said, "Are you afraid to die, Cecil?"

"Well, it's not something I'm looking forward to."

"That's no answer. Tell me the truth."

"I was at first," Cecil said carefully. "By George, I could hardly get into my airplane. I was shaking so hard just thinking about getting bullets in the brain or burning up. But I had to get over that. You can't fight if you're shaking like a leaf."

"How did you get over it?"

"Well, two things. First there were a few lines from Shakespeare . . ."

Logan grinned. "I thought there might be. You have to quote Shakespeare before you brush your teeth. What were they?"

"They're very fine lines. They didn't mean much to me until I got into this line of work. You don't face death as a university don—unless some student you fail comes after you with a pistol. But anyway, the lines go like this:

> 'Cowards die many times before their deaths;
> The valiant never taste of death but once.
> Of all the wonders that I yet have heard,
> It seems to me most strange that men should fear;
> Seeing that death, a necessary end,
> Will come when it will come.'

"Those are fine lines, and when I read them, I realized there was nothing I could do about death. So that made an impact on me."

"What was the other thing?"

"I realized that I was in God's hands," Cecil said simply. He was an Anglican who attended services every week and at times even gave brief talks on the Scriptures to groups arranged by the bishop. Now as he sat there, a smile came to his long lips, and he nodded. "I realize that as I love my own children, God loves me more than I love them. So I'm trusting Him to do the right thing for me."

Logan sat there silently for a moment, then finally said, "I think that's a good way to look at things, Cecil."

"You know, everyone's worried about you, Logan. You act very foolishly at times. I mean, we all take chances, but lately you seem to look for difficult situations. Like when you went at those two Fokkers today. You should have waited for the rest of the squadron."

"I got them both, didn't I? Or one of them."

"Yes, but they could have gotten you just as easily."

Logan suddenly stood up. "I don't know what's the matter with me, Cecil. I guess it's just this war. Nobody behaves rationally during a war, do they?"

"I think we have to look at it a little differently. Especially those of us who are believers. We have to believe that God has His hand on us, and that for this part of our existence, we are doing what He would have us to do." Cecil rose and took the pipe he had been puffing on out of his mouth. Gently he said, "Take care, Logan, my boy. I would hope God has a great life planned for you. Don't throw it away."

Logan watched as the gangling ex-professor made his way out and thought about what he had said. *He's a pretty sharp cookie, that one. But I can't make myself feel better.* He had been in the grips of a bleak despair, and he knew that somehow it was connected with his feelings for Danielle Laurent. But there seemed to be no help for that. With a sigh, he sat back down and began reading the book, but it had no meaning for him.

* * * *

Jo was waiting for Logan when he came out of his quarters. She went up to him at once, saying, "You got a minute?"

"I guess so."

"Come along. I'll buy you lunch."

He climbed into the sidecar of her motorcycle and was amused at the astonished glances they got as she roared into town. She took the corners almost at full speed, so that he had to hang on to his hat to keep it from being blown off. "Hey, take it easy! I'm not used to this sort of thing!"

"You'll be all right, Logan," Jo said. "I've never lost a passenger yet. Bedford takes it better than you do." She pulled up in front of her favorite small café, and the two went inside. They both ordered, and while they were waiting for it to be prepared, Jo said, "I received good news from home. My book's been accepted by a major publisher."

"Congratulations, Jo! You worked hard. You deserve it."

"I don't know. It's too soon to publish the book. I've tried to capture what I've seen, but I'm not happy with it."

"I'm sure it's great. I'm glad for you."

Jo shrugged, but her heart was not in talking about the book. She began, instead, talking about Bedford, who had some sort of stomach upset. She saw Logan paying polite attention, but his mind seemed to be far away. It was something that would not have happened before, and finally she said, "Lance is completely recovered. I'll bet all of you fliers see a difference in him."

"Yes. It's strange. He always kept his distance from the pilots, but now he plays poker with them, or squash, and it's quite a change. I'm glad to see it."

"Have you been to the Laurents' lately?"

"No. Been too busy."

This was not true, Jo knew, but she did not argue. "It's amazing how close Lance has gotten to Gabby. He needed this time away from the war. I'm so happy for her and for him."

"I guess they're all a family now, Pierre, Katherine, Gabby, Lance, and—" He hesitated and then said, "And Dani."

Jo did not miss the look that flickered in Logan's eyes. "They're all happy that Lance is doing better. They were very concerned about him. I think he's finally accepted his wife's death."

Logan did not answer. He sipped the cup of coffee the waitress had brought and said, "They can't fix coffee like they do back in the States, can they?"

"What's wrong with you, Logan?" Jo asked, leaning forward and speaking with an intense voice. Her eyes were fixed on his, and there was an urgency in her manner. "I talked to Pug Hardeston. He says you scare him to death when you're out on patrol. He told me about how you charged a whole flight of Germans with just Pug along. He grew absolutely pale telling about it."

"We came out of it all right."

"Pug doesn't see how. He says it was a miracle of God that the two of you weren't both shot down."

"Pug exaggerates."

The waiter brought their orders and interrupted their conversation. Finally, when he left, Jo said, "I'm worried about you. Of course, I always have been. I've been afraid you might get shot down, but now it's something else. Something is eating away at you, Logan."

"Leave me alone, Jo!" Logan shoved his food aside and stood up. "I didn't come here to get lectured on what's wrong with me!" He turned abruptly and walked out, leaving Jo staring after him, shocked.

"He's worse off than I thought," she murmured. She got up and left the restaurant after paying the bill. Down the street she saw Logan's tall, athletic form moving away, but she knew there was no point in going after him. "Something's terribly wrong, and I don't know what it is. But I'm very much afraid for him."

★ ★ ★ ★

The sun was low in the sky, and Logan, who was leading the flight over Sector R, signaled to his wingmen, Jerold Spencer and Harold Holmes. The three planes banked and headed toward home base. They had seen nothing during the flight, and Logan found that his attention wandered when there was no action. Now as they flew along high over the earth, he found himself thinking of how he had behaved with Jo and felt ashamed. *I didn't have to treat Jo like that*, he thought. *She's been my best friend here except for Rev, maybe.*

His eyes constantly searched the horizon, and every few minutes, he looked in the mirror in front of him and twisted his neck to look high in the sky. At this height, though, he was unlikely to be attacked from above, so he grew lax.

The engine was running smoothly, and the sound of it had a hypnotizing effect on him. He had not been sleeping well, and he knew his behavior to the other pilots was abysmal. Somehow he could not control the dark moods that had come over him. He had found himself taking long walks and avoiding the company of the other pilots. He had seen Danielle but once, and his short conversation with her had been stiff. She had been hurt, he had seen that, but he could not seem to control the jealousy that had taken possession of him.

What's wrong with me? he thought. *She's got a right to love who she wants to. She never made me any promises. I think I must be going crazy.*

He wrenched his thoughts away from Danielle but found them going back to her often. He had reached the point where he could call up her face almost instantly, every feature and line of it that he had learned to love. The thought of not having her, he knew, had driven him into this depression. He had known men before, and women as well, who were jealous, but this was the first time for him. It was almost like a sickness, and he hated himself for his behavior, yet he seemed consumed by it.

Suddenly he was aware that Spencer had pulled up, almost touching wing tips. He glanced over, and the ex-jockey was pointing down.

Looking over the cockpit, shock went over Logan, for there below was a flight of at least a dozen bombers.

They'd never send out a flight of that many bombers without fighter cover. He looked around the sky, and sure enough, hovering under a cloud bank shadowing the bombers were at least fifteen fighter planes.

Ordinarily Logan would have known better, but he was not thinking clearly. He had to strike out at something, and he jabbed his thumb down at the bombers. He saw shock run over Spencer's face. The ex-jockey shook his head, and his lips framed the words, "Too many, Cowboy!"

Suddenly Logan did not care. He forgot about Spencer, and he forgot about Harold Holmes, who was on his right wing. *I can get at least two of those bombers before the fighters can get to me,* he thought. He put the Nieuport into a steep dive.

Behind him, Spencer watched helplessly, then motioned to Harold Holmes, his baby-faced companion. "Come on!" he yelled, although he knew the pilot could not hear him. "He's gonna kill himself!"

The action took place very rapidly. The German fighter planes had seen the three Nieuports and were just waiting. As soon as the planes dived on the bombers, the leader of the flight signaled, and the entire squadron dropped into a screaming dive. The leader watched as the lead Nieuport tore into the bombers' formation, racking one that burst into flames immediately, then shifting and pouring tracers into another, killing the pilot.

What happened next happened so quickly that it was over in a few seconds. Spencer and Holmes both turned to cover Logan, who had seemingly lost his mind. He was dodging in and out among the fighters as the gunfire from their guns flickered and struck his plane. His two companions were left to take the incoming flight of Fokkers.

It was not a fight but an execution. All twelve of the Germans hit the planes of Spencer and Holmes with their guns blazing. They had been newly fitted with cannons, and both of the Nieuports were torn to shreds and both pilots killed immediately.

Logan suddenly glanced up to see Jerold's and Harold's planes practically disintegrate, and the shock of losing his comrades because of his actions slammed into him. He had no time to think, for the Fokkers were headed straight for him now. Logan threw his plane into a steep dive. The one thing the Nieuport could do that the Fokkers could not do was achieve great speed in a dive. He had discovered that this was the quickest way to shake off the enemy, and as he headed for the earth, he did not care whether he lived or died. He could see the baby-faced Harold Holmes, who had led a sheltered life and now had died at the age of nineteen. Spencer, who talked constantly about going back to his racing career after the war, was now dead, too.

"And I killed both of them," Logan screamed. He gunned straight for the earth and pulled out only a few hundred feet above the level of the trees. He glanced back and saw that the Fokkers had gone back to shepherding their bombers. He saw also the two black trails of smoke as the Nieuports with his dead companions scored the sky.

★ ★ ★ ★

Logan never remembered landing the plane. He had flown back automatically and landed almost without thinking. When he crawled out, Rev was there at once and so were Captain Winslow and Copper Jennings.

"Where are Spencer and Holmes?" Winslow asked quickly.

"Dead."

A shock ran over all three of the men who stood waiting. It was always a tragedy when a man went down, but these two had been the favorites of the squadron. "How did it happen?" Copper Jennings demanded.

Logan was filled with guilt. "It was my fault," he said. He related, without sparing himself, what had happened, and Jennings' face hardened.

"You fool! You killed two good men," he said, then turned and walked away without another word.

Lance was appalled. "You're a fool, Logan," Lance said angrily. "I've tried to talk to you about taking these awful chances. None of the pilots will want to fly with you now."

"I'll fly alone then!"

Lance shook his head. "This isn't knights in tournaments, Logan. We've talked about this before. There's no such thing as a flying cavalier. That's what the newspapers call you. Cowboy Smith, the flying cavalier. But you know and I know that's not how it is. We've got to work together and fight together."

Logan listened as Lance spoke, but he heard none of the words. He could see nothing but the faces of his two fallen comrades. Regret, grief, and dread filled him, and he shook his head, saying, "I couldn't help it, Captain. I'm no good." He turned around and walked away.

Lance turned to Rev Brown, who was standing alongside. "What do you make of it, Brown?"

"I've seen it before, Captain. He blames himself, and I'm afraid he'll try to get himself killed just to make up for it."

"We can't let that happen, Brown. You're his friend. Stay close to him. I'm his friend, too, although he doesn't believe it."

"I'll try, sir, but he's a very stubborn fellow. He's never had a thing like this happen to him. I believe God's brought him to this point, and God will have to bring him out!"

CHAPTER TWENTY-THREE

THREE ARE BETTER THAN TWO

★ ★ ★ ★

"You're his friend, Brown. You know him better than anyone else." Lance had called Revelation Brown into his office and now stood beside the window looking at the gangly mechanic. Over the months Lance had gained great confidence in the strange American. It was not only that he was the best mechanic anyone on the base had ever seen, but Rev had a heartfelt faith that, without question, was real. True enough, he irritated some with his direct approach, but he never grew angry and had a meek spirit such as Lance had never seen. "What do you think is eating on Logan?"

Shifting his feet nervously, Rev put his hands behind him and locked his fingers. "I don't know for sure, Captain, but he's got to get over it. I know that much."

"You're right about that. He's going to get himself killed."

"Have you tried to talk to him, sir?"

"Yes. But it's like he's built a wall around himself. I'm worried about him, Brown. He blames himself for Spencer and Holmes, and, of course, the truth is that he is wrong."

"Yes, sir. He won't talk about it at all. The rest of the pilots are down on him. Some of them anyway. They hate to fly with him. They think he's a suicide pilot."

Lance shook his head and ran his fingers through his hair. "Do you suppose it would do any good if Jo talked to him?"

"She already has, sir."

"What did she say?"

"About the same as we say. He's got a wall built up and won't listen to anybody."

"Well, we've got to try harder, that's all. We can't lose a good man. He's got some problems, but I've always known that he had a good, solid foundation—" He grinned suddenly and added, "For an American, that is."

Rev was thinking, *This is a different kind of Captain Lance Winslow. He would never make a joke with an enlisted man, and he really cares for the pilots.* "Yes, sir," he said. "I'm fasting and praying, and I believe God is going to show him the way."

"I'm going to take off. I've got business, so I'll be off the base for the rest of the afternoon. There are no missions planned for the next few days, so perhaps we've got a little time."

"Yes, sir. And, sir, thank you for being concerned."

Lance nodded and shrugged his shoulders. After Revelation left, Lance plucked his cap off the peg and settled it on his head. Taking a sheaf of papers, he stuffed them into his briefcase and left. As he got into his car and started for the house, he thought suddenly, *When I start for home, it's different now. I used to dread going there, but now I can't wait to be with Gabby.*

He drove quickly, and after parking the car he got out eagerly. He was met at the door by Katherine, who said, "Jo's here. She's in the sitting room with Gabby."

"All right. I'll just look in on them."

Katherine hesitated. "Have you talked to Logan?"

Lance grimaced and shook his head. It seemed that everyone was interested in Logan—except Logan himself. He seemed not to care at all. "I talked to Rev about him. He's worried just as we are."

"You've got to do something, Lance," Katherine said. "He's lost. He's not the same Logan that we first knew."

Desperation ran through Lance. "I know it, Katherine, but what can I do? I've tried to talk to him, but he won't listen. He flies like a crazy man. It's like he wants to get shot down."

"Dani's very worried about him. He used to come see her, but now he seems to be avoiding her," she said.

"I think he's avoiding everyone."

"Try to get him to come to supper."

"I have tried, but it doesn't work." He shrugged his shoulders, then said, "Well, as Rev said, God will have to work this out." He went to his room, hung up his cap, and deposited his briefcase on the small desk. For a moment he stood there and looked at the picture of Noelle he had framed and hung on the wall over his desk. Always before, up until recently, just looking at her picture gave him such pain that he could not bear it. He had kept the picture tucked away, hidden from himself. But now he found that he could look at it without the desperate grief that he had felt for years. The memories that came were good now, and he thought, *You gave me the best years of my life, and I'll never forget them.* He stood there half waiting for the agony of grief to come rushing back, but it did not, and his eyes shifted to the picture of Gabby that was also mounted over his desk. In the picture she was playing with Bedford. The big dog was licking her face; her eyes were closed with ecstasy, and she had a big grin on her face. "I wish you could see her, Noelle, but I'll do the best I can to take care of her. Just as you would."

Turning, he left the room, and as he moved into the hall toward the sitting room, he heard Jo's voice. The door was open and he paused there. Her side was to him, and she was sitting in a chair holding Gabby in her lap. It made such a beautiful picture for Lance Winslow. He stood there simply gazing at them. Sunlight came through the window, lighting Gabby's hair and falling across Jo's face. Her red hair gleamed, and there was a peace on her face as she spoke quietly. She was a good storyteller, and Lance stood there listening, pleased with the sight.

"And so the knight rescued the princess from the evil dragon."

"And did they get married and live happily ever after?"

"Oh yes!" Jo said. "They loved each other very much, and they were very happy."

Gabby's voice was sleepy, but she persisted. "And did they have any little boys and girls?"

"They had one boy and one girl."

"What color was their hair?"

"One had red hair," Jo smiled, "and the other had blond hair. They were the most beautiful children in all the world."

"Did they ever fight?"

"Sometimes they had disagreements, but they loved each other, and they always worked them out."

"Tell me another story."

"Which one?"

"Tell me a story about when you were a little girl just my age."

Jo began another story, a simple tale of her childhood. As her voice went on, Lance thought, *She's a beautiful woman and has a heart filled with love.*

When the story was over, Gabby sighed and held closely to Jo. "I like your stories."

"I'm glad you do, Gabby. I like to tell them to you."

"You know," Gabby said slowly, and with some hesitation, "when you're around, it's like having a real mother. It really is!"

Lance was moved by the simple statement of his daughter. He saw Jo hold her close, and he also saw that her eyes were gleaming with tears. He must have moved because Jo suddenly looked up, and a startled expression crossed her face.

"Oh, it's you, Lance."

"Papa!" Gabby was off of Jo's lap in a moment and came flying to Lance. He caught her outstretched arms, and lifting her up, he waltzed her around the room. "Well, you two have been having a good time, I see."

"We've been telling each other stories," Gabby said, "but Jo knows more than I do."

"Well, she's older than you are. By the time you're an old lady like she is"—Lance winked at Jo—"you'll have so many stories you won't get through them all."

"You tell us a story, Papa."

"Oh, I'm not very good at that!" he protested.

"Yes, you are. Come. You promised."

"Yes. Let's hear one of your stories," Jo smiled. "You've been listening to mine. Tell us a story about Lance Winslow and what a naughty boy he was."

"You don't know who you're talking to," Lance said. He sat down on the sofa while Jo resumed her seat in the chair. He held Gabby on his lap and said, "There was once a young boy named Lance Winslow. He was the very best boy in all of England. He never did anything wrong, and his parents were very proud of him. He got many medals for being the best boy in town, and pretty soon they were so heavy he couldn't wear them all."

Jo smiled as Lance went on with his outlandish story. Her eyes went to Gabby's face, and she thought, *She loves her father so much, and it's a miracle to see how she's blossoming with the attention he pays her now.*

Finally Lance ended the story and said, "So the king proclaimed Lance Winslow Day for the best little boy in all of England."

"Were you really that good, Papa?" Gabby's eyes were large with astonishment, and her mouth was wide open as she waited for his answer.

"Well, maybe I stretched the truth a little bit. As a matter of fact, I wasn't that good at all. Next time I'll tell you a story about what a naughty boy I was. Now, suppose you tell us a story. Both Jo and me."

The storytelling went on until suppertime. Pierre Laurent could not help but be happy as he saw how Lance had changed so completely. His eyes met those of his wife more than once, and when he was helping her later with the dishes, said, "Lance is a completely different man. He's like the old Lance, isn't he?"

"Yes, he is," Katherine said. She handed him a dish and added, "It's not that he's forgotten Noelle. He talks about her quite naturally now, but he's accepted the fact that she's gone. I never thought he would, but God has brought him through it."

After supper they sat around and played records and Lance played several games of draughts with Gabby, allowing her to win quite often. Her squeals of delight every time she jumped a man filled the room.

Finally it was bedtime, and Gabby insisted that both Lance and Jo put her to bed. They supervised as she brushed her teeth, and Jo helped her put her nightgown on. When she was in bed, she begged for another story. Lance said firmly, "Tomorrow I'll tell you the best story you ever heard as soon as I get home. As a matter of fact, tomorrow's Sunday. I'll be here all day. I'll tell you what. We'll go to church, and afterward we'll go on a picnic, and then we'll come home and fix supper. Just you and me and Jo."

"Oh, Papa, that would be fine! Would you say a prayer for me?"

Lance bowed his head and suddenly felt Jo's hand come into his. He squeezed it and said, "Father, I thank you for our family. I thank you for this daughter of mine who means so much to me. I pray that she will grow up to be a fine handmaiden of the Lord just as her mother was." He hesitated and then added, "And just as Jo is." He felt Jo's hand close on his, and when he said amen, he turned to see that her eyes were glistening with tears. She turned away and left the room. After he had tucked Gabby in and shut the door, he went back downstairs to the parlor. When he walked in, he said, "Is something wrong, Jo?"

Jo had obviously been moved, for she shook her head. "No. Just a silly woman." She hesitated and said, "Would you like to keep me company?" Lance smiled, and she said, "Sit down, Lance."

"No. You must be tired and want to get home."

"No. I haven't worked any today. I gave the day to myself. Bedford and Gabby and I went down to the river. She had the best time. I wish you could have been there."

"We'll go back tomorrow," he said.

A stillness came over the room, and Jo felt that Lance was withholding something. He had been happy, but now something seemed to be troubling him.

"Is something wrong, Lance?" she asked.

The lamp on the end table threw its reflections on Jo's features. Her face was seemingly touched by a sliver of the light, and her eyes seemed to reach out and touch him. She was warm and beautiful before him, fair and constant, and somehow he knew that she was waiting for him. He spoke her name quietly, and then saw a flicker of hope come into her eyes.

Jo was aware of his nearness. She stood and waited for him to come to her. His arms went around her, and she put her own arms around his neck. When he lowered his head and put his lips on hers, she suddenly realized, *I've been waiting for this so long.*

The kiss was not prolonged, and Lance was the first to draw back. He stood looking into her eyes and knew that she was stirred even as he was.

"Do you feel what I feel, Jo?"

Jo did not have to ask what he meant. Faint color stained her cheeks, but there was a possession in her expression, a look of joy and excitement. "I love you, Lance. I think I have for a long time."

Lance simply held her again. They stood there for a long time holding each other, and then he drew back and said, "You know what this is like, Jo?"

"What? What's it like?"

"It's like a melody I heard long ago but had forgotten. Now it's all come back."

Jo said quietly, "I know you loved Noelle very much."

"Yes, I did, and I nearly destroyed myself when I lost her. I will always have a place in my heart for her. Does that bother you?"

"Of course not, Lance. I honor you for it. If you loved one woman that much, I think you can love another."

"I do love another," Lance said. He kissed her again, and the two sat down.

Then they began to talk, making plans, and there was life and excitement in Lance Winslow such as Jo had never seen, and she was glad for it. She knew that the same happiness was bubbling up in her, and she held his hand tightly, feeling a love she had never known.

CHAPTER TWENTY-FOUR

DEADLY MISSION

★ ★ ★ ★

Commander Samuel Steel stood bolt upright and refused the chair Lance Winslow offered him. He was the epitome of what an RFC officer should look like. As a matter of fact, his likeness had been used on recruiting posters with a few wrinkles taken out and the silver hair in his temples removed. He had piercing blue eyes that his pilots swore could penetrate one inch of tool steel, and his jaw was as strong as the Rock of Gibraltar. He had the reputation of being a man as tough as any of the armies that were lined up against each other, and now he said abruptly, "Who's the best pilot on your station, Captain Winslow?"

For a moment Lance hesitated. "Do you mean for steadiness or for daring?"

"I would like to have both, but let's say daring."

"I would have to say that Lieutenant Logan Smith would fit that description, sir."

A light touched the frosty eyes of Commander Steel. "The one they call Cowboy Smith. He's compiled quite a record. How many kills does he have now?"

"Twenty-nine, sir."

"Well, if he's survived this long, perhaps he has the other element besides skill and daring that the man I'm looking for must have."

"And what's that, Commander?"

"Luck." Commander Steel's lips suddenly grew even tighter, and he lowered his head slightly, as if he were about to ram it through an oak door. "I've got to have a man who's tough and lucky. I hate to put it this way, but the man I'm looking for has got to be able to lay his life on the line."

"My pilots do that every time they go up, Commander Steel," Lance said testily. "I think you know that."

Instantly Steel apologized. "I didn't mean to put it that way. Of course you're right. The only thing is there's a special mission that has to be accomplished. I'm sending out six pilots, all from different aerodromes. They won't fly in formation. Each of them will fly alone."

"May I ask what the mission is?"

"The Jerries are building up their forces somewhere west of Verdun," Steel said. His eyes half closed, and he shook his head doubtfully. "You'd think they had fought themselves out. They must have lost half a million men at Verdun, but our informants tell us that they're shifting around. We think they're going to hit us again, this time even worse."

Alarm swept across Winslow's face. "If it's worse than Verdun, I'd hate to think about it."

"Exactly. So we've got to find out what they're doing. But the problem is, from all reports, they're screening their movements. Every fighter aircraft they can put up is flying full patrols. It wouldn't do any good to send a mass attack to get them. Half of our fellows wouldn't get back, and what we need now are not new Aces but information." He stroked his mustache thoughtfully and said, "Cowboy Smith. An American, as I understand it."

"Yes. He was an actual cowboy. Very fine pilot."

"What's his temperament?"

For a moment Lance hesitated. "I'm afraid it's deteriorated. He was a sunny, good-natured chap when he arrived. Came through the Foreign Legion, don't you know. He's gotten—well, hard. As if he doesn't care."

"I know what you mean. Many of our pilots get that way. They don't last long, usually, when that happens. In any case, if you recommend him, I'd like to talk with him."

"Yes, sir. I'll send for him."

Fifteen minutes later Commander Steel stood face to face with the pilot who had come through the door. He prided himself on being a man of quick and instant judgment, and he was favorably impressed with this one. He took in the lithe, smooth, muscled body, the darkly tanned skin, the crisp brown hair with a slight curl, and most of all the strange, indigo-colored eyes. *Never saw eyes that color,* he thought. *Most unusual.*

"At ease, Lieutenant. We'll make this rather informal, since it's a strange request I have to make."

Logan allowed himself to lose his rigid pose. He had been lying on his bunk staring at the ceiling when an orderly had come with the message, "The captain wants to see you at once."

Now as he stood there, his eyes darted once to Lance Winslow. The captain, he saw, was tense. *Must be bad if Winslow's having difficulty with it,* he thought.

"Lieutenant, look at this." Steel walked over to the map on the wall that showed the entire war zone, all the way from Switzerland, where the trenches began, up to Ghent, close to the North Sea. "You've been keeping up with what went on at Verdun, of course?"

"Yes, sir. Bad business. A lot of good men lost."

"Exactly, but we're afraid that we're going to have something else come at us, but we don't know where from." Steel went on to explain the situation, stressing the importance of gaining information on troop movements.

"At first I purposed to send every plane we had in a mass flight, but we would lose so many that way and, perhaps, find out nothing. The value of the Air Service, partially, at least, is to gather information. So what we're going to do is send out a number of planes, six or more, from different aerodromes. We've already discovered that the Huns are guarding most of this area more carefully than usual. As a matter of fact, our fliers found out that it's like sticking their heads into a beehive."

Staring thoughtfully at the map, Logan nodded. "That means they don't want us to know what's going on."

"Exactly right! But we've got to know what's going on. Our men are scattered out over a four-hundred-mile area. If they're going to be hit by the Jerries, we've got to move them quickly. If they break through, they could take Paris. I don't know. Perhaps it could mean the war."

"And you're asking me to be one of these pilots, I take it, Commander?"

"I'd like to put it on a volunteer basis if possible. If not, of course, I shall have to name someone."

"No need for that," Logan said quickly. "I'll do the best I can, Commander Steel."

Pleasure washed across the commander's face. He came over and put his hand out. "You come highly recommended from your commanding officer, Smith, and you've made quite a name for yourself. This time I will be personally very grateful for what you're doing."

"Yes, sir. That's why I came to France."

"I must warn you of one thing. This is no time to increase your score. We want your plane to be in absolute top condition, and if you are spotted, run for it. Hide in the clouds. Shake them off. Then go back and see what you can spot. Is that clear?"

"Yes, sir. Certainly."

"Now, I will have my adjutant, Lieutenant Carruthers, instruct you on what exactly to look for. Some of it, of course, you will already know, but we need specific information. I want troop movements, trains, artillery being moved. Lieutenant Carruthers will fill you in."

"Yes, sir."

"Well, I'll send my aide over right away."

"When would you like for me to leave?"

Steel made a grimace. "I'm afraid right away. It's an urgent matter. Is your plane in fit condition?"

"Very fit, sir. No problem about that at all."

"Very well. You will take off several hours before dawn. Go over the enemy lines and at first fly high. You won't be able to make out all that you need to see. That'll mean going down, and that will mean being spotted. I have no advice to give you, Lieutenant Smith. You're a pretty tough fellow, or you wouldn't have compiled your record. I'll talk to you later."

Both men saluted as Steel returned it and then left the room.

"Well, Logan, it looks like a tough operation," Lance said slowly. "I would take it myself, only . . . well, I feel you're better fitted for it."

"No need for that, Captain."

"You understand he asked me for my best pilot before he told me the mission, and I gave him your name. If I had known, I might have—"

"I'm pleased that you trusted me, Captain Winslow."

But Lance Winslow was troubled. "It's going to be a touchy thing. Don't take any unnecessary chances. Just get the information. Run and hide. It's not a matter of cowardice. Those are orders. I know you're impulsive, Logan, but this time the information is more important than anything else."

"Yes, I understand that, sir. I'd better go, if you don't mind, and go over my ship with Brown."

"Better have him say an extra prayer for you, and I'll be doing the same myself."

"Thank you, Captain."

★ ★ ★ ★

"What's wrong, Lance? You haven't said a word all night."

Lance looked over at Danielle, who had come to sit down beside him. "I'm sorry," he said, "Dani, I was just thinking."

"Is it trouble?" Danielle asked quietly. "I know it's always trouble. There's nothing easy about your job."

"Just something going on with the squadron that I have to deal with." He tried to smile and said, "Well, you told me once that you never had a brother, and that you always wanted one. I'd like to think that you have one now. That's what I'd like to be. I always did."

"I know," Danielle nodded and then laughed slightly. "I can accept that now. So you have to take care of yourself, big brother." She saw that he was still troubled and knew that there were some things he could not share with her.

"Good night," she said. "I'll see you in the morning."

"Oh, I'll be leaving very early. Probably about two or three."

"So early? I'll get up and fix your breakfast."

"No need for that," he protested. "I don't mind a bit."

She ignored his protests and left him. She set her clock that night, and by the time she woke up and dressed and went downstairs, she found Lance already stirring. "A big breakfast this time," she said. "Just sit down and let me pamper you."

Lance nodded. "I'll take all I can get. I hope you'll instruct Jo on the care and feeding of a husband."

"Well, I haven't had any experience, but I think she's got your number already."

Lance grinned. "I think she has."

The two talked for a time, and when she set the meal before him, she drank coffee while he finished the eggs and ham and toast. He suddenly looked over at her after he had finished and said, "I shouldn't tell you this, Dani, but Commander Steel came to see me yesterday. He asked for my best pilot for a very difficult mission."

Instantly Danielle stiffened. "It was Logan?" she whispered.

"Yes."

"Is it . . . more dangerous than usual?"

"There's no telling. He may pull it off without any trouble at all. On the other hand, it may be very . . . difficult."

"I get afraid every time he goes up."

"I know that. I think everyone has noticed it. You two aren't hitting it off so well."

"No. He's cut me off, Lance. I don't know why."

"Would you like to send him a note?"

"Do you think I could go see him?"

"Are you sure that would be a good idea? It might—well, he's not speaking much to anybody, and you say he's even cut you off."

"I'd like to go just for a moment. Just to wish him well."

"All right. Come along."

The two got into Lance's car and drove to the aerodrome. It was three o'clock and Lance nodded. "There are lights on over in the hangar. I expect Revelation's working on the plane. If I know him, he'll want that thing to hum like a well-oiled sewing machine."

Lance's words proved to be true. Revelation was going over the engine, tapping at it, listening, and making minute adjustments. When he heard footsteps, he turned around and jumped off the platform. "Good morning, Captain. Good morning, Miss Dani."

"Is the plane in first-class shape? But then I know it is."

"She runs like a dream," Rev said. He hesitated, then said, "The lieutenant wouldn't tell me much about his mission. So I take it it's a tough one?"

"Where is he?"

"I think he went back to get another cup of hot coffee while I was finishing up here."

"I think I'll go see if I can find him and wish him good-bye."

As the young woman left, Revelation said, "Miss Dani's worried about Logan, isn't she, sir?"

"So am I."

"Is it that bad, sir?"

"It's always bad. He's going over enemy lines, and you know what that's like. And worse, I think the whole German air force is over there." Lance saw no harm in telling this much to the mechanic. "Keep it under your hat, Rev," he said quietly. "He's not looking for a fight. Just to bring back information. The Germans are out to stop him."

"I reckon they're up to something, and the commander wants to find out."

Lance grinned slightly. "Yes. That's about it." He turned and looked in the direction where Danielle had disappeared. "I'm concerned about her and about Logan too. I had the idea that they cared for each other."

"Why shore they did and still do, but something's come up. Seems like there's a law that love never runs smooth."

★ ★ ★ ★

Logan looked up from the cup of coffee the cook had made for him and stood up at once when Danielle came in. "Hello," he said awkwardly. "I didn't expect to see you here."

Danielle went over to him. They were alone in the room, for the cook had disappeared back into the kitchen. Now that she was there she hardly knew what to say. "Lance told me you were going out early this morning. I just wanted to come to . . . to wish you well."

"Well, that was nice of you. You shouldn't have done it, though."

Danielle felt shut out, as if he had thrown up a barricade. She looked up at him, and her lips were tremulous. "What's wrong, Logan? What have I done to drive you away?"

Now that the question was in the air, Logan wanted to come out with it. He almost said, *You fell in love with Lance, that's what's wrong.* But now that Lance was engaged to Jo Hellinger, he was even more confused. Several times he had seen Danielle and Lance together in an intimate fashion. Innocent enough, it was true, but they seemed to be closer than ever. He had concluded that Dani was still in love with him and was covering it up.

"I guess I'm just in a blue funk," he said. "I haven't been fit to live with."

"Is it something I've done?"

"No, Dani. Don't think that." He could scarcely bear to look at her. He had always seen her as a young woman filled with vitality and imagination. But now her expressive mouth seemed soft and vulnerable, and her eyes seemed to be pleading with him. Her features always had been quick to express her thoughts, but now he saw a grief in them, and he knew there was pride in her that could keep her going when all else failed. He had always thought of her as a serene young woman, but now some sort of trouble stirred her expression.

"I've got to go, Dani," he said. "I'll see you when I get back."

Overwhelmed by confusing emotions, Danielle could not speak.

Her throat was full. She had come hopeful that whatever was in his heart would thaw, but he left almost at a run, and she bit at her lip fiercely to still the trembling. There was a fear mixed in with her feelings, and she knew her aching heart reached out toward this man who had come to mean so much to her. She left the mess hall and went to stand at the edge of the field. She watched as Logan spoke briefly to Lance, then turned to climb into his plane. Rev went to the propeller, grasped it, and prepared to start it.

An impulse came to Danielle then. She scrambled through her purse and found a pencil and a pad. She quickly wrote a few words on it and then ran across the field. The engine burst into life, and she heard Lance saying, "Wait, don't go out there, Dani!" but she ignored him.

She reached the plane, and the prop blast caught her. She ran right up, and Rev stared at her with astonishment. She saw Logan catch his glance, for he turned and saw Danielle as she came to the side of the plane. She held up a tiny slip of paper, and he reached out and took it as she said, "God bless you, Logan, and keep you."

He read her lips, and then she turned and ran off the field. Logan quickly jammed the paper into his shirt pocket, grasped the stick, and advanced the throttle. He took off quickly and gained altitude. He turned toward the northeast, and when he had reached five thousand feet, he threw the throttle back. He had worked on the timing carefully with the commander's aide, Lieutenant Carruthers, and knew that he wanted to be on the far side of the German lines by dawn. He expected to be spotted, but he hoped his plane was in top condition, and he was good enough to avoid them.

The stars overhead sparkled as if they were bits of fire. A hunter's moon lit up the sky, and as he sped along he thought of Danielle. Reaching into his pocket, he pulled out the slip of paper. It was too dark to read, of course, but he kept a flashlight beside him. Switching it on, he unfolded the paper and read the words.

I love you, Logan—believe me. I love you with all my heart.

Suddenly Logan Smith seemed to see what had happened to him. *I've been a fool!* he thought. He knew his depression had been brought on by his foolishness when Spencer and Holmes had been killed. He also realized he had been unfairly jealous of Lance Winslow. Looking back, he suddenly recognized that he had behaved in a way that was not rational.

As he pressed on through the darkness, he folded the paper carefully and stuck it in his pocket. He began to pray then. "Lord, let me do this job—and if you let me get home again, I'll take Dani as a gift from you."

As he flew steadily on, part of him thought of the job ahead, while another part of his mind thought of Danielle. There was a certain amount of fear in him, as there always was, but he remembered Revelation Brown's last words before he climbed into the cockpit. *"The Lord Jesus is flying with you, Logan."*

Those words seemed to burn themselves into Logan's mind, and he felt a sudden peace. "Lord Jesus, you'll have to help me fly this mission. I'm not able to handle it, but you are."

★ ★ ★ ★

The mission went almost too easily. Logan reached the North Sea just at dawn, turned, and started back. He kept one eye on the sky above him and one on the ground. He kept a notebook on his lap and made many notes concerning the troop movements he saw beneath him.

"The commander was right," he muttered, looking down at a long, serpentine line of artillery followed by masses of troops. "The Germans are moving eastward. They're all headed toward the center of the line."

His suspicions were confirmed by what he saw. From both directions, both north and south of the trenches, the roads were filled with marching men with a new weapon called the tank and massive artillery such as he had never seen.

I've got to get back with this information! he thought.

He put his notebook away and knew that that part of his mission was over. He was over Charleville, located on the Meuse River, where he had seen a few formations of German planes, but they had been almost out of sight. He had flown so low they could not have spotted him. Now he turned east and determined to fly between the German aerodromes at Rethel and Vervins. "If I just follow the Aisne River, maybe I can sneak through all these aerodromes."

His heart grew light, for by the time he passed Bergnicourt, he felt that it was going to be one of those missions that went perfectly.

And then a movement overhead caught his eye. There, about two thousand feet over him and headed straight for him, was a large flight of German craft. Instantly he kicked the rudder, moved the stick, and turned the Nieuport into a steep turn. But as soon as he did, he saw that he had turned almost directly into another flight of seven Fokkers. There was no escaping them, although he tried. As they made their first pass, he saw that the lead plane was painted sky blue and had a skull on the fuselage. "Hans Macher," he said grimly. "I would have to run into him!"

In the sky blue plane, Oberleutenant Hans Macher saw the single plane. His keen eyes picked out the cowboy hat on the fuselage and he laughed aloud. "So, it is the Cowboy! This time he will not get away!"

Macher's thumb was on the trigger mounted in the top of the stick, and he managed to get off a burst that missed narrowly as Logan threw his plane to the left. Macher had been expecting a turn to the right and Logan's maneuver had confused him.

Two of the other planes loosed bursts of tracers that also missed Logan.

Logan Smith knew that only a miracle could get him out of this. The seven Fokkers were the new three-wing variety that were more maneuverable than the old. It was the same model flown by the Ace, the Red Baron.

There was no time for thought. All was action and time flew by. Time and again the Germans loosed bursts, but they were so thick they were afraid of hitting each other. Macher gasped, "He flies like a madman! I never saw such reactions!" Grimly he tried to stay on Logan's tail, and then suddenly he was caught off guard when the plane in front of him suddenly *decreased* speed. It never happened in combat, at least not to Hans Macher. He had to push downward on the stick to keep from colliding with the American. And even as he shot by, he thought, *That puts him on my tail!*

It was the last thought that Oberleutenant Hans Macher ever had. He heard the hammering of the guns behind him and started to turn, but the bullets struck him in the back, shattering his spine, and he was dead instantly.

Logan felt no triumph when he saw Macher slump over. He was too busy trying to avoid being hit. The other pilots, infuriated that their great leader had been shot down by the American Cowboy, doubled their fury. There was no escaping them this time, and two of them were waiting as Logan tried to pull away to his right. He felt the Nieuport shudder, and then the engine began to emit vapor fumes.

That's it! Logan thought. He was horrified at the thought of burning, as most pilots were. His only hope was to get down quickly and crash-land, so he put the plane into a steep dive. The speed of the

Nieuport enabled him to leave the Germans behind, and he pulled out just as the engine gave a tremendous crash, and then more white fumes poured out.

Logan jammed the notebook into his jacket, buttoned it up, and then loosened his belt. His eyes searched the ground, and he saw what appeared to be a field of corn.

He actually had very little control of the Nieuport, which was gliding in at a terrific speed. He braced himself and felt the wheels hit the ground. The Nieuport bounced high into the air, and he held on as he would to a wild bull. The smell of petrol and castor oil was gagging him, and then the plane hit again. This time he felt the undercarriage shatter, and the Nieuport went skittering across the field on its belly.

Suddenly the bottom seemed to drop out. The airplane nosed up, and Logan threw his arms out. There was a hissing sound, and Logan thought, *I've got to get away. She's going to blow!*

He crawled out of the cockpit and fell toward the earth. The plane had hit a ditch, and he rolled into it. He knew that one spark would set everything off. Scrambling to his feet, he ran in a stumbling gait after getting out of the ditch. He had gone no more than fifty or sixty yards when a tremendous explosion shook the ground. He threw himself down and felt the heat of the blast. Looking back, he saw the Nieuport had turned into an inferno. A sadness came to him. *Well, she was a good plane while she lasted.*

He got up and started walked steadily, his mind working furiously. He was now in German territory and knew that he was only a few miles from Bergnicourt.

"I've got to avoid the patrols," he said.

He broke into a run and turned around a copse of trees. Standing there in front of a house was a man with a shotgun pointed directly at him. He spoke in French, and at once Logan threw his arms up. "Je suis Américain!" he yelled.

The farmer came forward, his eyes suspicious. He was wearing baggy overalls and was an older man with white hair and faded brown eyes. He spoke in broken English. "Who are you?"

"I don't speak much French."

"I speak English. Who are you?"

"I'm Lieutenant Logan Smith of the British Royal Flying Corps. My plane's been shot down."

Logan did not know what to expect. There were divided loyalties in this country. Some still were of German sympathies, and the old man might well be one of them. *If he turns me over to the Germans, that'll be it. I'll have to try to get the gun away from him,* Logan thought.

But then the man lowered the shotgun. "Come with me," he said.

Logan was shocked. "You're not going to give me up to the Germans?" he asked, moving to stand beside the man.

"Never to them, those swines!"

Logan followed quickly. The man was in his late sixties, but he was active. As they trotted across the field toward the house, he said, "My name is Jacques Carteau." They stopped at the door of the house, where a woman with black hair streaked with white was waiting. "This is my wife, Marie. Marie, the Germans will be coming. We will have to hide him."

"It will be trouble for you, Monsieur Carteau."

"Trouble. No. It will not be trouble."

"Come inside," the woman said. "Quickly, before you're seen."

Stepping inside, Logan's eyes swept the room. It was a humble farmhouse, and on the mantel he saw a picture of three young men.

Following his gaze, Carteau said, "These are my sons. This one, Charles, the Germans took him for a hostage. They shot him, although he had done nothing!"

"I'm sorry," Logan said quietly. "He's a fine-looking boy."

"My other sons are fighting the Huns."

"They'll be sending someone. A flight of planes saw where I went down."

"It will be hard for you to escape," Marie Carteau said. "They're used to hunting for fliers that are down. They never escape. None of them."

Suddenly an idea blazed through Logan's mind. "There's one way," he said, "if you're willing to risk it."

"What can we do?"

"The Germans must think I'm dead."

"But they will look in the wreckage of the plane for a body."

"I know, but there is a way, if you are willing."

"I am willing to do anything against the filthy Bosche," Jacques Carteau said fiercely. He leaned forward and held his hands out almost in claws. "I wish the Bosche had one throat and I had my hands around it!"

"Be quiet, Jacques!" Marie said.

He turned and said, "My son was studying to be a minister. Now he is dead. Tell me what we can do to help you. . . ."

★ ★ ★ ★

Lance heard a yell and straightened up at once. "Who's yelling like that, Corporal?"

"Don't know, sir."

Lance walked to the door and stiffened. There flying down the field at top speed, no more than forty feet off the ground, was a German fighter. He could not move for a moment, and then he saw something thrown out of the plane. It had a weight, and there were red streamers attached to it.

"He's got a nerve, don't he, sir? Deliverin' mail like that," Corporal Simms said.

Lance did not answer. He ran quickly, but Revelation Brown was even quicker. He had picked up the object and turned and saw Winslow. "It looks like a message, sir, in a jar of some kind."

It was a heavy steel bottle with the red streamers attached. Lance unscrewed the top and pulled out a single sheet of paper. He unrolled it, and Revelation saw the officer's lips go tight. "What does it say, Captain, if I could know?"

"I wish you didn't have to," Lance said slowly. He read the message out loud: " 'Lieutenant Cowboy Smith was shot down over German soil. He had scored a victory over Hans Macher, our great German hero. We give honor to Oberleutenant Macher, but we also give honor to the man who scored the victory over him. Lieutenant Smith was buried with honors at St. Anne's cemetery in Bergnicourt.' "

CHAPTER TWENTY-FIVE

A TIME TO EMBRACE

★ ★ ★ ★

For three days following the notification of Logan's death, a cloud of gloom hung over the aerodrome. The pilots were all shaken, and most of all, they grieved over the fact that they had shut Logan out and blamed him for the death of the two pilots. Pug Hardeston left the station without permission and got blind drunk. When Cecil Lewis and Clive Bentley were sent by Captain Winslow to find him, Clive had said, "I can't blame him, Captain. I feel like doing the same thing."

"Will there be charges, sir?" Lewis asked quietly.

"No charges. Just stay with him and make sure he doesn't hurt himself."

Lance found that he missed his distant kinsman more than he had thought possible, and every time he went to the house, everyone was somber and quiet. Pierre and Katherine had become very fond of Logan. Jo wrote the story up as best she could for the papers back home. She could not find the words, however, and struggled to put what she felt into the story. She had spoken with Rev, and the two of them had been filled with memories of how they had met.

"I just can't believe it's true," Jo said, biting on her lip. "It's hard to believe he's gone."

Revelation Brown said, "I *don't* believe it."

Jo stared at him. "What do you mean you don't believe it?"

"I mean I don't believe it, and I won't until I see the body!"

"But, Rev, why would the Germans do such a thing?"

"I don't know anything about that. All I know is I don't have any kind of go-ahead in my heart for grieving for Logan. And that ain't natural. I can't explain it, but I'm just going to keep on believing the impossible."

It was Danielle who took the loss of Logan the hardest. She could not eat, and she slept only fitfully. She went about her work at the hospital mechanically, and her father said more than once, "Take a break, daughter. Go somewhere on a trip. Get away from all this." He had put his arms around her and said, "You cared for him. We all knew that."

"Yes, I did, Papa," she said. She clung to him for a time and then straightened up and pulled her shoulders back. "I grieve over him more than I thought possible."

"Did you tell him you loved him?"

Danielle thought of how she had slipped the paper into Logan's hand. That now seemed a frail and pathetically unacceptable gesture. "No," she whispered, "I didn't tell him—not as I should have."

Every day after getting off from work, Danielle took long walks. She found that walking in the countryside somehow, at least, made the grief bearable. Still she could not help going over and over in her mind her relationship with Logan. It was like seeing the same scene in a movie again and again. As she made her way down the country lanes, oblivious to the beauty of the natural world, she could see plainly now how she had fallen in love with Logan almost against her will. *I had to get Lance out of my system*, she thought. *What a foolish girl I was, and it didn't end with childhood. Why couldn't I see what I was doing?*

Each night she would go to bed reluctantly, dreading the long hours she would lie awake keeping her eyes closed by force of will. Once again she thought of how she had met Logan and disliked him at first. Slowly she began to unravel their relationship, and she began to realize that it was the depth of his character she had grown to love. He was handsome enough, but she was wise enough not to let that be the basis of her relationship. There was something in him strong and good, and now she knew that she had been foolish to be so slow to recognize those qualities.

Tossing on her bed, she remembered the kiss they had shared, and grief swept over her then like a turbulent river. Once she awoke from a nightmare drenched in sweat when the dream had been so vivid. He had been holding her in his arms when suddenly a huge hand had jerked him away. She had seen him disappear as she cried out, "Come back, Logan! Come back!" She had awakened to find herself calling out "Come back!" aloud, and then as recognition of the dream came over her, she began to weep. It was the first time Danielle had wept since the news had come. Forcing her face into the pillow, her body shook with the ravages of grief that now pierced her broken heart.

The sun dawned bright the next morning, and Danielle rose and dressed. She sat down in the chair by her bed and read a chapter in the Book of Psalms. It had become a precious book to her, and she had gotten to the sixty-ninth psalm. The first two verses seemed to reach out and go right to her heart. "Save me, oh God; for the waters are come in unto my soul. I sink in deep mire, where there is no standing; I am come unto deep waters, where the floods overflow me."

She had that sudden feeling that God was speaking to her somehow, and she continued to read. When she got to verses sixteen and seventeen she read them aloud. " 'Hear me, O Lord; for thy loving kindness is good: turn unto me according to the multitude of thy tender mercies. And hide not thy face from thy servant; for I am in trouble: hear me speedily.' "

A great weight came down upon her, and she fell on her knees and for some time simply prayed the prayer over and over again. And as she prayed, the heavy burden miraculously seemed to lift, and the dark grief, almost palpable, that surrounded her seemed to break. She had the Bible before her, and as she read verses thirty-two and thirty-three, she began to know some strange sort of assurance. " 'The humble shall see this and be glad: and your heart shall live that seek God. For the Lord heareth the poor, and despiseth not his prisoners.' "

For a long time Danielle knelt with her eyes shut, and at times she cried out in her spirit to God. She repeated the promise, " 'Lord, you will hear the poor and despise not your prisoner,' and, Lord, I'm a prisoner. I have been foolish, but I pray that your Spirit would bring peace to my heart."

Finally Danielle arose. There was a stillness in her she had never known before. Trouble had come in her life, and she had prayed and found some relief. But what she now sensed was different. She left the house, went to work, and all day long it was as if God had put a hedge of protection around her. Outside there was trouble and grief and sorrow, but inside Danielle felt calm and a sense of the presence of God.

As she did her job, her father noticed there was a new spirit in her. He said nothing but thought to himself, *She's learning to accept Logan's death. Thank God for that.*

When Danielle got off her shift, she went home at once, and Katherine said, "Lance called. His car won't start. Could you go pick him up?"

"Of course," Danielle said quickly. "I'll go right away."

Leaving the house, she got into her car and drove out to the airfield. As she drove by, she noticed that the late afternoon sky was a beautiful azure blue. She even noticed the greenness of the earth and the smell of the trees and the earth itself as she passed by open fields.

Pulling into the aerodrome, she parked the car and started for headquarters. She passed by the hangar and saw Rev, who was sitting outside reading his Bible. She stopped long enough to say "Hello, Rev."

"Why, hello, Miss Dani," Revelation said, getting to his feet. "Just been getting a little word from the Lord here."

Danielle said, "It's a strange thing. I was reading the Scriptures this morning when I first got up. I've been in pretty bad shape, Rev, but God seemed to come to me and give me peace in spite of everything."

"That's His business," Rev nodded quickly. "And we have to live with that day by day. When we get saved, we get the Spirit of God in us, but every day we have to go back for more. The children of Israel didn't eat manna once. They went every day and gathered it, so we have to keep going back to the Lord Jesus. The Scripture says, 'My flesh and my heart faileth but God is my strength and my portion forever.' "

Smiling, Danielle reached up and patted the gangly mechanic on the shoulder. "You must come out and spend some time with Gabby. She misses you."

"I'll do that, Miss Dani. I'll surely do that."

Moving toward headquarters, Danielle entered and found Lance seated at his desk. He got up and went over and took her hand. "Sorry to be such a bother," he said.

"It's no bother. Are you ready?"

"Just let me get a few things together." He moved swiftly, putting papers into a briefcase, then snapped it shut. "All right. I'm ready."

The two stepped outside and started across to where Dani had parked. Suddenly Lance stopped dead still. "Wait a minute!" he said and stared at the south end of the airfield.

"What is it, Lance?" Danielle asked curiously. She saw his face tense up, and she watched an approaching plane as it came in.

Lance did not answer for a moment, and then he exclaimed, "Why, that's a German plane!"

Shocked at his words, Danielle stared at the plane. She had never seen one like it. It had three wings and was painted a violent yellow color. "A German!" she exclaimed. "Are you sure?"

"Of course I'm sure! We don't have anything that looks like that. It's a Fokker triplane." Lance began running and shouting orders. Men began to pour out of the hangar, and he yelled, "Get some guns, rifles, shotguns, whatever you can find!"

The triplane came down to a graceful landing, and Rev suddenly came running up to stand beside Lance. "You think he's come to surrender, Captain?"

"I don't know, but be careful." A peculiar expression swept across his face. "Since the German's here, we've got one of those planes now. Headquarters has been wanting to get ahold of a Fokker triplane. We can try it out and find out its weakness. Then maybe we can shoot more of them out of the sky."

Everyone watched as the triplane taxied up the field, and then the engine shut off. Lance glanced quickly around to see that several of the mechanics had side arms, and he said quickly, "Don't shoot now! He's probably run out of fuel or come to surrender. Who knows."

The pilot climbed out of the plane, and Rev said, "I never saw a pilot dressed like that."

Danielle saw the pilot was wearing a pair of baggy overalls and rough shoes like many farmers she had seen.

Everyone watched as he came to the ground and turned, then started toward them. He was no more than thirty feet away when he reached up and pulled his goggles off and then his helmet.

Danielle stared and shock ran over her. Then she cried out, "Logan!" She flew at once across the tarmac toward him and threw herself into his arms.

"I thought you were dead!" she cried, and tears stung at her eyes. She clung to him fiercely and felt his arms around her, holding her fast.

Logan held her, smelling the sweetness of her hair and feeling the strength of her womanly figure pressed against him. He could not speak for a moment, then he said, "I read your note a thousand times, sweetheart. It changed everything for me. Up until that time,

I didn't do anything right. But afterward I knew I had to live."

Lance had warned the others, "Stay back! Give them a minute, will you!"

Rev Brown said, "Looks like they're gonna need more than a minute, Captain."

Logan turned but kept his arm around Danielle. "I guess I'd better report in, but you stay with me. I'm not letting you get away."

"No. I won't go away," Danielle whispered. She held to his hand and clung to him as he advanced. He saluted with his right hand. "Reporting back, Captain Winslow."

"Well," Lance said, trying to keep an even tone, "I see, as the American Mark Twain said, the reports of your death were greatly exaggerated."

"Yes, sir. I couldn't get word to you any other way." He fumbled in his pocket, releasing Danielle's hand as he did so. "It may be a little late, but here're the reports I got."

Lance took the reports and said, "What happened, Logan?"

The other fliers and mechanics came and gathered around, insatiably curious. Logan grinned and repeated how he had crashed and the French couple had taken him in and hid him.

"I asked Jacques to make a coffin and bury it. And then the Germans came, and they had to dig it up again. Wanted to give their *noble adversary*, as they call me, a formal military funeral at St. Anne's."

"But what if they had looked inside?"

"Oh, there was something inside," Logan laughed. He seemed younger now, and his eyes were clear. He suddenly reached out and pulled Danielle close into the embrace of his arm. "We burnt a rotting pig until it was crisp and put it inside. Anybody expecting a body couldn't face that. I don't think they opened it, though. They took Jacques' word that he had removed the body and buried it."

"But how did you get this airplane?" Lance demanded.

Pug Hardeston said, "He copped it, that's what he did! That's the way these Americans are."

"That's about the way it was, Pug," Logan said. "Jacques took vegetables over to the German aerodromes. He dressed me up like a helper, and we peddled the vegetables. He told them I was a half wit and a deaf mute, so I didn't have to give myself away." He glanced at Rev and said, "I did a lot of praying, Rev, and the mechanics were tuning up this Fokker. They started it up and were listening to it. I waited until the mechanic got out of the cockpit, then

I bopped him over the head with a wrench and jumped in and took off."

"I bet that gave the Jerries quite a shock."

"Well, as it happened, I got out of there before they started a pursuit. Anyway, that's my story."

"I'll have to have all this in writing, Lieutenant," Lance said.

"Could you wait until tomorrow? I think I'm suffering from some sort of battle shock." His face was straight, but he kept his arm around Danielle. "The nurse here probably needs to take me to the hospital and have me looked over."

A laugh went up, and Cecil said, "Hospital, my foot!"

Then everyone came rushing around to beat Logan "Cowboy" Smith on the back. Lance stood there letting the pilots and the mechanics have their time. He moved over to Danielle and said, "It's like one risen from the dead. Don't let him get away."

"You can count on that, brother," Danielle said, and her eyes shone.

★ ★ ★ ★

They did not go to the hospital nor did they go back to the house. Instead, they drove out to the river where they were now sitting together. Logan's arm was around Danielle, and they had fallen silent. They had talked, it seemed, for hours and now she looked up and said, "I've been so foolish, Logan."

"No more foolish than I, but God loves foolish people just like He does the smart ones." He saw that the curtain of reserve that had once kept her back from him was gone, and there was a teasing expression of gaiety and joy in her eyes. He thought again what a complex and striking woman she was. His arm tightened, and he said, "One of us is going to have to change."

"What do you mean, Logan?" Danielle asked.

"I mean either I'm going to have to become a Frenchman, or you'll have to become an American."

"Are you saying that you want to marry me?"

"Of course. I wish I were a poet. I could say it other ways and better ways." Logan pulled her close and kissed her. Her lips were sweet, soft, and yielding beneath his. He drew back and said, "I love you just as you are right now. Young and beautiful, full of fire, and whatever it is that makes a woman so necessary to a man. And I'll love you just as much or even more when I'm walking with a cane and you have an ear trumpet. I'll have to shout into it, 'I love you, Dani, more than a man ever loved a woman.' "

His words touched her, and she pulled his head down and kissed him again. Her hands stroked his cheek, and she said, "Which will it be? Shall I become an American, or do you want to become a Frenchman?"

And then Logan Smith laughed. He pulled her to her feet and swung her into a wild dance until she gasped for breath. Then he caught her up so that her feet left the ground. He held her tightly against his chest and looked down. "I can't eat snails," he laughed, his eyes sparkling, "so I reckon you'll have to become an American."

Then he lowered her, and she put her cheek against his chest, holding to him tightly. "Never let me go, Logan."

"I'll never let you go, and you'll never let me go," he said. "Come on. We've got a lot of business to take care of."

They walked back over the soft grass, and overhead the sun beamed down on the pair as they got into the car and drove away.